ROGUE WAVE

Cake Series Book Five

J. BENGTSSON

Rogue Wave - Cake Series Book Five

Published & printed in the United States
Edited by Dorothy Zemach
Proofread by Kimberley Weaver
Cover by Steamydesigns
Book design by DJ Rogers Design

Published & printed in the United States.

ISBN-13: 978-1-949975-15-4

Dedication

Dedicated to all the wonderful readers and listeners who have embraced the Cake characters and made this book series the success it is today.

And a special thank you to the Chiquitas in *The Banana Binder* for always making me feel like I know what I'm doing.

Prologue: Keith

My hands jammed safely in my pockets, I kept my head down as I made my way across the quad on legs as spindly as sticks. I could feel the sea of unfamiliar faces sizing me up as I passed. Flinging my hair back, I relocated the unruly strands littering my forehead. Little good it did me, as the fringe tumbled back into my eyes seconds later.

In the combat zone that was middle school, appearances were everything and mine was just shy of embarrassing. At a time when other guys were making gains in both height and body mass, my little boy body was still hopelessly suspended in time. *Be patient,* my father would say. *The later you go into puberty, the taller you'll be.* It was easy for him to say, when he was over six feet tall, but for a thirteen-year-old trapped in a nine-year-old's body, patience was hard to come by.

And, as if the physique of an elf wasn't already a huge strike against me, relocating to a new school nearly two months into the semester put the nail in my social coffin. Initially stoked when my parents announced we'd be moving out of our shoebox three-bedroom rental and into a fixer-upper five-bedroom home of our own, I quickly soured on the plan when I discovered the catch – school zoning. As in, we were now in a different one. The move only affected me because my mom worked at the elementary school my siblings all attended. With a few favors called in, the principal signed off on their transfer.

I hadn't been as lucky, and here I was now slinking around the lunch tables at Barnum Middle School like a jittery rabbit. But now was not the time to waver. I could almost feel the starving wolves licking their chops. If they smelled weakness, I was done for.

Drawing deep gulps of oxygen into my lungs, I lifted my eyes to the challenge, determined to find the group I belonged in. Although not as defined as in high school, cliques were already forming in middle school. It made sense. Like-minded individuals naturally gravitated toward one another, and that was what I was banking on now.

The sporty crowd was the first to catch my eye. Cooler than snot, this pack had always been off-limits to me. On the top of the food chain, these guys would soar in high school and become the jocks we all knew and loved. They were the gravity that drew in the masses, but also the brick wall you ran into trying to get in. I wasn't big enough, clean-cut enough, or coordinated enough to fit into that select group.

Nor was I going to sit with the Einsteins. Sure, the book jocks would welcome me in with open if undefined arms, but once you went down the nerdy path, there was no turning back. Equally unacceptable were the geeks. Some might lump them together with the nerds, but geeks were an entity all their own. Instead of challenging books, geeks played Pokémon at lunch and carried around pocket-sized light sabers because, you know, you never knew when a last-minute intergalactic duel might break out.

My eyes followed the line of succession until I directed my gaze at the 'blue hairs.' These kids would eventually become the artistic, theater-loving crowd in high school. They were talented and quirky enough that social norms didn't necessarily apply to them. These were the kids who sang a Disney song at the top of their lungs as they spun in circles on the black top, or the thespians who randomly spewed lines of Shakespeare during a math final with no fear of retribution. But despite coming from a musical family, I hadn't an ounce of talent in my skinny bones.

I moved down the rows with surprising efficiency. The budding hipsters. The blossoming preps. The inevitable goths. They were all represented. And let's not forget my personal favorites: the outsiders who would someday wear black overcoats and assemble hit lists a mile long. I nervously chewed my fingernails as realization dawned on me: I didn't fit anywhere. What was I going to do – spend the rest of seventh grade with the loners? No question spots would still be available at their sparse table.

Pushing the panic aside, I continued to wander through the lunch area, sizing up the segregated students until, as if answering a call from the wild, my eyes narrowed in on the prize – my tribe.

The skaters.

It surprised me that I hadn't pinpointed them earlier, as this was the crowd who were not conventionally sitting on the bench eating their sack lunch. No, these guys were all over the table. Some sat on top of the interwoven metal lattice while others were suspended upside down, their heads resting where their butts should have been. I smiled, feeling even more certain that these eccentric rebels were my future.

Like my group back home, these were the guys who held some stature in the school. While not necessarily part of the popular crowd, skaters tended to have just enough looks, smarts, and athletic abilities to keep them relevant. I let out the breath I hadn't realized I'd been holding and allowed my tangled nerves to unravel.

Thank god for the skaters. I was saved.

Picking up the pace, I made a beeline for the group, confident in my ability to be accepted at face value. After all, I was a skilled skateboarder, and had been dealing with dudes like these my whole life.

"Hey." I offered my greeting in the least unobtrusive manner possible. Skaters hate posers.

The guys barely acknowledged me. I stayed put – waiting for the invitation I was sure would come. Finally, their leader, a guy with long, shaggy hair, took me in from his upside down position. He looked older, like the guy who'd been held back by well-meaning parents who balked at starting their little precious in kindergarten too early, but the joke was on them when he was held back later in his educational journey for being too dumb for words. Now he was just an acne-pocked smartass with a gaggle of young, impressionable followers at his beck and call.

"Who are you?" he asked.

"Keith. I just moved here."

"New kid, huh?"

"Yeah."

"You got any weed?"

Before I could stop myself, my eyes widened, undoubtedly giving away my position on the subject of pot. At my old school, the skaters and stoners hadn't yet joined as one. Come to think of it, the only stoner I knew, Brett Valentine, had been suspended long ago.

"Wait a minute." The dopey giggle came from my left. "I know you."

And there he was.

"Hey, Valentine. I haven't seen you for awhile."

"Well, yeah, you know. I did that stint in juvie."

No, I didn't know. This was just great. The one person I knew in this entire shithole school had a record.

Valentine vouched for me. "He's cool, guys."

How could it be that Brett Valentine, of all people, was suddenly my lifeline? And did I want in his group badly enough to brush aside the morals my parents had drilled into me since birth? Surely these guys would respect the truth. "No, I don't have anything."

"Yeah, you don't look like you got any edge."

Or not.

Their talking head continued to diss me. "You probably don't even get baked, do you?"

Ah, shit. This wasn't a test. Drug use was apparently a prerequisite for hanging with these dudes. The desire to lie my way in was strong. After all, who would it hurt if I pretended to be a pothead just until they accepted me? I was a fairly funny guy and, once they knew me and saw my skills on a board, I was confident they'd like me enough that it wouldn't matter if I filled my lungs with poison or not. This was a whole new world, with new rules and requirements. I had to do what I had to do to stay alive.

But even though I was totally prepared to lie, the truth inexplicably tumbled out of my mouth. "No. I don't smoke."

"Sucks for you, newbie," the upside down guy said, before turning his attention away from me.

My fingers clenched into fists. Who said this guy got to decide my fate?

"That's it?" I challenged. "You have the final say?"

"Nah, brah, the guys can do whatever they want. But this is my spot, so if they decide to hang with you, they'll have to relocate too. But hey, lucky for you, there's some room over there at Tweezer's table."

My eyes followed his finger until they settled on the lone figure sitting a few tables over with black, dyed bangs hanging down over his face. Tweezer was passing the time by plucking the coarse hairs out of his forearm. I cringed. All it would take was one gust of wind to ruin lunchtime for me forever.

Swiveling my head back, I scanned the group of skaters, hoping some of the others might show their support, but not one of them met my eye. Even Valentine, my damn lifeline, was looking away. Hell, no. That's not how this would end. These skaters were my group – they had always been my group. I refused to be turned away only to join the ranks of some hairless arm dude. There was no harm in telling a few lies to get me where I needed to be.

My mother's voice played on repeat in my ear. *Keith, you're stronger than this.*

No. No, I wasn't. Mom didn't understand. I had to survive. It's not like I wouldn't have loved more options to choose from, like my siblings had. A jock? Sure, I'd have loved to be one, but I wasn't Mitch. Aligning myself with the popular crowd would be awesome too, but I wasn't Emma. And having the musical abilities of a child prodigy? Hell, yeah! Sign me up! But only Jake wore that crown.

If I wasn't special in my own family, how could I expect to be distinctive within a group of strangers? Never had I felt more insignificant than I did today – as the scrawny new kid begging for acceptance.

Looking out over the cache of students, I searched for someplace, anyplace, to land, but my feet refused to deliver me to safety. For better or worse, this was my crowd. I belonged with the guys who would never be more than average.

I took a step toward my destiny.

"Dude, I'm totally down to try."

The leader flipped upright, his eyes scanning me with newfound interest. "Well, okay then, Newbs. Welcome to Barnum."

Five Years Later

CHAPTER ONE

SAMANTHA

Hey You

"Did everyone pick a number?"

I glanced down at the slip of paper in my hand and unfolded the parchment. My eyes widened. Number twenty-nine. That couldn't be good.

"Numbers one and two, you're at lab table 1. Three and four, lab table 2." Mrs. Lee flitted around the room, way too excited for such a mundane activity. "You get the idea. Let's go. Get to know your partners, and be nice. Barring an outbreak of a contagious disease or an explosion that takes out the lab, these will be your partners for the entire semester."

Obediently, I grabbed my bag and moved all the way to the far back corner of the classroom – lab table 15. I practically needed binoculars to see the whiteboard from there. Nothing good ever happened after midnight, went the wise old saying. That applied to the back of the classroom as well, the favored spot of troublemakers and slackers. In these parts, pant loops were routinely zip-tied to the back of seats, and if there were spitballs to be hurled, they'd originate in this far corner of the world.

Blessed with a top of the alphabet surname, Anderson, I'd spent the majority of my life inches away from the teacher's desk. And even when seating charts disappeared in high school, I still migrated north. I was just comfortable there – with the smart kids who were as predictable as they were dull. Trust me, I wasn't dissing the academic overachievers. On the contrary, I was lumping myself in with them. Dull and predictable – yep, that was me. Still, being boring meant there was no need to worry that other front row dwellers would tie my shoelaces together during a pop quiz.

Of course, the fact that I had the eyesight of a cave-dwelling bat also might have contributed to my affinity for the head of the class. Sure, I could wear my particularly unfashionable specs to school every day to correct the problem, but why advertise my super-geek status?

Before moving to this beach town last year, I honestly hadn't cared what people thought of me. Sweats, ripped tees, no makeup, ponytails – I rocked the 'no style' style. I even went so far as to sport highly practical, yet exceedingly dorky, light-adjusting glasses that allowed me to seamlessly move from indoors to out.

Sadly, the 'anything goes' approach wasn't sustainable at Pearl Beach High School, where beauty was the norm, and students would rather not see at all than be caught dead in a pair of spectacles. It went without saying that corrective glasses of any kind were a fashion no-no here – viewed with the same distaste as, say, wearing corduroy pants.

I had contact lenses, of course, but was also blessed with oily skin, which regularly caused an inflammation of the eyelid called Blepharitis. You heard right. In addition to my sight woes, I had the occasional smattering of pimples, too. I was one lucky girl indeed. So, due to my poor eye sight, zits, and vanity, I squinted my way through class most days, struggling to make out the simplest of words on the board; even though, if I wanted to be totally honest with myself, I was such a nobody that expectations of beauty probably weren't even attached to me.

Sliding onto the stool, I opened my bag and tried to appear busy as I waited for number thirty to arrive. A nervous flutter attached itself to my chest as it always did when I was dropped into a new situation. I'd never been a great communicator, but it had only gotten worse since transferring into a school with working swimsuit models populating every few feet of Main Hall. I didn't walk like them, I didn't talk like them, and I sure as hell didn't look like them, so I kept my mouth shut as much as possible to limit the possibility of ridicule.

Already uncomfortable, I looked around at the others who'd pulled the short end of the stick and was at least comforted to see fellow front-rower Sanjay Evani over on table thirteen. He caught my eye and we traded similar disgruntled expressions. It was still early in the process, but so far it appeared he had it worse than me. Sanjay had been partnered with Thad, the basketball player who was already high-fiving his buddies over the good fortune of being paired with the supposed class valedictorian. No doubt my acquaintance's presumed intelligence was based solely on the fact that his hair was parted down the middle and he still carried around a lunch pail and a pencil pouch in high school.

But Sanjay was nowhere near valedictorian status, that coveted crown jewel celebrated by nerds the world over. Last I heard, his class rank was somewhere around twenty-six… out of close to five hundred juniors. Respectable, sure, but certainly not superstar level. Of course, I couldn't talk. My ranking slid in there at a measly number thirty-nine. It was too embarrassing to talk about, so when the other smart kids were swapping their success stories, I kept quiet – just as I did when the 'pretties' were discussing their beauty routines.

Laughter burst forth from table thirteen. Poor Sanjay. In the minute or so it took for him to relocate to the back of the classroom, he'd already managed to earn himself an unflattering nickname: V-Dicky – short, of course, for valedictorian. No one could claim the jocks weren't creative when it came to ridicule. I could only hope and pray their attention would not somehow divert to me.

It was humiliating enough that I was in a college prep chemistry class instead of Advanced Placement, so the last thing I needed was for my nose to be rubbed in my failures. Sanjay was like me – one of the smart kids who didn't excel in the sciences. I know it sounded like an oxymoron, but students like us did, in fact, exist. We'd calculated the risks and determined our best bet for admittance into a high-ranking university was to take, and excel, in the lower-level college prep classes for the subjects we weren't as strong in. And while I shone in reading, writing, and the arts, that special area of the brain used for scientific thinking had never fully developed in me. Any mention of a pop quiz in this study area was enough to send me to the nurse's office to ride out a series of faked menstrual cramps.

"Number twenty-nine!" the teacher hollered back to me. "Tell me your name, please."

Every set of eyes in the classroom swiveled in my direction, and I cringed. Great, just what I needed – to be singled out on the day I hadn't shaved my legs.

"Samantha Anderson."

"Louder, please. I can't hear you."

What did she expect? I'd been banished to Siberia.

I repeated myself, this time giving my voice the push it needed to project across the great divide.

"Well, Samantha, I'm sure we'll get another student in here at some point, but until then, you get the best partner of all – me."

Finding herself hilarious, Mrs. Lee giggled like a schoolgirl. I realized my teacher was trying to be light-hearted and funny, but there was a time and place for adults to be comedians, and this clearly wasn't it. The longer she drew this out, the pokier the hairs on my legs became.

Before the Bunsen burner lottery began, I'd just been hoping not to be partnered up with Nosebleed Nathan. Legend had it he'd once pulled a blood clot from his nostril the length of his forearm. And yet, still, I'd prefer daily bloodletting over being best buds with my chemistry teacher.

Mrs. Lee moved onto the classroom rules, allowing me to relax a bit and take in my new surroundings. Table fourteen sported two girls who were getting to know each other by talking non-stop throughout the teacher's speech. As annoying as they were, I envied them. Not because they were interrupting class, but because of the ease with which they apparently made friends. I was the girl in school with one friend, and sadly that one friend had severe allergies that kept her out of school on a regular basis. So, when she was home on one of her many sick days, I was the girl who sat in the library and read a book.

It's not that I was necessarily a weird kid; I'd just never managed to find a place to belong. Maybe it was because I'd come in late to the game – midway through sophomore year – and long after all the social cliques were filled. I wandered for weeks before Shannon, in all her sneezing glory, swooped in and saved me from complete social annihilation.

The door to the classroom opened just a smidge and hovered there a moment in suspended animation. A voice could be heard laughing on the other side. All heads swiveled toward the interruption, forcing Mrs. Lee to stop enjoying the sound of her own voice and swing her head toward the source of the commotion.

Lips pressed in a thin line, she grimaced as she called out. "Excuse me."

The voice on the other side of the door continued to chatter away, not in the least bit concerned he was disrupting the class fifteen minutes after the start bell had rung.

Mrs. Lee, who'd been resting her newly minted 'best friend' rump on the front of her desk, stood up and walked to the door, yanking it inward with all the strength her tiny body could muster. The reason for the resistance was the male arm attached to the door handle on the other side. The wider the door got, the more of the body attached to the anonymous arm followed, and into the classroom stumbled a boy, laughing as if he hadn't a care in the world. There was no mistaking that face. Or that laugh.

Every person in the room sat up a little straighter, smiles already brightening their faces. Pearl Beach High's very own Jeff Spicoli had just entered the building in the form of Keith McKallister – arguably the most disruptive student in school. Don't get me wrong, he wasn't a bully or anything like that – but he was always ready with a sarcastic remark or a perfectly timed interruption. If this guy managed to find his way into your classroom, you just knew you were in for an entertaining semester.

Needless to say, Keith was a hit among the student body. Guys loved him because he made them laugh, and girls loved him because he made them swoon. I myself didn't have an opinion on him one way or another. He'd never spoken to me. He'd never looked at me. He'd never even breathed in my direction, so any judgment I might have of him was based solely on hearsay from those in the know.

There were so many words circulating around campus to describe Keith McKallister, but some of the most common ones were dumb, stoned surfer and hilariously hot fuckup. Again, I couldn't confirm or deny these character assessments, but they seemed fairly accurate to me, given the alarming rate at which girls at the school fell victim to his doped-up charms. Sure, he was a good-looking guy, but Keith McKallister was not boyfriend material. He was the guy you hit up if you needed some weed or if you wanted a guaranteed good time at prom. He was not, I repeat, not the guy you wanted to bring home to meet Mommy.

Not like such a scenario would ever pertain to me. I stood so far outside of Keith's realm I might as well have been in a different solar system. It wasn't just that he was a senior and I a lowly junior, but in order to have a shot at enjoying Keith's unpredictable company, you'd have to be in the first or second tier of popularity. That ruled me out immediately, as I was down there on the fourth out of five tiers. Yes, I'd raised myself up a notch because, please, I had to be at least a level above the guy who pulled snot taffy out of his nose.

"Are you in my class?" Mrs. Lee asked, taking a decidedly defensive stance with one hand wedged on her hip. It probably goes without saying, but the teachers and staff at Pearl Beach High weren't as fond of Keith as the student body was. It was rumored there were bidding wars at the beginning of the semester to see which unlucky educators would get stuck with him.

Keith stood motionless, appearing uncertain himself if this class was where he belonged. His confusion was understandable. He was one of those guys who routinely wandered around the halls until someone on staff pointed him and his fellow potheads in the right direction.

"I don't know," he answered in a low drawl. "What class is this?"

"I don't know," she mimicked. "What class do you think it is?"

"Um… Chemistry?" he tried, as if he truly were just taking a wild guess.

Giggles erupted as my fellow students salivated at the possibility of having Keith amuse them on a daily basis. However, Mrs. Lee was clearly not one of his admirers and resisted allowing him passage into her sanctuary.

"You're not on my student list, Mr. McKallister."

"Are you sure?" he asked.

"Trust me. I check at the beginning of every semester."

"Yeah, so, Mr. Friend said he didn't have room and that I'd been transferred to you."

"Oh, did he now?" Mrs. Lee asked, crossing her arms defiantly over her chest. "How convenient for Mr. Friend."

Keith shrugged, not picking up on the diss at all. "I guess."

"All right, well, go sit. We'll get this straightened out later. Don't get too attached to my classroom, because you're going right on back to Mr. Friend first thing tomorrow morning."

"Dude, I don't think so." Keith shook his head. "He said something about having a doctor's note excusing him from having me repeat his class another semester."

Mrs. Lee sighed so loudly even I could hear it all the way in the back of the classroom. "We'll just see if that will be enough to save Mr. Friend. All right. I'll get this all straightened out later, but for now you're number thirty – last table left side. Move along, dude."

Number thirty? Oh, no. I couldn't be Keith's partner. I sucked at science. I needed someone who could help me or, at the very least, someone who wouldn't drag me down with him. Mr. Friend had to take him back, even if it meant my circulating a petition on Keith's behalf.

With every step he took in my direction, I could sense my list of choice colleges shrinking. Panic rising, I sat transfixed in my seat as Keith confidently strolled through the classroom, high-fiving and hugging everyone along the way. I did notice, however, that he wisely sidestepped Nosebleed Nathan.

My brand spankin' new lab partner stopped at table fifteen.

"Hey you," he said, flashing me his most disarming smile. "Can I sit?"

Saliva dried in my throat, rendering me speechless. Say something. Anything. But I just sat there staring, fighting the horror of my predicament with a smile that flatlined before it ever formed.

And if that wasn't bad enough, my body reacted in a similarly embarrassing fashion, heating up areas I'd prefer stayed frosty. Perspiration instantly squirted from my pores, flattening my hair to my forehead. Suddenly I wished I were Thad's partner. I'd take the nickname V-Dicky any day over this.

Keith kept his eyes on me, a knowing smile settling onto his face. And even though I kept that weird killer clown smile on mine, I cringed inside as I waited for the nasty comments I was sure were about to befall me. I'd heard them all before, but the ones that hurt the worst were the ones hardest for me to change.

I wasn't pretty or skinny or engaging, I knew that, but to constantly be reminded of my faults was like a dagger to my heart. And boys like Keith, ones who slayed with their tousled good looks, did not suffer fools easily, especially not sweaty, unshaven squinty-eyed ones. Sadly, mortification seemed the only realistic path forward.

"I like your necklace. That's an agate, right?"

I blinked in shock, trying to process his words and the friendly way in which they'd been spoken. Glancing down at the security blanket dangling around my neck, I blushed. Rubbing the stone in times of stress had become a habit of mine, one I wasn't aware I was doing until someone pointed it out to me… someone like Keith. Keith McKallister. My lab partner. Lucky number thirty. Oh, god, I think I might pass out.

Somehow in the sea of sweat and stubble, I found my voice. "Yes, blue lace agate."

Keith, his eyes bloodshot and rolling just slightly in their sockets, replied in a clear tone of voice. "I dig the triangular shape – it looks like a guitar pick. And those colors in yours, dude, they remind me of totally iridescent waves."

Was I supposed to answer? Agree? Ask about the weather? Aside from the cool ocean patterns racing through the smooth stone surface, there was nothing outwardly special about the leather cord necklace I wore. Inwardly, however, well... that was a different story.

Gripping the stone tighter, I rubbed the hell out of it like the little freak I was. "Um... thank you."

Taken aback by the compliment, I nonetheless steeled myself for the assault. Come on, skater boy, hit me with your best insult. Just get it over with. I've been through way worse than anything you could dream up. Deflecting a few rude comments from a stoner was all in a day's work for me. Yet that affable, glazed-over expression of his never faded and, slowly but surely, the tension eased from my bones.

"Can I sit?" He repeated his earlier question as if he required my permission. This guy could do just about anything he wanted in this school with very little consequence. He was, after all, Keith McKallister, dope-dealer extraordinaire, and that made him about as close to a celebrity at Pearl Beach High School as one could get. Everybody knew of him, but few actually knew him. That's not to say he was some complicated guy who kept the world at arm's length. On the contrary, Keith was just high a lot of the time and a little difficult to have a conversation with.

"Um... yeah... sure." I swallowed hard, observing him with broad, unblinking eyes as my chem partner slid onto the stool beside me. Surprisingly, the faint pong of weed clinging to his clothing took a backseat to the smell of salt and seaweed. As a rule, I hated the smell of seaweed… but not on him. The scent was a surprisingly pleasant one when it was clinging to his bronzed skin.

Unsure what to do with myself, I opened my notebook and stared at the blank page. I needed to do something, anything, but I was nearly paralyzed with indecision.

A silly giggle erupted from the boy beside me. "I had the weirdest dream last night," he began.

My first instinct was to ignore him – not to be rude, mind you, but because I had no idea how to respond. Was he just musing, or was he looking for an in-depth analysis of his nocturnal adventures?

His continued amusement piqued my curiosity to a point where it could no longer be denied. "What was your dream about?" I asked, cautiously.

"A platypus."

I cast him a sideways glance as a spontaneous smile jumped to my lips. Why did that not surprise me? This guy was all kinds of weird. Or stoned. Or a combination of the two. But I didn't care because it had been a long time since I'd met someone quirky enough to pull me out of a nearly two-year funk. Simply put, Keith was a breath of 'not so' fresh air.

"A platypus?" I questioned, always the analytical one. "Like the animal?"

"No, like the breakfast cereal." He chuckled. "Of course, the animal."

And then I did something I hadn't done in ages: I laughed. Unencumbered by self-doubt, endorphins skipped their way from one neuron to the next. I felt almost weightless.

"You're funny," he said.

No. I was so far from funny that even old people with their hearing aids turned down didn't chuckle awkwardly at me. But you know what? I'd accept Keith's compliment and blush over it for days.

"So, um..." Come on, Samantha. You can do this. Deep breath. Talk. "Platypus dreams, huh? They can't be all that common."

He laughed, nudging into me with his shoulder as if we were the oldest of friends. "I know, right?"

I giggled – actually giggled. What was happening here? How on earth had I gone from sad, lonely number twenty-nine into a tittering dream analyst for Pearl Beach's hottest stoner? A lifetime of self-preservation, and now suddenly I was throwing caution to the wind with the guy who kept my fellow classmates in a steady supply of mind-altering drugs. I should fear him. Why didn't I? He was the school stoner. By definition, that made him the least trustworthy person in town.

Yet here I was finding actual words to speak. "So, what exactly was this platypus doing in your dream?"

Keith leaned in, a grave expression transforming his goofy face. It was as if what he was about to say was of critical importance to the security of the nation. "She wanted her baby back."

Never had I been as riveted by a story as I was this one. I matched his serious face and whispered a response of my own. "Where was her baby?"

Number thirty tilted upright once more, returning to me the personal space he'd just stolen. He shrugged. "How would I know? It was a dream."

Gaping openly at him, I waited for the continuation of his story – willed it from his depths – yet nothing more was revealed. That couldn't be it! There were too many unanswered questions. "Wait, what?"

"Exactly, dude. Trippy, right?"

"That was..." I cocked my head, blinking at him. Was he for real? Being a lifelong reader, I knew a thing or two about plot holes, and his tale was littered with craters. "I'm sorry, but that was the worst bit of storytelling I've ever heard."

Keith laughed as he folded his arms on the table like a pillow, laid his head down, and smiled up at me from his relaxed position. Holy crap, he was handsome. My heart did a little somersault. I guess maybe I'd never given him the credit he deserved, but in my defense, I'd also never been this close to such perfect imperfection. Keith's shoulder-length sandy brown hair, streaked by the sun, was a tangled mess, and his deeply tanned skin was strewn with sun splotches and road-burn-style scratches. His tattered clothing completed the haphazard picture.

Yet, that face.

It was like something out of a teen dream magazine, and I could easily picture him smiling back at me from a poster on my wall. Thankfully, my goggling didn't seem to register with my lab partner; either he was used to the reaction or he just didn't care. But a strange thing happened to me in that moment – a feeling of weightlessness came over me, filling me up as the stress I'd been holding onto for so long suddenly evaporated. Two years I'd tried to rid myself of the strain, and this wild, handsome boy waltzed in with gemstone compliments and unfinished dreams and suddenly I had a reason to laugh again.

His eyes twinkled with mischief. "I'm Keith, by the way."

"Samantha."

"Cool. I'm gonna take a nap now."

I nodded.

Summer school, here I come.

CHAPTER TWO

KEITH

Wasted Space

"Kali, wake up."

Hands jostled my slumbering frame. Keeping my eyes firmly closed, I groaned my displeasure while swatting blindly at the annoying gnat-like creature invading my privacy.

"You got any skunk on you?" the voice slobber-whispered into my unprotected orifice. I cringed as his spittle slow-dripped into my earhole.

"Can't you see I'm napping?" I grumbled, irritated that my pot-laced brownie high had worn off after such a short amount of shuteye. I really needed to sell better shit.

"Well, you might want to wake up, because the bell's rung, and as we speak, Mrs. Lee's on her way over to kick your ass."

My eyes flew open as I raised my head and looked around. The class was indeed empty, and the little drill sergeant of a chemistry teacher was stalking her way to the back of the classroom.

"I'm going," I said, catching her eye as I hastily grabbed my backpack and bolted to my feet. But in the melee, the strap of my pack caught on my lab partner's stool, tipping it, and me, sideways. I tumbled ungracefully to the floor.

"Oh, my god." Mrs. Lee hurried over and pulled the stool off me. I was about to thank her for her concern when I noticed her checking the chair for damage instead of me. Well, okay then. At least now I knew where I stood in this awkward threesome – squarely behind the inanimate object.

Rising to my feet, I dusted myself off, grinning. "Yes, I'm fine. No worries, Teach."

Teach wasn't amused by the shortening of her title, or maybe her distaste was with me in general. She pursed her lips as if I were a particularly unsavory flavor in her mouth. "You've been in my room thirty minutes, Mr. McKallister, and already you've disrupted the class, enjoyed a siesta, and destroyed my property."

"Actually" – I directed her attention to the unscathed stool – "I don't mean to be a stickler for detail, but technically the chair landed on me, so I think it's fair to assume I cushioned its fall."

A steely-eyed glare was her only response.

"Look, I'm sorry," I said, attempting to ease the rising tension between us with a little schoolplace humor. "My lab partner dropped the ball on this one. But don't blame her. She's new to this whole thing, and evidently I forgot to outline her duties, which include waking me up at the bell."

Like a rocket flaming on the launch pad, Mrs. Lee exploded. "Out!" Her finger shook as it pointed me toward the front door.

"It was a joke," I mumbled. Jesus. She needed to take a chill pill. Come to think of it, I probably had one in my pocket for her. "I'm leaving; relax."

Exhaling audibly, my chemistry teacher appeared worn and, dare I say, disappointed in me. "Why are you here, Keith? You obviously don't care about your future, so if you don't want to learn, go home. All you're doing is wasting your time and mine."

Normally I would have responded with a snarky comment, but her judgment bothered me enough that I was left speechless and feeling like a fool. With heat burning up my cheeks, I turned and exited the classroom. That's when the anger set in. Who was she to talk down to me? It was her job to deal with wastes of space like me. If she didn't like juvenile delinquents, then why the hell was she a teacher in the first place? Poor career planning, if you asked me.

Still, Mrs. Lee's words knocked me off my game. I hated getting lectured by authority figures, maybe because deep down, I thought of myself as a good kid – redeemable. Although I suppose I could understand how others might not see me in the same light.

"So..." Gnat buzzed in my face as I stormed down main hall. "You got anything?"

"Not for you," I answered, without even the benefit of a sideways glance.

"I got money," he whispered, at least smart enough to keep his voice down to an almost inaudible squeak. "I can pay."

"Fuck you," I scoffed. Like I needed Gnat's money. There were a hundred more insects just like him hovering in the wings ready to throw cash at me for a good time. Besides, after Mrs. Lee's diss, I was in a foul mood, and someone had to pay. "You ruined my beauty sleep, Dipwad. Thanks to you, I'm going to be twenty percent uglier for the rest of the day."

His buddies laughed. Gnat did not. "Come on, Kali. Don't be a dick."

Clenching my teeth, I fought the urge to pop him in the jaw. This was the downside to being Pearl Beach's bagman. They never left me alone. And shits like Gnat really irritated the hell out of me. He knew the rules: no money or drugs exchanged hands within these walls. Everyone in the loop knew where to find me after the bell rang.

But he wouldn't stop; kept pestering me for a dime. I'd had enough, so I grabbed Gnat by the shirt and pushed him against the wall with enough force to wipe the smirk right off his face. Careful to keep my voice low, I growled in his ear. "I'll be sure to let my boss know who to thank for getting me kicked out of here."

Horror swept across the kid's face. "No. No, that's not..."

"If you think you can do it better, take your paisley ass downtown and make the deal yourself. Have fun playing with the big boys, Gnat."

If possible, his eyes grew even wider. These rich boys never wanted to get their hands dirty. They paid someone else to take the risk. Someone expendable, like me.

I let Gnat off the wall, and as he flew away, my eyes passed over several students glancing warily in my direction. Ah, shit. I hated that look. I wanted people to like me – no, I wanted them to love me. I wasn't a heavy; never had been. But one thing I'd learned in this business was if you gave gnats a little space to spread their wings, they'd take over the world.

"Nice, Keith." A slow clap accompanied a sarcastic female voice. "Way to make a scene on day one of senior year."

I flipped around only to find my sister Emma standing before me with her flowing blonde hair, a dangerously short and low-cut flowered dress, and beach-ready flip-flops. Good lord. Could she get anymore cliché California girl?

"I see you left the Uggs at home," I said. "Good for you."

"I see you left your comb at home. Honestly, Keith, you look like you just stepped out of one of those 70's communes where the leader was trying to poison everyone and you were only set free when the place was raided by law enforcement and then the cops gathered all the kids of the sister-wives together, sprayed them down with a hose, and sent them to the local school to be ridiculed and picked on."

"That's…" My brain took a moment to process her incredibly visual description of my hairstyle. "Very detailed."

Emma nodded, and we exchanged nearly identical grins. I could feel the tension ease after the confrontation with Mrs. Lee. Sometimes I just needed my sis's unique brand of humor.

"So, Jethro," she said, now assigning me a cult name. "Do you have a problem with my outfit?"

Of course I had a problem with her outfit. Where to begin? Too much makeup. Too much leg. Too much boob. Too much of everything I liked to see on other girls – just not on her, my little sister.

Emma was only a sophomore, after all; too young for the attention she was receiving from the guys my age. More and more, I was finding myself in the unenviable position of shutting down conversations centered on my sister's body parts. It was creepy, and it needed to stop.

"No way did Mom green-light this get-up."

"Of course not. I changed in Lydia's car on the way over."

I pushed my backpack into her arms. "Here, wear this – on your front."

"It's not *that* revealing, Keith." She glanced back at her posse, as if to get their reaction to my ridiculous request for modesty. "Until I'm dress-coded, the outfit stays. Geez, Keith, since when did you get so conservative?"

"Well, you know, back in the commune…"

Emma threw her head back and laughed. This was the sister I knew and loved – the one I could hang with and not worry about having to kick the ass of every guy who gave her a sideways glance. If only we lived in a chilly climate, my life would be so much easier.

Suddenly serious, Emma grabbed my arm and steered me away from her gaggle of friends, all while still impressively micromanaging the team. "Go on ahead. I'll catch up with you guys in a few."

A chorus of giggles erupted from Emma's squad. "Bye, Keith."

I waved and smiled at the departing herd parading themselves down the hallway. I swear you could almost see the little animated hearts pulsing from their eyeballs.

"Stop encouraging them," Emma complained once they'd gone.

"What? I'm telling you, Em, it's the whole cult thing. Chicks love it."

"Yeah, well, I don't like that my friends think you're hot. It makes me want to throw up in my mouth."

I nodded, her comment making perfect sense. "I get the same shit about you, only instead of throwing up, I punch people."

"Yes. And speaking of punching, you need to be careful, Keith. Strong-arming a hundred-and-twenty-pound sophomore is not up to school code. You can't afford to get in trouble."

I mimed a perfect pout. "He started it."

"Well, you finished it, and that's all administration needs to kick you out of here with a backpack full of pot."

Emma never sugar-coated things, always telling me how it was whether I wanted to hear it or not. And since I didn't have the type of friends who were up for deep conversations, Emma had become my go-to confidant. Contrary to what her appearance said about her, Emma was no mindless beach-bunny. In fact, she was the smartest person I knew… although to be fair, that wasn't saying much.

"And not only that, but I overheard Mom and Dad talking about how to deal with you, and they were throwing around the idea of some family bonding and communication class. I mean, why should the rest of us kids suffer because you're a dim-witted pothead?"

"Right, because god forbid we get closer as a family."

Emma rolled her eyes. "We live in a shoebox. How much closer can we get? Look, all I'm asking is that you don't be stupid. Can you do that for me, Keith?"

"Sure Em, I'll give it a shot."

"Good." She patted my shoulder, smiling. "Now get to class. The bell is about to ring."

The first rule of high school: never run. A tardy was always preferable to dashing across campus like an overeager freshman. Besides, getting to class on time had never been my thing. It just extended the amount of time I had to spend learning. And for that reason, instead of taking a direct path to my classroom, I ducked into the bathroom first, followed by a quick detour to the C-wing to check in on a hot chick I hadn't seen since I'd made out with her at a party last week. She was happy to see me. Her teacher? Not so much.

By the time I wandered into fourth period, I was in trouble again. It was an endless cycle made possible by the fact that I couldn't make a good decision to save my life. My irresponsible behavior could all be traced back to one very damaging character flaw – impulse control. Or rather, the lack of it. If something seemed like a good idea at the time, I did it, no questions asked and no costs considered. I'd always been of the mindset that it was better to deal with the consequences *after* the fact than to never have done it at all. And, while that approach had proved epic for me in the short run, long term it wasn't nearly as satisfying… or safe.

Case in point – my side business. I could see now that I probably should have remained a gnat. But, no, I just *had* to become their king. It had all started out innocently enough. Last year, after my former dealer was arrested, I'd had no choice but to make my way downtown to refresh my supply. And since I was already going out of my way to get a dime bag for myself, why not pick up some extra herbage for my homies, right? And then, if I was taking that additional step for my friends, it would just be rude not to pick up a little something extra for the cheerleaders and jocks. I was a giver that way.

Of course, the downtown dealers knew a sucker when they saw one, and before I knew it, a smarmy dude named St. Nick was promising me riches and filling bags of weed in a sack like some stinky Santa Claus.

No. No. NO, my brain screamed at the time. *Run, Keith. Run.*

And, of course, that would have been the correct response – the smart choice. But the rewards – oh god, the rewards. They sounded amazing. Money. Popularity. Truck loads of cannabis. What could go wrong?

"So are we all in agreement? Vacation starts tomorrow?" Valentine asked. "First stop, Universal Studios?"

Warning lights immediately flicked on, blinking and swirling in my brain. My thoroughly exhausted, and whiny, voice of reason desperately tried to talk me out of it. *There is no reason for a vacation, Keith. Senior year only started today. Don't be a dumbshit, Keith.*

My buddies and I, we lived for these mini vacations. They were the highlight of every school year. But never had we tried one this early in the game. It was a ballsy move, for sure, but the risk was what made it extra fun. Plus I was still smarting from Mrs. Lee's comments, so anything that got me out of her class for a couple of days was a good thing in my book.

"I'm in," I impulsively blurted out. And just like that, another shitty decision was born. "But if I'm taking the Surfmobile, you guys better lay flat in the truck bed this time. I'm not getting another ticket because of you."

"You hit a pot hole," my fellow stoner Walt complained. "We weren't sitting up, we were levitating."

"Yeah, well. No levitating in my fucking truck. You know the rules."

The others grumbled, but since I was the only one who owned a vehicle with the capacity to stack bodies on top of one another, they had no choice but to agree to my conditions.

"Hey, Kali, you want to hear the coolest story ever?" Screensaver asked. I glanced his direction, surprised by his participation. This was the guy who'd gotten his nickname because he literally did nothing all day, and that included talking. Screensaver typically rode out any discussion in a haze. He was what we called perma-fried, meaning he acted high even when there was no drug residue in his system. It was almost as if he had backup reserves of the stuff floating around in his lungs. But today – well, he was just extra giddy with excitement, which in turn sparked my curiosity.

"Sure. Hit me."

"Last night I asked my dad if we could get a cat and he said no. I asked why and he said it was because Mom has allergies."

Oh-kay. He lost me at cat. I turned in my seat, no longer interested in his shitty kitty story. I should have known better than to get my hopes up with this one.

Yet despite my completely ghosting him, Screensaver continued with his tale of tails. "So I said to him, 'Once Mom dies, *then* can we get a cat?' And Dad said, 'Sure, bud, just as soon as she dies.' I mean, is that like the coolest thing ever? I'm getting a cat. Dude, I'm so stoked right now."

Raising a brow, I glanced back over. Holy shit! He was for real. I burst into a fit of hysterics, which only served to confuse my dopey friend.

"You do realize," I said through the laughter, "that you'll have to sacrifice your mom to get that cat, right?"

Screensaver pressed his lips together, not appreciating me questioning his reasoning. "Are you not listening to me, Kali? I'll have *a cat*. God, sometimes you are so stupid."

I could have argued with him, but what was the point? He wouldn't remember it in the morning. Hell, he wouldn't remember it in three minutes. Pulling my hood up, I took to scanning the lunch tables for intelligent life forms. If Screensaver was any indication, I'd need to look well outside the perimeter of my immediate circle.

In a school of over two thousand students, there was a wide world to explore. Too bad I never did. An interesting phenomenon had occurred with the jump from middle to high school. The stereotypical groups remained, only now the popular cliques had joined forces, their masses occupying a third of the outdoor quad. Dubbed Utopia, entry was strict. Either you were in, by belonging to a certain group, or you were hand-picked based on your athletic ability, your good looks, or some other value deemed worthy by the powers that be. I was in, and so were my boys, because of what I brought to the table – literally. Every group needed their friendly, local pot guru. But because Utopia was like an ecosystem all its own, it was easy to forget that three quarters of the school population lingered on the outside looking in.

My eyes narrowed in on my lab partner at a table located well outside of the coveted zone. What was her name again? I searched my memory banks but came up with nothing. Granted, I'd been seriously baked when I'd made her acquaintance earlier in the day. And even though I couldn't recall much of our conversation, the part where I sounded a lot like Screensaver came to mind. *The platypus dream? Really?*

She was sitting with her friend, the kinky-curly haired sneezer with the perpetually red nose. Now hers was a name I remembered. Everyone in the school knew who Shannon O'Malley was – the girl who had freakish allergies as well as the highest number of paramedic visits in the history of Pearl Beach High. She was the reason peanuts were banned from the lunch tables and epi pens were strategically placed throughout the campus. If ever there were a candidate for "The Girl In The Bubble" program, it would be poor, wheezy Shannon O'Malley.

My lab partner was deep in debate with her friend and hadn't yet noticed me staring. I didn't know what it was about her that caught my eye, but it probably had something to do with the way she was so engrossed in the conversation she was having. I wished I could say the same thing about the company I kept because the current discussion going on behind me would entice no one.

"Dude, I dare you to deep throat this pickle," said Jordy, a.k.a Fire Crotch. He'd gotten his nickname from… well, I think you get the idea.

"You're on," Valentine agreed without hesitation. "Hand me that girthy fella."

Those two were a powerful argument for abstinence. Distracted, I kept an eye on the girls who were still hunched over the table talking. What was so damn important? They acted like they'd just discovered the cure for cancer. Incidentally, such a medical breakthrough probably wouldn't be all that farfetched for those two. Based solely on their unfashionable clothing, I guessed their IQ's were at cancer-curing levels. There was no doubt in my mind that these two were going places – if Shannon didn't contract a deadly virus first.

"What are you two talking about?" I whispered under my breath, surprised I even cared. Maybe I was just starving for something different. After all, eighty-four percent of the conversations I'd had with females today revolved around Starbucks. I hated that I knew the Frappuccino flavor of the month.

Movement on the dork front caught my attention, and I sat up a little straighter. Both girls came out of their huddle and, as if perfectly choreographed, turned their heads at the exact same moment. Suddenly two sets of eyes were staring directly at me. I almost diverted my own just from the shock of being caught, but then it occurred to me they'd been talking about me, so really *they* should be the embarrassed party. And, oh lordy, were they ever. Both immediately shifted their gaze, my lab partner even going so far as to shield her face from view with a carefully placed, unmanicured hand.

Fuck the kitty cats and the pickle head, this was the conversation I wanted in on. Just exactly what were those nerdy girls saying about me? I had half a mind to break out of Utopia and stalk over there myself. And I would have, too, if it wouldn't have been social suicide. So instead, I kept my eyes glued on the girls, waiting. I knew my lab partner would be back, too curious not to check if I was still watching her.

A full minute passed before she lifted her eyes just enough to see me staring. I waved. The girl's eyes widened as she slowly swiveled her head around, checking the space behind her to determine if there was, perhaps, another intended recipient of my greeting. Finding no one there, the girl gestured toward herself, before mouthing *Me?*

A smile tugged at my lips and I nodded. "Yes, you."

Chapter Three

Samantha

Spooned

I nearly floated from my seat on a wave of euphoria. Keith. Keith McKallister was smiling at me. This just didn't happen – not to me. And even though I'd done a sweep of the perimeter to confirm there hadn't been someone else passing behind me at that exact moment, I was still having trouble processing the sudden turn of events. I mean, what were the chances that moments after I'd given Shannon the rundown of events in chemistry class that we'd look up to find him staring?

In a perfect world, I would have remained calm and composed – maybe even offered him an upper class wave or a sexy toss of my tangled mane. But, of course, I'd done the opposite, and now I had to deal with the burn spreading through my cheeks from the embarrassment of being me.

As quickly as the excitement surfaced, my questioning mind chased it away. Why single me out –the chubby chick from chemistry? What was his angle? The more I thought about it, the more I realized his actions made no sense. With him sitting over there in his posh zip code, there was absolutely no reason for him to acknowledge my existence.

Reality smacked me squarely in the face: Keith was mocking me. Of course he was. It was the only logical conclusion. He'd probably made some bet with his buddies – devised some plan to humiliate me in front of the entire student body. I could almost picture the pig's blood dripping down my face. I should have known better. 'Nice' in my world was never just nice.

Heat burned up my spine and spread through the extremities. I was teetering dangerously close to an emotional collapse. I didn't have a lot of reserves to pull from in the first place, but this had the makings of a full-scale disaster. Peace was all I asked for. Why couldn't people just leave me alone?

Willing back the sobs threatening to burst unchecked, I grabbed my backpack and ran from the lunch tables. It never even occurred to me that I'd just abandoned my best friend until Shannon caught up with me at the end of the first set of lockers.

"Samantha! What happened?" she asked, panic gripping her as she checked me for injury. She wouldn't find anything. The damage was buried too deep.

Tears brimmed on my lashes. "He waved and smiled at me."

"What are you talking about?"

"Keith. He waved and smiled at me."

"Keith McKallister waved and smiled at you?" Shannon repeated, and I could see her trying to process the gravity of my words but finding nothing alarming in them whatsoever. And then came the stunned smile. "For real?"

"Yes, for real."

"Then why are you crying? That's the best thing that's happened to either of us in high school, and I'm including the time that guy said I might be pretty if I could get rid of all my freckles."

Exactly my point. That was the type of garbage she and I dealt with on a daily basis, and it was the reason I was now convinced of Keith's deception. I dropped my gaze to the floor. "He was making fun of me, Shannon."

"By waving and smiling? Apparently you've never had people fake-blow their noses when you walk by or ask you how many *miles* tall you are."

It was a joke, but there was no mistaking the pain behind her admission. It wasn't easy being misfits in a world of health and beauty, but Shannon and I did our best, minding our own business until someone felt the need to rub our noses in all our faults. I hated feeling unworthy, but maybe that was just me. Shannon apparently was made of sterner stuff.

"It's not fair. You're the nicest girl at this school. If people just took the time to get to know you, they'd love you as much as I do."

The way I saw it, there was someone for everyone in this world, and at this point in my life, Shannon was my only someone. Already emotional, I failed to stop the tears from rolling down my cheeks. Maybe I was just overly sentimental because this was the last 'first day of school' I would ever share with my friend. Shannon was a senior, so by this time next year, she'd be in college, off living the dream, and I'd be confined to the four walls of the library praying the librarian had done a heavy restock over the summer.

Shannon's eyes softened as she wrapped her arms around me and squeezed. "Don't add me to your list of woes. And stop obsessing over what others think of you. Who cares? You are you. I am me. We can't change that. But what we can do is surround ourselves with positive people."

I cringed just thinking about the support system I had at home. Shannon picked up on it right away, holding me tighter. "It's not as simple for you. I get that, but just know it will get easier. High school doesn't last forever. And has it even occurred to you that maybe Keith's smile and wave was just that – a friendly gesture? There are still good people in this world."

I leaned back, considering my best friend's words before grinning. "He's a drug dealer, Shannon."

"A drug dealer with a heart of gold, Samantha." She winked. "With a heart of gold."

I spent fifth period hashing over Shannon's version of events. Was I so warped in my thinking that I'd misread what happened at the lunch tables? Was Keith really just being friendly? And if that were the case, what did it say about me? I had a sinking feeling if I continued down this skeptical path, I was going to live a lonely, distrustful life.

Maybe it wasn't so far off to think Keith liked me – in the most platonic sense of the word. We'd had a fairly interesting conversation, and I had actually felt a connection to him. Not a romantic one, of course, because that would just be, well, pathetic wishful thinking. No, the connection I'd made with him was a human one. Keith had seen me – the invisible Samantha Anderson – and, for only the second time since moving to this town, I'd felt like I belonged. Like I was a part of something bigger than myself. I felt welcomed.

Not that it was going to last. If my disappearing act at the lunch tables hadn't put a wrench in our unlikely pairing, Keith's inevitable transfer back into the other chemistry class certainly would. I mean, what were the chances of Mr. Friend's doctor's note holding up in a court of law? Odds were, by tomorrow morning Keith would be returned to his rightful home, and, in true Samantha fashion, my good fortune would have only lasted a class period – even less if you counted Keith's late start… and the nap.

As the school day drew to a close, all thoughts of Keith and chemistry were set aside for the real life drama that plagued me. Home. As in, I had to go there after school. I drew in a deep breath and tried to settle my nerves. Would it ever get easier walking through the front door?

After the bell rang, and all the other students flooded into the surrounding streets and headed back to their humble abodes, I would quietly make my way to the library and settle in for the afternoon. It had become my after-school ritual since moving to town last year, and I wouldn't leave until the lights were turned out in my sanctuary. Only then would I make the anxiety-inducing trip home. You'd think I was going to a funeral the way I went to that dark place in my mind during the five-minute drive.

Because I never knew what to expect when I walked through the front door, my stomach always churned as I stepped onto the front porch. Today was no exception. I silently turned the key in the lock before opening the door and poking my head in to check the situation. The coast was clear, and I sighed in relief. Slipping off my shoes, I tiptoed to my room. Almost there. This might be a good day after all.

"Samantha! Is that you?"

My mother's shrill words rang in my ears, and I stopped dead in my tracks, contemplating my next move. I could ignore her and pretend I hadn't heard, although nobody within a half a block radius could have been spared her piercing screech. Besides, evading her was only a quick fix. She'd still find me, and I'd be right back here where I started.

Shoring myself for the assault, I answered. "Yes. I'm home."

"You care to explain this?"

She always did that, pointing to an issue in another part of the house where I couldn't possibly know what she was referring to. Not that it mattered. Whatever was upsetting her was my fault. It always was. I felt a tingling of dread travel up my spine as my feet obediently moved toward the sound of her voice. I wondered how long she'd been stewing over the perceived slight. As I rounded the corner to the kitchen, I saw her standing with the dishwasher door open.

"I cleaned it out this morning," I said, jumping in to defend myself. "Just like you asked."

She slammed the dishwasher closed, and I jumped in place like the skittish colt she'd raised me to be. Mom yanked open the silverware drawer and the wood hit the stopper with a loud crack. I was surprised the flimsy rubber held. My mother presented me with Exhibit A: a spoon.

"What is this?" she asked, her eyes blazing.

I was too far away to see a problem, but I could guess the issue. I thought back to my brother, Sullivan, who'd taken the brunt of her fury for a similar spoon-related issue. Before he'd gone off to college, our failures split her disappointment in half. Now it was just me dealing with her. And *her* was a mentally unstable perfectionist who forced her unnamed disorder on the rest of us like a demented Martha Stewart.

My mother's tyranny was the reason Sully moved halfway across the country the first chance he got. The reason he'd never once come home to visit that first year in college.

The reason he…

Tears immediately flooded my eyes, and I swallowed them back as quickly as they started. I wouldn't give her the satisfaction. Like a human wrecking ball, my mother had driven away everyone I loved. I was the only one left standing – but just barely. My thoughts turned toward my father. *I can't take it*, he'd said. *She's dangerous. She's crazy*. And yet he'd had no trouble leaving Sully and me behind with Mommy Dearest to go marry the secretary he'd been banging at work.

He'd had no trouble washing his hands of his *old* kids when the new ones came along. And certainly, he had no trouble bitching about the child support payments he was court-ordered to pay. Never mind that it was the only day of the month mom was in a good mood. Sadly, today was not one of those days.

"Spots!" she screamed, the spoon shaking in her hand. "There are spots, Samantha."

"Sorry," I answered feebly, wishing the safety stone around my neck had the ability to erect a shelter large enough for me to crawl inside. "I didn't see them."

"Did you even bother to look? What about this one? Spots, too! Look!" Mom tossed the offending spoon at me before lifting another one from the drawer, examining it. "And this one? I take it you didn't see this one either?"

"I… no…"

Mom let out an aggravated growl before flinging that one at me as well. There had been a time when Mom could nail a fly on an opposing wall with a butter knife, but luckily for me, her aim was all over the place nowadays.

"Get it together! What's wrong with you? How hard is it to wipe down the silverware *before* you put it away? Do I have the only kid on the planet who can't follow simple goddamn instructions?"

"I'll fix it, Mom," I answered, my lip quivering from the force of her fury. I hated living this way. I hated being weak and accommodating, but what choice did I have? Lashing back never accomplished anything except more yelling and more screaming and more punches landing on my body. Appeasing her was the only feasible option. "Go get your stuff done. When you get back, your silverware will be as shiny as a freshly cut diamond."

"Are you mocking me, Samantha? Is that what you're doing?"

"No…no," I hesitated, my voice lowering to a bare whisper. "I'm going to fix this, but I can't if you're throwing silverware at me."

Mom's eyes narrowed as I stood in place like a shaky puppy waiting for the big dog to pounce. If she did, I knew it would hurt, but I'd gotten to a point where I'd become numb to her beatings. At least when they were over, I'd be safe for another day.

But today would prove to be a good day. Instead of engaging, my mother spun for a dramatic exit but dizzied herself in the process and had to get steadied with the support of the kitchen counter before stomping off in a huff. I slumped against the wall, letting out the breath I'd been holding, and those pesky tears returned. Her moods were becoming more erratic. Who was to say the next thing she threw at me wouldn't be a butcher knife that would slice me clean in half?

Maybe I needed to rethink Auntie Kim's offer of asylum. But I barely knew her. Who was to say I wouldn't be trading one bad living situation for another? It was a matter of choosing the devil I knew; although, to be fair, the choice really wasn't mine to make. My mother wouldn't willingly give up daily maid service. And if I didn't have the voice to stand up for myself when it came to smudged spoons, how could I stand up in front of a judge and speak of years of abuse and threats? No, I could make it another year and a half. It would be tough, but I'd survived so far. Once I graduated, I'd be off to a far away college, and I'd never have to lay eyes on that woman again.

Like Sullivan.

A vice tightened around my heart.

No. Not like Sullivan.

Chapter Four

Keith

The 'T' Word

The trip to Universal Studios on Tuesday had seemed like such a good idea – at the time. And ditto to yesterday's outing to Hollywood. Even today's planned beach day hadn't raised any red flags in my mind, and trust me, I'd had plenty of time to ponder the dangers while climbing out my bedroom window and pushing my car to the end of the street to avoid detection.

Certainly I could see how my adventures might not endear me to authority figures, like principals and parents… and cops. Case in point – my father, who was currently clutching the steering wheel with such force that his fingers were turning a sickly shade of white. A few minutes earlier I'd spotted him trudging his way through the sand, dressed in all shades of postman blue. The Terminator grimace he wore on his face told me all I needed to know. I was in big trouble.

It was currently eight-thirty in the morning. He was supposed to be at work. I was supposed to be in school. And now neither of us was where we were supposed to be because I couldn't make a good decision to save my life.

Dad was an infinitely patient man, but even he had his limits. And judging by the demented swearing under his breath, I'd not only hit that limit but had busted through it. He was mad. I got it. Dealing with me couldn't be easy. I was one of those people who never made the same mistake twice. Instead I made it like five or six times; you know, just to be sure.

The garbled mumbling coming from the driver's seat motivated me to get my story straight. I'd screwed up and was going to have to dig deep, employing every last alibi in my depleted arsenal of excuses. What had I been thinking? Skipping class one day, sure, but three? How could I have overlooked the obvious? By not being in my first period seat by the time the bell rang, I was marked as absent. Those absences would generate a report. And that report would produce a call. And that call would prompt my father to leave work and go in search of me. Truly, with all odds stacked against me, it was a miracle I'd made it to day three.

Even as I tried to avoid direct eye contact, I could feel his glare burrowing into me. Dad hated getting called by Principal King almost as much as I hated being sent to his office. It wasn't the first time he'd been forced to take a detour from his postal route to drag my ass off the beach. And, in all honesty, it probably wouldn't be his last.

I cleared my throat. Once. Twice. Eleven times.

"Do you have something to say?" His voice was high-pitched and jittery, like a jacked-up clown preparing to end my life.

"Yeah, I just want you to know how sorry I am, Dad."

And I was. Truly. I never set out to make his life difficult; it just happened organically nearly every day.

His jaw clenched. Nothing in his distressed demeanor favored my survival. "Three days, Keith! You haven't been to school in three days! What the hell have you been doing… for three days?"

Oh, man. The real question was what *hadn't* we done? We'd been all over the Southland, and this morning's surf break had just been the start of another epic adventure. Left unchecked, my buddies and I would have had a kick-ass day at the Santa Barbara Zoo followed by some highly illegal pier jumping. Of course, that seemed like information my father probably didn't want to hear. He was simply too agitated for the truth.

"Just chillin'."

"Just chillin'," he repeated, nodding like one of those loony bobble-heads. "Well, how nice for you. I sure hope you're feeling rested."

Actually, I was, but certainly I wasn't stupid enough to admit that to my father – not when his own stress levels were through the frickin' roof.

"Well, while you were *chillin'*, Principal King was screaming at me over the phone. Something about incompetent parenting and… oh, yeah, he was throwing around the 'T' word."

Dad knew better than to toss puzzles at me so early in the morning. I scratched my head, searching my brain. "Tits?"

A blast of energy escaped him. "Truancy!"

Oh, right. That made more sense than tits.

Dad didn't let me finish my thought before he was asking a follow-up question. "And what follows the 'T' word, Keith?"

My brows furrowed in concentration. So much thinking so early in the morning. "U?"

He slammed his hand against the steering wheel. "Stop playing dumb, Keith. The 'S' word. The 'S' word follows the 'T' word."

What the hell was with all the letters? He knew damn well I couldn't recite the alphabet without singing the song.

"Suspension!" he blurted out. More beastly growling followed. "And, after what happened last year, if your mother even gets wind of that word again, you'll be on your way to military school. I hope you like scrubbing toilets."

I ignored his baseless intimidations. I'd been threatened with military school more times than I could count. The truth was I'd probably already be off to boot camp boarding school if my parents had the money to send me. As it was, my interventions were typically of the bargain basement variety. For example, instead of the Scared Straight program, where a group of my equally doped up peers got screamed at by murderers in prison, I got poison oak from a weekend narcotics prevention camping trip. And instead of pricey drug counseling sessions with a trained professional, I got Justin, the twitchy ex-addict who praised sobriety while pulling strands of hair from his head.

Yes, my parents tried, but I prided myself on staying a step ahead of them at all times. I mean, who said potheads weren't creative? Give us a bud and nothing to smoke out of and we'll turn into frickin' MacGyver.

"Last year wasn't my fault."

"No?" My father violently flung his body back into his car seat as if he were absorbing the jolt of running over a dead body in the road. He was laughing now, but it was the type of dark amusement that preceded a full-on mental breakdown. "I drove you to school every morning. I walked you onto campus practically holding your hand as I personally deposited you in the principal's office, and yet still somehow during school hours, you inexplicably broke into the basement of the ice skating rink with enough pot to kill a medium-sized animal."

He took a moment to gather his wits before continuing on in a calmer tone. "So tell me, Keith. Whose fault was it?"

Obviously mine. But conceding defeat so early in the negotiations was a rookie move. Think. Who could I make the culprit when we both knew all fingers pointed in my direction? "Um… I blame Schwarzenegger."

"Schwarzenegger?" Dad's eyes widened, my innovative answer momentarily taking his mind off premeditated murder. "As in, the governor of California?"

"Yeah. He needs to get tough on education. Do you have any idea how easy it is to sneak out of school?"

Dad sighed heavily, appearing weary of my antics. It took him long enough.

We sat in an extended silence before I asked, "Does Mom know?"

"No, I'll break it to her tonight. Do you have any idea how lucky you are that the school called me today and not her?"

I had some idea. Last time they called my mom, suddenly I was enrolled in a teen drug prevention program with a bunch of tweakers who chased their shadows. I didn't belong there. Just because I was a pothead didn't mean I had a problem with drugs. So I liked to relax with a puff or two, no big deal – well, until I made it a big deal by turning my pastime into a flourishing business.

I traced my finger along the dashboard before meeting my dad's eye. "Luck had nothing to do with it."

"What do you mean?" he asked.

"The office. They won't call her."

Dad couldn't contain his curiosity. "What makes you so sure?"

"Last time I was in the office, the school caught fire."

In response to his shocked expression, I replied, "I know. It surprised me too. Anyway, while they were evacuating the building, I took the liberty of changing her phone number on the emergency form."

My father's mouth dropped open, his eyes darting back and forth between the road and me. "So you're telling me that your first thought in the middle of an emergency was to tamper with official documents?"

I shrugged. "What can I say? I'm good under pressure."

A reluctant smile formed on his lips. "Was there an *ac tual* fire?"

"A small one, in Home Ec. Nothing I couldn't handle."

"No," he chuckled. "Of course not."

I flashed him a brilliant smile, wondering if we were good now. Had I sidestepped punishment?

But his smile faded away as quickly as it appeared. Dammit, he was fighting back. I still had work to do.

"You know, Keith, if you put even half as much effort into school as you do into ditching it, you'd be headed to an Ivy League school."

"Oh, you'd love that, wouldn't you? I could be Mitch's errand boy and keep all his trophies nice and shiny."

The venom that hissed from my mouth surprised even me. Usually I was better at keeping my feelings on that matter to myself, because criticizing Mitch around my father was the equivalent of condemning the Pope. My older superstar half-brother walked on holy water.

Dad shook his head, a sour look on his face. "Knock it off."

"What?" I asked, but already knowing I'd crossed the Mitch-line.

"Stop blaming your brother for your shortcomings. He's worked damn hard for everything he has. You think he ditched three days of school just to chill?"

"No."

"You're damn right, no. You could learn a thing or two from his work ethic, Keith."

"I have a work ethic," I mumbled, even though the truth was, I only worked hard getting myself *out* of trouble. Everything else was approached with half-assed efficiency.

Dad scoffed, raising a brow.

"Okay, fine," I conceded. "Mitch is a saint. Is that what you want to hear? Let's all rejoice."

Looking ready to burst, my father abruptly swerved the car off to the side of the road, then clicked off his seatbelt and turned to face me. "Is that what this is all about? Mitch?"

Stunned by the rapid turn of events, I stumbled over my words. "Wh…what? I have no idea what you're talking about."

"You think I love him more, don't you?"

Of course he loved Mitch more. Anyone in his or her right mind would love Mitch more.

"No," I lied.

But the dumbfounded expression on my father's face told me he was connecting the dots for the very first time. "Keith, listen to me. I've never shown your brother favoritism. I treat all my kids the same, and you can't say otherwise because it's not true."

Oh, how I wanted to believe him! Maybe Dad didn't treat us differently, but it was in the way he looked at Mitch. That told the real story. When my brother was around, my father was like a kid meeting his idol for the first time. With me, there was no excitement. I was just a problem that constantly needed fixing.

It was an injustice I'd watched my whole life, so he could say what he wanted, but I knew the truth. Anger simmered just below the surface, and if my father continued down this treacherous path, I wasn't sure I could prevent an explosion. "Drop it!" I warned.

Maybe Dad sensed my instability because he backed off immediately. We sat in silence for a minute, neither one of us knowing what to say.

Finally, he lowered his voice to barely more than a whisper. "You're in trouble, kid. Big trouble. At this point, I'm not sure if they'll let you stay in school or even graduate."

I scoffed. "I'll graduate, Dad. Jesus. In California, even the biggest idiots earn a high school diploma."

"Yeah, well, California hasn't met *you* yet."

The diss was so unexpected and hilarious that it had us both in stitches and allowed us to bury the hatchet, if only for a short time. Sadly, the lighthearted moment didn't linger.

"I'm being serious now, Keith. Have you even thought about what you want to do with your life after high school? And don't say pirate. That's not an actual profession."

"It is in Somalia."

"Yes, well you live in America, where pirating is frowned upon."

Dad's eyes sharpened on me as he reached over and gripped my shoulder. "Look, kid, we need to turn this sinking ship around before it's too late. This is your last year in high school, and you've already missed nearly every day. And if you do miraculously show up to class, you're stoned. I'm worried about you. I'm afraid you're going to get lost. There's a big, wide world out there ready and willing to swallow you whole."

I knew that. Of course I did. Seeing my father look so troubled pained me. We'd always been close, and even though he didn't approve of my lifestyle, my father had always stuck by my side. During those tough middle school years, he was there. Through my ice-skating rink arrest, he was there. But the fact remained that I was my father's greatest disappointment.

"I'm not going to get lost," I whispered. "I've got it all under control."

"No, you don't. Skating by just isn't going to cut it anymore. You're turning eighteen in a few of months, and once that happens, nothing I say or do will protect you. Don't think I don't know you're dealing, Keith. Mom and I, we don't know how to help you any more, and we're both terrified. If you continue down this path, there's a real good chance you'll end up in prison."

I shifted my gaze out the window, shame coloring my cheeks. It was a fear, for sure. I wasn't strong enough to survive behind bars. "I know."

"It's not too late. Mom and I can get you through this, but you have to do your part too. No more skipping school. You have to pass all your classes and get a high school diploma. And, Keith – no more drugs. No more dealing."

That last one was a taller order. Ridding myself of whatever leftover drugs I had was one thing, but there was also the matter of my side business. Not only were the students at Pearl Beach not going to be happy with a hiatus, neither was my supplier. I'd been making us both good money as of late, and separating myself from the trade wouldn't be as easy as just stepping away. But I had to try… for him.

"Okay."

"Okay?" He flared like a freshly struck match. "Are you saying no more drugs?"

"Yes. I'll clean up my act, for you."

"No, Keith. For *you*. It has to be for you."

Although I didn't really see the difference, it seemed important enough to him that I nodded my agreement. His happiness filled me. Like no one else in my life, my father understood me. He'd once been me – the loveable loser. I wanted more than anything for him to be proud of me the same way he was proud of Mitch. Maybe if I could get myself clean… Maybe. Because, at the end of the day, I was still a daddy's boy, desperately seeking his love and affection.

Chapter Five

Keith

For Me

Although my father and I had come to a shaky agreement, he still didn't trust me enough to allow me to walk into school by myself. Not that I blamed him, after the numerous times I'd strolled in the front entrance to the high school only to slip out the back as soon as his car left the parking lot. This time he refused to allow me out of his sight, gripping the back of my shirt as he guided me through the halls and into the main office.

And now here we were, sitting side by side on the bench outside the principal's office, just two rebels awaiting our sentencing.

Clasping my hands behind my head, I turned toward him. "So, dude, what're you in for?"

Although he tried, there was no suppressing the smile that transformed his face. Still, he refused to humor me with a glance in my direction. "This had better be the last time I come to the principal's office, Keith."

"It will be."

"Because every time I'm in here, it shaves like five years off my life. At this rate, I'll die at fifty."

Patting his shoulder, I reassured him. "And you'll have lived a good, long life."

"You're a piece of work, you know that?" He laughed. "I hope someday you get to experience the joy of having a kid just like you."

"One can dream."

The door opened and Principal King sighed as he narrowed his gaze on me. There was no love lost between the two of us. I estimated I'd taken up more of his time than a thousand normal kids combined. In fact, by the looks of his weathered face, I might eventually have a hand in his early death as well.

"In my office." His clipped voice dripped with contempt.

The desire to flee was strong, but I'd run out of options. This shit was what I'd created. Dutifully, I rose to my feet but, before disappearing into the principal's office, I turned toward my father, in need of a strength I knew I didn't possess. But what I found in his eyes stopped me dead in my tracks – hope, disappointment, love, fear. He'd been beaten down, and his face was distorted with worry. Dad hadn't been kidding. This was killing him. *I* was killing him. I fought the urge to go to him, throw my arms around his shoulders, and bury my head into his neck like I had when I was young and things were still easy.

Regret burned deep as I dropped my head and shuffled into the office.

Thankfully, the browbeating was short-lived. Principal King was more straightforward than my father had been – no cryptic alphabet clues hinting at my fate, just stark warnings about my future at Pearl Beach High School. Never had it been spelled out so clearly. The wiggle room I'd always banked on was gone. Either I got with the program or I was out.

Yeah. I'd heard it all before. The same threat had played out so many times over the years I could recite it in my sleep. So why did this one leave me feeling so edgy? Had it been that glimpse into my father's soul, or was it just that I could finally see the future in front of me, and it wasn't looking pretty? Continuation school – I thought not. I was either going to graduate from Pearl Beach or not at all… and 'not at all' seemed to be the prevailing wind.

But now I had the power to shock the hell out of the masses. The choice was simple, really: clean up my act and empty my lungs of poison, or become the nothingness everyone considered me to be. I'd been at a similar crossroads a few years before in the lunch area of Barnum Middle School. I'd had the option to walk away then, but I'd chosen the wrong path. And now, once again faced with a decision that could very possibly seal my fate, I was still waffling. What was I waiting for? All I had to do was pick what was behind door number two… and give myself a future.

It occurred to me then that I'd all but given up on myself. I myself had bought into the common belief that I was a fuck up, and I was living up to that expectation smashingly. To everyone else, I was a joke. The only people who could still see *me* inside the caricature I'd become was my family. My dad. My mom. My siblings. I was still something to them, even though I could feel myself losing ground there too.

This had to stop. I didn't want to be *that guy*… the one people laughed *at*, not with. I didn't want to be Pearl Beach High's well-loved slacker anymore. I knew if I put my mind to it, I could turn this around. Certainly my people skills and proclivity for money should be enough to carry over into a legitimate job whose employee benefits didn't include jail time.

So while I listened to the principal talk about the future he believed I'd never have, I made what I hoped would be a life-changing decision. Instead of walking toward danger, like I did so many years ago, I would allow my feet to carry me in the opposite direction – to a place where my father could be proud of me again. And maybe even to a place where I could be proud of myself.

Principal King marched me out into the main office just as the passing period bell rang. Through the large windows that spanned the entire wall, I spotted a welcoming committee of sorts. Somehow, the friends I'd left on the beach less than an hour ago were on the other side of the window, sliding their nostrils in grotesque displays along the glass.

I had to hand it to them. They hadn't left me behind. Instead of being halfway to the zoo, my buddies had made the side trip to school to spring my sorry ass. With students flooding the hallways, how easy would it be for me to disappear into the crowd?

King grabbed my arm, pulling me back. "I'll be waiting for you in Mrs. Lee's class in seven minutes. I expect you to be there. If you make the wrong choice and follow them out the back door, I'm going to recommend you for transfer. Do we understand each other?"

I jerked my arm out of Principal King's hold. He might own my ass, but that didn't give him the right to manhandle me. Besides, he didn't need to worry. I'd already made my choice, and it didn't include skidding my nasal passage along single pane glass.

"Yeah, I understand."

King adjusted his tie and, before he could turn back toward his office, I asked, "You're not going to call *them* in?"

He followed my eyes and we both settled on my friends, two of whom were now suggestively pressing their nipples to the window.

"What's the point? None have enough credits to graduate even with intervention. Besides, they'll be gone by lunch."

"So that's it? No ultimatums? You're just giving up on them?"

"They've given up on themselves. Do you know that I personally called every one of their parents this morning? One after another, I dialed up the emergency numbers on file, and I got through to a parent or guardian of every single one of them. Your father was the only one who brought you back."

With that little doozy of a parenting truth ringing in my ear, I stepped out into the arms of the worst influences on the planet. Valentine was escorting me down the hallway before my right foot had even left the office. He clapped me on the back, his bloodshot eyes rolling in their sockets as he spoke. "I've got the back door to the gym propped open. Let's roll, boys. Party time!"

I ground to a halt. "Wait. I thought we were going to the zoo."

"We are," Fire Crotch confirmed. "But it's by the beach, brah. It's a total party zoo."

"Less chit chat and more walking," Valentine prodded. "We only have a few minutes to disappear before the bell rings."

This didn't seem the right time to tell him about my life-changing revelation or that I was going to have to part ways with his dopey ass if he continued to try leading me astray. Besides, I needed to tread lightly with Valentine, seeing that he was about to become Pearl Beach High's newest dealer. But that conversation was going to have to wait because I had neither the time nor the colorful crayons to explain everything to him.

"Dude, not today. King busted me. I'm in some trouble. I need to lie low for a while."

"Lie low? What the fuck? We're always in trouble. Why is today special?" He gripped my arm much like Principal King had and pulled me along.

Again, I came to a standstill. "Look, I promised my dad I'd stay in school, and" – I lowered my voice, feeling suddenly embarrassed by my pending future – "graduate in June."

By the perplexed expressions on my friends' faces, you would have thought I'd just explained to them that some restaurants don't serve all-day breakfast.

Valentine blinked once. Then twice. Maybe even three times before responding. "Wait, like, *this* coming June?"

"Yeah, man, we're seniors, remember?"

"I know," he said, his brows slanting in a downward trajectory. "I just… I thought we all agreed we were going to be Super Seniors next year. The five-year plan, bitches."

"I think the term Super Seniors only applies to the mentally challenged," I said.

Proving my point, Screensaver jerked his head up as if he'd just been awakened from a deep sleep. "Oh, man," he whined. "Five more years?"

"Yes." I nodded at my little friend who had the IQ of a deck chair. "You'll be twenty-two when you graduate."

"Oh." He gripped his chest, exhaling a sigh of heavy relief. "That's not so bad then."

"Not for you, bud." I patted his shoulder. "Not for you."

"So, what exactly are you saying, Keith?" Valentine asked.

"I'm saying I'm not leaving school with you today… or any day. I've got to graduate, dude."

"And smokeouts?" he asked cautiously, as if fearing my response.

I shook my head. "Done."

"What the fuck? What about the business?"

Brett Valentine had been my right-hand man for a while now, so he was my natural successor. I nodded toward him, and his eyes widened. Maybe he hadn't believed me before, but now he understood this was no passing phase. For me to give up the kind of money I was making, there had to be a compelling reason.

"Shit, you're serious. You're just walking away from everything? For what? A piece of paper that says you aren't as dumb as you look?"

"I'm walking away for my dad."

He and I stared each other down until Valentine shrugged and looked away.

Screensaver came back to life. "What's going to happen to the Three Musketeers?"

Fire Crotch scratched his temple. "There are four of us."

"Yeah, but everyone knows you never count yourself."

My eyes widened. Jesus Christ. Please tell me I wasn't as slow-witted as them when I was high. I mean, everyone was entitled to be stupid, but these dudes were abusing the privilege.

"Listen, guys, I've got five minutes to get to chemistry. I'll see you later. Oh, and if you go to the zoo," I said, addressing Screensaver, "no petting the kitties."

As I walked away, I could hear him trying desperately to save his earlier argument. "One. Two. Three. See? The Three Musketeers."

Not only did I meet Principal King's deadline, I beat it by two minutes. Maybe I should have been late, though, seeing that Mrs. Lee blocked me at the entrance, all ninety pounds of her.

"Not so fast, Mr. McKallister. I need a note from the office first."

"King is on his way." And just as the words left my mouth, the principal rounded the corner, and I stood by awkwardly as the two exchanged a hushed conversation about me. She requested my reassignment but was emphatically denied. As the big man took his leave, I attempted to make myself as inconspicuous as possible by slinking back to my lab table.

"Hold up there, Keith," she called to me. I turned around and she walked up, leaning in and speaking for my ears only. "Just so we're clear. You're forbidden from disturbing my class unless you're bleeding, vomiting, or on fire."

A laugh burst from my gut. Well, hell… Mrs. Lee had a sense of humor. I could work with that.

"Is there any wiggle room when it comes to fire?"

This time *she* laughed. "No, Keith, there is not."

"Fine. I'll do my best not to burst into flames."

"Thank you." A smile fluttered to her lips.

I met her smile and raised her one. "Oh, and Mrs. Lee?"

"Yes?"

"Mark my words, I'm gonna make you proud."

"Keith, nothing would make me happier."

My lab partner was already there when I arrived at the table, and she seemed about as happy to see me as Mrs. Lee had been – although I suspect for an entirely different reason. The poor girl was a blusher. I'd found that out at the lunch area on the first day of school when I'd waved at her for no other reason than I was bored. Big mistake. First came the aforementioned blushing and then the strategically placed hand hiding her face. Then for some inexplicable reason, she'd freaked out and ran from the lunch tables in an overly dramatic fashion.

In hindsight, I should've been less friendly. I mean, I knew nothing about the nerdy crew or where their triggers might lie, so who was to say a wave in the Star Trek crowd didn't mean something entirely different? Smart girls were tricky like that. From what I'd gathered through trial and error, the higher the SAT score, the less impressed a female was with my overall being. Not that I had a ton of experience with them to begin with. Typically, the honors kids refrained from interacting with me. Maybe they feared my stupidity would rub off on them, I don't know. But what I did know was this girl, with her divided, color-coded binder and back as straight as an arrow – she was definitely part of that extra credit crowd.

"Hey there, partner." Hair tumbled over my forehead as I tipped my head in her direction. After the day I'd had, I wasn't feeling particularly charming, but I needed to win this girl over, and quickly. Normally I wouldn't give two shits about someone I had zero interest in, but given the promise I'd made to my father, my priorities would need to change. People who'd been merely background players before were about to take center stage in my life. If I had any hope of passing chemistry, this little ball of tension sitting before me needed to be unraveled.

"Hey," she answered in a voice that sounded both hesitant and hardened. There were none of those embarrassed giggles from a few days ago. It was as if the dopey conversation I'd had with her the other day hadn't registered at all, and now I was back to square one.

Okay, first things first: establish a connection. "Sorry, I forgot your name."

"Samantha Anderson."

"Oh, right – Sam."

"My name is Samantha," she said, all business-like. "No one calls me Sam."

I fought the urge to smile. Samantha Anderson was trying so hard to be badass, but she just didn't have the street cred to pull it off. And even though I needed to tread lightly with this girl, I couldn't help a little subtle teasing.

"Uh-huh. So, Sam, what did I miss?" I asked, taking my seat.

"Samantha," she corrected once more. "And… you missed three days."

That was not the response I'd been expecting from my straight-laced partner. Damn, she was a ballsy little brainiac. I was impressed. Yet still, I had to call bullshit on her timeline. I knew for a fact I'd only missed two days of chemistry. "Your tally is off."

She shook her head, the tiniest of smiles finding its way to her lips. "I counted the nap."

What the fuck? I couldn't help but laugh. This girl had more spunk than I'd given her credit for. Maybe using her for my own benefit wouldn't be as painful as I'd imagined. I might even go so far as to say I sort of liked her – not in the lusty 'Hey baby, you wanna sharpen my pencil?' kind of way, but the more cerebral, 'Can I copy off your homework and then maybe eat some of your nutritionally sound homemade lunch items?' kind of way.

And even though she wasn't my type at all, I could certainly see her potential. She was a curvy chick, maybe a little pudgy around the middle, but her legs were long and she sported a natural, make-up free face that honestly wasn't half bad. Really, Sam was just one of those girls who was packaged all wrong. With a few tweaks, like a decent haircut, a tan, and some fashionable clothing, she might actually have a little something. Not for me, mind you. I didn't have the patience to put into her transformation…

not when there was an ample supply of bona fide hotties that came with no assembly required.

Sam actually laughed with me after realizing she'd made a funny, and I was happy to be making some headway with her. Although she still didn't appear to be my biggest fan, unlike fifty percent of the company I'd kept today, at least she didn't look like she wanted me dead.

Step two to winning her over: reference a shared experience. "I have a bad feeling I told you about my platypus dream on Monday."

"Oh, you told me all right." She laughed, and I watched as her body began to unwind. "That story… it haunted me. I couldn't sleep – I had to actually get up in the middle of the night and do some research. Did you know that platypuses are one of only two mammals that lay eggs?"

My eyes ran the length of this girl, intrigued that she'd cared enough about the inner ramblings of my incapacitated mind to actually investigate my claims. "I did not know this."

For the briefest of moments, she made eye contact with me, and we exchanged a smile.

"I thought you'd been transfered back to Mr. Friend," she said.

"Nah, Mr. Friend was prepared to take his claim to the Supreme Court."

"You must have made quite the impression on him."

"Uh-huh. Like the impression I made on you. Be honest: how much do you know about the lifecycle of a platypus now?"

In the most deadpan voice imaginable, she replied, "I could sweep the category in Jeopardy."

I eyed her, laughing. Dang, she was more amusing than her very uptight exterior would suggest. And even though it wasn't like me, I was sort of digging having an intelligent conversation. She might have disagreed about that.

"Hey, I'm sorry about missing class." Honesty? From me? What the hell?

She nodded, accepting my apology. "Why were you gone?"

What could I tell her that didn't make me sound like a douche? Wracking my brain, I came up with nothing. It was just best to own up to it. "I took a vacation with the boys."

Narrowing in on me with intuitive eyes, she sounded puzzled. "A vacation? Summer ended four days ago."

"Right, but I had summer school, so in a way, I go to school year round."

It was a joke – one she clearly didn't get. Or maybe she just didn't find it funny. Either way, it didn't sit well with her, and as hesitation hung thick in the air, Sam nibbled on her bottom lip. Obviously she had something more to add. Why was this chick making *me* feel insecure?

"What?" I blurted out.

"Look, Keith, I envy your carefree lifestyle, I really do. I mean sometimes I wish I were you, but I can't afford for my GPA to take a hit. College is really important to me. If it's okay with you, I'd prefer to work separately."

No, it's not okay. What the hell? Most girls would jump at the chance to give me a little one-on-one attention and this... this... *nobody* was making me work for it. My first instinct was to be pissed. She just assumed I was going to be a shitty partner without any evidence to the contrary. Okay, well, maybe she had a whole arsenal of evidence; but was it too much to ask for the benefit of the doubt?

Seconds away from blasting her for her bias against stoners – we had rights too – I caught sight of her rueful eyes and stopped dead in my tracks. This wasn't a diss. For Sam, her grades weren't a luxury, they were a necessity, and based on past performance alone, I'd given this girl no reassurance that I'd be anything but a strain on her resources. How could I blame her for wanting to put some distance between herself and my stupidity? Hell, I'd do the same if her nerdiness were to suddenly start rubbing off on me.

I should have left the chick alone and accepted her request at face value. But desperate times called for desperate measures. I needed this girl. She was the difference between a passing grade and a drawer full of F's. I couldn't take no for an answer.

Step three: show my hand. "What if I told you I was going to get serious about education?"

She lifted a brow. "I'd say 'Good for you,' but I hope you understand, getting an 'A' in this class is imperative for me if I want to get accepted into a good university."

"I get it."

Actually, I didn't. College meant nothing to me. I wasn't cut out for higher education, so I'd never paid much attention to all the hoopla surrounding admissions. For the life of me, I couldn't figure out why anyone would want to subject themselves to more schooling. To each his own, I supposed; but in some ways, Sam and I wanted the same thing.

She exhaled. "Thank you for understanding."

Not so fast. I caught her eye and offered up something I'd always been reluctant to share: sincerity. "I need to graduate, Sam."

She studied me with more interest now. Maybe I'd finally ceased being a caricature in her eyes. I didn't know, nor did I care. I just needed her on my side.

"Do you have enough credits?" she asked, thawing.

"If I pass all my classes with a C or better, I can walk in June."

"And that matters to you?"

"It matters to my dad."

"But does it matter to you?" she replied.

I was taken aback by her question. Why did people keep asking me that? Try as I might, I couldn't see the difference. "Why does that matter to you?"

"Because if you don't care, then it's just a waste of my time."

Her ultimatum rendered me speechless. Right here. Right now. I had to decide who I was doing this for, because Sam was right – it did matter. If this was all being done for someone else, I was bound to fail.

What exactly was it that I wanted? I mean, obviously I didn't want to end up in prison with a bar of slippery soap as my only friend; but more long term, what about that? I thought about my father. He was a hard worker, devoted to family, and liked by everyone. The man came home every day whether he wanted to or not. And I can attest… there were times he definitely did not. But like clockwork, he walked through that door and became the man we all needed in our lives. That was what I wanted.

I lifted my eyes to meet hers. "It matters to me."

Chapter Six

Samantha

My Loss

Oh, man, was I a sucker for sincerity or what? Maybe it was naïve of me to think someone like Keith McKallister could be honest about a request for help, but I believed him if for no other reason than I desperately needed to believe in something. In no way was my decision influenced by the fact that he was a dreamy guy who smelled of seaweed. No, I'd like to think I was principled enough that I would have helped him even if he'd had a face full of acne and reeked of week-old nerd.

But when the hot guy in question went all heartfelt on me, speaking of his father and recommitting himself to his studies, I was a goner. Actually, I was surprised I'd shown any gumption at all. Making him dig a little deeper for my help was inspired. Now he knew I meant business. He was using me – of course I knew that – but I'd weighed the pros and cons and decided I was intrigued enough with this guy that it was worth my time to help him. After all, I needed to find out what had changed since Monday and why my lab partner, who could barely complete a full sentence without drifting off, was suddenly clear-eyed and ready to make a change.

As he settled in beside me, I resisted the urge to sniff him. With his hair wet and tangled, it was clear he'd just stepped off the beach and into the classroom. And given that this was third period, I had to assume he'd skipped out on his first two classes.

"So, I'm assuming your dad didn't know you were on vacation."

"You assume correctly."

"How'd you explain your absence to your parents?"

"I didn't. We took day trips. Kissed my mom good-bye at breakfast and was home for dinner every night. If done right, Sam, truancy doesn't have to be an unpleasant experience."

"Wow." I smiled. "How very resourceful of you."

"Right? People just assume stoners are lazy, but I'm like, guess what assholes, the blunt doesn't pass itself."

His comment had me giggling up a storm. I'd never met someone so easy to talk to, and the idea of tutoring him was becoming more intriguing with each passing minute. If Keith could give me just a little of this giddy feeling every day, I'd come out of this partnership a winner.

Surprising even myself, I kept our conversation going. "How were the waves?"

A calm instantly settled over him. "Gnarly. Thanks for asking. Do you surf?"

"Me?" I laughed. "No. I don't like the idea of the flesh being ripped from my bones."

Keith groaned, pretending to pound his head on the desk. "Everybody blames the sharks. You do realize that the chances of getting killed by a shark is like one in three million? You have a better chance of getting hit by lightning."

"But, see, I don't go out in storms, so my chances of dying either way is 0. Who wins now?"

"Not you."

I cocked my head, confused. "How do you figure?"

"Because, Sam, everything that makes life worth living carries a risk. If you eliminate that, you might as well start collecting cats now."

"I like cats," I protested.

"I'm sure you do."

He caught my eye and we smiled. I can't overstate my surprise that Keith hadn't already tired of our conversation. The truth was, people typically just looked right through me.

"Think about it, Sam. Is there any cooler way to die? I mean, like cancer would be a sad way to go, but getting trampled by the bulls in Spain – epic."

"Or spontaneous combustion," I added, rolling with the theme.

"Yes!" Out of nowhere, Keith high-fived me. It was the first time a guy outside my family unit had ever touched me, and my skin flushed accordingly. "That's some gnarly shit there. You're just hanging out watching a little TV when BAM – you frickin' explode. That's just all kinds of awesome."

What the heck was happening here? Somehow I'd been witty enough to warrant the attention of a member of Pearl Beach High's ruling class. Shannon would be proud.

Leaning in, Keith lowered his voice. "You want to hear my evil revenge plan?"

Oh, boy, did I ever! At this point, anything that came out of his mouth was gospel to me. Wide-eyed and rapt with interest, I nodded.

"If I get killed by a shark, I want a memorial bench erected in my name right next to a garbage can."

That sounded like a horrible idea, but I encouraged him to continue with an awkward tilt of my head. "Why?"

"To make it easier for the seagulls to crap on people resting on my bench."

Again, pretty terrible idea. So far, Keith's evil revenge plan was going in the direction of the platypus story. "Why would you want that?"

"Because Sam…"

"Samantha."

The way in which he completely ignored my earlier request told me he'd never be getting my name right. And while it usually annoyed the hell out of me when people shortened my name for their own convenience, when Keith did it, with just that little bit of snark, I honestly didn't mind all that much.

"Whatever. Anyway, how do you get people to remember you after you die?"

Thinking about his question, I shrugged. No one would remember me if I died, so it was sort of a moot point. But for someone like Keith, yeah, I could see him inspiring a candlelight vigil in his honor.

"I have no idea," I finally conceded.

His affecting smile slayed me. "Drop a little bird doodoo on them. No matter how old you get, you'll always remember where you were the first time a seagull crapped in your mouth."

I choked out a laugh. It really was a brilliant way to be remembered. "The Keith McKallister Memorial Bench. I like it."

He nodded, pleased his plan passed muster with me.

"Well, sadly there will be no memorial bench in my honor because, sharks aside, I don't go in the ocean."

"You can't swim?"

"Actually, I'm a really good swimmer," I said, before adding a series of completely irrelevant supporting facts. "I have long arms and a long torso. It's a great combo for swimming."

Keith accepted my reasoning with no push back, which I was happy for because I totally couldn't back up my baseless claim.

"So what's the problem then?"

I shrugged. "I just hate the ocean."

"You can't hate the ocean," he said. "You live in a beach town."

"Through no choice of my own. My grandmother passed away two years ago and left her house to my mom. That's how we ended up in this crap town."

"Whoa, hold up there, Slugger. This is so *not* a crap town. Any place where you can wear shorts year round and surf as the sun comes up qualifies as paradise."

"According to who?"

"According to *everyone.*" His voice peaked in amusement. "The world fucking over!"

"This town is not real life, Keith. It's a fantasy world filled with bikini-clad airheads and trips to the beach."

"That's exactly what I just said." He nodded empathically. "Paradise."

"Yeah, well, enjoy it; but I for one will be gone the minute I graduate, and I'll never look back."

"Seriously? What about your family?"

"They don't care."

"I'm sure that's not true," he said with the confidence of a guy who'd never experienced the betrayal of his loved ones.

I didn't argue the point because it would require explaining my living situation, and that was something I did not intend to share with the likes of Keith McKallister.

He slapped his hand on the table. "Okay, I got it."

"Got what?"

"How I can pay you back for helping me out with my classes."

Classes? I'd thought I was just helping him with chemistry, but apparently I was now tutoring him in a wide variety of topics. Okay, well… I had nothing better to do, so why not? So was payback even required for my services? I honestly didn't mind doing all the giving while he did all the taking. But certainly I could hear him out.

"I'm going to teach you how to surf," he said, all bright-eyed and bushy-tailed. "That way you'll never be afraid of the ocean again."

The laugh that shot from my mouth might have sounded exaggerated and ridiculous, but it matched his absurd proposal. "Um, thanks, but I think I'll pass. Besides, Keith, you don't need to pay me back. I already said I'd help you – no strings attached."

"Are you sure? Because I don't make this offer to just anyone. Surfing is a way of life, dude. You have no idea what you're missing. The beach. The waves. It's freedom like you've never experienced."

The far-off look on his face told me he truly believed his words, and his passion might have been enough to sway someone else, but not practical Samantha Anderson. I wasn't sure what terrified me more, the dark abyss of the unruly Pacific Ocean or the idea of standing in front of this hot surfer boy in a bathing suit. Either way, it was a hard 'Hell, no.'

"I really appreciate the offer, Keith, but let's just focus on getting you to graduation."

Keith studied me for longer than I felt comfortable with. Anything I had for him to look at only took a few seconds. He needn't linger. I squirmed in my seat until he finally diverted his eyes to the assignment in front of him.

"Okay." He shrugged. "Your loss."

Yes, I silently agreed, *my loss*, but then I was used to losing. What was one more time?

Chapter Seven

Keith

Homemade

Mom breezed into the kitchen, a waft of perfume following her in. She smelled like home, which apart from the beach was my favorite scent. I took in her bright, billowy outfit and was struck by her beauty. Mom was a put-together woman on a daily basis, but today she'd put in the extra effort and it showed. This was the first woman I'd ever vowed to marry, and today I remembered why.

Standing up, I kissed her cheek. "You're looking fine, Mamacita."

"Well, thank you, sweetheart. You're looking…"

Her eyes passed over me, no doubt ready to return the compliment, but got stopped up on my t-shirt, which read, 'This guy likes bacon.'

"Keith, come on. I thought you changed."

"I did. You should have seen my other option." Something told me she'd have been even less enthusiastic about the shirt with 'Vegetarian' across a giant pot leaf.

She sighed. "We're going to a nice restaurant. Would it kill you to put more effort into your wardrobe choices?"

I glanced down at my clothing. I'd been going for whimsical fun, but clearly my mother had no sense of humor. "This *was* effort. I even applied deodorant."

Mom laughed. "Oh, well then, that more than makes up for the dead pig parts on your shirt."

"Exactly. Who's going to care what I look like when I smell Arctic fresh?"

"Off you go," Mom said, physically turning me in the direction of my room.

"Fine, but I'm warning you, I can't guarantee my next choice will be any better."

Her lips tipped in amusement, she answered, "I believe in you, honey. Surely you can find something in your closet without words."

"Actually, I'm not sure if I can."

"I need you to dig deep into that closet of yours. Remember the Christmas clothes I buy you every year? Why don't you see if you can find those?"

Ah yes. Christmas – that special time of year when my parents tried to turn me into a golfer. I might not have been Pearl Beach's drug dealer anymore, but I still had a reputation to uphold, and that did not include clothing with buttons.

I could stand there holding my ground for as long as I liked, but that didn't change the fact that I wasn't going anywhere until I was wearing something that passed her inspection. Without a word, I headed down the hallway.

"And hurry," she called out after me. "We have reservations in fifteen minutes. If they figure out who the party of eight is before we get there, we're screwed. Oh, and Keith, do something with your hair."

My hair too? I reached up to run my fingers through my mop, but the digits got stuck in the tangled strands, forcing a pain-filled squawk from my throat. I'd hit the point in my hygiene where nothing short of a head shave would fix the ratty strands of hair occupying my head.

"Oh, my god, Mom," I hollered at her from down the hall. "It's your birthday, not the crowning of a new president."

Emma passed me in the narrow passageway, always ready with a sarcastic reply.

"Yes. Because the coronation proceedings of our elected officials are always the highlight of American politics."

I had absolutely no idea what she'd just said, but it was annoying enough to warrant pushing her into the wall. I thought that squared us up, but Emma had never been one to play by the rules. Retaliation was swift, in the form of a knee to my ass. She'd been going for the crown jewels, but I knew a thing or two about her combat skills and twisted my body away in the nick of time.

Emma grinned mischievously, her face flushed from the fight. "You give up?"

"Never," I panted. And then, with a swiftness I hadn't been expecting, I was avoiding her jabbing knees as if my balls were the target in a whack-a-mole game.

"Okay," I laughed. "I give up. You win. Jesus, you're ruthless."

"Emma," Mom hollered from the kitchen. "Leave your brother alone. He's going to need every second of the fifteen minutes I gave him to be presentable."

She opened her arm to let me pass, but I didn't trust her for a minute. "You heard Mom. Go."

Pressing myself against the wall, I slid past her and darted off down the hall. I'd almost made it to my room when a list of demands was volleyed down the narrow passageway.

"Remember, Keith. Clean shirt, nothing offensive, no words, no holes, no shorts… and as for your hair, just pull it off your face. That's all I'm asking."

I shut the door on her requests. Short of sticking a post-it note to my forehead, there was no way I was remembering that lengthy list. But I got the general idea of what she was expecting. As I rummaged through my drawers, my brother Jake let himself in. He didn't say anything, just plopped himself down onto my ratty beanbag chair and watched.

I could understand the interest. Jake was viewing this as an entertainment opportunity. It wasn't every day I was called upon to improve my overall looks.

"Can I help you?"

"Not really. I'm just curious what you're going to come up with," he said, that lazy grin of his hard to ignore.

"Well, be curious in another room," I replied, pulling out a white Hanes t-shirt and holding it up for inspection. From the corner of my eye, I saw Jake cringe.

"What?" I asked.

He shook his head. "You're not going to wear that, right?"

"Maybe. Why? What's wrong with it? This shirt checks off all the items on her list. No holes. No words."

"I'm pretty sure 'no pit stains' would have made her list if she'd had more time to compile it."

Upon closer examination, I could clearly see the yellow underarm rings. "Well, shit."

Slanting his gaze to mine, Jake smirked. "Why do all your clothes look like they came out of a dumpster? Doesn't Mom take care of you?"

"Most of my clothes are damaged from climbing out windows. Occupational hazard." I shrugged.

"I thought you weren't climbing out windows anymore."

"I'm not, but my clothes haven't caught up yet."

"It's not rocket science, Keith. Pick a shirt, get your gift, and let's go. I'm hungry."

Ah, shit. My gift. I'd totally forgotten the gift. Thankfully, my younger brother had reminded me numerous times of Mom's upcoming birthday, which was the only reason I actually had a gift to give her.

"Bro," I answered, stripping off my bacon shirt and tossing it at him. "You saved my ass."

"What's new?"

Kidding aside, there was nothing new. Jake had single-handedly kept my worth in this family high even when I should have been devalued long ago. While everyone else jumped into Mitch's gleaming red wagon, Jake remained behind, helping me pound the wheels back onto mine. His loyalty had gotten me though some tough times, so if he wanted to enjoy the Keith show, I was inclined to allow him.

"If you're so smart, Pretty Boy," I said, gesturing to my drawers. "Be my guest."

"Screw you. I'm not the one with lady hair."

"It's pirate hair, and everyone knows pirates are cool. Now, help me find something Mom will like. God knows you're the biggest kiss-ass in the family."

Ignoring the diss, Jake rose from the beanbag and, as if he were filming an episode of *Queer Eye For The Straight Guy*, my little brother effortlessly whipped out a button-down shirt from my closet.

"Oh no. No way!" I protested, waving my hands around to illustrate my utter distaste for his choice. "Mom didn't say a dress up shirt, she just said a clean one."

"Do you want to make her happy on her birthday or not?"

"Not. Definitely not."

"Fine. Whatever. Wear the shirt with the pit stains. I'm sure she'll love it," he said, heading for the exit. "And don't forget the gift."

Ah, shit! The gift! How had I already forgotten it? Eyeing the shirt Jake had chosen for me, guilt clouded my better judgment. He was right – she'd love it, and it was her birthday. I just had to hope no one I knew would be in the restaurant to see my embarrassing prep boy transformation. I'd already lost all street cred after giving up my side business, and now this.

Slipping on the shirt, I buttoned it to the second to top position before taking on the rat's nest that was my hair. This was the result of whipping my head around after surfing but never actually combing it out. The matting was getting out of control.

Sighing, I pulled it back into a short ponytail and checked my appearance in the mirror. Oh, she was going to love this. Plus, it was a look I could get behind for the night. I was presentable while still retaining my pothead, screw-up flair.

Turning off the light, I jogged down the hallway before making an abrupt turn and heading back toward my room. I'd forgotten the fucking gift.

"Scott, make sure Jake and Kyle are separated," Mom said, as we were led to the table at the fancy restaurant. In reality, it was an Olive Garden, but for us, that was the height of culinary excellence. "You take one, I'll get the other."

My brothers both dove for the seat next to our dad, Kyle edging out Jake by a hair. He then proceeded to rub it in by whooping in joy as if he were an Olympic champion. A disgruntled Jake punched him.

"Hey." Mom raised her voice to get their attention. "Stop it right now. This is why we can't have nice things."

I snickered. Clearly Mom was kidding, but there was some truth behind her words, and it had nothing to do with Jake or Kyle's antics. See, Mom wasn't like the rest of us. To say she had married down would be an understatement. My mom hadn't just grown up wealthy. Her family was the type of rich that owned half the city. She'd been destined to live her life in the lap of luxury when a chance encounter with a sandy-haired beach boy changed her life forever.

It was your typical poor boy meets rich girl love story, only this one came with the added twist of lawsuits, fistfights, and a lifelong disownment. In moments like this, when the best we could afford was a night out at Olive Garden, I sometimes wondered if she regretted her decision all those years ago. Sure, she wouldn't have us, but she'd have everything else she'd ever dreamed of, and more.

Mom tapped the seat beside her, letting Jake know she wasn't taking the slightest bit of crap from him. "Now."

Pouting all the way to mommy jail, he flung himself onto the open chair. "That's not fair. Why am I being punished? I didn't do anything wrong."

"Yet," Mom corrected him, not taking any offense to the suggestion that sitting beside her was the equivalent of prison. "You and Kyle haven't done anything wrong *yet*. And Dad and I aim to keep it that way."

"That was just one time," Jake protested.

"Which time are we talking?" Emma asked. "The time Kyle went head first into the barrel of peanuts, or the time the two of you set the tablecloth on fire?"

"The fire was an accident… and the peanut incident was on Kyle. He's the one who wanted to know if he could breathe under all those peanuts. I was only helping him with his research."

"And just so you know," Kyle pitched in, "they packed those peanuts in tight."

"Anyway, I just want a nice, quiet evening with my family," Mom pleaded. "No fire trucks or CPR. Do you boys understand?"

A moment passed with neither one agreeing to the terms of the evening. It took a harsh glare from Mom to force reluctant nods from the troublemakers.

Dinner went on without incident, and as it wound down, Quinn wiggled restlessly in his chair. "Mommy, I want to give you my gift now."

"Ahh, so sweet. Okay. I'm ready."

"I'm going to sing you a song."

Mom clapped, genuinely moved by the effort her youngest son was putting into her birthday.

With a mischievous grin, five-year-old Quinn began his own unique rendition of the Yankee Doodle song. "Yankee Doodle went to town, riding on a baby. Accidentally turned around and saw a naked lady!"

Eyes widening in surprise, Mom looked around to make sure no one outside of our family unit had heard his song.

"Quinny, where did you learn that?" Mom asked.

"Kindergarten."

"Wonderful." She and Dad exchanged amused smiles.

"So happy the education is well-rounded."

"Ooh," Kyle teased. "Quinn saw a naked lady."

My baby brother's tanned skin flushed a bright crimson color, and he immediately backpedaled on his birthday song. "That didn't really happen, though."

"Uh-huh, right, sure," Kyle goaded, not letting Quinn off the hook he was now dangling helplessly from. "Did you see her boobies and everything?"

The humiliation was too much for young Quinn to handle. With gritted teeth and clenched fists, my baby brother swung out, pelting Kyle with a series of punches. If there was one motto us McKallister boys lived by, it was that the quickest way to settle a conflict was through combat.

"Was that supposed to hurt?" Kyle blew on the area of his arm where the strikes had landed. "'Cuz it felt like a bunch of bird pecks… but maybe that's because you're exhausted after looking at sooo many naked ladies."

Quinn burst into tears, running to Mom for comfort as the rest of us boys laughed at his pain. Hey, we all had to toughen up at some point. Quinn's education just started a little earlier, based solely on birth order. As the newest male member of the McKallister clan, he had to pay his dues.

"Kyle." Dad grabbed him by the collar in an attempt to wipe the smirk off his twelve-year-old face. "That's enough."

Kyle had a quick wit as well as a propensity for trouble. Like me, he rarely learned from his mistakes. But Kyle took it to the next level, adding that extra little bit of comic relief to his performance. Really, he'd missed his calling. Kyle should have been a child actor because he could easily be mistaken for the bratty kid brother on any television sitcom series *ever*. Granted, I was a lot of work too, but at least I could sit through an entire dinner without uttering 'naked lady' like forty frickin' times.

"Don't blame me." Kyle shrugged. "I was just pointing out the flaws in his composition."

"SHUT UP!" Quinn screamed, raising the eyebrows of the patrons at the tables nearest us.

I swung my head toward Mom, knowing she'd never let such a display go unanswered, and I wasn't disappointed. Lowering her voice, Mom leaned in, instantly transforming from mild-mannered mommy to scowling beast before our very eyes. "If I have to warn either of you again to be civilized in the restaurant, I'll drag both of you by the ear into separate corners of the dining room. Would you two really like to face the wall in front of everyone?"

Ah, yes. She'd gone with public humiliation. Excellent choice. It had always been a favorite of hers. And, I must say, from past experience, it was a surprisingly effective punishment. Having faced that wall myself once or twice, I knew she wasn't bluffing. If Mom promised us a toddler timeout in the middle of a restaurant, that's exactly what we'd better expect. Only as a wily teen had I figured a way around Mom's combatant parenting style – sneak out and ask for forgiveness later. It wasn't the best strategy, as I spent a significant portion of my life on restriction, but again, that's what windows and early morning escapes were for.

Both Quinn and Kyle heeded the threat, wisely sealing their mouths shut and adopting a shaky truce for the sake of their respective dignities.

Satisfied with their compliance, Mom smoothed out her dress and transformed into the lovely woman she'd been moments before the altercation. She was a frickin' rock star when it came to parenting.

Focusing her attention back on her youngest son, Mom offered him the loving relief that only a mother could and he sank into her arms, nestling his head into her neck.

"Me next. Me next," Grace said, her shiny golden locks glowing in the recessed lighting. She hopped off her chair and crowded onto mom's lap beside Quinn. Just shy of four years old, she was the baby of the family, and unlike Quinn's tough love indoctrination, Grace enjoyed around-the-clock adoration. "I drew you a picture."

"Oh, wow. I love it," Mom said, glancing around the table at her older kids with a comical grimace on her face. "Sweetie, is this… um… blood?"

"No, Mommy," she said in the cutest little voice. "It's red flowers."

"Okay, right, now I see it." More cringing. "Are those *people* lying on a concrete slab?"

Grace nodded, clearly not understanding the word as she rattled off all the names in our family. "That's Mommy and Daddy and Mitch and Keith and…"

Mom interrupted her to hold up the picture so the rest of us could get our first look. It was a gasp heard around the room. Baby Grace had drawn a bloody massacre. Bodies with stick arms and legs broken at forty-five degree angles littered the wide-ruled canvas. Setting aside any worries about her mental health, we oohed and aahed the budding assassin and made her feel like the most talented artist ever to slaughter her family on a birthday card.

"Kyle," Dad asked, prying his worshipping eyes off his baby girl, "do you have anything for your mother?"

"Yeah." With zero enthusiasm, he pulled a wad of stapled papers from his back pocket and tossed it across the table.

"Not the coupon book again," Jake groaned. "You get her that every year."

"Stop it, Jake." Mom elbowed him. "I love it. Kyle's coupon book is the gift that keeps on giving."

Kyle's eyes rolled on cue. "Yeah, well, just so you know, I added a terms and conditions section this year. Now there are time limits. No more twenty-minute massages or unlimited compliments."

Mom smiled. "Understood. Come here and give me a hug."

"A free hug is on page four. You have to rip it out first, otherwise I'm not coming over."

Mom laughed as she extracted page four and held out the coupon to Kyle, who made a show of being annoyed even though he dutifully accepted the coupon and hugged her. He even waited patiently as she smothered his neck in kisses before setting him free.

"Yuck. I need to come up with a different birthday gift next year – one that doesn't involve slobbering."

"Here," Jake said, sliding a notepad over to our mother. "My gift."

Mom opened the notebook and read whatever it was that Jake had written. Within seconds, her eyes misted over, and she placed a hand to her heart. When she was done reading, she didn't say anything. Instead she slid her arm around his back and gave him a kiss on the cheek. See what I mean? Kiss-ass.

"My turn." Emma reached into a bag with an ear-to-ear smile as she passed an immaculately wrapped gift over to our mother. My eyes darted back and forth, taking in the unbelievable scene. Wait, what was happening here?

I glanced at my brothers, all of who wore the same horrified expression. Cheesy, stupid, last minute, homemade gifts – those were the rules.

Ripping off the gift-wrap, the birthday girl squealed in delight. "You didn't!"

Emma clapped, her eyes glowing with excitement.

"The purse I saw in the store?" Mom giggled, then went so far as to hug the handbag to her chest and give it a little snuggle. "Emma, it's simply gorgeous."

Oh, no. No. There was absolutely no need for pomp and circumstance. Mom had always been fine with the bare minimum. My sister was single-handedly ruining everything we'd worked so hard for! How could Mom ever go back to ground beef now that she'd had a taste of filet mignon?

"Sweetie," Mom said, scaling down her excitement as she demurred. "I don't need something this fancy. It's too expensive."

Of course it was, *EMMA*. No money was allowed to change hands! Like I said – ground beef. That hugged purse was going to go back to the evil place it came from. That's what my sister got for trying to show us up… no, for trying to bury us. Give it to her, Mamacita!

But Emma's voice shook with emotion. "I wanted you to have it. I bought it with the money I earned from babysitting the neighbor kids. You're the best mom in the world, and you deserve to have pretty things."

Oh, no. Don't do it! Don't you dare cry! And then came the tears. Once sis employed the waterworks, I knew the boys and I were officially doomed.

"Oh, Emma, I don't even know what to say. I love it so much. Thank you, honey. I'm so lucky to have such a thoughtful daughter."

They hugged for an uncomfortably long time. Jake, Kyle, and I looked on in disgust. Emma had risen the bar – the one we'd now forever have to hurdle over.

I could no longer hold my tongue. "Um, I don't mean to be a stickler here, but the rules state we're supposed to give homemade gifts. Emma's cheating."

"No, Keith," Emma answered. "It's supposed to be *heartfelt* gifts, not homemade. You mixed up the words. Right, Dad?"

Dad jerked his head up like a skittish deer seconds before the fatal shot was fired. "Well, I uh… I…"

Come on, dude. I urged him with my eyes. *Stand strong with your sons!*

"Technically, Keith, Emma is correct. The word used was 'heartfelt.' You boys always just interpreted that to mean homemade, and since your mother seemed okay with pasta necklaces and Popsicle stick photo frames, I saw no reason to correct you."

"Kids, listen, I love all my gifts. They mean the world to me." Tears pooled in her Caribbean blue eyes. "When I was growing up, there was always a pile of gifts on the table on birthday morning, but no one was ever there to watch me open them. There was no love or joy. That's why it doesn't matter to me if the gift is homemade or bought. I just want the idea to come from a place of love and to have all of you right here by my side. That's all I want for my birthday."

I sighed. How nice for everyone that went *before* mom's profound speech. Now I had to follow it up with my crap gift. I fumbled with my shell photo frame. Yes, it was a step above the Popsicle sticks, but not by much. Instead of Emma's fancy wrap job, mine looked pathetic wrapped in paper towels and scotch tape. Out of options, I slid the gift across the table. "Happy birthday, Mom."

She smiled as she peeled the wrapping back with meticulous fingers. Mom examined my offering, running her fingers over the delicate shells, ones I'd spent about thirty minutes collecting. Probably not my best effort, but no matter, because she appeared pleased regardless. "You made this?"

I nodded.

"It's beautiful, honey."

"Did you see what was inside?"

Mom checked the photo before bursting into a fit of hysterics. "Who took this?"

"I did," Dad replied. "And might I add, I now understand why other species eat their young. It was a nightmare, Michelle. Do you have any idea how difficult it is to get all six of these kids in the same shot? And then that one" – he pointed at Grace – "just when I had them all in place, boom, she's gone, scaling the back fence. Her white dress was ruined. That's when Keith suggested that instead of taking a perfect photo, why not take one as they really are

– a bunch of shi…" Mom's glare stopped the swear word from fully forming. "Poopheads. So, there you have it."

In the photograph, each of us was mugging for the camera, but in our own unique way. In my arms, Gracie was hanging upside down in her dirty dress. Quinn was brandishing a plastic sword, a look of steely determination forever captured on his face. Kyle was performing the splits while suspended in midair. Jake was strumming an air guitar as his left pointer finger reached for the sky. Emma was showcasing her best *Charlie's Angels* kissing pose. And there was me, wagging my tongue as my signature pirate hair blew in the wind.

We weren't a perfect family, not by a long shot, but as Mom had just proven in her speech, perfection was overrated. She wanted heart. She wanted love. And she got all of that with her tribe of well-meaning delinquents.

"This right here, Keith." Mom smiled. "This is what I'm talking about."

Chapter Eight

Samantha

My Favorite Word

Keith was knee-deep in a geometry worksheet when he disintegrated before my very eyes. First from somewhere in the recesses of his throat came a pitiful groan, and then the fake cry, and finally, he buried his head in his arm and loudly declared, "I'd rather slam my flaccid penis in the car door than satisfy one more Pythagorean Theorem."

Such meltdowns were not unusual for my lab partner, but this particular one had me chuckling behind my book. No one could say he wasn't creative in his self-expression.

"Shhh, Keith, we're in a library."

"Who cares? It's a ghost town in here."

That wasn't entirely true. There were a few hardcore studiers spending their after-school hours in the library. And each one of them was eyeing us now.

"What are you looking at?" Keith challenged, spooking the timid souls, who quickly disappeared back into their books.

Not satisfied with his tantrum, Keith rolled himself up on top of the long table and stretched out on his back, making a show of miming a very elaborate stabbing death scene. Only after his eyes had rotated back and his tongue had lobbed out was his sheer and utter misery accurately portrayed to his rapt audience.

It set off a frenzy of giggles in me that echoed through the room, although one glance around told me that not everyone was as entertained. One skittish student even packed up and left. The type of kids who frequented the library were still a bit uneasy having the infamous Keith McKallister in their midst.

"So mature," I said, pushing his twitching carcass.

My lab partner had a way of easing my troubled mind. Before his flare-up, I'd been stressing hard over midterms and maternal tantrums. After his theatrics, I was smiling and breathing easier. It was hard to say why I completely relaxed around Keith, but I did. In fact I'd go so far to say

I'd laughed more in those past weeks than I had in my whole life.

Shannon kept insisting I was falling for him, and although I vehemently denied it, there was no refuting my crush. Keith was cute. He was funny. And he was the first boy to ever really want to know me. So yes, I had it bad, but I refused to admit it in words – not even to Shannon. Such an admission could only end in disaster because no matter how fun and flirty the boy was, he would never fall for a girl like me.

Still, that didn't stop me from experimenting with different techniques to improve my overall appearance. Studying hair and makeup tutorials on YouTube had become an after school ritual, and I'd even started watching my calorie intake and upping my workout routine in hopes of dropping some of the extra weight I was carrying. Seven pounds were already gone, and my normally makeup-free cheeks were now dusted in a fine powder.

Not that Keith noticed. He seemed oblivious to my transformation. To him I was just a buddy – no, I wasn't even that. Buddies acknowledged each other in public. Keith never did. Outside of the safety of the library, we were strangers, and as much as I wanted more from him, I knew it would never happen. We were just too different.

I knew where I stood – on the outside, where I'd always been. And I was okay with our friendship remaining firmly in the educational realm as long as I could stay relevant in his life. Pathetic, yes, but that was the reality of being me.

Keith lifted his head off the table. "Why do you always have to say shitty words like that?"

"Like what? Mature?"

"Yeah. We're seventeen. This is the only time in our lives we get to be imbeciles. Embrace it."

"Hey, you're using the vocab words in sentences. Way to go!"

"I can't help it. You're a bad influence on me."

"Some might argue I'm a good one."

"Yeah, well, I don't hang out with those people. Anyway, I'm not itching to be a genius. How about we just aim for functionally competent?"

Keith's fears of becoming a genius were unwarranted. He still had a ways to go just to make the 'utterly ordinary' category of scholastic achievement, as evidenced by some of his recent zingers like 'So you're saying Egypt *isn't* a religion?' or 'Are you trying to tell me that parallel lines never meet? How do they end?'

"You want to aim *that* high?" I teased.

He grabbed my arm and pulled me toward him, grinning that flirty smile of his. "You're a lippy little thing today, aren't you, babe?"

"Yes, I am. And stop calling me *babe*." I pulled my arm out of his hold.

"Why? You are a babe."

"Not according to my mirror, I'm not."

Keith flipped over onto his stomach. "Well, according to my eyes, you are."

A flush crept over my cheeks. His words registered, but they didn't make sense. Not once had he ever indicated that I qualified for babe status. Why all of a sudden was he acting weird? I slid back in my seat, away from him.

"Stop making fun of me, Keith. Now get off the table. I need to study. Unlike you, I can't aim for 'functional' if I want to get into a good college back east."

"Why can't you just go to school in California?"

"Because it's not far enough away from…" I stopped myself before revealing the truth behind my school choice.

That was enough to pique his interest, though, and Keith sat up on the table, tilting his head like an eager dog waiting for a bone. "Not far enough away from what?"

I looked down at my paper. "Not from what. From who."

Although I could no longer see him, I knew Keith was staring at me, intrigued. I'd just given away more than I'd intended to part with.

"Sam?"

I didn't look up.

"Saaamm." This time he sang out my name and nudged me with the toe of his sneaker. I looked up only to find him assaulting me with that heartthrob smile of his. I didn't stand a chance.

I made a scene of laying down my pencil and sighing. "What, Keith?"

He leaned in, his hot breath inches from my tingling skin. "I feel like you're keeping secrets from me, babe. I mean if you can't trust a reformed drug dealer, then who can you trust, am I right?"

Despite all my reservations, I laughed. "Fine. I'll tell you my secret if you tell me why you're always looking over your shoulder."

Pulling away from me, Keith returned to his crisscross applesauce position on top of the library table. I wasn't certain, but I thought I saw him flinch. For all his positivity, the past few weeks had not been easy for him. He had an addiction that needed breaking, and that wasn't something that disappeared overnight. And as if that weren't bad enough, he also had to untangle himself from the drug trade. Keith talked a good game, but I knew him well enough to know when his insecurities came calling.

"You know who Brett Valentine is, right?" he began.

"Yeah, your friend."

"Well…" Keith grimaced. "I'm not sure I'd call him that anymore. You know how when a dictator comes into power, he executes anyone who poses a threat to his authority? Well, if Valentine is the new ruler, where does that leave me?"

My eyes widened in response to his question, but then fear overlapped the surprise. "You think he wants to *execute* you?"

"Well, not in the chop your head off kind of way – at least I hope not – but Valentine wants me gone. And he has the backing of my former boss. So, yeah, I'm a little freaked out."

"Keith, this isn't a joke. You need to say something."

"Right, because tattling on the bully is absolutely the best thing to do in a situation like this. No, I just need to lie low and not draw attention to myself, that's all. Okay. Your turn. Who are you trying to get away from?"

My shoulders slumped as I spoke the words. "My mother."

"Your mother? Why? Does she not cut the crust off your sandwiches?"

"She's not a good person is all. Now let's drop it and get back to work."

"Well now, hold up. You want to move thousands of miles away because your mom's a bitch? If that were the criteria, there'd be an annual pilgrimage into the heartland."

"She's worse than a bitch, Keith."

I fought the tears pushing their way to the surface. I couldn't let him see me cry. Exposing my weaknesses would give Keith the ammunition he needed to destroy me, if that was his desire.

"Hey…" He reached over and touched the back of my hand with his fingertips. It was just the quickest little contact, but it meant more to me than he knew. "You okay? I didn't mean to make you cry. I'm sorry."

"No, it's not you. My mother… she just – she makes me feel worthless."

His fingers now slipped around my hand. Keith stared deep into my eyes before lowering his voice. "Why haven't you said anything?"

"To you?" Telling someone like Keith, who had what seemed to be the perfect family, that my mother was verbally abusive... and worse… well, that would just bring all kinds of shame to an already embarrassing situation. If he only knew what a coward I'd been.

"Yes, to me," he replied seeming slightly offended. He dropped my hand, making me long for the warmth of his touch. "Why not to me? We're friends, aren't we?"

"I…"

Even though he hid me from everyone in his life, he'd been more a friend to me than every other student in the school, with the exception of one curly-haired superhero.

"Yes," I smiled. "We're friends. And I guess I haven't said anything to you for the same reason you haven't told me about your dictator issue. I'm just lying low and not drawing attention to myself until I get into college and…"

"Move as far away from her as possible." Keith caught my eye as he finished my sentence. Did I hear disappointment?

I nodded. "Next week I turn seventeen. That's one year closer to escape."

"Well, that's one way to look at a birthday." He grinned.

"It's the only way to look at it… when no one cares if you turn another year older."

Keith tucked a pencil behind his ear, considering my dilemma. "Then make them care. Throw a party. Live it up."

"With who, Keith? I don't have a squad."

"Okay, but you have *some* friends, right?"

"I suppose I know four or five people who don't want me to die."

"Well, there you go." He slapped my shoulder. "That's a start."

And despite my melancholy over a deadbeat mother, I smiled. I loved talking to him. There was no coddling, no politically correct wording. Keith was brutally honest, and after a lifetime of walking on pins and needles, it was a refreshing change of pace.

The librarian cleared her voice loud enough for us to hear. She motioned for Keith to get off the table with the flick of her head. It surprised me that Miss Markel had allowed him to linger this long, when even an overeager rustling of papers could bring her over in a frenzy of flaring nostrils.

"Keith," I whispered. "You'd better get down before she sends you to detention."

"Yeah," he scoffed. "Miss Markel wouldn't dare."

The fact that he was so sure of himself had me instantly intrigued. "And why not?"

Keith looked around before lowering his voice. "Can you keep a secret?"

"Sure."

"Miss Markel is a former client of mine. Turns out she likes to let her hair down with a little of the devil's lettuce, if you know what I mean."

Miss Markel – a pothead? I didn't believe him for a second. With her polo shirts and twisted buns, she was more strait-laced than me. I grinned. "You're such a liar."

"Believe what you will." He shrugged. "All I'm saying is I have enough dirt on her that I could take a crap in the middle of the library and there'd be nothing she could do but hand me a roll of toilet paper."

My mouth dropped open as I glanced between Keith and my one-time book-buying hero. Yet just the fact that he was still perched on the table as she wandered around the library was indication enough that there might be some truth to his claim. "How many more secrets do you have about our fine institution?"

His eyes sparkled with mischief. "Let's put it this way – if the superintendent of schools tortured me for information, half the teaching staff would be gone."

"Damn." I giggled. "Where have I been all my life?"

Without skipping a beat, he answered, "Saying no."

And with those two little words, Keith McKallister perfectly summed up my last two years. There was no way to defend myself because we both knew he was right. When 'no' had become my favorite word, I couldn't say, but it was now my way of life. I'd even turned him down the first time he'd asked for my help. Had he not been persistent, I would have missed out on getting to know him, and that would have been the biggest mistake of my short life.

Perhaps he sensed my turmoil, and he backtracked. "I was kidding. Relax. Hey, you know what you need?"

"If you're going to say I need to get laid, I'm going to blow my rape whistle… right here in the middle of the library."

He lifted his arms. "Whoa that escalated quickly. No, I was going to say you need to get drunk – let the liquor take your mind off everything for a few hours."

"Right, but then afterward, I'll just be right back where I started."

He scratched his head. "Huh. So that's how addiction works? So simple."

I laughed. "Yes, Keith. That's how it works, and I don't need to add that to my list of woes."

"One drunken binge does not a habit make, Sam."

"Okay, if I were to go with your plan, how might an almost seventeen-year-old purchase this booze you speak of?"

"How might?" Keith mimicked me. "How come you talk like a character in a prehistoric novel? Newsflash, Sam. You live in the 20th century. Act like it."

I cringed. We had such a long way to go. I considered correcting him on his centuries, but he seemed a little overwhelmed by the heavy influx of learning, so I let it be. "I know. I need to loosen up. I wish I were more like you. Sometimes I feel so old."

Again, Keith reached out and glided his fingers over the back of my hand. Aside from the occasional nudges and arm punches, he'd never touched me, and now all of a sudden my study buddy had octopus tentacles. What was happening and why was my body shuddering under waves of heat? Was it so wrong to ache for affection from him… or really just from anyone?

"Keith," Miss Markel interrupted, her eyes gliding over him in a knowing manner. This woman had been aiding in the delinquency of a minor. I had no respect left for her. "Off the table, please."

They exchanged a glance before Keith morphed into a sloth-like creature and, in the slowest most deliberate movements possible, returned to his chair. I watched his whole show in amusement. Clearly he was making a statement, and Miss Markel had no choice but to allow it.

I met Keith's eye, questioning. He grinned, shrugged, and dove back into his geometry homework. Reluctantly, I returned to my AP English assignment.

Several minutes passed before he nudged me and whispered, "Hey, Sam?"

I tilted my head. "Yes?"

"I care."

"What?"

"That you're turning seventeen. I care."

Chapter Nine

Keith

Trust Me

Sam was in the library when I arrived for my tutoring session, papers spread out around her. Her shiny brown hair grazed the table as she concentrated on the task at hand. Sensing me, she glanced up from her work and smiled. Not the kind of smile to simply acknowledge one's presence but a wide, glowing one that worked in conjunction with her sparkling eyes. My pulse quickened, as it did more often now. I wasn't exactly sure what was happening but the uptight girl I'd met a month and a half ago was mutating into my dream girl before my very eyes. How did she keep getting hotter?

Clearly, I'd underestimated Sam. At the start of our partnership, I'd viewed her as nothing more than a pass off, a way to get to the end zone with the least amount of work possible. But there was no willy-nilly homework copying with this girl. Oh, no. Sam wasn't like most girls, who seemed perfectly happy caving to my will. This one always had to push back, make me think. I'd never worked harder or thought deeper.

As strange as it sounded, she was single-handedly rewiring my brain. Aspiring to become a pirate just wasn't going to cut it anymore. I wanted more for myself. She'd opened my eyes to a future I might not have known about had I never met her. To Sam, I wasn't Kali, the drug-dealing stoner. Instead, I was the guy trying to rebuild the life he'd nearly thrown away. And the distinction hadn't escaped her. She was proud of me, and that was validation I clung to.

And now for the weird part: the more she challenged me, the deeper I fell under her spell. She was like every wicked teacher fantasy I'd ever had come to life. Who knew I liked girls with brains? Not me. But the way my timid cottontail bunny morphed into a quick-witted Jessica Rabbit, I could do nothing but become a believer. Suddenly, taking my sexy nerd behind a rack of hardcovers and teaching her a few things she wouldn't find in any of her dusty books was all I could think about.

I stopped in front of the table, tilting my head and flashing what I hoped would be my most affecting smile. "Hello, Sam."

"Well, hello yourself, Keith." She smiled. "Are you ready to get started?"

"Actually, no." I held out my hand to her, urging her to take it without complaint. "Let's get out of here."

"What? Where?"

"It's a surprise."

She eyed me suspiciously. Because Sam was a calculating person, every decision took time and careful consideration. I knew this and patiently waited for the refusal I assumed would be coming. 'No' *was* her motto, after all. Only today, on her seventeenth birthday, I wouldn't be accepting that as an answer.

"What about your test this Friday?" she asked.

"What about it?" I shrugged.

She put her pencil down, staring at me with an intensity I hadn't expected. "What about your friends? What if they see us together?"

I flinched, embarrassed she'd even needed to ask such a question. As much as I was digging this girl, I had kept her hidden from my buddies, knowing if I revealed my connection to Sam, they'd rip her – and me – to shreds. I told myself it was to protect Sam, but I knew better. My position in Utopia was precarious now that I no longer had my fledging business to fall back on, and one misstep was all it would take to be cast out. And so, to protect myself, I kept the connection between Sam and me a secret from everyone but the mega geeks in the library, who couldn't give a Millennium Falcon fuck about the status quo.

"Who cares?" I said. "Let's go."

The glow that passed over her face twisted a knot in my stomach. She thought I was finally ready to present her to my world, when in reality, I'd arrived at the library fifteen minutes late, allowing ample time for my crowd to disperse. I was such a dick.

"Well, okay then." She slapped her book shut and neatly placed her papers in her folders before sliding them all into her backpack. "Why not?"

Exactly. Why not? And then I said a silent prayer to the reefer gods – wordlessly pleading for my glazed-over posse to have passed out by now. I sighed at my utter douchiness.

Forgive me, Sam, for I have sinned.

My hands gripped her hips as I held her in place. Like a baby giraffe learning to walk, Sam's legs splayed at unnatural angles, making it impossible for her to stand up straight. I laughed with abandon. Damn, she made me happy. It was like we were mismatched socks in this weird static cling world.

I shook her playfully, but what I really wanted to do was sink my lips into the crook of her neck and watch her fall apart under my touch. "What's with the loosey-goosey shit?" I teased, like a booger-laced nine-year-old crushing on the cute girl at the next table over. "Stand up straight, Nostradamus. You're embarrassing me."

"Keith, I think you might mean Hunchback of Notre Dame."

Did I? My eyes rolled up, thinking. Was there a difference? Since meeting Sam, it seemed like I was wasting an awful lot of time looking shit up.

"Anyway, I'm doing the best I can here, given the fact that you chose to bring one of my greatest fears to life on my birthday."

"It's ice-skating." I shook my head. "How terrifying can that be?"

"Plenty of people are afraid of ice skating. Just because you're not afraid of anything doesn't mean the rest of us aren't."

"I'm afraid of things."

"Yeah? Like what?"

"Sinkholes."

"Sinkholes?" Sam's voice rose to comical levels. "Let me get this straight. You're okay with shark attacks, being trampled by the bulls, and spontaneous combustion, but sinkholes in California – where it never rains – *that's* what you're afraid of?"

"Is that weird?" I squinted, playing it for laughs. "I feel like you think that's weird."

She laughed, which caused her to bobble and, that in turn, resulted in Sam digging her icy hands into mine with bone-breaking force.

"Well, since the chances of me falling on my butt are higher than the chances of you getting swallowed up whole by the earth, I think it's fair to tell you that if you let go of me, I'll personally see to it that you fail every single class for the rest of the semester."

"Oh, no, Sam," I gasped in mock horror. "Not academic ruin, please! Anything but that!"

"You laugh now, but…" Sam stumbled on the ice, screaming as she pushed back and burrowed her shapely ass into me. As cute as her terror was, the contact produced a chain reaction in my jeans. Shit, she was going to be so pissed if she felt my overeager woody building a bridge between us.

In an effort to keep the evidence from poking her in the butt, I moved her to my side, wrapping my arm around her dwindling waistline. The swift movement startled her, and she dug her nails even deeper into my flesh.

"I don't like this position," she protested.

"No?" I dropped my head into her neck. "What position do you like?"

"Are you flirt…" Sam swept her eyes over me, landing on my very noticeable hard on.

For safety reasons I widened the gap between us, but in my haste, my skate collided with Sam's. She stumbled forward, and as I tried to right her, I lost my balance as well, and the two of us tumbled to the ice. I landed missionary style on top of her, my steel beam now at a 90-degree angle and poking into her pubic bone. Sam's shock was so complete that I willed a sinkhole to open up and save me from her wrath. But instead of anger, her eyes crinkled in the corners and the purest, most untainted happiness burst forth. Her laughter was so infectious that it spread to other skaters, who smiled as they whizzed by.

We stayed like that, in each other's arms, until the slush bled through her jeans and forced us off the ice. I grabbed her around the waist once more, ready to begin skating with her in my protective embrace, but she grabbed my hands, and as our eyes met, I saw a change in hers. The fear that lived in them was wavering.

"I can do this on my own," she said, a new determination steeling her resolve. And just like that, Sam took her first tentative glides forward.

After skating around and around for a good hour, we finally called it a day, collapsed onto the benches, and removed our skates.

"That was..." Sam's smile lit up her face. "The best birthday ever."

"Hold on," I said, remembering the surprise I had for her in my backpack. "I have something for you."

Dipping into my bag, I found what I was looking for: a plastic container holding a cupcake decorated just for her. Peeling the lid back, I cringed at the remains of the confection stored inside. Instead of my proud creation, there was only a pile of cake crumbs and a ring of frosting around the walls of the plastic. The #17 I'd formed was smeared into a clump of nothingness. I shut the lid and slipped it back in my bag.

"Never mind," I grumbled. "I guess I don't have anything for you."

"What was that? I want to see." She reached around and snatched my bag.

"I wouldn't do that if I were you."

Sam pulled the lid off the plastic and choked back a laugh.

"It was a chocolate cupcake," I rushed out the words. "Not, um… roadkill."

"You made me a *cupcake*?" Placing a hand to her heart, Sam visibly swooned.

"My mom helped me, but yeah, of course… it's your birthday."

Sam continued to fixate on the remains until, unexpectedly, a single tear rolled down her cheek.

I hooked my arm over her shoulder. "I'm sorry, Sam. I know it looks like shit now, but I promise when I packed it this morning, it looked nice. In hindsight, maybe I shouldn't have stored it upside down in my backpack."

Tucking a strand of hair behind her ear, she shyly lifted her gaze to meet mine and I gulped her in. She was gorgeous and vulnerable and everything I never knew I wanted. This wounded girl was reactivating my brain and, like a speeding train barreling toward me, there was nothing I could do to stop it.

"Don't apologize," she said in a halting tone, her hand reaching out to grip mine. "You're the best birthday present I ever got."

CHAPTER TEN

SAMANTHA

Crocodile Tears

They mill around in gloomy clothes, their somber faces offering each other solace in this time of mourning. I should be grateful they came at all, but I'm not. I'm angry. Furious. Where were these people when he needed them? Not here, that's for damn sure. In fact, they'd have been hard-pressed to answer his call had he rung them up in the middle of the day to talk. But now – now they come to pretend. 'So sad,' they say. 'Such a tragedy.'

Go cry your crocodile tears somewhere else.

There she is, my mother, front and center, the martyr. She looks frail under all the black, her hands shaking. No tears are shed. 'She's strong,' they say. 'She'll get through this.' Oh, yes, I have no doubt she'll survive. In fact, instead of bearing the blame that should fall squarely on her shoulders, she will come out looking like the victim. 'He was weak,' she says. 'All he had to do was ask for help.'

Go spew your hateful lies somewhere else.

My father's there too, tears spilling from his eyes. 'Why?' he asks. "My boy was so happy.' Yes, he was. When he was ten! Before we were left alone – with her. I can barely look him in the eyes. Traitor. He cradles his four-year-old son in his arms. The six-year-old circles his feet. The replacements. He'll never let those ones go. Where was that commitment seven years ago, when his other son could still be saved?

Go pretend you're Father of the Year somewhere else.

These people are nothing but imposters. They don't care. They didn't love him – not like I did. They can grieve without me. I'm done. Slipping out the front door, I walk over to the tree – our tree. Sinking to the ground, I rest my back against the weathered trunk and remember. Him. Us. Tears cascade down my cheeks. He'd once been happy here.

The mailman, passing on the street, makes awkward eye contact as he slips letters into our mailbox. Does he know my heart has been ripped from my chest today? Does he care? Once he's left, I rise to my feet and move to the box. Who else wants to pretend to care? I riffle through the Hallmark-sized envelopes, tossing them back into the mailbox. I don't want their pity. I want Sullivan.

Something catches my eye – an envelope. Just a standard letter, but there's no mistaking the handwriting. The gasp that rips from my throat startles even me. To Samantha. From… him.

With shaky fingers, I open the letter. Something bulky is wrapped in paper and taped shut. Attached is a post-it-note. "I'm so sorry, Sis. I tried, I really did. I hope this gives you more strength than it gave me. I love you always. Sullivan."

He was my brother. My best friend. And now he was gone... forever. I tore through paper and tape, already knowing what was inside before the contents were revealed. Sobbing, I fixed the agate pendant around my neck, then looked up to the sky in thanks as I rubbed the smooth stone.

The door swung open to my room, startling me from the daydream that was currently destroying me. I wiped the tears from my eyes. Why had Sullivan chosen three days after my birthday to do the horrible deed? There was no good time to die, but casting a shadow over the day of my birth felt like a punishment.

My mother swept in. "What are you doing, Samantha? It's a school day."

"I know, but I can't go. Not today."

"Yes, you can. Now up, out of bed." Mom yanked the sheets clear off me before opening the blinds and flooding the room with light. "Today is no different than any other day."

Oh, but it is.

"Today is the two-year anniversary," I whispered. "I can't."

Although she tried to suppress it, I could see just the slightest tremble of her lip. Somewhere deep inside, she still felt.

"He chose to leave us, Samantha. We don't mourn weakness. Now, get up. It's a school day, and you don't want to be late."

With every step I took, I could feel the heaviness, like weights circling my ankles. I wanted to drop to the ground and sob, but that was a luxury I was not allowed. Weakness was not allowed. That mantra had followed Sullivan into his grave. He hadn't been allowed to feel. *Be a man, Sullivan. What's wrong with you, Sullivan?* Why couldn't she see he was perfect as he was? Why couldn't he? My sensitive big brother had suffered in silence, choosing the worst possible way to make his voice heard. He was only nineteen.

Sometimes, I wondered what it would be like to join him. How easy would it be to just cease to exist? No more pain. But then I'd be just like Sullivan – a memory hanging around Shannon's neck – and I refused to do that to her. She was like a sister to me, and I would not place on her the burden Sullivan had placed on me.

Hundreds of unsuspecting students passed by as I opened my locker, leaning into it for support. What would they think if I died? No doubt they'd be scratching their heads and saying, *Samantha who?* Just like Sullivan, I'd die in obscurity, no one mourning my passing.

Sudden warmth spread as arms wrapped around me from behind. My knees nearly gave way from the force of the hug.

"You're okay," Shannon whispered in my ear. "I'm so sorry, Samantha. I forgot the date. I'm so sorry."

Shannon's strength was what I needed now. It would get me through the day, and then tomorrow, I'd wake up and move on… again. Slowly I turned and transferred some of the overwhelming weight onto her devoted shoulders. Thank god for Shannon. I often wondered if I'd been there for Sullivan at that exact moment when he'd made the decision to end his life, would he still be here today? Or would my intervention only have pushed his death forward to another day, another time? Could you really save someone determined to die?

Touching my fingers to the stone, I imagined Sully's last moments. In my mind, I watched as he solemnly removed the necklace, carefully slipping it in the envelope, and quickly scribbled the note. Getting the necklace to me had been important to him in his final minutes. Maybe he knew the stone would be the one thing I would cling to when he was gone. Maybe it was a way to purge his guilty soul. After all, he was doing what he'd promised never to do. *I won't leave you Samantha. You're all I have.* And, of course, I'd repeated those lines right back to him.

We'd had a deal. He broke it.

I squeezed my eyes shut, trying – but failing – to block out the thoughts of his final minutes. What had he been thinking? How had he made his legs move across campus to post my letter? And why had the person who loved me most in the world climbed the stairs to the top of his dorm and jumped?

I hurried to third period, hoping to arrive before Keith in order to fix the protective goggles over my bloodshot, puffy eyes. But when I walked in the classroom, I saw he was already there, holding his hand over the open flame, a defiant smirk across his face, and as miserable as I felt, my suffering eased just a pinch in his presence. He had, after all, made me a cupcake.

"Ouch," he yelped, yanking his hand away from the flame. "Sweet merciful crap, that's hot."

What did he expect? He was literally playing with fire. I shook my head at his antics, the smile typically reserved for him slow to take flight. Normally I adored Keith's youthful exuberance, even envied his middle school mentality. He was so full of life, and I wished I could have stolen just a smidge of his energy and passed it on to Sully before he died. Maybe it could have saved him.

Blowing on his sizzling hand, Keith lifted his eyes to acknowledge me.

"Hey there, Sammy."

I cringed. Sammy was even worse than Sam, and today was certainly not the day to assign me a new nickname.

"Samantha," I snapped.

Unaccustomed to my harsh tone, Keith looked me up and down. "Okay, wow. Maybe this isn't a good time to ask you why islands don't float away. I mean, they're surrounded by water."

I held firm to my scowl, determined not to let Keith's stupid questions cheer me up. Not today. My sour face seemed to wise him up.

He leaned in closer, the sparkle gone from his eyes. "You okay?"

Caring about my birthday was different than caring about me as a person. People who cared didn't take the long way around the school parking lot to avoid running into their buddies with a nerdy girl by their side. I mean, if Keith couldn't even make the trip across the lunch tables for me, then he certainly wouldn't have my back if I really needed him.

"I'm fine," I replied, looking back toward the door that I desperately wanted to escape through. But then what? Home? Her? My mother's bullying was getting progressively worse, forcing me to spend the majority of my time at home barricaded in my room for safety. Spoons were the least of my problems. Bruises littered my arms and back, and my grandmother's china, once considered an heirloom, was now just a worthless pile of broken shards.

Staying home, curled up in my bed, and sleeping my sadness away – that's all I asked. But even that request had been denied. It wasn't that my mother cared if I missed school; she just couldn't allow me even the tiniest of victories. Not that mourning Sullivan's death would have been a victory, but at least I wouldn't be subjected to the lunch line on the very date my heart had been ripped clean out of my chest.

"You don't look fine," he said, interrupting my internal rant.

"Neither do you," I replied. "Are those third degree burns on your hand?"

"Don't change the subject."

I grabbed his hand and turned it over. His palm was red but otherwise uninjured. I blew on it as a mother might do to heal her small child.

"Hot," I warned in a cautionary tone. "Ouchy."

He laughed, yanking his hand away.

"Hasn't anyone ever told you not to play with fire?" I questioned.

"Not since I was eight and lighting matches in the bathroom."

"Obviously, *that* message didn't stick. Why were you lighting matches in the bathroom in the first place?"

"To watch them burn. Duh."

With Keith, often the simplest answer was the right one. Untouched by adversity, he knew the world to be a good place. I wasn't as convinced.

"I also enjoy blowing things up. Does that make me a pyromaniac? I don't think so."

"Actually, yes, it does," I answered, no longer able to suppress a smile. "How often do you blow stuff up, anyway?"

"You know." Keith ran his fingers over his stubbled jawline. "A fair amount actually."

We exchanged amused glances, and I could feel the sadness begin to fade. Some might say Keith was the only beneficiary of our tutoring sessions, since his rewards were clear to see. They could be measured in higher test scores and passing grades – tangible evidence of our partnership. But what Keith gave to me was far more powerful a force. Every smile, every laugh I attributed to him was another day I kept moving forward – kept breathing. So did it really matter that he refused to be seen with me in public? After everything else he'd given me, how important was it that he sit opposite me at the lunch table?

"Here's today's lab," I said, passing him the assignment. "Take a look. If you have any questions, just ask."

Without skipping a beat, he raised his hand.

I tried to block out the frantic arm waving, knowing he couldn't possibly have formulated an intelligent question in the short amount of time he'd been allotted. Ignoring him, I dipped into my bag for my own work, all while keeping an eye on my smirking lab partner. I wished he weren't so attractive. It would have made it so much easier to ignore him.

I sighed. "Yes, Keith?"

"I have a question."

"Okay, go."

"Is this the experiment where we boil acid to prove it contains hydrogen?"

I rocked back in my seat, surveying him with curiosity. Keith had come a long way from the boy who'd met me in the library after school that first day with just an unsharpened pencil to his name. Now, when he slid onto the seat beside me, he was prepared and thriving, as if a low-voltage light bulb had switched on inside his head. Yet Keith loved to get under my skin with stupid questions. The whole floating islands bit was just the tip of the iceberg. And whether his ignorance was real or faked mattered little, as Keith had an arsenal of dumb queries at his disposal.

"Wow, Keith," I said, in deference to his intelligent inquiry. "You've done your homework. Good for you."

He shook his head. "Nah, this is one of my do-over classes. I remember this experiment from last year. It was gnarly." He pointed to the diagram on his sheet. "Gas is going to come out of this tubing, and when it does, get me a match – I'm gonna light this place up like the Fourth of July."

"Uh, I think not," Mrs. Lee intervened. She'd been standing nearby when Keith had made his loud declaration, and now she was on high alert. "Remember your promise, Keith. No fire."

"Actually, I believe the deal was *I* couldn't be on fire. No mention was made of the classroom."

"It was implied." She grinned, laying his test facedown on the table. "Let's not ruin the good thing you've got going on here."

She patted his shoulder, and as she walked away, Keith and I both dove for the test. I got to it first and flipped it over.

"An 88%," I whispered, gripping his wrist and shaking it. There was no hiding my pride. Keith was proving no obstacle was too great if you set your mind to it.

"Are you crying?" he asked, skirting his eyes over me. "You're that shocked by my grade?"

It was only then I felt the tears trickling down my cheeks. Swiping them away with the back of my hand, I tried to cover for my slip-up with a faked smile, but found that once the tears had started, there was no stopping their descent.

"Hey, what's wrong?" he asked, for the first time realizing I was crying for something unrelated to him. "For real, Sam?"

"I'm fine."

"No, you're not. You're rubbing the stone."

I wanted desperately to trust him, but the people in my life had made it hard for me to take that leap of faith. My bottom lip trembled. "I'm struggling."

That was all Keith needed to hear, and he leaned in close until we were nearly touching. If there had been any doubt that he cared about me, it was put to rest when I searched his eyes and saw pain in them – for me. "What can I do to help?"

I shrugged, unable to form a sentence without sobbing and alerting the students around us of my meltdown. My gaze shifted to my trembling fingers.

"Hey." He nudged me. "Sam, look at me."

I lifted my eyes.

"Ask me anything. I'll do it."

Only one person in Pearl Beach knew my history… and all the secrets that went with it. Even then, Shannon only gained access after touching her hand to my bruised shoulder and watching me wince. Yet here was Keith, a guy I'd known mere weeks, edging himself into my life with ease. But how much headway had I made in his? Then it occurred to me. Maybe the fact that he kept me from his friends, spoke more to his insecurities than to my deficiencies. Maybe Keith didn't know who he was any more than I did.

"My brother died two years ago today."

The background noise fell away, and for a moment it was just the two of us sharing a deeply personal moment.

“Ah, Sam,” he said, shaking his head. “I’m so sorry. I had no idea. If I’d known, I wouldn’t have been joking around.”

“Then I’m glad I didn’t tell you before. Please never stop making me smile.”

He nodded, staring down at his wringing fingers. “How did he…?”

“Die?” I finished the question.

“Yeah.”

“You don’t want to know.”

“Oh.”

That was enough information to catch Keith up. Typically conversation ended there. Suicide was never a comfortable topic, but he surprised me by pushing deeper into my gloomy past. “How?”

How? Why did it matter how? He’d killed himself – end of story. But I knew better. The way people chose to live their lives mattered, and so did the way some chose to die. Sullivan had made a statement with his death, however misguided it might have been. He could have gone quietly, drifting into oblivion with a cocktail of pills alone in his dorm room, but instead he’d chosen to go public in the most terrifying and messy of ways. And the worst part of it all was, I understood his reasoning. Like me, Sully had spent his life in the shadows. In death, he wanted to be seen.

Through jagged breath, I told Keith the story, every sordid detail, and the more I unloaded on him, the easier it became to breathe. When I came to the end, Keith seemed the one who couldn't catch his breath. We sat quietly, staring at the empty worksheets on the table.

"Hey," he said, lowering his voice for my ears only. "What can I do to make this day easier on you?"

He already had made it easier just by being there for me. But Keith was searching for something tangible, something he could roll his sleeves up and fix. I had an idea, a thought that had been brewing in the shadows of my mind for some time now. It was something he'd once offered, but I'd been too afraid to take him up on it at the time. Now it seemed as if there was nothing left to lose.

"Actually, there is something you can do for me."

His eyes lit up, and it struck me that my happiness meant something to him. It was the first time I realized that this beautiful, fun, kind boy might actually like me for something other than my tutorial skills. As crazy as it seemed, I thought… maybe… possibly Keith McKallister might be falling for me.

And as the first butterflies bore down on my belly, I bit back the elation and said, "I want you to teach me to surf."

A rapid-fire succession of blinks spoke to his surprise, but to his credit, Keith recovered quickly and nodded as he smiled. *Challenge accepted.* And then Keith raised the stakes even higher when his long, strong fingers reached for mine under the protection of the table. I lifted my eyes shyly, meeting his. He smiled, but it wasn't his normal happy-go-lucky grin. No, this one was soft and warm and glowing with affection. What had I done to deserve this? Whatever it was, I was beyond grateful. Keith had taken one of the saddest days of my life and made it bearable. I wouldn't forget.

"I promise you won't regret this," he whispered, his lips dangerously close to my ear as if he didn't care who was watching. And then, with his breath tickling my skin, Keith made me a final guarantee. "I'm about to change your life forever."

Turning my hand over, Keith's fingers braided seamlessly with mine, and I held his hand with a purpose I'd never felt before. His words, his protective hand gripping mine, and those unwavering promises all conspired to set my heart on a collision course with destiny. It was in that moment I knew: I would love this boy forever.

CHAPTER ELEVEN

KEITH

The Shakedown

"I'm pushing twice what you did. You hear me, Kali? Jules thinks you were either lazy or rippin' him off."

I didn't bother responding to Valentine, as he was just trying to goad me into a confrontation I could not afford to be in, at least not if I wanted to remain at this school.

"Did you hear me?" he asked; only this time he smacked me upside the head.

"I heard you," I responded, carefully controlling the spite threatening to spew from my gut. "And can I be the first to congratulate you? I think you and Jules make a beautiful couple."

"Fuck you," Valentine replied, his features twisted in irritation.

Getting under my skin was priority number one for him these days, and it took everything in my power to keep my cool. His passive aggressive behavior had started almost immediately after he'd taken over my weed route, and since then it had only escalated. Although there were times, like now, where I wanted to pummel him to a bloody pulp, my hands were tied. Not only could I not afford a blow up at school, but also he had the backing of some unscrupulous dudes who'd been threatening to beat my ass simply for existing. Staying under the radar was a matter of survival.

Drunk on power, Valentine had made me his cocktail of choice. Like any bully, he figured that emasculating me in front of a crowd would raise him up, but the truth was, my very existence was a threat to his rule. Valentine and I ran our businesses in vastly different manners. For the most part, I'd kept my dealings light and pain-free – a joke here, a laugh there. No reason to make a drug transaction an unpleasant experience. A little money and dope would change hands, and then we'd all go back to our lives like nothing nefarious had happened.

Not so with Valentine. He went with the threat and intimidation approach, and had already alienated a large portion of my former cliental. In fact, many of them were begging me to come back, and that only further served to irritate the new king. If it weren't for the loosely tethered ties I still had to the other guys in our group, I would probably already have been cast out of Utopia.

Sometimes I wished Valentine would just do it and get it over with. I existed in a state of limbo anyway – not really here or there, and since meeting Sam, I was slowly coming to the realization that life would be easier for me as an outcast. Hell, I already was one. My reputation had taken such a hit that I held no real status in the school anymore anyway. And the further I got away from the popularity trap, the harder it was to figure out why I'd needed it so much. Maybe it was time to make that final leap and just accept that I wasn't special enough to occupy a seat at the cool kids' table.

Pinpointing Sam across the quad, my gaze softened. She was like a beleaguered flower struggling to blossom in unyielding darkness. Her story today had shaken me, but it had also given me newfound respect for the girl who'd risen above the adversity with grace and kindness. Her strength dwarfed me – dwarfed every person in this school – and I'd already decided that I'd do whatever it took to help her through - starting with surfing and ending with... well, anything else she'd allow me to do.

I'd liked girls before Sam, but not like this. Sometimes I even forgot to eat I was so wrapped up in thoughts of her. That's how I knew she was different. I had plenty of female friends. We met at parties. We got wild. We got it on. But I'd never cared about their lives. I'd never hung on their every word. And I sure as hell didn't call them up to ask how their test went or frost them a damn cupcake on their birthday. That was reserved for Sam… the bookish tutor who'd unexpectedly wound herself around me.

Checking on her again, I saw Sam huddled over the table with her friend, much like she had been on the first day of school. I smiled, knowing exactly what they were talking about – me. Ah, damn, how I wanted to be over there immersed in their deeply dorky conversation. Even though I felt I knew her, Shannon and I had never met in person because I'd balked at walking over there and introducing myself. It was like I was still that uncertain 7th grader making decisions based on my shaky self-worth. Maybe I'd been trying so hard to fit in that I'd missed the obvious. I was born to be an outsider, skirting the fringes, and the sooner I could respect myself for it, the better.

Sam looked up from her conversation and caught my eye. She smiled. My stomach tightened like a vice as shame gripped me. How could I speak of respect when I wasn't willing to show it to the one person in this school who actually mattered to me? Sam deserved better. So why, then, was she over there and me here? Why was I not still holding her hand? Because I was a goddamn coward, that's why. I was keeping us apart for no other reason than I was afraid of being judged and ridiculed by the people who claimed to be my friends. If they truly were, they'd be happy for me. They'd welcome her in with open arms.

But that wasn't how my crowd rolled, and I'd allowed myself to be a slave to their rules because I didn't trust in myself enough to stand up for what I believed in. And, as long as I wore my insecurities around my neck like a shock collar, I'd never be good enough, smart enough, or confident enough to ever truly belong. It was the story of my life… and it had to stop. All I was doing was delaying the inevitable because if there was one thing I was certain of, it was that Sam and I were going to be together.

Change was in the air, and it was up to me to make it happen. It's not like I had much to lose anyway now that the number of skaters at Pearl Beach High had been drastically reduced after a drug-sniffing dog wiped out half our herd. You would have thought the cops were raiding a Mexican drug cartel's warehouse the way my buddies were being lined up and marched off campus in handcuffs. That would have been me – should have been me. But I was one of the lucky ones, and that girl over there was the reason I was still here today.

Valentine had survived the purge only because he'd been on a weeklong suspension after being caught stealing a test from the teacher's desk. Screensaver lived too, but only because he was convincing enough in his stupidity to get out of all charges. Sadly, Fire Crotch hadn't been as lucky. As bad luck would have it, one-fourth of the Three Musketeers had been kicked out of school, never to return.

"Are you into that chick?" Valentine asked, his eyes trained in the direction I was looking. The smug smile on his face instantly irritated me. She was a joke to him.

"What if I am?" I challenged.

"Wait." His brow rose as he darted his eyes between Sam and me. "I was just kidding. Are you being serious right now?"

I clenched my fists, scowling at my nemesis. "Very."

"Dude." He snorted out a laugh, nearly falling off the table in the process. "If you think that's hot, you need to do more drugs. "

I shot to my feet, lunging for Valentine. My only goal was to physically wipe that smirk off his face, but before I could get to him, Screensaver jumped between us, pushing me back.

"Don't do it," he warned. "It's not worth it, Kali. You've come too far to risk it all."

Blinking, I let Screensaver's words of wisdom sink in. No way could I let the likes of Valentine ruin the good thing I had going on. Drawing a deep breath, I unfurled my fists and addressed my friend by his given name. "You're right, James. He's not worth it."

James glanced nervously between the two of us. He'd been smart enough to keep in the neutral zone of this particular pissing match. "Well... that's...uh... not really what I said."

Now that he was secure enough in his safety, Valentine puffed out his chest before dispensing with more trash talk. "You'd better watch your back, Dickweed, that's all I'm saying."

"Yeah? Why wait? I'm right here." I drew my arms to the sides in invitation. "Give me your best shot."

He wouldn't. The biggest talkers always had the least to show. For all his bravado, Brett was not a fighter. I'd watched him cry on the street from road burns after falling off his skateboard, and run into the bushes when trouble came calling. Trust me when I said he didn't want a punch to the face any more than I wanted to deliver it.

"No? Okay then. Leave my girl out of it, and you and I have no problem. Are we good?"

No response.

I took a step forward and repeated myself. "Are we good?"

His shoulders slumped. "Yeah, man. I don't know what your problem is."

Just what I thought. Nothing to show for it.

Gripping James's shoulder, I smiled. "Thanks for talking me down."

"Dude, always." Screensaver nodded his bobblehead before lowering his voice. "And, uh, just for the record – she's hot. I'd totally hit that."

It was meant as a compliment, albeit a backwards one, so I let it slide because this was Screensaver, the guy who still made bunny ears when tying his shoes.

As I strode off, Valentine called out. "Where are you going?"

"Where I should have gone five years ago. See you around, Valentine."

Each step I took away brought with it renewed vigor, and crossing the threshold of Utopia, I breathed in the fresh air. Finally, I knew just where I was headed.

Sam and Shannon watched my approach open-mouthed in awe. I came to a halt at their table, the eyes of those around us burning into my back.

"Hey, Shannon." I nodded my head in her direction, smiling. "I'm Keith."

"Yes, you are." She giggled, the flush only multiplying her endearing freckles. "I've heard a lot about you."

I made a show of cringing. "Any of it good?"

"A very, very tiny bit." She used her fingers to emphasis the point.

Sam slapped her arm and they laughed. There were no pretenses here, no one-upping each other. It was this type of friendship I needed to aspire to.

"It's nice seeing you around these parts, Keith," Shannon said, glancing behind me. "But you might want to get back before your friends stage an intervention."

My eyes now locked on Sam's, I didn't bother to turn around. I knew what I'd find – lots of spectator eyes straining in my direction. Who cared? Let them stare. I wasn't going back. Ever.

"Can I sit?"

Sam nodded, smiling as she held my gaze with her warm, honey-hued eyes. "What took you so long?"

Chapter Twelve

Samantha

The Turtle Roll

6:30 Saturday morning. That's what he'd said. I glanced at my watch. 6:32. Yep, he wasn't coming. I should have confirmed with him last night. Best case scenario, he just forgot. Worst, he'd decided I wasn't worth the effort. I mean, what did I expect? One day at my lunch table and suddenly I was trust falling into his arms.

I should go. In fact, I never should've come in the first place. Stepping into that ocean would be my nightmare come true. Something about the uncharted depths of the unknown terrified me. My fear had only grown over the years, and I somehow associated the ocean with death – my death. And since Sully's suicide, I stayed clear of danger, preferring to exist in a bubble wrapped world.

I checked my watch again. 6:33. *Screw you, Keith McKallister – making me sit on a bench, next to a garbage can, in the parking lot of your choice!* If he thought I was going to tutor him after leaving me here to be dive-bombed by his shitty memorial seagulls, he'd better think again. *Good luck passing geometry now, you jer*k. I mean, good lord, everyone knows parallel lines don't intersect!

As I sat humiliated on a park bench at 6:34 in the morning, my body began to rebel. I tightened the sweatshirt around me as a wave of shivers swept through me. I wasn't sure if the reaction was due to the cold or if I were quivering with fear. I lifted my head and looked around at the fine layer of mist. The sunshine we enjoyed on a daily basis had yet to burn through the coastal fog, making the air extra chilly today.

My teeth were chattering. How had I even considered submerging my body in the unruly Pacific Ocean? Tourists tended to believe the California coast sported nice, lukewarm waters to frolic in. Um…no. This was not the Caribbean. The Pacific was too deep, too wild, and too inhabited by dangerous creatures to give off that warm, fuzzy feeling.

The revving of an engine in the distance caught my attention, and I froze in anticipation. *Please be him. Please save my faith in humanity.*

"Sam! Hey, Sam!" Keith yelled my name out the window, adding a horn to his noisy entrance. And just like that, I forgot how much I'd despised him. Or how cold I was. Or how terrified I was. He'd come for me, and that was all that mattered.

I jogged over to him and slapped the arm he had dangling out the window. "My name is Samantha, jerk."

"Sorry I'm late. I couldn't get the damn truck to start. Are you pissed? You look pissed."

I shook my head.

"Liar. You were plotting my death, weren't you?"

How accurately he knew me. I laughed, nodding. "Yes."

He hopped out of his truck, gave me a hug, and then went around the back, pulling two surfboards out of the flat bed.

I ran my hand over the rust bucket he called a truck. "Nice ride. What happened to your piece of shit car?"

"Well, see, as it so happens, there are plenty of shitty vehicles to choose from at my house. This particular one works well for trips to the beach. Surfboards. See?"

"Ah." I nodded. *Be still my heart.* Keith was being so adorably chatty – just the way I liked him. "I see."

"Officially, I'm only allowed to drive the Surfmobile to and from the beach because every time this baby hits fifty miles per hour, things start flying off. Can you believe my dad has had this truck for over twenty years?"

I glanced over the ancient beast. "Yes. Yes, I can."

With his winning personality and those affecting eyes of his, I'd almost forgotten that Keith was about to blow my predictable world all to hell. "Relax, Sam. You look like you just found a severed finger in your chili bowl."

"I wish. I told you I don't like the ocean. "

He shoved a wetsuit into my hands. "And I told you, I'm about to change that. Go put this on."

I held up the tiny suit, seriously beginning to question not only my sanity but his as well. Did he really think I could fit more than a thigh into that itty-bitty wet suit?

"It's my sister's," he explained.

"The four year old's?"

"No," he laughed. "Emma's."

Oh, well, that explained it. I'd seen his sister around school, and even with my now ten-pound weight loss, there was no way I was fitting into a suit she wore. She was sun-kissed perfection. I was like her pale, plump, fraternal twin.

Keith seemed to pick up on my hesitation. "It's supposed to be snug fitting."

Oh, yes. It'll be snug, all right.

"Come on. Let's go, Anderson. Stop wasting time. I'll give you three minutes to get the wetsuit on. Any longer than that and I'll meet you at the beach."

I wanted to remind him that he was the one who'd been late, but that impatient expression on his face told me Keith wasn't playing around. He intended on leaving me if I didn't get with the program. Maybe him playing hardball was what I needed because, instead of second-guessing myself for all eternity, I raced into the bathroom and began the arduous process of pulling the suit up over my baby-making hips. That was the hard part, requiring a delicate dance of back and forth redistribution before the rest of the suit fell into place with organ-pinching perfection. And, like a seal in a very tight-fitting second skin, I waddled out to Keith with seconds to spare.

His eyes passed over me, landing squarely on my sealskin suit and nodding.

"What? Did it rip?" I asked, crossing my arms over myself. I was so out of my element.

"No. I was just… damn, you look hot."

"I do?"

Curving his arm around my waist, he yanked me into him, and our bodies pressed together seductively. Keith's lips hovered close, teasing and tempting me. To say I was out of my element would be an understatement. Last week a boy held my hand for the first time. Today he wanted to kiss me. It was a moment I'd daydreamed about, but now that the boy was here, eager for the taking, I had no idea what to do with him. I ducked out from under his embrace.

"What's wrong?" he asked, brows furrowing.

"Nothing's wrong. It's just – I've never been kissed before. If, you know, that's what you were going to do. Maybe you weren't, and I totally misread the whole thing, and if I did, I'm sorry, but…"

Once I caught the grin on Keith's face, I stopped rambling.

"I *was* going to kiss you, but I didn't realize you needed to make an outline first."

"More like a rough draft," I added playfully.

"I'm thinking getting you into bed would take a full dissertation."

"Whoa. You need to slow down, Keith. I won't go past a term paper with you."

"We'll see about that," he answered confidently.

His playfulness drew a smile to my lips. "No, we won't."

He grabbed me again, and before I could think, he pressed a quick kiss to my lips. "There. Now you've been kissed. Stop making it weird."

He let me go, picked up his surfboard, and started jogging toward the water.

My fingers found my lips and I grinned like a loon before picking up my own board and chasing after him.

Exhausted, waterlogged, and seriously tested, I paddled my way out the back, past the broken waves, to position myself in the right spot to catch the perfect ride. Getting to this point had been a battle of both body and soul. There was nothing like gasping for air while being tossed about in the waves to point out the obvious – I was seriously out of shape. By dropping a fair amount of weight, I'd fooled myself into believing I was a lean, mean fighting machine, but one day on the beach proved I was anything but. Even if I never caught a wave, from this day forward, I would make it my mission to get fit.

The battle with my soul proved easier to overcome, since the minute I dipped my big toe into the frigid Pacific, all brain activity slowed to a crawl. I couldn't remember which way was up, much less concern myself over silly stuff like death and dismemberment. My mind had one goal: surf. Somehow I just knew if I could get my unathletic body up on that board, all the world's dysfunction would be solved. I had the power of the universe in my hands… if I could just get over the next swell.

But as I was preparing my victory speech, a wall of water hit me in the face. I gagged on the salty concoction flooding my nose. Every swipe of my hands to clear the water away only made my face wetter. I pawed at myself, coughing up a swell of water before I turned to see Keith eyeing me in amusement.

"You doing okay there, champ?"

"Aside from swallowing a school of guppies? Sure."

"It's the surfer's version of sushi."

"Yes. Yum."

Keith dropped onto his stomach and started paddling away. "Gotta watch for those rogue waves, Sam. They'll get you every time. Now, let's go. We don't want to lose our place in the lineup."

"Right, because it would be a shame if I couldn't get up there in time for the other surfers to laugh at me."

"Nothing's for free, Sam. You've got to earn your respect."

And then suddenly Keith was gone, having flipped his board underwater only to suspend himself upside down until the wave had passed.

"Oh, crap." I gripped the side of my board and followed him below the water line. The dreaded turtle roll. No matter how many times I'd done it today, the maneuver elicited panic every single time. Holding my breath under water was one thing, but holding it while dangling upside down was quite another.

Once the whitewater had passed over me, I flipped the board back around and ungracefully scooted my stomach back onto the smooth surface. Keith was already back, bobbing on his board as if the effort of battling the current hadn't affected him at all. He pointed toward the horizon. "You see it, Sam? It's coming."

I followed the direction of his finger to see the perfect wave developing. It was mine. I could feel it. Never taking my eyes off the redemption forming not far in the distance, I nodded to Keith. This was what I'd needed all along – something to focus and challenge me. For the first time since Sullivan's death, I was thinking clearly, and everything finally made sense. We weren't put on this earth to survive. We were put here to live. Sully's suicide had dragged me down below the waterline, but instead of resurfacing, I'd remained suspended upside down. It was like the turtle roll of my life and I'd never completed the flip.

Today was the day I'd resurface. I was going to stand back up on my own two feet, and when that wave came, I was going to ride it all the way to shore, so help me god.

Keith twisted on his board, staring me in the eye, the thrill of the moment not lost on either of us. "It's beautiful, Sam, and it's got your name written all over it."

"Samantha," I corrected with a wide smile.

Keith gripped my arm and pulled me toward him. His hands took hold of my neck and he pressed his salty lips to mine. This time I wasn't shy and timid. This time I kissed him back with all the excitement this moment meant to me. Breaking our connection, Keith pushed my board toward the wave.

"Go earn the respect you deserve, Samantha."

Wetsuits off, Keith and I lay on our backs at the base of a sand dune, baking in the sun. I was flushed with accomplishment, and a feeling of euphoria had settled over me.

"Why didn't I do this earlier?"

Keith flipped to his side, resting on his elbow before proceeding to run a finger along my neckline. "It's called, 'no.' I told you surfing would change your life."

His touch was so casual, as if he regularly caressed me and it had become an afterthought to him. But me? Yeah, my body didn't take it so nonchalantly. I shivered like I'd just collided with an iceberg.

"Are you cold?" he asked, the slightest hint of a grin turning up the corners of his lips. He knew damn well why I was shaking.

"No. I'm confused."

"Confused?" Keith pushed a little higher up on his elbow, but instead of ceasing and desisting, his fingers just kept slipping further down my neck until they were nestled in the crevice of my cleavage. "About what? I think I'm making my intentions pretty fucking clear."

"Oh, you are," I replied, sucking in a breath as his hand dipped lower still. "I just can't figure out what your angle is."

Keith laughed. "You say that like I'm some complicated guy, Sam. I don't even know where the sun goes when the moon comes out. I don't have some master plan. I can assure you that when it comes to seduction, I'm a simpleton."

"So, that's what this is all about? You're trying to seduce me?"

"If you have to ask, then I'm not doing my job properly. How about this?" Keith nestled a little closer until I felt his 'angle' pushing into my thigh.

"Yeah, I get that you're a fuckboy, Keith. That's common knowledge around school. What I don't get is why me? I'm not your typical one-night stand skank whore."

"Oh, Sam." Keith smirked, his hand sliding over my breast and down the length of my stomach before coming to rest inches above my sex. "If the guy is doing it right, every girl's got a little skank whore in her."

His hand relaxed on my mound, and I pulsed with excitement. Never having been touched by a member of the opposite sex, this was like going from zero to blast off in seven seconds flat. Oh, god, how I wanted to be part of lift off. Keith applied just the slightest bit of pressure, and I trapped my lip under my teeth and moaned. What was happening? How was my body so easily betraying me? I quivered, meeting his touch with the tilt of my hips.

The sounds of kids frolicking on the beach roused me from the trance when I realized that, in nine months time, I could be the proud owner of one of those noisemakers myself.

"Keith." I sat up, covering myself with my arms. "Too fast."

"Sorry. I got excited. You weren't stopping me, so I was like, 'Hell yeah.'"

The idea that I excited him was such a new concept that I had trouble believing it to be true. Anxiety played out over my face, catching Keith's attention.

"Hey, I'm sorry. My bad. I shouldn't have pushed so hard."

"No. I liked it, it's just… I need to know what we are exactly."

"Do you need a definition?"

"I'd prefer one, yes."

"We are…" His fingers trailed over my leg. "Whatever you want us to be."

"What I want?" I asked. "I think we both know what I want."

"Then that's what we are."

"Can you be more specific?"

Keith flipped over and was on his feet in seconds. I watched as he grabbed a stick and began to write in the wet sand. Inside a roughly drawn heart were the words, Will you be my girlfriend?

Turning back to me, he opened his arms wide and yelled, "Is this specific enough?"

As he perched over me in the cab of his truck, I glided my hand over him with slow, sure strokes.

"Sam," he panted.

It wasn't a question or a command, just my name forcibly stolen from his throat with every agonizing touch. I had the power to bring him to his knees and I did, whenever the opportunity arose. Pulsing with ecstasy, I reached my free hand to his sinewy stomach. Aside from his grabbable ass, it was my favorite part of him. Strong and lean from the surf, his abs would dip and swell under my manipulations, sending a surge of pleasure through me.

This – what we did in the confines of the Surfmobile – brought us together in ways I'd never imagined. It took us from friends to lovers, yes. But it was so much more. I wasn't a sad little girl anymore. Now when Keith trailed his fingers over my skin, I had the confidence to enjoy his touch. My body, once a vessel of lethargy, had transformed into something I'd never thought possible. Not only had my sun-deprived skin bronzed up under the warm rays, but also something resembling muscle had begun to reshape my arms and legs. Even my stomach muscles were showing signs of waking from a deep sleep.

Now when I walked through the halls of our high school with my very own surfer boy glued to my side, I was the picture of confidence and poise. Being with him, feeling his love, gave me the courage to blossom into a new me. For the first time in my life, I was choosing my own path, and it was with Keith.

Two months had passed since he'd asked me to be his in the sand, and we hadn't looked back, not for a minute.

The beach became our home, and every minute we spent together on the waves brought us closer together. We talked a lot, bobbing on those boards, about my family situation and about his dreams of one day owning a surf shop with his brothers. And the more we talked, the more my college escape plan began to waver. I wanted to stay here with Keith forever.

The only person not celebrating my transformation was my mother. The more I grew to love myself, the more she seemed to hate the new me. When it became clear she could no longer control me with intimidation and force, she'd shifted strategies and now regularly employed sabotage and sneak attacks.

Keeping Keith a secret had become a necessity. If she discovered what we were doing in the cab of his father's twenty-year-old truck, I feared for our safety. She was unstable and getting worse. Twice in the last couple of months, erratic behavior had nearly gotten her fired from the real estate agency where she worked. If she hadn't been such a prolific agent, they surely would have rid themselves of her long ago. Still, she was currently existing on a third strike policy, and I had to wonder how much longer she'd be able to pay the bills.

"Hey," Keith whispered, flicking his tongue lightly across my nipple. "Are you with me?"

As he sucked the taut peak into his mouth, his free hand slid to my other breast, fingers toying with the nipple.

Yes, I was with him. Of course I was. Always. Keith was the one constant in my life, and no one could ever convince me what we were doing was wrong. I loved Keith. He loved me. That was all that mattered.

"I'm with you," I answered, shivering as he continued to work me over with his tongue. Dangling one foot over the truck bench, I opened my legs wide, inviting him in. So close, only a thin layer of fabric separating me from what I desired.

Keith knew what I wanted. He didn't have to ask. After all, he'd been the one to introduce me to such pleasures in the first place.

We'd started off slow, each night taking us further and further until I was a quivering mass of desire, ready and willing to surrender. And when I awoke the next morning, I could feel the difference. The power. It was as if I were seeing the world through a different lens. I felt stronger and more determined. No one would be using me for target practice ever again.

Keith trailed his fingers along my inner thigh and over my pulsing mound. I strained upward, willing him to probe deeper, my body a series of currents, electrified under his touch. His hand moved under the edge of my panties and found me wanting; slick and hot and ready. He slid along the crease before dipping inside my folds. Writhing against him, I matched him stroke for stroke, unable to keep my body still or my cries muffled. And then it happened. The world splintered into a thousand pieces and took me right along with it.

Spent, I fell back against the seat, shuddering and panting. Keith rested his head on my chest, watching with a small smile.

Threading my fingers in his hair, I pressed a kiss to his lips. And he knew. I was ready. With his eyes on mine, Keith popped open the glove compartment and, finding the foil packet, ripped the condom packet with his teeth. And then he was above me, and I could feel the weight of his love. See it on his face and in his smile.

Placing a hand on his shoulder, I gave him a gentle nudge.

"No," I whispered. "My turn."

CHAPTER THIRTEEN

KEITH

The Metamorphosis

Heaven was the only way to describe the sweet little handful of buttocks currently cozied up against my erection, slowly rubbing against me in agonizing fashion. Sam did not require my help or guidance as she positioned her body over mine, and that can-do attitude was one of my favorite things about her – well, that and her shapely ass… and her killer bod… and her silky smooth skin. Don't get me wrong, I liked her personality too, but at the moment that took a backseat to her physical perfection.

Nothing in this world beat watching my girl writhe and moan and tip over the edge with lust. Yeah, that was absolutely my favorite thing about her—like to the point where if I died today, the memory of her climaxing would be what floated through my mind as I wandered off into the light.

I was inside her now, and Sam was moving slowly, teasing me. Her face contorted as the pleasure overpowered her. Fuckin' A, she was beautiful. My impatient fingers trailed the length of her bronzed skin that had been sculpted by the waves. Her body was now a toned machine, but somehow she still felt as soft as butter—unblemished and smooth to the touch. If I lived a thousand lifetimes, I could never get enough of her body.

Leaning in, she pushed me into the upholstery. A storm gathered at the base of my spine as I thrust inside her. She tipped her head back, keeping pace with me as I dipped into her neck with a frenzy of kisses. Draping one arm lazily over my shoulder, Sam caressed the arc of my neck, while her other hand slipped around to lightly stroke my back. With my palms molded to the swells of her breasts, I traced my fingers over her nipples. Ragged breaths eased from her throat, and my name escaped in a raspy moan. Encouraged, I slid my tongue along the rise of her nipples and lost myself to the frenzy. She squeezed tighter, and I bucked with abandon.

Her mouth found mine, and as our movements quickened, Sam's tongue became the aggressor, tangling with mine in a fury. She finally pulled back, her lips swollen and wet and wanton. And shit – the way she looked at me – I was so not worthy.

"You're killing me, Sam."

Trailing her tongue along my collarbone, her lips curved into a smile. She knew what she was doing to me, the way my body convulsed with every slippery stroke. The overhead light illuminated the steaks of gold in her long brown hair. Sam looked like a heaven-sent angel… and felt like one, too.

"I love you so much, babe."

She didn't respond – couldn't respond, because a strategically placed thumb accompanied my declaration, sending her reeling against my touch. With her lip tucked between perfectly straight teeth, Sam threw her head back and whimpered.

Nothing had ever looked so good. So appetizing. So right. A rush of euphoria raced through me. I'd never felt so alive.

I rocked with her as the frenzy built, and when I met the end of her with one final thrust, I erupted deep inside. With every movement, every spasm that traveled between us, our connection was sealed.

Because Sam was hiding my existence from her crazy mother, I dropped her off at the grocery store where she'd parked her car earlier in the day. This was where we'd part ways until the day the two of us could bring our relationship out into the open. My birthday was fast approaching, and Sam feared if her mother caught wind of what we were doing in my truck after hours, she'd try to have me arrested when I came of age. I hadn't met her mom, but I wasn't going to mess around. I'd come too far, changed my ways too much, to get thrown in the slammer for loving her daughter.

My family was another story altogether. They'd love Sam, and I wanted to introduce her to them, but she was understandably nervous around parental figures. It had taken some convincing, but she'd finally agreed to meet them on my upcoming birthday.

One place we no longer had to hide was at school. There, everyone knew we were a couple; well, a couple with a 'plus one' in the form of one very tall and very skinny best friend named Shannon O'Malley. If ever there was a cock blocker, it was she. But because Sam refused to be that girl who abandoned her best friend for a guy, Shannon had become a constant fixture in our relationship. Luckily, we got along like dysfunctional siblings.

"Are you sure you can't hang out tomorrow?" I asked, already knowing the answer but testing her for fissures.

"You know Shannon and I are having a girls' day. But you'll meet me on the beach Monday morning, right?"

"On a school day?" I asked in surprise, because even though Sam had become a bit of a bad girl, she never neglected her studies. "You rebel!"

"Think, Keith. What have you been talking about for two weeks now?"

"That we should be allowed to bring pillows to class?"

"No," she laughed. "In what world would that be a good idea? I'm talking about Staff Development Day. We have it off, remember?"

"Oh, fuck yeah!" I slapped the top of my truck. "I totally forgot! We get to spend all day together."

"We do," she said, cuddling up to my side. I bent down, smiling as I planted a wet kiss on her lips. Man, I couldn't ever remember feeling this good. With Sam, the possibilities were endless. I'd already decided that wherever school took her, I'd follow. That was how committed I was to us. But I'd do my part and make something of myself, so I could be the man she deserved. Things were falling into place. Our future looked bright. Gathering my girl into my arms, I nuzzled her neck and whispered sweet somethings in her ear, and then with our surf date confirmed, I gave her a quick kiss goodbye, and we parted ways.

Had I known it would be our last day as a couple, I would have savored the moment, but hindsight was a fickle bitch.

CHAPTER FOURTEEN

SAMANTHA

I Know Him

Shannon and I had spent the day in Los Angeles with her mother, returning late evening after shopping, eating dinner, and watching a movie. Nothing seemed amiss until I stepped through the doors to my house and my mother came at me like a bullet from a gun.

"Oh, my god." I jerked back, hitting the wall behind me. What had I been thinking? Why had I let my defenses down? Normally I opened the door a smidge and peeked inside first, but my day had been so light and easy I forgot about the loaded weapon inside my house.

"Where have you been?" she screeched, coming straight for me.

I sidestepped her; these days I didn't allow my mother to get the upper hand. She seemed to understand that I was stronger than I'd ever been, and the days of physical tyranny were over. She could assault me with her words, but her fists would never touch me again.

"I told you I was out with Shannon. You knew that."

The television was blaring in the living room, and I took in her anxious face. "Well, I figured you'd come home early, under the circumstances."

"Under the circumstances?" I questioned. "What are you talking about?"

My phone rang then. I checked – it was Shannon. I'd just left her. What could she possibly need from me three minutes later? I ignored her call. It rang again.

"Do you have any idea what's happening out there? There's a madman on the loose! And what has my daughter been doing – traipsing around like some whore?"

If she only knew. As far as my mother was aware, I was as pure as the day I was born, so those insults were meant as character assassination and nothing more.

"Wait. What are you talking about, a madman?"

My phone rang again. Shannon. Now I was getting a bit worried, but I knew my mother would go ballistic if I interrupted our little scream session for a personal call. Once again, I ignored it.

"The kidnapper?" Her voice reached the highest crescendo. "How do you not know? Honestly, Samantha, I'm surprised you're not lying in a ditch somewhere yourself."

She was too kind. My mother always did have a way with words. But I was too interested in the details of this madman to lash out at her. "What kidnapper? What are you talking about?"

"The boy, Samantha, the one who was snatched off the street a few hours ago right here in our little town. It's all over the news."

In the living room I could see a press conference happening on the television, and I bypassed my mother's reporting to get a more accurate take from the professionals. A line of reporters was firing off questions for the officer in charge.

Not wanting my information to come from anyone but her, my mother stepped in front of the TV and rushed out the details. "It happened right down the street at that business park off Jenkins. Thirteen years old. He was skateboarding with his brother, and some guy just snatched him up. I'm sure he's dead by now."

I fought the urge to blast my mother for her insensitivity when a picture flashed on the screen and I took a step back. The kidnapped boy… he looked like Keith, but he wasn't. I blinked in horror.

"What… what's his name?"

"Who?"

"The kidnapped boy! His name?" I raised my voice past acceptable levels and I braced for her fury, but my mother seemed too stunned by my outburst to retaliate on cue.

"Jake McKallister."

The weight of a monster wave clobbered me and I stumbled backward, barely keeping myself from toppling over the coffee table. My phone rang again. Shannon. That was why she was calling. She already knew what had happened. Tears gathered in my lashes, preparing to splash down my face. *Keith.*

"Samantha!" My mother's shrill voice burst into my thoughts. "What in the world is wrong with you? You look like you've seen a ghost."

"Are you sure?" I whispered, black dots spinning through my vision and threatening to take me down. "The name. Are you sure about the name?"

"Yes. Like I said, it's all over the news. What's gotten into you?"

"I… I know him."

"You know the kidnapped boy?" she asked, shocked by the turn of events. "How?"

"I mean, not him. I know his brother. From school."

But in a way, I did know Jake because Keith talked about him all the time. I knew of his musical talents; Keith swore he'd be a rock star someday. I knew he was the brother Keith was closest to, and that he sometimes felt unworthy of his devotion. I knew these things because there were moments on those boards when we were bobbing on the ocean that we swapped truths. If what my mother was saying was true, Keith had just lost his Sullivan.

My first call was to Shannon to confirm what I hoped to hell wasn't true. The second was to Keith. When it went unanswered, I steadied my shaking hands on the kitchen counter and bit back the fear – for Jake, and for Keith. This had happened several hours ago, but he hadn't reached out to me. Not even once. We talked all day, every day, sometimes even late into the night. If Keith wasn't contacting me over this, he either physically couldn't, or worse, he'd already mentally checked out. I had to get to him.

Despite the fact that it was already past my curfew, I grabbed my car keys and sprinted to the door. Leaving my mother's fervent protests behind, my only focus was getting to Keith before he did something he couldn't take back. I prayed my fear was misplaced, but Keith had more pharmaceutical skeletons in his closet than others knew. Those weeks leading up to his decision to leave that whole life behind, Keith had not only been smoking weed but also popping pills and huffing. Had he not gotten out when he did, things could have gotten very far out of control.

But now, mere months after escaping that life, his sobriety was being tested in the worst way possible, and I wasn't sure he had the discipline to keep from coming unhinged.

I was a block away from Keith's house when it became apparent I wasn't going to be able to get there by car. Two police cars were blocking the entrance to his street, which forced me to park and walk the final distance. What I saw when I arrived drew me up short. A line of dark, unmarked vehicles mixed with police cruisers. Reporters. Lights. And screaming – so much screaming.

I came to a halt several houses down, a rush of ice hardening my veins. A woman, who I could only assume was Keith's mother, was wailing from somewhere inside his house. I was familiar with that sound. I'd sobbed the same chorus the night I'd learned about Sullivan. I remembered it like yesterday: that terribly personal moment when the truth seeped in with a sickening thud.

Had the sadness already gripped Keith's heart? Would my sweet, goofy surfer boy ever be the same after suffering the dire consequences of tragedy? Keith was inside that house, and he needed me. I pushed forward through the crowd.

"Miss, I need to ask you to back up," a young officer said, herding me away from the scene. No more than a few years older than me, he looked like he was playing dress-up in his father's uniform. "No one is getting through unless you have proof of residence."

"No. I don't live here. I'm just… that's my boyfriend's brother who's missing."

I didn't miss the flinch that skipped over him. Maybe with more years on the job he would develop his poker face, but for now, the officer looked as horrified as I felt.

Did he know something I didn't? Was that what he was so unsubtly trying to hide? A gasp ripped from my throat. "Oh, god, Jake's not dead, is he?"

The officer turned his attention to the house before twisting his head back toward me. "I don't know, miss, but I figure he probably wishes he was."

CHAPTER FIFTEEN

KEITH

Rug Burn

It was strange the things that mattered when everything was right in the world – like the internet dropping out in the middle of a game or someone forgetting to replace the roll of toilet paper. When life was easy, even the slightest irritant became paramount, and it wasn't until hell rained fury down upon my cushy little existence that I was able to see what was really important. Family.

And now part of us was gone – stolen into the night. I didn't know where to go or how to conduct myself. Activity swirled around me, but I experienced none of it. The fear was all-consuming. Jake was gone and, after the story Kyle told of his last moments, there was a good chance he wasn't coming back – at least not without a goddamn miracle. And I had my doubts whether my family, as a collective whole, had done enough to warrant such blessings.

While my distraught mother wailed at the top of her lungs, a feeling of doom incapacitated me. I knew instinctively if Jake didn't come home, our family would not survive this. My thoughts shifted to Sam. How had she kept her head above water? What reserves had she tapped into to keep going when her world fell apart? I'd been there for her when she'd poured her soul out to me. I'd given her comfort and the reassurance that she wasn't alone. But I'd had no idea what I was talking about – no idea of the pain that was attached to her loss. When it came right down to it, we all walked through the darkness alone, and, god help me, if this nightmare was real, I wanted to be the first one blazing the trail to oblivion.

So as the hours ticked by with no sign of my little brother, and with no glimmer of hope, I began looking for an out. And, oh man, was I ever ripe for the plucking. It would take nothing for the bad influences to wrap their hands around my neck and drag me under. I hadn't been clean long enough to adopt any new coping mechanisms, and even though I'd thought that life was behind me, it was actually still there, just lying dormant and waiting for the right trigger to relight the smoldering itch inside. And what could be more igniting than losing my little brother to a demon?

The phone vibrated in my trembling hand. Sam. Again. Why couldn't I just answer her call? I needed her right now. She loved me. I loved her. If anyone could talk me off the ledge, it was my girl. So why then was I refusing her help? The answer was obvious. I refused to allow myself the luxury of her voice because Sam would want me to face the reality – to deal with it clear-eyed. But with clarity came pain, and if I'd proven one thing in life, I wasn't strong enough to endure tough times. Hell, even mildly uncomfortable ones were enough to push me over the edge.

I shoved the phone in the drawer and sprawled out on my bed, regret burning a swath through my tormented brain. Instead of savoring the minutes I'd had left with Jake, I'd spent those final hours as I did any other given weekend in the McKallister household – arguing with my brothers. It was our unique way of beating back the boredom. Today's squabble had been nothing extraordinary... except now, in hindsight, it made me want to throw up.

Like the bratty little brothers they were, Jake and Kyle had snuck into my room while I was playing video games and rearranged the entire floor plan. They'd pushed my bed under the window and wedged my dresser into the closet. They'd even removed the posters from my wall and flipped them upside down. I'd been livid and felt justified teaching them a lesson. Jake was first, and like a caveman,

I'd dragged him down the hallway of our family home. Not that he'd taken offense. Jake was a McKallister boy, after all. Retaliation was not only expected but anticipated. In fact, he'd acted as if sustaining a series of rug burns was the most fun he'd had all week.

On any other day, our argument would've faded away like all others. But now that it was possibly my last memory of him – and maybe Jake's last memory of me – all I wanted to do was rewind the whole day, before he and Kyle decided to go out skateboarding, before a gun was pressed to his head… before my little brother had become a statistic.

Smothering my face with a pillow, I tried to block out the images of Jake and what he had to be going through – if he were even still alive. Of course he was. I couldn't give up on him. There was always hope, right? Jake had only been missing for about eight hours, and that meant we had time for a miracle. He could still be set free and come home – not unscathed, of course, but we could deal with the aftermath later. I think I spoke for us all when I said we'd take any outcome that didn't end in death.

Mom's wails had died down. I knew I should be out there offering her my support. Or I could be at the hospital where Kyle was currently being treated for the injuries he'd sustained in the kidnapping. At the very least, I could be with Emma on the couch quietly deflecting her offers of serving me up the now-cold dinner still sitting on the kitchen table. But I wasn't hungry – well, not that kind of hungry, anyway. The only thing that could satiate me now was tucked away in a shoebox in the far corner of my closet. I'd meant to rid myself of its contents long ago, but like that Ho-Ho hidden away in a yo-yo dieter's pantry, it was still there, patiently awaiting my relapse.

As the night turned to dawn with no news of my brother, I crawled from my place of safety and retrieved the box. Sam's beautiful face filled my vision, that sun-streaked hair of hers blowing in the breeze as she told me she loved me. I could lean on her. She'd understand and help me face the challenges ahead with clear eyes and a functioning brain. I clutched the box, the one that promised sweet relief from the pain.

I'm so sorry, babe. So damn sorry, but I've got to wipe you from my memory banks – just for tonight.

Deep down I think I already knew it wouldn't be just one night – not for me. This was one more crossroads, and I was about to make another very bad decision.

With regret already tearing up my gut, I opened the lid.

Chapter Sixteen

Samantha

To A Head

I sat in my car watching the house. Nothing had changed in the three weeks I'd been coming here after school to do my homework and stake out the McKallister family residence. Jake was still missing and Keith was still gone, lost to a world I didn't understand.

Those first few days after Jake's abduction, I was convinced Keith would come for me. We would talk and cry and hold each other. I would help him through whatever obstacles were keeping us apart. But that day never came. It was as if he'd vanished off the face of the earth. Well, not totally. His stoner friends knew where he was, but they weren't talking, which left me scrambling to find my boyfriend before the dark forces swallowed him whole.

My daily searches at the beach turned up nothing, and even my stakeouts of his family home – the ones that got me a talking to by the FBI - hadn't yielded any clues. As everyone searched tirelessly for Jake, no one seemed to notice that the boy I loved appeared to have dropped off the face of the earth. And I wasn't entirely sure anyone except me was looking for him.

Slowly but surely, life in this sleepy coastal town was returning to normal… for everyone except the McKallister family. And me. Once reality set in and the likelihood of recovering Jake alive diminished, the reporters dropped away, and the police and FBI, once a large contingency, trickled to a handful.

As I did everyday, I debated whether to knock on their door. Some days I did, with no response, and other days I left them alone with their grief. Coming to my decision for the day, I exited my vehicle, walked up their front stoop, and knocked. I knew Keith wasn't there, but I felt I needed to be his advocate – to be sure they were aware of his absence. Plus, if they did have any information about him, it might just ease the anxiety clenching knots in my stomach.

When there was no response, I knocked again. It was what I always did – gave them some time to answer, hoping today might be my lucky day. I startled at the sound of movement on the other side of the door, and then suddenly it opened a crack and a little boy stared up at me. His hair was a wild mess, and he was wearing nothing but a pair of what I assumed to be hand-me-down pajama bottoms that were hanging off his little body.

"Hi." I leaned down to address him. "You must be Quinn."

He peered up at me, squinting in the sun, and I wondered how long it had been since he'd left the house.

"Who are you?" he asked, much too suspiciously for a child his age. "I'm not allowed to talk to reporters."

"That's smart thinking, but I'm not a reporter."

"Are you coming to take me away?"

His question was unsettling enough that I bent all the way down to his level before I asked, "Take you where?"

The little boy's eyes dropped to the ground, and then I understood. Quinn wanted to know if he was next – if I had come to steal him. He was too young to grasp what was happening, and so he had come up with his own conclusions.

"No, sweetie. Don't be scared. I'm Keith's girlfriend. My name is Samantha."

"Quinn!" A young female voice cut through our conversation. "What are you doing? What did I tell you about opening the front door?"

Keith's sister Emma appeared in the doorway, grabbed Quinn's hand, and protectively pulled him back and away from me. "Who are you?" she demanded. "What do you want with us?"

"It's okay," Quinn said, peering up at his sister through impossibly long lashes. "It's Keith's girlfriend. Maybe she knows where he is."

Emma's gaze narrowed in on me. "You're Sam?"

"Well, yes. Samantha."

She continued to evaluate me, and for a moment I was afraid she would send me away. What I hadn't anticipated was her arms wrapping around my back and pulling me in for a hug. A few months ago, such a scenario would have seemed impossible; the moors of popularity would have kept us a good distance apart. But I no longer felt inferior to this girl. Yes, she was still physically perfect, but life had a way of evening the score. And Emma McKallister had been humbled.

I'd seen her around school recently and had been shocked by her transformation. Once the leader of the most popular sophomore posse in the school, Emma now wandered the halls alone, preferring to spend her lunches in seclusion in the school library.

"I've seen you around, and I thought maybe you were her, but because sophomores have a different lunch period than juniors and seniors, I never actually saw you and Keith together. He showed me a picture of you months ago. You've changed so much since then I wasn't sure."

"Yeah, I..." I was about to explain to her the reasons for my metamorphosis but figured she had too much on her mind to sit through a drawn-out explanation, so I just asked the most pressing question. "He told you about me?"

A smile highlighted her beautiful face, letting me know she and Keith had, in fact, discussed me at some point. "He did, and I just want to thank you for all you've done for my brother."

Tears sprang to my eyes. "It wasn't enough."

"There's nothing more you could have done. Keith... he likes to take the easy way out. That first night, he didn't even wait for the sun to rise before he was flying high. I get he's trying to numb the pain, but what he doesn't understand is, it's not going away. He'll have to deal with it at some point, and by then, it will just be so much worse."

As I'd done every day since this nightmare began, I wished there was more I could do, because I was confident that if I could just get my hands on Keith, I could help him. "Do you know where he is? I can't find him anywhere, and he won't answer my calls. I'm scared for him, Emma. Really scared."

"I am too." She sighed, and it was a heavy sound. "He does come by once in a while, usually at night, but he never stays long. I haven't seen him in probably five days now. It's not good, Sam. He's in a bad way."

"Do you know what he's taking?"

"I don't, but I'm guessing pot isn't his only vice anymore."

None of this came as a shock, but at the same time, it wasn't what I wanted to hear, either. I dropped my head. "That's what I was afraid of."

"Everything's just gone to shit." Her voice crackled with emotion. "Keith's figured out a way to deal with it by numbing his brain. Honestly, I'd envy him if I didn't want to beat the living shit out of him for abandoning me. I mean, we all know where this is headed for him. I thought maybe..."

I reached out for her, offering what support I could. "You thought what?"

"I thought maybe he'd pull it together for you. I don't know if he's told you, but he loves you, Sam. Like head over heels in love. Before... *this*... he was all in. He even talked of moving away to wherever you went to college. That's how committed he was to you. I know you're disappointed in him – I am too – but if I can find him, will you help me? Maybe together we can do something."

Relief buoyed my spirits. Of course I would help. I was the one standing on his doorstep pleading for information. "I'll do anything, Emma. Take my number, and the next time he comes home, call me. It doesn't matter how late. I'll sneak out if I have to."

And I would. I'd do anything for Keith. The question nagging at me, though, was would he? Because when it came right down to it, none of this was up to me. Stoned-out Keith was running this show now, and if he hadn't leaned on me for support weeks ago, what were the chances he'd change his tune now? I loved him, but I wasn't sure that would be enough to save him – or us.

"Okay, thank you," she replied, her shaky voice growing stronger. "Whatever you do, Samantha, please don't give up on him."

I gripped her arm, and an understanding passed between us. "Never."

Worn but hopeful after meeting with Emma, all I wanted to do when I got home was veg out in my room, but life with my mother never went according to plan. I hadn't even stepped one foot through the door before an object whizzed by my head, smashing against the wall.

"What the…?"

The second time I wasn't so lucky, taking a direct hit to the head. I stumbled back in shock, my hands clawing at the wound. Blood dripped from my hairline.

"Did you think I wouldn't find out? Did you think you could just hide your whoring ways from me? Is that why you lost the weight – so you could screw some boy behind my back?"

My mother was waving a pregnancy test in front of my eyes. I'd used it a week before when my period was late.

It had come back negative, but that didn't stop me from promptly hiding the evidence of its existence at the bottom of the outside trash bin. How in the hell had she found it? Upon closer inspection, however, I realized she was holding the second pregnancy test, the one I hadn't peed on yet. I thanked my lucky stars for small miracles. Yet the fact remained, she'd been rummaging through my drawers… and I was bleeding from the head.

"Where's the other test, Samantha? Are you pregnant? Who is the boy?"

"I'm not pregnant. And the boy is none of your business."

She rushed me, and I was too dazed to flee as her open palm connected with my cheek, knocking me over the side table. I landed in a heap on the carpet. Eyes glazed over in crazy, my mother jumped on my stomach, pinning me down. The power she derived from insanity was a force I couldn't dream of fending off. But even as uncontrolled as she became in moments like this, I could not have predicted what came next – a pillow placed over my nose and mouth. At first it didn't seem real, like she was playing a game, but as the pressure increased, I began fighting for my life.

The head wound slowing my defenses, my breath became labored as panic set in. My mother, the woman who'd given me life, was now trying to smother it out of me. I struggled mightily under her iron grip, but she was too crazed with anger, screaming obscenities at the top of her lungs. My nails ripped into her hands, trying to dislodge her, but I could feel the life draining away. *I never thought… I never…*

And then suddenly air flooded back into my lungs. The pillow was gone, my mother plucked from my deflated body by a force I was slow to understand. But as my vision, and wits, slowly returned, I could see who'd saved me from certain death: a nameless next-door neighbor.

"Calm down!" He yelled to my flailing mother who'd taken to using her teeth to dislodge herself from his grip. "Call the cops. She's psycho."

It was only then I noticed the woman kneeling beside me cradling my head in her lap. She was already two steps ahead of her husband, a phone pressed against her ear.

"You're okay," she said, repeating those two words until help arrived on the other side of the line. "Yes, my husband and I heard screaming. The neighbor's front door was open, so we ran over to see if we could help, and found the mother trying to suffocate her daughter. The mom is crazy. The girl is bleeding. We need an ambulance… and the police."

There is no greater love than that of a mother for her child. She can cure her baby's sadness with a hug or lift a car off her trapped child or jump into the ocean to save her toddler from certain death. Once upon a time, I'd had that mother. Although faint, it was still a memory I carried inside. She'd once been loving and kind, and Sullivan and I… we were happy. I remembered in elementary school her picking us up from school, a radiant smile gracing her face as she embraced us and asked about our day. I was proud to be her daughter then.

But gradually something changed in her. Some evil force had grabbed hold and turned her into the monster I knew today. Instead of love, she spewed hate. Instead of building us up, she tore us down. What had happened to her? Where had the mother I remembered gone?

By middle school, Dad had all but disappeared, and Sullivan and I were living behind her cloak, quietly taking the abuse because we'd become conditioned to accept cruelty as a way of life. Maybe if she hadn't been so sneaky, reserving her abuse for private times so others couldn't see it, my brother and I wouldn't have been so afraid to speak the truth.

Sullivan did finally speak the truth… but only after his body hit the ground.

And now it was my turn. I had to find my voice… to stop protecting her. That mother I remembered was gone, and she was never coming back. I had to look out for myself now. And so I spoke my truth – at the hospital to the officers who had arrested and escorted my mother to the county jail. With her vile words still ringing in my ears, I spilled my secrets to the sympathetic duo. Only after the cut on my head had been stitched up and the ER doc on duty cleared me was I released to the care of Shannon's sympathetic parents.

In the coming days, my life would be turned upside down but, for now, I was safely cuddled up beside Shannon in her twin-sized bed. I knew this arrangement couldn't last indefinitely. The O'Malleys were more than willing to take me in for a week or two, but I doubted their charity would last a school year or more. I needed a more permanent solution because even if my mother made a deal that got her home before dinner tomorrow night, I would never return.

Moving in with my father was not an option; I knew he'd never make space for me amongst his new family. My dear ol' dad had checked out long ago. That left only one family member I could turn to – Auntie Kim, my mother's estranged stepsister. Although not a blood relative, she was the closest thing to family I had. The case worker assigned to me had already contacted her and she'd agreed to take me in. But going to her meant leaving behind Shannon and Keith and the beach I'd come to love.

Speaking of Shannon, she turned suddenly in the bed, nearly catapulting me to the floor.

"Oh, geez. Sorry," she giggled, grabbing my waist and pulling me back from the brink of disaster. "I'm not used to sharing my bed with a hot surfer chick… or, you know, just with anyone. Not that I'm a prude or anything. I mean, I'm into guys, but I'd totally go for you if I wasn't."

"You really didn't need all that explanation," I said, adopting my best pouty face. "I get it. I'm not your first choice."

"Well, now hold on there." She snorted. "You twisted my arm. Why not? Come here, chicky."

We rolled around, laughing, as I swatted her grabby hands away.

"Honestly, though." Shannon flipped herself onto her back. "Is it not possible for an awkward six-foot-one redhead to get a date in this town? I swear I even put my feelers out to that greasy-haired nerd Pete in AP English – you know, the one who gets spontaneous erections during the reading of *Hamlet*? Anyway, I'm not lying, Samantha, even he wasn't interested."

"Because he was probably too nerdy to know you wanted him to ask you out. You need to find a guy with at least an ounce of swagger."

"Says the girl who has options."

How wrong she was. Yes, maybe since my transformation there'd been an uptick in interest from the male species as a whole, but the only boy I'd allow to lay his hands on me had simply vanished from my life.

And very soon, my speckled bestie would be gone too.

Shannon sat up, gasping. "I'm so sorry. I didn't mean that you weren't still with Keith. I just meant you could do better than me."

"I could never do better than you," I replied, biting back the emotion threatening to overcome me.

Brushing her fingers over my bruised cheek, my best friend provided the comfort I needed.

"Shannon?" I whispered, depleted.

"Yes?"

"It's not safe for me at home anymore. I have to leave."

Her eyes instantly filled with tears. "I know you do, Samantha."

I turned one of her spectacular spiral curls through my fingertips. "You will forever be the best friend any girl could ever ask for."

"I know," she replied. "I'm pretty special."

"Yes, you are." I wiped the tears rolling down her cheeks.

Her voice heavy, she asked, "Where will you go?"

"My aunt was already contacted, and she agreed to take me in. By next week, I'll probably be gone."

"Okay, then," she said, putting on a brave face. "If that's the case, we need to find Keith and let him know."

"How would I do that, Shan? I've been looking for him for weeks. He doesn't want to be found. Maybe… maybe it's best to just go."

"But you love him."

"Yes. But sometimes that's not enough."

"That's not how romance novels end, Samantha."

"Yeah, well, mine sucks. The end." I gripped Shannon's hands and looked her in the eyes. "But enough about Keith. I need to know if you'll be okay by yourself at school. I hate the thought of you sitting at the lunch tables by yourself. Can you sit with Mia or Nicole maybe?"

Shannon lowered her gaze and looked away.

"What?" I asked.

"Nothing," she hesitated. "It's just… I've sort of been lying to you. I don't have a fifth period class. I can actually leave school before lunch. I just stayed so you wouldn't have to eat alone."

The space in my heart reserved just for her expanded. I might have been unlucky in family and unlucky in love, but I was a winner when it came to Shannon O'Malley.

CHAPTER SEVENTEEN

KEITH

The Debt

I was too out of it to hear him coming. It wasn't until hands were lifting me off the sofa and throwing me across the room that I got the memo that Steve was in the house. After hitting the wall and sliding to the floor, I struggled to pick myself back up, but it was useless. I was too wasted.

"Where is it?" he demanded, before the toe of his boot connected to my stomach. I could pretend I didn't know what he was talking about, but we'd both know it was a lie. I owed him money, which he in turn owed to his bosses and so on and so forth. We were all heads on the same totem pole, mine being the one at the very bottom.

Placing my hands in front of me in hopes of calming him down a little, I said, "I was given three days, dude, and I still have one to go."

"No, idiot, *I* was given three days. *You* were given two. The way it works is you pay me, I pay them, and everyone's happy. But see, now you're breaking the pattern, and that doesn't make anyone happy."

Once I'd started using again, I found it wasn't as easy to get my supply as before. Brett Valentine was bitter over my abandonment and resistant to feed the newly resurrected habit of his rival. He'd all but driven me out of his district, forcing me to go straight to the source for my stash. And sadly, that source was a smarmy dude named Steve who was always there to offer bigger and better highs, all at a price that was getting harder and harder to afford. But I was willing to do anything to ease the pain and keep my brain in a perpetual state of lethargy. I'd found my way out… but at what cost? Because cannabis wasn't doing it for me anymore, I'd been forced to move on to opiates, and from there, I'd worked my way down the ladder to hell.

Another swift kick to my ribs smacked the breath clean out of me.

"Get up so I can beat your ass to the ground again."

"Come on, man," I tried reasoning. "Look, you know I've got issues right now. My brother, he's missing, and

I'm doing my best to keep it all together. I promise, Steve. Tomorrow you'll have your money."

Jake. I hated myself for dragging his good name into my mess like it was some excuse. He deserved better… so much better. Weeks had passed with nothing. No miraculous reunion. No waking up from a horrendous dream. Not even a body to bury with a proper goodbye. Jake's absence had left a gaping hole that was getting wider every day.

"Jake? Are you talkin' about Jake?" He laughed each word, inciting the beginnings of a riot inside my head. "You're so dense. Your brother's not missing, Keith, he's fucking dead. Everybody knows it. He was probably offed the first night."

Steve wasn't saying anything I hadn't heard before. Nor was he saying anything I hadn't thought myself, but damned if I was going to let some lowlife speak my brother's name like he didn't matter. Steam rose through my body like a teakettle ready to blow its top, and when it hit the surface air, I came up swinging. My fist connected to his nutsack without a second's warning, and he dropped to the floor beside me, cupping his battered balls and stinking up the place like the pile of filth he was.

Gathering what strength I had left, I picked myself up off the floor and stood over Steve, ready to pummel him. I'd never been an angry person… selfish and resentful, yes, but not angry. Now I wanted to hurt people for speaking the truth. Yes, the likeliest scenario was that my brother had met a grizzly death, but the alternative was equally as horrifying. If Jake was still alive, he was suffering, and there was no way my brain could go there. It's not that I wished him dead, it's just I didn't have the mental toughness to wish him alive.

"Don't you ever say his name again, you got that? Ever!"

I continued beating on the recipient of my rage until his colleagues ripped me from his body. Steve, of course, was furious, and how could I blame him? His ball sack had just absorbed an entire month of my pent-up rage, and now he was itching for revenge. Apparently roughing me up on site wasn't intimidating enough, so I was thrown into the back of Steve's vehicle for what was sure to be a wild ride.

Belying the seriousness of my situation, a smile stretched wide across my face. That little loss of control was probably going to get me beaten to a bloody pulp, yet I welcomed the pain. Craved it. At this point I really didn't have anything left to lose. My family had detonated the minute Jake was forcefully dragged away from our lives. Some of us held on longer than others. Actually, I take that back. Emma was the only dangler left. The rest of us let go from the start and were now just bodies littered on a concrete slab like Grace's birthday drawing had foretold.

No doubt reacting to my smiling profile, Steve warned, "I don't think you fully understand the seriousness of the situation, Keith. Outstanding balances don't sit well with my boss."

"Well, I hate to tell you this, but I don't have any way to pay my debt this second, so this little trip of yours isn't going to help your cause. Like I said, I can get you your money tomorrow, and then both our problems will go away."

"That would be swell, Keith, if I trusted a word out of your mouth. It's time you learned a lesson."

I sat in silence the remainder of the way, my mind retreating back to an easier time – a time when I was still a fuck up but at least a lovable one; a time when my family was imperfect but mercifully intact; a time when I had the girl of my dreams on top of me in my truck. Now I was just a junkie, no better than the tweakers I'd thumbed my nose at months ago.

God, I was pathetic. I shouldn't be here now, about to get the snot beaten out of me. I should be holding strong with Sam by my side, the two of us helping Emma hold what was left of my tattered family together. But the second I pulled that box from my closet, I'd lost all claims to her. Sam deserved better than the likes of me, and the sooner I let go of what we'd had, the better.

I sat fidgeting on my chair. The man circled around me, speaking to himself under his breath as his fingers followed the lines of the chair. When you lived in the hallucinogenic world I did, bizarre behavior was the norm. So, even though I was alone with him, I wasn't all that worried. I mean, it wasn't like this wasp of a man, in his forties, balding, and missing a couple of teeth, was some imposing character. I was seriously questioning how he'd risen to a middleman position in the first place. I mean, I wasn't some muscle man myself, nor was I in the best physical shape after the month I'd had, but even I could blow the guy over with one puff of air. A beating from this guy was going to be about as painful as getting whacked by a fly swatter.

"Do you know who I am?" he asked, all cocky like he was some high-profile celebrity and not the piece of shit he truly was.

No, I didn't know who he was, nor did I care. My high was fading, and I needed to get back and find a friend who could keep me going until morning. *Let's get the beat down over with, shall we?*

"My name is Paulie. I'm the guy you're stealing from."

"I'm not stealing from you, dude. Like I was telling Steve..."

Before I could finish my line of bullshit, Paulie back-handed me across the face, and I had to admit, it smarted more than I would have expected from a skeleton.

"Keeeithhhh," he said, elongating my name in a breathy, creeper sort of way. "Here's how it's going to work from here on out. I talk. You listen. Got it?"

I nodded.

"Excellent. Now, I hear you have a bit of a unique situation. I know who your family is and what happened to your brother. Now, I'm not heartless, Keith. I'm not. I get that you're going through a rough time. But I'm also a businessman, and I expect to be paid what I'm owed."

"And I'll get it to you tomorrow, like I told Steve."

Pain exploded through my eyeball and I could feel it swelling up on impact. Jesus, this feather of a man had a hell of a right hook. My head was spinning from the violence, and suddenly I wasn't feeling as confident in my ability to escape this man's clutches with minimal damage.

"What did I say, Keith?"

"No talking," I answered, my face tingling as it puffed up.

"Exactly. You don't follow directions well, do you?"

"No, that's never been my strong suit."

Another blow rocked my world. He was confusing me. I thought we were having a conversation. I mean, why was he asking me questions if he didn't want an answer? Jesus, you'd think he could be clearer. I tried shaking off the pain spreading through my face, but it was no use. I was in a world of hurt.

"Here's the problem, Keith. You say you're going to pay me, but I don't believe you. So, now I'm forced to take a different approach."

Paulie walked to his desk and flipped the computer around. What was on the screen knocked the wind right out of me: photographs of my family. Some had been taken at the press conference and others snapped at close range of my father and siblings entering and exiting the house. Even Grace and Quinn weren't spared in this shakedown.

"What is this?" I asked, in little more than a whisper. "Why do you have these pictures?"

"Insurance, Keith. You have until 3:00pm tomorrow or I'll be making a house call I guarantee you won't like."

Maybe I'd assumed things couldn't get worse, but of course I'd been wrong. I'd always been able to count on my stupidity to lead me astray, but it had only been myself that got hurt. This was different. I'd led these people to my front door… endangered those I loved. It was my soul that needed to pay the price. Lowering my gaze to the ground, I nodded. The debt would be paid.

I was flying high as I inched closer to the edge of the cliff, keeping my eyes firmly focused on the rubber toecap of my tattered white Vans. It was as if my shoes had a life of their own, pulling me feet first toward oblivion. How easy would it be to end it all? Just step off the ledge and all pain would cease. Oh god, how nice that sounded! Such a relief. I inched closer, and pebbles cascaded over the ridge.

"Whoa." A nervous cackle escaped me as I slid my feet back a smidge. I wasn't thinking right. I didn't want to die… did I? No. I couldn't do that to my family. They'd already suffered enough. But, if I thought about it, what did I really add to the mix? Nothing – especially now that I could add breaking and entering to my list of crimes.

After Paulie's threat of retaliation, I'd taken to procuring money by any means necessary, first from my dad, and then, to continue feeding my habit, by stealing easily pawned items and swiping prescription drugs off the shelves of the homes I burglarized. I'd justified my behavior by telling myself I was doing it for my family, but my debt had been paid the first day, and now my exploits were just being cycled back into my system.

I should've stayed home. After calling Emma for help following the beating, suddenly I found myself at home fearing an impending visit from Paulie. I'd had no choice but to tell my father. He'd taken care of what I owed, and I'd promised him I'd stay home. But withdrawal kicked my ass, and when he'd given me a moment to myself, I'd climbed out the window and hadn't returned.

Whatever pill was inside me now was filling my head with dangerous thoughts. I felt weightless and ready for flight. Raising my arms to the side, I crept ever so slightly forward until the tips of my toes touched air again. The deliberate movements sent small rocks and other dusty debris tumbling to their demise over the rocky ledge. The Devil's Plunge; that's what locals had ominously dubbed this soaring patch of earth, and it lived up to its gloomy moniker. Every year it beckoned lost souls, and every year scores of them were silently claimed by the clutches of hell.

I could easily join their ranks. And once that happened, I'd be nothing more than a number, forgotten by all but a select few. There'd be no Keith McKallister Memorial Bench because I wouldn't be dying in some badass way. There would be no horrifying shark attack for me. No, just a calculated and weak death, one that would serve its purpose in silencing my own demons… but would cast fresh new ones at the people I left behind.

Taking a quick peek over the rock face, I settled my gaze on the assembly of rocks piled high at the base of the cliff. Ocean water crashed, filling in the gaps between the boulders, and then, almost as if the water was changing its mind, the surge rushed back out to the sea in a swirl of waves. It was a sign. *Back away from the edge.* Yet my feet stayed put, teetering on the edge of death.

I could feel it – the pull for silence, for death. Whatever was in that pill I'd taken was making it so easy. I thought of all the other cliff jumpers who'd come before me and wondered what had been their final straw. Had they stood in this very spot contemplating their life up until the point they'd given up?

A familiar voice cautioned me. *Back up, Keith. Don't do this.* Her face materialized before me, so clear. Sam.

"What are you doing here?" my altered brain asked. And then I remembered her brother, Sullivan, and his similar flight to oblivion. The rocks began to give way below my feet and I could feel myself slipping. I was going to die. Fear stole the haze from my brain, breaking my trance. I took a step back. Then another. Soon I was free from the cliff's edge and from a death that was not meant to be mine.

A safe distance away, I dropped to my ass, burying my head in my knees as relief rocked my soul. Sam's hologram rested beside me, her transparent fingers covering my own. *You're going to be okay*, she reassured me. If ever there was a wake-up call, this was it. My tweaked-out brain had nearly forsaken me. If Sam hadn't appeared when she did, I'd be dead. I took a deep breath and closed my eyes. This had to end. I had to pull myself back off the ledge – somehow.

"KEITH!"

The scream came from somewhere down the path. I lifted my head to the shouts of one of my new druggie friends whose name totally escaped me. There was a desperation in the way he was calling to me that sent me scrambling to my feet. Something was wrong.

The scruffy dude rounded the bend, his eyes wide and face beet red from the trek up the mountain. As soon as he caught sight of me, he dropped his hands to his knees, drew in puffs of air into his lungs, and said, "Jake."

Even though I couldn't remember who the fuck he was, I felt certain he should know not to speak my brother's name. Hadn't I made that perfectly clear? I narrowed my eyes on the traitor before brushing past him, away from the ledge, away from death.

"No," he panted, grabbing the back of my shirt. "Keith. Wait. It's all over the radio. Jake's been found."

Chapter Eighteen

Samantha

Shoreline

I'd only been at Shannon's for two days when her mother's frantic voice traveled down the hallway calling for our attention. Her tone was jarring enough that we'd both jerked our heads up and out of our books and exchanged alarmed glances before racing into the living room. Her mother and father were huddled around the television when we arrived, and Shannon's mother reached her hand out to me.

"He's been found," she said.

My first thought was that she was speaking of Keith, but when a picture of Jake filled the screen, the full scope of her words hit home.

"He's alive, Samantha."

Jake's escape would soon become the biggest news story ever to come out of our town. The details were so extraordinary that it reached a worldwide audience. If we thought the media had gone wild over the kidnapping, it was nothing compared with his return. Overnight our town's population quadrupled as news organizations moved in, once again setting up shop on the McKallisters' front lawn, in front of the hospital where Jake was currently fighting for his life, and at the home of Ray Davis, the man responsible for it all.

For the next several days, I sat glued to the tube with the O'Malley family and, along with the rest of the world, watched as the miracle of Jake's return was twisted into something dark and sinister. Learning of the horrifying details of his imprisonment and subsequent escape was like a live action horror movie come to life – and that was before the police started digging up bodies.

Burrowing my feet into the warm sand, I pushed those graphic images from my mind. Today was about finding peace and appreciating this place I'd called home for the past two and a half years. By tomorrow night, I'd be settled into a new life down the coast in San Diego with my aunt and her two young daughters. And although my heart was sad for those I'd leave behind, I was ready. Living a life free of fear was all I'd ever wanted, and now that it was within grasp, I clung to it with newfound vigor.

But nostalgia was in the air as I sat at the base of the sand dune and looked out over the vast ocean, committing to memory this beautiful place. It only seemed fitting that I come here for a final goodbye. This was the spot that had started it all – where I'd fallen in love but also where I'd gone to nurse my broken heart. And it was where I'd come in search of Keith, hoping that someday he'd find his way home.

Movement in the distance caught my eye, and I followed the figure of a man as he made his way along the shoreline. Like an intruder, I sat quietly on my towel, spying on his private moment. I watched as he dipped his bare toes into the water and occasionally bent down to pick something up from the sand. Then, after careful inspection, he'd cast whatever was in his hand back into the ocean. I wondered what he was looking for and why it was so important to him.

At first he was just a stranger wandering along the water's edge, but as he drew closer, my heart rate quickened. I sat up a little straighter, attempting to bring his face into view. And even though he was too far away to see clearly, I knew. It was Keith. Wrapping my arms around my knees protectively, I continued to study him. He was walking with a heavy gait now, but that distinctive sway of his body was unmistakable. I'd draped myself around it enough times that now just the memory of our intimacy brought with it a quiver of need.

The promise to Emma had been made before Jake's return, before my mother's assault, and before Keith had returned home without ever picking up a phone and calling me. I had no choice but to give up on us – especially now when holding on would do neither of us any good.

As Keith drew closer, I startled at his gaunt appearance. His hair was longer than before, and instead of the shaggy mane I loved to run my fingers through, the strands were now stringy and lifeless. And his shoulders, once so proud and strong, were slumped forward, as if an invisible weight were dragging him down. This wasn't the boy I remembered. My Keith walked with a spring in his step and a smile permanently stamped onto his face. My heart ached for him. I wanted to wrap my arms around him and cure his sadness, but I was no longer enough for Keith. He had a new lover, and she was dragging him into the ground. I wanted to steal him back, but I knew I couldn't hold onto him. He required help I was unable to provide, especially given that I was leaving for a new life. Anything I could give him today would only add to his sorrows tomorrow. No, I wouldn't go to him now. It was best to leave him be.

But that was before he dropped to the sand. Before he laid his forehead against his folded knees. And before his entwined fingers rested behind his head with a heaviness I knew all too well. I wasn't sure if I'd ever witnessed such a lonely and conflicted moment. Keith was a broken soul, on the edge, and I imagined Sullivan at this same desperate moment in his life. There was no way I could walk away now.

Rising to my feet, I dusted myself off and made my way across the sand. Would he welcome my intrusion or cast me aside like he'd been doing for weeks now? Not that it would matter. He would get my help regardless. Not wanting to startle him, I kicked a little sand in his direction to announce my presence. Keith followed the gravel's flight path before twisting his head in my direction. It took a moment for recognition to flash in his eyes.

"Sam?"

Oh, my god, he was gutted. Bruised and battered. I didn't even want to know what had happened to him since he'd been gone. Swallowing back a sob of pity, I corrected him – as was our way. "Samantha."

A tiny smile traveled to his lips, and regardless of the fact that I'd spent the last month wanting to physically throttle him for leaving me, I hovered over him from behind and wrapped my arms around him like a comfortable blanket.

Keith grabbed my arms, now crossed over his chest, and tipped his head back against mine, and we stayed in this position for as long as it took for the tension to release from his body. Only then did I take a seat beside him, and our shoulders pressed into each other like old times.

The two of us sat quietly looking out over the ocean. It was only later that I felt his gaze upon me. Slowly I turned my head, and our eyes connected. Reflecting off the water's glow, his were a fusion of blues and greens and grays – like the swirling colors of my stone. Behind all that pain was the exuberant boy I'd met in class, the one who'd swept me off my shaky feet and deposited me back on solid ground a changed person.

He reached up, gently touching my cheek. "Damn, you're a sight for sore eyes."

I froze, craving his touch but understanding I could never have it again. Reaching up, I removed his hand. I wasn't his any longer. He'd seen to that weeks ago when he'd gone off to fight the battle alone.

"It didn't have to be that way," I replied. "You knew where to find me. I would have stood by your side."

His gaze dropped, and a frown tightened his features. "If you're disappointed in me, Sam, get in line."

It went beyond disappointment. I loved him, and he'd basically thrown me away for a pharmaceutical lover. I could spend this time tearing him apart for what he'd done, but that would leave Keith worse off than when I came.

I'd had plenty of time to come to terms with the disappointment and could set it aside to keep this boy afloat. "I was worried about you. Where have you been? What about school?"

"What about it?" he grumbled.

"Did you give up on graduating? Because I don't think it's too late. I'm sure, given the situation with your brother, the school would work with you."

"It's more than a situation." Keith raised a brow. "Or maybe you haven't been following the news."

"Oh, I've been following it. It's a little hard not to. But I'm not talking about Jake right now. I'm worried about you."

"Why?"

"Why wouldn't I be?"

"Because you hate me, Sam. I can see it in your eyes."

"I don't hate you. Maybe I don't particularly like you right now, but I could never hate you." And it was true. No matter where life took us, I'd always have a special place in my heart for my first love.

We went back to staring at the shoreline. Cupping sand in my palm, I let it funnel out over my bare feet.

"For what it's worth," he said, "I'm sorry."

"I know."

"Do you?" Keith let a breath out, deflating like a balloon. "I wish… I wish I could take it all back. I wish I was stronger."

I covered his hand with my own, knowing in my heart he hadn't intended to hurt me. He was just lost and alone and in need of healing. "Look, I've been where you are. I get it. But now it's time to pull yourself together and fight against the forces trying to drag you down. This is your life, Keith – the only one you're ever going to live. Are you who you want to be?"

Keith considered my words for the longest time before shaking his weary head. "Not even close."

"Then make the change. Reach in there and find your strength. And then once you've got it, pass a little on to Jake. He needs his big brother."

Keith dropped his head and slumped his shoulders. "He doesn't need me. He needs a miracle."

"He already got his miracle."

"Did he? I'm not so sure of that."

"He's alive."

"Barely. And what's left of him…" Keith shook his head.

"He's alive," I stopped him. "And that's more than I can say for Sullivan. As long as Jake's still breathing, as long as you're still breathing, you have the power inside you to turn this around. But Keith, listen to me – you've got to stop messing with Fate. It's not going to give you unlimited chances."

"I know," he replied, raking his fingers through his patchy stubble.. "Maybe I just needed to hear it from you. You're good for me, Sam. So good."

I ignored his words because they did us no good now. Redirecting the conversation, I asked, "What are you doing out here, Keith? What were you collecting?"

Reaching inside his pocket, Keith pulled out some seashells, dumping the fragmented pieces into the sand between us. "They're for Jake. I'm going to see him for the first time this afternoon. He loves the ocean, and I wanted to bring him something...."

Keith stopped abruptly, tears brimming. "But I can't find any whole ones, Sam. Everything's broken."

"Hey," I said, gently touching his face. It was meant to be comforting, but the minute our eyes met, Keith gripped the back of my neck and drew me in, his lips crashing into mine. There was nothing sweet or loving in the way he kissed me. It was laced with anger and lust and need. Yet, despite the fact I wanted to hate him for leaving me, I responded in kind, pushing my lips forcefully against his. With his tongue sparring against mine, my body, which had lain dormant for weeks, suddenly roared back to life. The thrill of being wanted again clouded my judgment, and as Keith brushed a hand over my breast, I quaked with desire.

The hypnotic connection was broken as he dipped me back into the sand. It was then I came to my senses. This could not happen. We could never be. Reluctantly, I eased my lips off his and sat up, pushing him away with my hands.

"No. I can't."

"Why?"

"There are just things…" I stopped in mid sentence. There was no point in telling him about my move, about what my mother had done. He needed to focus on what he could change – himself. I was already gone. "I just… I can't. I'm sorry."

"I get it," he said, his fingers walking softly across my cheeks. "I know I ruined us."

During these past difficult weeks, I'd imagined how easy it had been for Keith to make the decision to leave me, but now, looking into his defeated eyes, I finally understood. Keith hadn't ruined us; life had.

"I don't blame you. Maybe we just weren't meant to be together," I replied. "Everyone has a first love, Keith. That's why they call it 'first.' We'll both move on – and be better for it."

He slanted his gaze. "You really believe that?"

I bit down on my lip to prevent the tremble. Of course I didn't believe that, but lying to myself – and him – was the only way I could set Keith on a path forward as I started over in a new city, safe and alone.

Forcing a smile on my face, I climbed to my feet and offered him my hand. "I do. Now, let's go."

"Where?"

"To get Jake his ocean."

CHAPTER NINETEEN

KEITH

Making Contact

Sam had emptied her paper lunch bag, and we'd stuffed it full of shells and rocks. The plastic bags we'd used for water and sand. If Jake couldn't come to the beach, I could bring it to him. Not that I hung out there much myself anymore. In fact, it was the first time I'd set foot back on the coast since his kidnapping. Something had changed in me, and I no longer felt the pull toward the ocean. Maybe when Jake went back, I would too. Maybe.

I thought back to my time with Sam. She'd been different – remote – and I got that she was angry. Why wouldn't she be? I'd set her aside – wiped her from my thoughts like she hadn't existed. If I'd only answered her calls. Seeing her again brought everything back, all the feelings I hadn't allowed myself the luxury to feel. I loved her. Not past tense, like she'd suggested on the beach. I loved her present tense. But, due to current circumstances, it would be a long time before I'd be in a position to win her back. If I was lucky, she might wait.

Mitch, Emma, and I waited by the door for Kyle to finish his visit with Jake. By unanimous vote, he was the first in because, well, he'd suffered the most in Jake's absence. And as I waited my turn, I clutched Sam's beach bag like a lifeline.

Mitch leaned against a wall, looking tanned, rested, and healthy, unlike the rest of us ghostly beings who appeared to have just hobbled out of a nuclear war. At twenty-one years old, my half-brother was a collegiate athlete with the body to prove it. He was everybody's favorite guy. Handsome. Athletic. And nice – like Mormon nice. He'd always been an ideal I couldn't live up to, so instead of making him the hero of my story, I'd cast him as the villain, hating him accordingly.

When Jake went missing, Mitch had been in South America, building infrastructure for debilitated villages on an exchange program through his college. Word of the tragedy had been slow to reach him, and when he'd finally worked his way out of the developing country and found his way home, he was a month late.

No matter, though, because as soon as he arrived home, Mitch took over. Suddenly the piles of trash were gone, the holes in the walls patched up, and the dishes washed. Not only that, but superman gave poor Emma a break with the kids and managed to get Dad cleaned up and on the road to recovery. And then, boom, four days later Jake made the miraculous escape heard round the world, and Mitch came out looking like the good luck charm we'd needed all along. There had been no suffering for him, no late nights with the FBI ripping his home apart looking for clues, and no Steves telling him to stop hoping because his brother was dead. No, Mitch had shown up late for the game yet had still gone on to hit a grand slam.

The door to Jake's hospital room swung open and Kyle stumbled out, darting his head around as if he were a cornered raccoon looking for escape. I gripped his arm and he jerked back, almost as if I'd jarred him from some nightmare in his head.

"What happened?" I asked.

His voice broke as he forced out the words. "He's not there."

Confused, I asked. "What do you mean? That's not his room?"

Mitch grunted as if dealing with my stupidity was such an inconvenience. Pushing me aside, he grabbed Kyle and drew him into an embrace. "That's not what he means, Keith. Use your brain."

Then horror stamped out my confusion, and the full weight of Kyle's words hit me. *Jake. Wasn't. There.* In all my fantasy scenarios of him surviving the kidnapping, never had I thought up this one: that he would return to us… but not really.

Despite Mitch's diss, my slipup was somewhat justified. My siblings and I had not been privy to the specifics of Jake's condition. The details were kept far away from our bleeding ears. But it didn't take a genius to put the big pieces of the puzzle together once the bodies of Ray Davis's former victims began coming out of the cold, hard ground. Jake had not only escaped a prolific serial killer, but he'd taken that fucker down. A full-on knife battle at his final stand, and somehow my little brother had emerged the victor – sort of. I found it hard to declare him the 'winner' when the thirteen-year-old boy now lying broken and shattered just beyond that door had lost absolutely everything.

The door opened wider as my parents followed Kyle out of the room, looking grim as their eyes scanned the lot of us. Shit, they were going to scrap the whole thing. Mitch, Kyle, Emma, and I had waited eight days to see Jake, and I wasn't going down without a fight. I needed to see him, if only to ease my fear of what was behind that door. I knew Jake wouldn't be the same smiling, sarcastic kid he'd been before, but I needed to know he could get there again – eventually.

Mom gently slid her hand through what remained of Kyle's freshly shorn head of hair. "You kids can still visit, but just understand, Jake's on a lot of pain medication. He might be confused and have trouble remembering who you are."

Was that what had happened? Had he failed to remember Kyle – his partner in crime? Those two were like the same side of a coin. This was bad. It wasn't what was scarred onto Jake's body that worried me most, it was the matter of what couldn't be seen – the psychological violence that would stay with him a lifetime.

Slipping her arm around Kyle, Mom whispered something in his ear before leading him away.

Once they were out of earshot, Emma asked, "What happened in there?"

Dad's gaze lifted, and I took in the dark bags sagging under his eyes. He looked so tired; Mom too. Both had aged years in the last month and a half, and by the looks of it, they'd be continuing down this haggard path for a long time to come. I should have been there to carry some of the burden.

"Jake just sort of looked right through Kyle like he didn't even see him. It was heartbreaking. Your mother says to give him time, but…"

While Mitch offered Dad the emotional support he needed, Emma glanced at me, the fear in her eyes matching my own. If Jake couldn't remember Kyle, what hope did the rest of us have? My sister absently stroked the neck of the guitar she'd insisted on bringing for Jake. In her mind's eye, music would be his healing grace, but after what we'd just learned, maybe she'd wasted her time lugging it all the way here.

"No. He's going to be okay," Dad reasoned, pulling himself back together. "Once they wean him off the pain meds, he'll be okay."

Over the past week, I'd been weaning myself off pain meds too, but I'd never forgotten who Kyle was.

"He just needs time to adjust and heal. Keep your visit short and your expectations low. That way you won't be disappointed. Mitch, why don't you go next?"

Mitch? What the fuck? Why was he always first in line? It didn't matter that the amount of time he'd spent in our family consisted of summers and holidays, and that was only until he turned sixteen and decided we were no longer worth the visit. The last summer he'd spent with us was when Jake was only eight. And yet, still, Mitch got the coveted pimp spot.

Typically I just stewed in silence, but not today… not when I was feeling the sting of injustice. "Why does he get to go first? If Jake didn't know who Kyle was, what makes you think he'd recognize Mitch? He's not even Jake's real brother."

My words hit their mark. Mitch winced. Dad winced. Even Emma cringed before hastily looking away. My eyes bounced off every stunned face, and maybe I would have even celebrated the verbal victory had Mitch not swiftly pushed me up against the wall.

"Don't you ever talk to me like that again," he seethed, his grip tightening as he leaned in so close I could feel his breath on my heated skin. "He's my brother too."

In his dreams. Mitch was just the shiny trophy on the shelf – the one you went to for advice on how to be a winner. But I was the real deal – Jake's oldest brother, the one who'd been there for him when he needed defending against bullies or for advice on his first kiss. I was his hero – not Mitch. Not ever.

"Do you have any idea how that makes me feel when you downgrade me like that, Keith? Huh? Was it my fault Dad didn't marry my mom and give me full-blooded siblings? No! You're no more entitled to your brothers and sisters than I am, so shut your fucking mouth."

Mitch rarely lost his cool, but when he did, it was always spectacular – and always my fault. His piece spoken, he released me from the wall. Dad shook his weary head, staring at me with the disappointed look I knew so well. Fuck him. Fuck them all! I didn't need this shit.

"You know what? Go ahead, Mitch. I'll take a backseat... like always."

Pushing past my father, I made sure to drop my shoulder and barrel into my fake brother for good measure. As I stalked off, I turned and made eye contact with Emma. The pleading in her eyes did not escape me... nor did it alter my path.

The further away I got from the hospital, the worse I felt. I made it several blocks on foot before I realized what I was doing – I wasn't sticking it to Mitch, I was turning my back on Jake. This was not the person I wanted to be. And certainly not the person I needed to be to win Sam back.

When it came right down to it, Mitch was just an excuse – an easy target. Was it his fault that he shit gold bars? Some people were just destined to be on the starting lineup. It was written in their DNA. And by stomping off the way I did, all I'd done was prove I was a second-string player.

What was I doing walking away when Jake needed me? What kind of a douche did that? Me, apparently. Well, shit! If I was going to change myself for the better, I had to go back and apologize to Mitch. It was the only way out of the hole I'd dug for myself.

Sighing, I pivoted on the ball of one foot and trudged back to the hospital.

Mom was sitting in the small waiting area outside Jake's door.

"I knew you'd be back," she said.

"Yeah? That's one of us. Did you hear?"

"Oh, I heard."

"Where is he? I need to apologize."

"He left with Kyle, Emma, and Dad." Her weary eyes rolled over me. "Lucky you."

I shifted from foot to foot, shame heating my cheeks. "I shouldn't have said those things to him."

"No, you shouldn't have. Mitch is not your enemy, Keith. He never has been."

"I know. He didn't do anything wrong. I can barely control my pettiness around him."

"Trust me, you inherited that particular trait from me." She smiled, patting the seat beside her. I sank into it and laid my head to her shoulder. "I don't know how much I told you about the issues Aunt Mel and I had growing up. She was the perfect older sister. Everyone loved her. Sometimes I felt like an afterthought. I spent my life trying to live up to her, and it just damaged our relationship. It wasn't until I decided to be okay with who I was that we were able to put everything in the past. Because your situation was similar to mine, I tried extra hard to make you feel special, but obviously I failed."

"You didn't fail me, Mom. I made my own choices. You know I've never been easy to control."

"No." She chuckled. "You definitely have not. When you were a toddler, you used to flip over the coffee table because you thought you were the Hulk. At playgrounds, if I turned my back for a second, you'd strip down naked and pee on trees."

"Well, in my defense, that just sounds like crappy parenting. Way to go, Mom."

We laughed, and she leaned over to kiss my forehead as if I were still a small child. "I've missed you."

"I missed you too. So much. I'm sorry for everything."

She held her hand up. "We all have our crosses to bear, Keith. Anything you have done dwarfs in comparison to me. If it takes me a lifetime, I will make it up to you and the others, I promise you that." Mom's voice shook, and I could feel her body trembling.

I lifted my head back up, looking into her teary eyes. "Hey, what's wrong?"

Such a stupid question, seeing that currently everything was wrong. I hooked my arm over her shoulder, hugging her to me. She was frail under my touch. The strain was taking its toll. Jake was alive, and that should have brought joy, but little about the situation we found ourselves in was cause for celebration.

"I'm sorry, baby." A sob escaped her. "I let you slip through my fingers. You were still fragile, and I knew that, and I should have held on tighter. Now you've rewound and are back where you started."

I wish. If she only knew how much further I'd fallen. But I kept silent as we embraced.

"It's okay," I whispered in her ear. "It's not your fault."

Her body shook. "I don't know how to make this better, Keith. How do I fix Kyle and you and Jake?"

"I don't know, Mom. I just want our family back."

"Me too."

Mom took my hand and led me to Jake's door. She stopped before opening it and placed an unsteady hand to my cheek "Don't expect much. He didn't talk to the others."

"Has he spoken to you?"

"Not coherently, no. Listen, before you go in, I've spoken to a few people. We're going to get you the help you need. It's already set."

I wasn't surprised, but I wasn't happy either. "I don't want to be sent away. Not now. I need to be here for Jake."

"I know. It's outpatient. But it will become inpatient if you don't take it seriously."

I had no choice but to accept her terms, so I nodded solemnly as I tried to step around her.

"One more thing," she said, stopping me. "I need you to promise that you won't let what you see in there take you away from us again. We need you here. Strong."

Promises were easy. Keeping them was where I'd always struggled. But I would give whatever was required to walk into that room.

"I promise," I said, reaching for her hand and squeezing before pushing the door open and facing my fear.

If Jake saw me arrive, he didn't acknowledge it. In fact, he didn't even blink an eye. My brother just stared blankly at the back wall. The first thing I noticed about him were the patches of baldness scattered over his head. Had he pulled his own hair out or had that been courtesy of Ray Davis?

So many emotions passed through me in that moment, and I wanted to rage for all the injustices he'd suffered, but I knew that wasn't what he needed. Right now, if I had any chance of reaching him, I had to be the fun brother Jake loved.

"Hey, dude, it's me, Keith," I said, taking a step closer.

No reaction. Not even a twitch. And although I'd been warned of his condition, the reality of seeing him this way nearly brought me to my knees. Pale, emaciated, and covered in angry purple bruises, Jake was barely recognizable under all the tubes and wires sticking out all over his broken body. A constricting cast spanned his leg, reaching up to his thigh.

"I brought you something."

Still no response. No flash of recognition. Could he even hear me? Where was he? Locked somewhere inside his head? Now that I was closer, I could see his bones protruding from his skin. He was so thin. Did he ever get food? What kind of a fiend steals a kid, abuses him, and lets him starve? Flashes of his life in chains forced me to look away. I now understood why Kyle had run out. It was what I wanted to do too, but I couldn't leave him – not now. Not ever. Mitch might have been Dad's ideal son, but I was Jake's favorite, and I'd be damned if I left this room without him knowing my name.

Settling into the chair, I was careful not to touch him. That was a trigger, I'd been warned. Digging into my paper bag, I pulled out a seashell and placed it on the sheets beside him.

"For you. Courtesy of the ocean. It says hi by the way."

He didn't move or even swivel his eyes to look at my peace offering.

"Look, I get you've been through hell, and I don't blame you for acting like a zombie, but I'm going to give it to you straight, bud: you keep this shit up and people are going to think you're a few McNuggets short of a Happy Meal, you feel me? Before you know it, shrinks are going to be coming in here throwing around big words that end in 'ology'. So here's what I need you to do, champ. Wake the fuck up."

Apparently I'd been too engrossed in my inspirational speech to notice movement on Jake's part. It wasn't until the shell was flying through the air that I realized what had happened. I watched in shock as the fragile seashell hit the wall with a thud, shattering into a thousand little pieces as it fell to the floor.

"Whoa. Dude. That was gnarly. Nice arm. You're a destructive little shit, aren't you? You wanna destroy another one?"

Staring straight ahead again, Jake slipped back into his comatose state. *Oh, no, you don't.* Now that I knew he was in there, no way was I letting him go without a fight. I pulled another shell from the bag and placed it beside him. "Do your damage."

This shell lay idle by his side. I pushed it closer like a dog nudging a ball at its owner. Nothing.

"Okay, I get it. You need a joke first. Why don't oysters give to charity?"

I waited. Every joke needed a pause for effect.

"Because they're shellfish."

I laughed, and I knew if Jake felt better, he would have too. We'd been telling these jokes to each other since we were little kids, the stupider the better.

"Damn, dude. You're a tough crowd. Fine, time for more surprises."

Out of one of the plastic baggies, I pulled a clump of seaweed and placed the slimy concoction on his arm. "Did you know that seaweed has a mild laxative effect and is quite useful in maintaining healthy digestion?"

No response.

"Now, I know what you're thinking, Jake. Who's the poor sap who had to test *that* theory? Am I right?"

Finally, I got a reaction. Jake glanced up at me for the briefest second before looking away. The bruises circling his eyes were all shades of the rainbow, and his lip was lined with black stitches, but still I sighed with relief. I had him now, and I wasn't letting go.

Gently tracing the cool algae over his arm, Jake seemed fascinated by the slippery feel. After piling on more seaweed, I looked up to find him staring at me. Our eyes met, and even though no words passed between us, I understood what he wanted. When I was with him, there would be no sympathy – no tears. All that was required of me was to make him feel alive. That I could do.

And to reward him for the non-verbal deal we'd brokered, I hit him with another joke. "What does seaweed say when it's stuck on the ocean floor?"

Jake cleared his throat and, in barely more than a scratchy whisper, he spoke his first words to me in six long and grueling weeks. "Kelp. Kelp."

CHAPTER TWENTY

SAMANTHA

The Story of the Stone

After parting ways with Keith, I knew there was one last thing I needed to do. Driving back to Shannon's house, I sat down at her desk and began penning a letter for Keith on the only paper I could find, a notepad with the slogan, *Warning! Don't pet the redhead.*

My fingers flew as the words transferred from my brain to the parchment with ease. I'd always done my best writing when it really counted, and this was one of those times. Originally, I'd just intended to quietly leave town, but seeing Keith again had changed my mind. If I had the chance to say goodbye properly, why wouldn't I? Did Keith not deserve to know the truth about me – the girl he'd fallen in love with? I wished I'd had the courage to speak my truth while we were still together. Maybe if I'd been honest to him when it really counted, he might have reciprocated when it mattered most to him.

I started with the parts he knew, Sullivan's death and my father's abandonment, and then I moved onto the isolation I'd felt at school and how both he and Shannon had saved me in different ways. Then came the tough stuff, the part of my life I'd kept hidden from view – my mentally ill mother. Every nasty detail was described, all the way through to the horrible last day I'd spent with her. And when I was done, I was certain Keith would understand the reason I was leaving was not because of his abandonment but because I needed the chance to know what it felt like to be safe in my own home.

And finally I settled in for a story that needed to be told: the story of my agate stone necklace. It was more than just a pretty crutch hanging around my neck. It had special meaning; special protective powers. That's not to say the stone hadn't seen its fair share of failures, Sullivan being the biggest of all. Its healing powers hadn't been enough to save my brother, but they had been enough to save me. Toying with the stone, I slid it along the leather cord as I remembered the moment it came into my life.

I was ten and trembling. Sullivan was beside me, fidgeting in place. My grandfather was dying, and we'd been summoned for our final goodbyes. I'd never known death at that stage of my life, and I was terrified he'd take his last breath in front of me.

"It's time," my father said, his chipper voice masking the pain. "He wants to see you kids. Sullivan, go first."

I waited for maybe ten minutes before my brother emerged from the room shell-shocked and blurry-eyed. I tried to snag his attention, to ask what had happened, but he was in no mood to catch me up. In fact, he slunk off to use the bathroom, which had always been his go-to place for a good cry.

"Samantha?" Dad said, opening the door. I took a deep breath and stepped into my grandfather's hospital room. He was lying in bed, eyes closed, looking peaceful. *Please don't die on me.* As I stepped forward, he turned his head in my direction and smiled. I'd only met him a handful of times, but the one thing I remembered about him was his smile. I sometimes wished we'd skipped a generation and he'd been my father instead.

"Come, Samantha," he said. "Don't be afraid."

I tiptoed closer.

"Honey." His tired eyes were trained on me. "Can you reach around and unclasp my necklace?"

Doing as I was instructed, I removed the jewelry from his neck and laid it into his weathered palm.

"Sit." His bottom lip trembled as some unseen memory passed through his mind. "I want to tell you about this stone."

And then he began a remarkable tale of his time in Vietnam. While on a mission and hunkered down in a bunker, he found the necklace lying in the dirt. Thinking someone had dropped it accidentally, my grandfather affixed it around his neck for safe-keeping, fully intending to give it to the rightful owner as soon as he returned to base camp. But shortly after, he and his platoon came under attack, and my grandfather was one of only four survivors. The necklace, he'd said, was his lucky charm.

"And now it's yours, Samantha. You're special, and I know you'll do right by this stone. Do you understand?"

I remembered nodding, but at the time, I didn't really understand its significance or why my grandfather was giving it to me and not Sullivan. Maybe he knew life would test me and I'd need that extra bit of protection. Or possibly he just saw a fighting spirit in me and knew I'd keep going even when times got tough – just as he had done all those years ago. Whether the stone had magical powers or not wasn't as important as the wearer believing it did. And I believed.

My grandfather passed on a couple days later. And even though they'd never been close, Sullivan took his death hard. I did all I could to calm him down, but my brother was inconsolable. That was when I knew what I had to do. Even though he'd given it to me, I removed Grandpa's stone from around my neck and fastened it around my brother's neck. And as I told him the story of the stone, I watched in wonder as it eased his pain.

My story told, I sealed the envelope and addressed it carefully. Then I flipped it over and printed on the back, "Be who you want to be – Love always, Samantha."

And then I was out the door and in my car, determined to add closure to my departure. Pulling into the post office, I found a spot in the front and parked. As I walked to the mailbox, tears swamped my eyes, but I didn't let them stop me from doing what needed to be done. Kissing the parched envelope, I dropped it in the mailbox, and as I walked back to my car, I traced my fingers along my collarbone where the agate necklace had once hung.

Bobbing in the water, my board at the ready, I spotted the unbroken wave and paddled like mad to catch it. The last few swells had fallen out before I could get lift, but this one… I just knew it would be epic. And then I was up, my hair blowing in the breeze, a smile centered on my face. The ride was everything I knew it would be.

I felt so lucky to be here, to feel alive like this. Adjusting to life in San Diego hadn't been as difficult as I'd thought.

My two little cousins, nine and eleven, were old enough that watching them during the afternoons while their mom was at work was no hardship at all. I met a few friends at my new school and was thrilled to discover my aunt's house was a twelve-minute drive to this surf spot.

The ocean filled a void in my life that had opened up with the lack of a committed father, the stress of a mentally unstable mother, and the death of my big brother. It was as if being on the water leveled the playing field. Sure, I had been handed a raw deal, but look what I had – this ride, and then the next. Peace was what I'd been missing, and here on the waves, I'd found it.

Of course I knew who to thank for my newfound happiness – the boy with the stupid questions who smelled like seaweed. I smiled. That was another benefit of my new Zen lifestyle. Remembering Keith was no longer painful. Now when I thought of him, I didn't dwell on what could have been, but instead comforted myself in the knowledge that we'd changed each other for the better. When all was said and done, Keith had occupied only a very short chapter in the story of my life, but it would be remembered as the crucial turning point – the moment in time when I took back my life. Keith McKallister had not just given me my first love, he'd given me my passion.

"Hey," a male voice interrupted my daydream. I looked up, blocking the sun with my arm. He was college-aged, deeply tanned, and smiling at me with an affecting grin. "Sick ride."

"Thanks. The conditions are challenging today."

"Don't I know? I've been wiping out all day. I'm Drew, by the way."

"Samantha," I said, reaching for his outstretched hand. "But everyone calls me Sam."

Five Years Later

Chapter Twenty-One

Keith

Yogi

"Excuse me, people. Coming through."

"No, ma'am. Hands to yourselves, please."

"Easy, killer, let's keep the volume levels in the healthy range."

"Sir, I assure you no one wants to see that… no one."

The sea of quivering bodies parted as beefy security guards cleared the way for us to make it through the back gates where there would be sanity. As Jake's star had begun to rise, so had the crowds. And despite the fact that he was just eighteen years old, his followers weren't all giddy preteen girls – as the middle-aged woman flashing her nipple ring proved. From the very young to the very old, Jake attracted a wide range of music lovers, men and women alike. My job was to keep their hands, feet, breasts, and teeth off him. Not as easy as it sounded, I assure you.

"Hang on, bro. We're almost there."

As we pushed through the hordes, Jake dipped his head, acknowledging my words but saying nothing in return. He didn't need to. I was dialed in, able to understand his wants and needs without clunky conversations slowing us down. Before me, Jake had navigated these shark-infested waters alone. He'd had no one to read his non-verbal cues or make him smile when his day turned to shit. The people assigned to his team in the early days didn't care about him. He was a paycheck, nothing more, nothing less. Back then, Jake was more a zoo animal than a musician, placed on stage so people could gawk at the boy who'd survived a grisly high-profile crime. The suits didn't care if he could sing or write or perform. All they cared about was that paying concertgoers would fork out the money required to watch the infamous one-hit wonder perform his hit song, "Deception."

No doubt expecting Jake to crash and burn after his debut solo flight, the label was intent on milking his notoriety while keeping their expenses at a minimum. Why pour resources into a lost cause? So they dropped Jake into a debilitated tour bus, arranged for a forty-eight-year-old drunk to be his manager/handler, assembled the motleyest stage crew they could scramble together at a moment's notice, and assigned him Lassen, the most cantankerous bus driver known to man.

But the funny thing about underdogs was you could never really count them out, and while the bosses were totaling up their chump change, Jake was quietly building a devoted fan base. Before the studio heads knew it, their one-hit wonder had morphed into a two- and three-hit phenomenon. Followers arrived in droves, filling concert halls and gymnasiums and then later stadiums and arenas. Jake was a rising star who'd suddenly found himself in an enviable position of power. And to everyone's surprise, he wielded it.

After just one album, Jake turned the tables on his label, suing and claiming he'd been coerced into signing the contract as a minor. In an effort to avert a public relations disaster, Jake was let out of his contract. He promptly signed a favorable multi-million dollar deal with their biggest competition. It was a shake up heard round the musical world, made more fantastical because it was a kid just shy of his eighteenth birthday who'd choreographed it all. Well him, our two fed up parents, and Mom's lawyer friend, Larry.

Gone were the sloshed manager, the unprofessional roadies, and the decrepit tour bus he'd shared with the entire band. It was a total overhaul of the status quo. Well, maybe not total. There was, in fact, one unexpected survivor of the purge – Lassen, the jerk bus driver who was hated by all except for the one person who mattered. Jake.

And so as the empty ranks were filled to my brother's specific requirements, he was handed everything he wanted on a silver platter: a new manager, a professional crew, a private tour bus, and yours truly – personal assistant to the stars – Keith McKallister.

The security guards and I had Jake surrounded as we made our final push through the crowd. I wasn't paying attention to the people around me until a hand reached out and squeezed my package. Too stunned to respond, I turned to face the culprit, but she'd already dropped my dick in favor of palming either side of my face and aggressively shoving her tongue so far down my throat she was tickling my tonsils. I wished I could say the manhandling disgusted me, but that would've been a lie. In fact, the entire Jake-train was forced to stop so I could give my assailant a proper response. Cupping her neck, I pulled her in and planted a kiss on her lips that gave her a glimpse of what she was never going to get.

Then as swiftly as it began, I drew away and kept moving through the crowd.

"Holy shit!" the woman called out. "Come back. Don't set me on fire, baby, if you're not going to put me out."

I grinned, not looking back. There was a certain satisfaction in leaving my accoster in the dust. Chancing a glance at Jake, I worried he might be pissed at my pit stop, but instead, I was met with a smile of mad respect.

"Pirate hair." I shrugged. "The ladies love it."

After making it into the back lot where the busses and semi trucks were parked, the world around us returned to normal. No more grabby hands. No more screamers. Lassen was waiting for us at the door to the bus. He grunted something unintelligible to Jake, who nodded his own weird greeting.

I scratched my head, not understanding their primeval language. As far as I could tell, they genuinely seemed to like each other, but for the life of me I couldn't figure out why… or how… or when. Granted, the closest I'd ever gotten to an actual conversation with the man was when a bird unexpectedly splatted on the windshield of the bus.

I'd said, "Oh, shit, man, you hit a bird."

And he'd replied, "Yep."

The end.

Once Lassen was out of earshot, I spoke my mind. "You know, Jake, you really need to get some friends your own age."

"I know, but people my own age are way too young."

"Well, then, maybe we can get you a puppy or something. Anything's preferable to Lassen."

"Give him a chance. I didn't like Lassen when I first met him either, but he grows on you."

"Hmm, interesting, you mean like flesh-eating bacteria?"

"Yes," Jake grinned. "Just like that."

"Alright, well, as long as you've got some strong antibiotics, who am I to complain, right?"

Jake plopped down at the kitchen table and proceeded to stare at me while I was rummaging through the refrigerator.

Lifting my head I asked, "Do you have a question? Or are you just admiring my bubble butt?"

"Actually, I do have a question," he replied. "How's your girlfriend going to feel about you macking on that woman back there?"

"My girlfriend?" I asked scrunching my nose. "Are you referring to Sophie?"

"I thought her name was Sophia."

Now I had to think. Resting my jaw against the open refrigerator door, I wracked my brain for clarity. "No, I'm pretty sure it's Sophie."

"You're pretty sure?" Jake laughed. "You might want to get it straight."

"Why? She doesn't care."

"Oh, I guarantee you she cares."

"Yeah, well, she's not my girlfriend, so it matters not, my friend."

"See, the problem with that is *she* thinks she's your girlfriend. I caught her doodling something on a notepad the other day and once she left I saw that she'd written Sophia McKallister just above two entwined rings and an overload of puffy hearts. You might already be engaged, Jack Sparrow."

I scoffed. Not with Sophie, I wasn't. She was a trust fund groupie who drove from place to place, sleeping her way backstage because she didn't have anything better to do with all that money. That's where I'd found her a few weeks back, and we'd been getting it on at different concert stops ever since. But she was nowhere near marriage material.

"Trust me on this one. Sophie will never be a McKallister."

"Sophia," he corrected.

I shook my head, grinning at his persistence before tossing him a bottle of water from the fridge.

"Whatever. I need to break it off with her anyway. I need someone who's smarter than me."

"That shouldn't be a problem."

"You'd think, but the last time we were together, she was talking about seeing a psychic, so I made a joke, saying I wished she was clairvoyant. She got jealous, thinking Clair Voyant was an actual woman."

Jake chuckled. "No way is that true."

"Oh, but it is. And get this – she pronounces the 'l' in salmon. Who does that shit?"

"Women you date."

I nodded smugly, playing up the role of the perpetual playboy. My track record with women was legendary with my brothers. They thought I was a god of sorts, going from woman to woman, never deigning to settle down. But that was just a part I played to earn their respect. The reason I couldn't hold onto anyone for longer than a couple of weeks was because I was still stuck on the ideal of a very specific girl I'd lost long ago.

As I peered into the fridge, I shook off the image of Sam tracking through my brain. It did me no good to dwell on the past. Besides, remembering her put me in a somber mood, and Jake needed me to remain upbeat and fun. That was the role I'd played in my brother's life ever since that day in the hospital when I got him talking again. I was the comic relief, the person he turned to alleviate the darkness that still swirled just behind his troubled eyes. If I could get him to laugh a few times a day, I was earning my paycheck.

"You wanna hear my shower thought for the day?"

Every morning, while soaping up my meat sack, meaningless thoughts popped into my brain, creating the phenomenon commonly referred to in our family as 'shower thoughts.' My dad was blessed with the gift, as was I, but I liked to think my ideas were more profound.

"You know I do," Jake responded, amusement already spreading across his face.

"So, you know that commercial that says four out of five people suffer from diarrhea? Does that mean one person actually enjoys it?"

Jake coughed out a laugh, water spraying from his mouth and as he wiped it away. "You have the maturity of a ten-year-old kid who still laughs at fart jokes."

"I don't care how old you get, fart jokes are always hilarious. Besides, you should talk about maturity. You're eighteen years old and cradling a stuffed animal."

The squishy toy was one of the many gifts that were thrown up on stage every night. Why he'd swiped that one off the floor and carried it with him to the bus was a mystery to me, but Jake was like that – a walking perplexity.

My brother responded to my diss by pitching the fuzzy bear at me. I caught it in midair and proceeded to have my way with it. Rubbing its furry body against my face, I switched to kid's speak. "I'm going to name you Cuddles and we're going to be *best* friends."

My brother smiled but otherwise ignored my nettling. I tucked the bear under my arm, needing it handy for the counter assault I was currently plotting.

After a quick search of the shelves, I found what I was looking for. Yes! Frieda was my girl! She'd stocked the fridge to my specifications. Tucked in the back on the bottom shelf were the beer bottles I'd requested. Grabbing one, I popped the cap and downed a healthy gulp.

"You drinking?" Jake asked, as if it were an afterthought and not some calculated attempt to micromanage me.

I raised a brow. "One beer is not drinking."

Before he could respond, I performed a spin maneuver and pelted my brother in the right temple with the downy bomb. He tipped back in his chair from the force of the sneak attack.

"Jesus," he grumbled, rubbing his head.

"Besides, what are you, Jake, the fuckin' drink police?"

He actually gave my words some thought before countering, "I don't think that's an actual division of the police force."

I flipped him off with a smile on my face, pretending it didn't irritate the hell out of me that I was being questioned in the first place. I was twenty-three years old. If I wanted a drink, it was my goddamn choice. "Do you want me to pour it out, Officer Dickweed?"

"No." He shrugged, looking away. "Drink it. I don't care."

Well, fuck. Now I was pissed. "Clearly you do care or you wouldn't have brought it up."

My family had a way of doing this – policing my choices as if I couldn't be trusted to make the right ones. And, yes, fine, there had been an issue or two on the tour, but I had never lost control. Okay, maybe that one time. But otherwise I'd been clean. Regardless, it was no one's damn business what I did on my down time. I wasn't an indentured servant. I didn't serve Jake twenty-four seven.

My brother sat up a little straighter, boldly meeting my eye. "If you want to know the truth, I don't think it's the best idea to have alcohol in the bus when both you and Lassen are recovering addicts."

"Lassen?" My ears burned. The nerve. "I'm supposed to worry about Lassen now too? Is it my fault you hired a wacked-out bird murderer?"

"What are you so pissed about?" Jake asked. "I have no idea why we're fighting in the first place."

"We're fighting because you're being a condescending little shit. Don't tell me what I can and can't do. You're not the boss of me, asshole."

"Actually, I am, and I have a contract you signed to prove it."

He was right, and that fact made me want to smack that smirk right off his face. But the days of using physical force on Jake were over. There was no dragging him down hallways anymore. No swift punches to the arm. Even the curling of a fist could cause my little brother to flinch away. No, nowadays, I was reduced to using stuffed animals against him. And blackmail.

"Look at you puffing out your chest, big man. Just remember who carries the dirt on you."

"What dirt? The only dirt I have, the whole fucking world knows about, so the joke's on you."

He'd played his trump card. We never discussed *that* dirt, and I wasn't about to start tonight. But I had a few other cards up my sleeve. "I'm referring to the ancient porn stash you and Kyle found in that tree house in the woods when you were twelve."

A fusion of mortification and amusement crept over Jake's cheeks.

"Uh-huh, I knew all about it. Who do you think was swiping those antiquated magazines from your hiding spot under the dresser and rubbing it out in the bathroom like a pilgrim?"

His embarrassment turned to straight up laughter as any tension between the two of us diffused. Suddenly, we were back to our easy camaraderie.

"Speaking of pilgrims and porn," I continued, eyeing him as I made a show of dumping my remaining beer into the sink and then turning to His Majesty and presenting him with a shallow bow, "you do realize that, thanks to the Internet, we've seen more naked women than all our ancestors combined."

Jake's eyes rounded as he chewed on that shower thought.

"Shit, I never thought about that," he said, scratching his head.

"Powerful, right?" Now it was my turn to puff out my chest. After all, I'd just contributed to the smut sciences. "We're so lucky to be born in this century."

Nodding his agreement, Jake leaned down and swiped the stuffed bear off the floor where it had fallen after ricocheting off his skull. He examined it for the longest time before sliding it over the table toward me and pointing to the words and numbers written on its back in silver sharpie.

Call me. I promise you won't regret it. LeAnn.

I looked from the bear to Jake and then back to the bear before realization dawned on me. Oh, shit. He wanted to call her. This was a new development. In all the time I'd been with him on tour, sex with a groupie had never been a line item.

"You want to hook up with her? Is that what you're saying?" I tried to mask my astonishment. Really, I shouldn't have been surprised. He was, after all, a teenage boy. But things were different for him. He wasn't like everyone else. Despite being on his way to becoming a musical icon, privately Jake was isolated and reserved

"As long as that's what she meant by 'You won't regret it'. How am I supposed to know?"

Exactly. How would he know? Jake didn't come in contact with girls his own age very often; unless, of course, they were fainting at his feet. And it wasn't like he could just stroll onto a college campus and come out a winner.

I had to get this conversation into a place where Jake didn't look like he was going to spew his guts. Leaning in, I read the words etched upon the stuffed animal's back. "I mean, if I were a betting man, I'd say she doesn't mean you'll regret not listening to her talk endlessly for hours on end. But women are a goddamn mystery, so don't mark my words on that."

"What do you think I should do?"

"I think you should take your chances. The worst that can happen is you'll get a new chatty best friend. And the best – well, you know, you'll be on your way to pound town, son."

Just by the way he diverted his eyes to the ground told me I'd overestimated what he *knew*. The obvious question of his virginity now tottered on the edge of my mind – which he promptly read.

Shifting uncomfortably, Jake clipped me off before I could even ask. "No. I haven't."

"And, uh, you want your first time to be with Yogi Bear?" I asked, my eyes diverting to the stuffed animal in question.

"Not specifically with the bear, no." He grinned, breaking the tension in the room and bringing his eyes back up to meet mine. "The girl who threw the bear up on stage – yes."

"So you saw her, and there won't be any nasty surprises?"

"I saw her. She's hot."

"Oh, whew. I mean there's nothing wrong with the aesthetically disadvantaged. Like I always say, never be afraid to plow some 4's here and there."

"Really? You always say that?"

"What? It's clinically proven that having low standards automatically quadruples your chances of getting laid."

Jake shook his head, but there was no hiding the amusement. "I should have asked someone else for advice."

"Right. Because Lassen's a regular old sex guru."

"Actually, he is. Did you know Lassen's been married three times and, he hasn't said it in so many words, but I think he was married to more than one wife at a time."

My mouth dropped open. "Lassen was?"

He nodded.

The image of the sweaty, overweight bus driver getting it on with one woman was disturbing enough, but two? "Well, fuck."

Jake wasn't paying attention to me as he turned the bear over in his hands. "Do… do you think I should call her?" he stammered.

Multiple times a week I watched him take the stage with a maturity that defied his years. He was poised and talented. A star. Sometimes I forgot he was still a kid – in need of his big brother to show him the way. Pulling my chair out, I flipped it around and straddled it. Time to get serious.

I reached my hand out. "Give me the bear."

His fingers closed over the squishy animal. "No. Why, what are you going to do?"

"I'm going to call the number and get her over here, that's what I'm going to do."

"You? Shouldn't I call her myself?"

"If you were a normal guy, yeah. But Jake, you're a star. You don't call women."

"I don't?"

"No, you have people to do that for you. Now give me the bear."

Jake squeezed it tighter. "I don't know."

"Do you want to get laid or not?"

Myriad emotions passed over his face before his fingers loosened and the bear dropped to the table. The phone was out of my pocket and I was dialing her number before he'd even retracted his hand.

I set the call on speaker.

"Hello?" A female voice responded on the first ring. Perhaps she'd been anticipating the call. Jake jumped from his chair and signaled me to abort the mission with the subtle mime of slicing his fingers across his throat. I smiled and shook my head. *Not a chance, stud.*

Directing my attention back to the caller, I asked, "Is this LeAnn?"

She let out a high-pitched squeal as giggles from her friends filled the line with giddy little air bubbles. "Yes. Are you Jake? Oh, my god, I can't believe you called me."

Pacing back and forth, my brother was chomping down on his knuckle while emitting low groans like an animal caught in a leg clamp.

"No, I'm not Jake, but I work for him. He got your message."

"He did?" More squeals. "I saw him pick it up, but I never thought..." She stopped to breathe. "Does he want me to come over? I'm still at the stadium."

I sought Jake out and found him crouched near the ground, his hand covering his mouth. He appeared alternately horrified and enthralled. Our eyes met and I queried with my thumb – yes or no?

After a moment's thought, he removed his hand from his mouth and turned his thumb up, green-lighting the operation.

"Yes, LeAnn. Jake wants to meet you. I'm going to send you a text. Bring it to security and tell them Keith sent you. They'll get you to his bus."

By the time I hung up the phone, my brother was lying flat on his back on the tour bus floor hyperventilating. I got up and nudged him with my foot. "*This* will not impress LeAnn."

"Maybe *this* isn't a good idea," he groaned.

"Of course it is. Sex is like pizza...when it's good it's good, but when it's bad it's still pretty good."

I offered him my hand, and to my surprise, his fingers wrapped around mine. I pulled him to his feet.

"You'll be fine. Now, I'm warning you ahead of time, don't be too ambitious because chances are you're going to suck. I mean, dude, the first time is never pretty. Most newbies are 'two pump chumps,' if you know what I mean. Don't panic. It's totally normal to blow your wad before she's even gotten started. But here's the thing – at this stage of the game, her satisfaction isn't your problem any more than the safety of other motorists on the road is the concern of a 16-year-old with a newly minted driver's license."

Jake nodded, soaking up my wisdom. "But what if I want to make it good for her too?"

"It won't be, so there's no sense in worrying about it."

"Keith, I'm serious. I don't have much time."

I sighed. "All right, fine. A little trade secret – you can buy a lot of time with a well-placed thumb."

Once the knock came at the door, I made my exit. Wandering for a while in the dark, I resisted the sounds of riotous fun streaming from the band and crew buses. Jake was playing the same venue the following day as well, so we were camped out in the parking lot for the night. And overnights became tailgates. And tailgates became blowout parties. And partying came with shit I had no business ever getting involved in again.

Addiction had taken me down a treacherous path, and I found myself drifting that way more and more the further away I got from the protection of home. It was easier to stay on the straight and narrow when the people around me were as committed to my sobriety as I was. But on the road, the lines were blurred, and convictions became harder to abide by.

After Jake's return, I'd tried so hard to hold it together, having only to look to him for motivation. Withdrawal had been a bitch, but I knew if Jake could pull his life out of the shitter after everything he'd been through, then I sure as hell could do it too. That day in the hospital was the turning point for me. Whatever issues I had, Jake had them ten times worse, and the only way to support him was to keep myself in one piece. So that's what I did. For Jake. And for my parents who'd suffered enough. And for me – like I promised Sam all those years ago.

But long stretches of sobriety were routinely interrupted by nasty relapses, the last one even landing me in an outpatient rehab. I'd only been clean for four months when the offer to tour with Jake came along. His manager presented me with a very detailed list of duties; just as long was the list of don't-ies. I signed on the dotted line, knowing the risks involved but believing that entering into a binding contract would be the best way to keep me away from the bad influences. Wrong. In true Keith fashion, all it had done was drive me into the shadows. A drink here, a blunt there… maybe even a pill or two for good measure. It was all about moderation and keeping my head above water.

Sliding my hands through my hair, I walked toward the gate separating me from the real world. Fans were still milling around, perhaps waiting for an invitation to the crew party they could hear even from across the parking lot. I knew trouble lay on the other side of that fencing; and yet I went straight for it as if I were being pulled to the dark side by some hypnotic force. Shaking my head, I focused on what had happened a couple of weeks ago when Jake caught me flying high. I'd promised him then that it would be the last time. And he'd promised me then that there would be no more second chances.

"Hey, do you work for Jake?" a woman asked, pressed up against the fencing. She appeared only a couple years older than me, but the relatively short amount of time she'd walked this earth hadn't been kind to her. "Sounds fun back there, but you know, every party needs some entertainment."

I stopped. Why did I stop? "What type of entertainment are we talking?"

She perked right up, perhaps not expecting my sudden interest. "Honey, I'm my own talent agency. I can get you anything you need and more."

I cast her an eager glance. There was no doubt she was connected, and in only a matter of minutes I could have the drug of my choice in hand. Temptation called my name. I could find myself an empty corner of the lot and enjoy a little peace of mind for a change. *No. Keep it together.*

Any relief I felt would only be a temporary, and as soon as the euphoria faded, I'd be right back to chasing the high – and back to delivering pizzas to a different type of addict.

Walk the fuck away.

And, for once, I listened to that voice in my head and took two giant steps back. "Hey. Sorry. I was mistaken."

Perhaps sensing the loss of easy money, the temptress reached her arm through the fence. "No. Don't leave. I can get you the finest blow. Honey, come back."

As she kept calling for me, it became clear that merely walking was no longer cutting it, and before I knew it, I was sprinting frantically away from danger, back to the bus where I'd be safe. I skidded to a halt at the sound of Lassen's rough, husky voice.

"They're still in there," he warned, in an accusatory tone. "Give the kid his privacy."

"I wasn't going in," I replied, with an equal amount of antagonism. Did he really think the plan was for me to beaver dam my little bro on the day of his deliverance?

Lassen and I glared at each other like the enemies we were. Throughout our entire stare down, he was spitting sunflower seed shells from the corner of his mouth. A pile lay on the ground by his side.

"What are you running from?" he asked, more shells spurting out from the tiny opening in his lip.

"What do you care?"

He shrugged, a shell going airborne. "I don't. Just passing the time. Don't tell me if you don't want. It's not like I'm going to lose any sleep over it."

No, I didn't suppose he would. Lassen never had any trouble sleeping, as evidenced by the restless nights I'd spent listening to him snore and fart, fantasizing about silencing him forever. I glanced at the empty chair beside him. There was always an empty chair next to the Grinch Who Stole Happiness. Just to defy him I plopped down and made myself comfortable.

We sat in silence while he added to the pile of seeds between our chairs, and even though he had no interest in my drama, I felt the need to explain myself. "I'm running from my past."

Crunch. Spit. "And how's that going for you?"

"Well, I got back without pills in my pocket, so I'd call that a good day."

Lassen nodded, another mouthful of seeds spat into the landfill. Without commenting on my rather telling statement, he tipped the bag in my direction. "You want some?"

"Nah," I replied, waving off his offering. "I don't like sunflower seeds."

Spit. Spit. "I suggest you develop a taste for them."

"Why?"

"It'll help with the cravings."

"I don't need any help," I responded, defiantly.

"Suit yourself. But just so you know, I'm running from my past too."

Later, lying in my cot in the bus, my mind raced. I'd been so close to destruction tonight. Why did I always insist on cutting myself off at the knees? The urges were getting stronger, to the point where I was now actively sabotaging myself. Tonight, I'd walked right into the path of temptation. Something had stopped my forward motion… this time… but it was getting harder to resist.

I just wanted life to be normal again, like it had been before the kidnapping. Before the endless relapses. Before I lost her. Every day that went by, I drifted further from where I'd once been… from the man I wanted to be. It's not like I'd been a real prize back then either, but at least life had been easy and fun, and I had sunlight and dreams. I had the ocean… and Sam. Now, it was all gone, and finding my way back to that light was as daunting as retracing my footprints through a forest after a punishing rainstorm.

When I was feeling particularly down in the dumps, like today, I'd lie in bed and ponder what had made me the one degenerate in a family of champions. What had been different in my upbringing? Why had I felt the need to self medicate where my siblings seemed content inside their own heads? Even Jake, who clearly had the most to lose, seemed to be functioning on a level higher than me.

To the outside world, I was a flirty, outgoing guy, but inside there was darkness – an entity that refused to just let me be.

Left to my own devices, I'd be lying dead in a ditch somewhere; but I was a McKallister, and that meant every single person in my family was all up in my business, like Jake had been earlier. I knew it came from a place of concern, but until I was ready to accept the help, no amount of intervention would stop my downward spiral – not the counseling or the parent participation, and certainly not the outpatient rehabilitation programs that were routinely forced upon me. God knows, I'd figured out how to work that system like a champ. Never taking it seriously or trying to learn from my mistakes, I'd done nothing in rehab but dick around, charm the workers, and slip under the radar.

My loved ones tried, they really did, but fixing me was the equivalent of treating a gunshot wound with Band-Aids. By the time I completed the various programs they'd lined up for me, I was no better off than when I'd gone in. It's not that I didn't want to be the man they expected me to be, I just didn't know how. It was like a light had gone out inside me, and now that evil was lurking everywhere, I was content to just nestle myself in its shadows.

Reaching up to the little shelf over my bed, I pulled down the well-worn letter I'd kept with me all these years. Sometimes I read it when I needed a little extra perspective, like tonight. The edges were frayed, and the body of the text was now being held together with tape. But even though I'd memorized the words and could recite them in my sleep, I reread the letter anyway.

Once, I'd had a starring role in the story of Samantha Anderson's life. And I never got tired of reading and rereading the part where she described how I'd changed her for the better. Yes, I'd brokered a peace between her and the sea, but I'd done more than that – I'd loved her unconditionally, something she admitted had been lacking in her life. And I could feel with every word she wrote that Sam loved me back. With just the stroke of her pen, she elevated me beyond the screw-up everyone else saw. She made me real and flawed and worthy. And that was what I held onto in my darkest days. There was a girl out there somewhere who had loved me… and maybe, just maybe, she still did.

I'd made a huge mistake. I knew that now. Young and stupid, I figured she'd be around forever. But then, I hadn't factored in the kidnapping or the drug addiction or her mother's murderous ways. I knew I loved Sam, but I hadn't fully appreciated what she'd meant to me; nor did I realize the extent of her suffering until she was gone. I wished I could go back and change the decision I'd made the day Jake was taken… the day I reached for the drugs instead of her. Maybe if I'd made a different choice, I wouldn't be here today holding what I had left of her in my hand.

The urge to search for her was always there, but what would I do once I found her? I couldn't just drop into her life with a drug addiction. She didn't need that, not after what she'd been through with her mom. If anyone deserved peace and happiness, it was Sam. I would be nothing but more hardships thrust upon her, and I refused to be a burden. Besides, if Sam had realized her dreams of an East Coast school, then it was safe to assume thousands of miles separated us.

Maybe someday, when I was worthy of her love, I'd find Sam again – and then all bets would be off. I'd fight for her and stop at nothing to win her back. No obstacle would be big enough to keep me away. But that was when I was worthy, and I wasn't so sure that day would ever come.

Folding the letter, I ran my fingers over the flimsy paper before replacing it on the shelf and whispering, "Good night, Sam – wherever you are."

CHAPTER TWENTY-TWO

SAMANTHA

Genetics

"Samantha Olivia Anderson."

The sun was warm and I could hear the sounds of the waves crashing onto shore as I crossed the stage to accept my diploma at this university by the sea. No, I wasn't graduating from an Ivy League school, and no, I wasn't getting that English Lit degree I'd always pictured myself earning, but life has a way of changing you when you least expect it, and adapting was the only way to get ahead of the game. And that's where I was now – ahead. So far ahead of where I ever thought I'd be. My mind was challenged, my body was strong, and my soul was filled with happiness. Those old dreams of escaping to some far off place had faded away once I'd decided to live my life in the open, free of fear.

With that change in outlook came a redirection of my passions. Instead of spending my life analyzing the literary classics, I'd applied and was admitted to the biology program at UC Santa Barbara with a specialty in aquatic studies. I spent my four years studying ecology, marine botany, and deep-sea biology. Not bad for the girl who once hated science.

And now, here I was with my head held high as I walked across the stage to accept my due reward. This degree meant more to me than just a piece of paper. It meant I'd stopped living in the past and had embraced my future. Sure, there were a few key players missing from the celebration – namely, anyone blood-related to me – but I'd cultivated a small contingency of supporting players who meant more to me than some title. Who needed marrow-matches when you had friends like I did?

Making the trip from San Diego were my Aunt Kim and cousins Jennie and Joyce. We'd grown incredibly close in the year and a half I'd lived with them ... so much closer than I'd ever been to my mother the first seventeen years of my life. With them, I'd realized the full scope of who I could be as a person.

And then there was Shannon, the one constant in my life. She'd graduated with a bioengineering degree last year and had moved back home to work in the same lab where both her parents and one of her two brothers were employed.

"Samantha! Samantha Anderson." Her shouts reverberated through the crowd, but it wasn't just her voice I heard. Stewart, Shannon's boyfriend of three years, was screaming just as loud. Never in the history of soul mates had there been two people more suited for each other then Shannon O'Malley and Stewart Fitzpatrick.

Born on the same day, Shannon and Stewart could have been litter-mates. Their hair was the same shade of red, both were tall, skinny, and they both sported matching 'his and hers' humidifiers. Yes, that's right – if possible, Stewart was even more allergic to the world than Shannon.

And the similarities didn't end there. The two were Harry Potter fanatics who regularly dressed up like their favorite characters and wandered around town flicking their wands and performing fake spells in front of startled onlookers. Like journalists on the national news stations, they agreed on literally everything. They ate the same food, they liked the same TV shows, and they regularly finished each other's sentences, playing the whole jinx/double jinx game ad nauseam.

The two were in sync now as well, combining their vocals skills to catch my attention. As if their merged voices weren't enough, they'd taken it a step further with the simultaneous use of cowbells. Under the misguided belief that graduation rituals couldn't have enough of those handy little noisemakers, Shannon had brought four – one for herself, one for Stew, and two more for my cousins, who joined in the ear-splitting commotion.

"Samantha Anderson!" Cowbell. Cowbell.

I followed the sounds until I spotted my statuesque friend standing high up on a chair, her equally lanky beau beside her on the rickety contraption.

"Did you have any trouble finding us?" Stewart asked, trying to appear serious when you just knew he was laughing on the inside. Shannon's main squeeze was one of a kind. There were nerds, and then there was Stewart – their intergalactic commanding officer. Standing six foot three and weighing in at a breezy one hundred and fifty five pounds, his pale body was see-through in certain light, and if not anchored down, Stew could easily be blown to sea by a gusty wind.

"Were we loud enough?" Shannon asked, a smirk of innocence stamped upon her face.

"Yes, thank you. I think your cowbells may have disrupted the gray whale migration along the coast."

"Eh." Shannon waved dismissively as she climbed down from the chair and hugged me. "They're off the extinction list. If they swim around in circles for a few hours, it's a small price to pay for your utter joy."

"Such pleasure," I agreed with a wry smile.

"I don't think she's a*moo*sed." Stew snorted at his own wit. Oh, how he loved puns! and, someday, maybe I would too – in my late seventies.

Still, I laughed. Nothing, not even puns, could ruin this day for me...

"Congratulations, Sam. I'm so proud of you."

Except for him. I froze. What was he doing here? Slowly I turned, hoping he had a voice twin or something but, nope, there he was – my ex. Taking a very close second behind my mother of people I did not want to see, Preston was not a welcome sight. This was *my* day, not his to ruin. And, of course, he had to be standing before me all gorgeous and looking like he'd just stepped out of a J. Crew ad. With a winning smile and the Heisman trophy of all flower bouquets bundled in his arms, Preston was the upgraded package that women – most women – lusted after the world over.

"Hi, Preston," I greeted him with a forced smile. "What are you doing here? Do you know someone graduating today?"

Yes, I knew it was a long shot, but I was still holding out hope that he'd simply stumbled upon me by accident while searching for the true recipient of the oversized flowery casket spray.

He chuckled as if I'd made a funny. That told me all I needed to know. Despite the beatdown I'd delivered him a couple of weeks ago, Preston was back for round two.

"What do you think, Sam? Of course I'm here for you."

And suddenly, the flowers were shoved into my arms – all eight hundred pounds of them – and I was struggling under their weight.

"Thank you, they're beautiful," I said, trying to juggle the arrangement as Preston leaned in for a hug. My eyes connected with Shannon's. She was standing directly behind Preston and was dramatically mimicking an asthma attack.

"I'm surprised to see you here," I said as we stepped apart.

And truly I was. I thought I'd been pretty clear that we were no longer a couple, but lo and behold here he was again. I knew Preston was no quitter, but I didn't think he was a glutton for punishment either. Besides, he had a line of women waiting in the wings. What did he need with me?

"I know, and I'm sure you're devising some exit strategy in your head as we speak, but you need to hear me out, Sam. I made a mistake. I know that now, and I'm ready to do anything necessary to win you back."

I glanced around at all the interested faces. Even some strangers in the aisle behind seemed overly invested in our conversation. I shoved the blooms into Stewart's hands and grabbed Preston by the arm to lead him away.

"Um, Samantha," Stewart called to me. "Maybe this is a good time to tell you I'm allergic to absolutely every flower in this arrangement."

Steering Preston away from the crowd, I didn't stop until I found a spot where we could speak in private. "Thank you so much for coming. I really appreciate you thinking of me today. But I need you to know – it's over."

"I heard you the first time. I just don't accept it. When you love someone, Sam, you fight for them."

"Like you fought for me? With your family?"

"I was working on them. They were warming to you."

"Preston." I held my hand up to interrupt his make-believe retelling of the events leading up to our split. "Your mother invited everyone but me on a trip to the Bahamas. Hell, even your brother's fuck buddy was summoned – of course her daddy owns a Fortune 500 company, so she can be forgiven for being loosey-goosy with her morals."

"There's no reason to hash over the same details. Yes, I admit it. That was bad. I shouldn't have gone. I understand that now. It was just that I was getting pressure from you and I was getting pressure from them. I chose wrong, and I've apologized a thousand times."

He wasn't lying about that. Preston had felt guilty… after the fact. But I'd seen the Instagram pics he'd been tagged in. He wasn't sorry when he was drinking a Bahama

Mama on the beach, and, try as I might, I couldn't get the image of his smiling face out of my mind. Preston might be sorry now, but he hadn't fought for me when it counted, and that was where I drew the line in the sand.

Preston grasped my arms and drew me in. I blinked up at him, his face blinding me. *Oh, Preston. Why do you have to be so beautiful?* It made what I was about to do all the more difficult. I should have shut him down that very first day I met him at the beach. I was the surf instructor and he the unsteady pupil. Try as I might, I never did manage to get him to his feet. Preston was accustomed to winning quickly, and when it became apparent he'd have to work hard for every ounce of skill surfing demanded, he gave up – on surfing, that is, not me.

He'd pursued me hard, I'll give him that. Like a whittler, he'd chipped away at my resistance until I finally agreed to a date. And really, why wouldn't I? On paper, Preston was the perfect guy – a first place trophy. Five years my senior, he'd had the mature stability I was looking for. Handsome, wealthy, and a real go-getter, Preston was a rising star in his father's freight trucking business. He was going places, albeit with a little help from his friend named nepotism. Still, life with him promised to be steady and fulfilling – and boring.

But it was his mother's icky obsession with her first-born child that became the spur that split us apart. The jabs started upon first introduction, when Preston's injection-filled mother looked me up and down and asked if I'd had a nose job. When I replied 'no,' she'd patted my hand and said she'd give me the name of her surgeon. And the pin-prink insults continued unchecked. His mother had made it clear where I stood, and that was just behind the cat named Swanky who was deemed too homely to be included in the family Christmas cards.

I was never sure exactly why she'd thought me unworthy, but I assumed it had something to do with my lower social class. They were high society, beacons of the community with money to waste. I was a poor college student who drove a rusty old pickup truck. Let's put it this way: if we'd been on the *Titanic*, I would have been the throwaway character from the lower deck dangling off the side of the ship as it sank, while Preston and his family would have been safely snuggled under blankets on a lifeboat while his mother defended her brood by knocking stragglers off the side of the raft with an oar.

I grabbed his hand, not wanting him to suffer needlessly. I'd cared for him; just not enough. "It's not just your mother. You and me, I'm just not feeling it. You're an amazing guy, Pres, and you're going to make some girl very happy. It just won't be me."

"You're not feeling it?" His jaw twitched as he processed my words. "Yeah, well, you never really tried, did you?"

"What's that supposed to mean?"

"It means sometimes you're so cold. You're afraid to get close to people. I get that, but Sam? If you're not careful, you'll end up just like her."

I froze. Like her? No way could he be speaking of my mother. As far as he knew, she was dead. That's what I'd told him, anyway. But clearly, from the expression on his face, he knew more than he had let on. And then it hit me.

"You had me investigated?" I whispered, shock spreading through me at lightning speed. Jumping to that conclusion wasn't so farfetched, considering his family used private investigators in the get-to-know-you phase of any business transaction. It made sense they'd employ the same tactics on their soulmates.

He didn't reply, nor did he blink. The bastard.

"You... had... me... investigated." I repeated each word as if it were its own agonizing sentence.

He shook his head. "Not me."

My eyes narrowed in on Preston. Of course it wasn't him. This reeked of his meddling mother. I'd never wanted to maim someone as much as I wanted to maim that woman. How dare she dig into my past? That was mine, no one else's. At least now I knew why she wouldn't invite me into her stinkin' lifeboat. Who wanted to save the crazy lady's daughter?

"Sam, I get why you have trust issues and why you want to push people away – why you don't want kids."

I startled at that. "I never said I didn't want kids."

"Yes, you did. I asked you once what you felt about having children, and you told me you didn't want them."

Ah, okay, he was right. I had said that; but only because I thought *he* wanted them, and I was grappling for ways to make him less interested in me. I figured telling a family-oriented guy like Preston I didn't want kids would be the kiss of death.

He grabbed my hands. "But it's okay because I don't want them either."

Well, shit, that backfired on me.

"Look, Preston, I don't see why kids have anything to do with it, but I've never ruled them out."

"Maybe you should."

"What does that mean?"

"Mental illness runs in your family, Sam. It's not just your mom. Your grandmother was institutionalized repeatedly, as were two of her four siblings. And your brother..."

Why would he bring Sullivan into this? A tremble set my body in motion. Preston grabbed my arm to steady me.

"Look, I'm not trying to hurt you. I love you. And I know you aren't ill. I think maybe you've been able to ward it off by being in the water – surfing – and that's great, but it doesn't mean your children will be as lucky."

Preston was dropping one bomb after another. Did he not see that he was obliterating me? I fought back with the last of my strength. "There is no science behind that. No one can say for sure that mental illness is genetic."

"And no one can say that it's not. I'm not trying to knock you down. I'm trying to show you that we have the same goals and could have an amazing life together, just you and me." His eyes never left mine. "Babe, listen. Remember when I told you I fought cancer when I was younger? Well, the drugs rendered me infertile. It's … well, that's a deal breaker for most women."

My bottom lip began to quiver as the full scope of his words hit me. It was a deal breaker for normal, whole women, he should have said.

"Anyway, I can't have kids, and you…"

"Shouldn't have them." I whispered the conclusion to his statement. The happy bubble I'd existed in for the past few years had just burst. Preston, armed with my sordid family history, had just destroyed my future.

CHAPTER TWENTY-THREE

KEITH

Above The Haze

My eyes were open but unfocused. I existed in a fog. Where the hell was I? What had I done? And why did my bones feel so heavy? It hit me then: I'd been drugged. Wracking my brain, I tried to recall taking something that would make me feel this way, but I only had faint memories of the night before – and the woman from the bar. Oh, shit, what had she done to me? I remembered following her to her car. I remembered the party. I remembered the sex.

And then I remembered where I was supposed to be – on tour. With Jake. Oh, shit. Oh, no. My first chance had already been spent. I had to get back to him before he figured out I was gone… before his manager fired me for breaking the contract. But the more I fought to remember, the more I wished I hadn't bothered, because as the previous night spun into focus, I knew I'd fucked up royally.

Anxiously attempting to blink the haze from my eyes, the only thing I seemed to be able to make out was sterile whiteness and bags of liquid dangling from a hook. Goddammit! I was in a hospital. If they found out where I'd been and why, no amount of groveling was going to save me. But how was I supposed to get out of here when I was tethered to machines? Desperate times called for desperate measures, and I yanked on the tubing holding me prisoner. It was then I felt fingers grip my forearm and I jolted back, attacking like a cornered animal. More hands held me down. Whoever was with me in this drug-induced fog had better back the hell up.

"It's okay, Keith. Relax. It's an IV. If you pull on it, they'll restrain you."

Mom? What the hell was she doing here? We were in Massachusetts, right? How had she gotten here overnight? Was I hallucinating? Now clearing my blurred mind became a necessity. Either I'd fallen down a fucking rabbit hole or my mother happened to have a few extra thousand mileage points to burn.

As I blinked furiously, the world around me began to clear, and that's when I saw him too. *Dad?* If I was in a fantasy world, I'd done a fairly shitty job using my imagination.

"Keith, can you hear me?" My eyes shifted off the mirage of my parents and onto a man in blue scrubs who looked way too old and way too tired to not be real. But until I had proof I was in the here and now, I wasn't wasting my breath on words. So I grunted.

"I'm Dr. Hilton. You've had a rough couple of days, son. You were brought in here unresponsive. We're waiting on the toxicology reports, but based on your symptoms, we're treating this as a cocaine overdose. You arrived here tachycardic, and we couldn't get a blood pressure because you were fighting us so much. That's why you were sedated. You'll need to be monitored here at the hospital for a few days until your renal function returns to normal."

'Overdose' was the last thing I heard before conveniently tuning him out. I didn't need to hear the specifics; I was sure they would be played on repeat for a long time to come. My parents weren't an illusion. They were in Massachusetts because of me. I'd summoned them here through my sheer stupidity.

Everything came flooding back to me now. It had been an overnight in Springfield, and after arranging a 'fan encounter' for Jake, I retired to my hotel room. Yogis – our code word for casual sex – had become a regular thing. Not that it bothered me. Good for him. It was just that his extracurricular activities left me with more time on my hands and no good intentions to go with them. I passed the stretches with my own Yogis, and while that took the edge off, it was never quite enough to satisfy the itch.

That night, as with most nights, I'd hit the bar where I could drink in peace. But, of course, there was never peace. Scouting ants were always on the lookout for crumbs, and once spotted, reinforcements were called in. Chantal was her name, or at least that's what she claimed. She was gorgeous and exotic and persuasive, and I was the drunken sod with a wad of cash in hand and a seriously weakened resolve. Before I knew it, she'd lured me in with the heat of her touch and the promise of pharmaceutical pleasures. I was her crumb, and at that moment, I'd have followed her anywhere.

And I did.

As the shame settled in, I turned away from the doctor only to make direct eye contact with my little brother. He was standing near the exit as if he were prepared to bolt at a moment's notice. I didn't blame him. If I could just get this IV out of my hand, I'd escape with him.

My father swatted my fingers away from the tape and tubing. "Leave it!"

I kept my eyes trained on Jake. He didn't look as pissed as my father sounded, and that was a good thing. Maybe I still had a chance to make this right.

"I'm sorry," I said, the words scratching against my raw throat. "Don't give up on me. Just give me a day and I'll be as good as new. I promise you this will never happen again."

He shook his head, diverting his eyes.

Suddenly it felt like I was drowning in a sea of disappointment. Everywhere I turned, a wall of water threatened to submerge me.

Demanding his attention, I raised my voice. "Jake! Do you hear me?"

"Quiet. I hear you." The first traces of irritation passed over his face. "I gave you a chance, Keith. That was my fault. And now my hands are tied."

His hands were tied? What the hell did that mean? Had I just been fired?

"Who made you judge, jury, and executioner?"

"You signed an agreement," he continued, justifying his abandonment with clear-cut facts.

"So what? You and I both know who runs this show. You have the final say. You can rip up the agreement if you want to."

He and I stared at one another, but instead of folding to my will, as was typical in our relationship, Jake stood his ground, his resolve strengthening with each piercing glare.

Narrowing his eyes, he said, "Yeah, well, I don't want to."

It was as if my last safe passage had just been sealed shut. Jake, the brother who'd always had my back, had turned his on me.

That was all I needed to hear for the vitriol to spew forth. "So this is how it's going down? You're just going to throw me out?"

"Don't put this on me! I'm not the one who chose to get shit-faced. I'm not the one police found face down in vomit. You did this to yourself."

Of course, I knew what he said was true, but that didn't make the facts go down any smoother. I was angry, and he was my bullseye. "Fuck you, Jake! Do you have any idea what I gave up for you?"

"What did you give up, Keith? A delivery boy job? I'm so sorry for your loss."

"No, asshole. I gave up my girl for you."

Silence descended upon us. Every person in the room shifted uncomfortably. I'd gone too far. I hadn't lost Sam because of Jake. I'd lost her because of what happened to him. There was a difference. A big one.

"Keith." Mom broke the awkward pause. "You disappeared after the Springfield concert – that was two days ago."

I shook my head as the words sank in. *Two days?*

"The police have been looking for you," Dad continued. "Mom and I got here yesterday. Do you have any idea what it did to us to have another son missing? A maid found you this morning, unconscious in some sketchy downtown motel."

I glanced around the room at my morose audience, all nodding in unison. Even the doctor's head bobbed up and down, as if he too had a stake in my humiliation.

"You could have died, Keith. You almost did. My god, what were you thinking?"

Nothing. I'd thrown my life and my future away for nothing! Now I'd never get Sam back. Angry tears welled up but I refused them passage.

"Do you think I like being this way?" I growled, gripping the railing so tightly that my knuckles blanched white. "Self destruction is wired into me. I can't stop it. I hate living this way!"

"Good," Dad replied, refusing to allow me to wallow in self-pity. "It'll make this next part a whole lot easier to swallow. As soon as you're released, you're going into a ten-week drug rehabilitation facility."

Great! Now that we weren't poor, my parents weren't reduced to bargain basement treatment options. I slumped back against the pillow, defeated. I'd do their rehab, sure. It was to be expected after what I'd put them through, but I knew what they didn't – that it would never work.

"I'm not saying I won't go, but what's the point? As soon as I'm released, I'll be right back at it. Face it, I'm too far gone."

"No." Jake stepped forward. His eyes bore into mine. "You're not. Trust me when I say no one is ever too far gone."

Doodling on my notepad, I tried to ignore the conversations going on around me. Two weeks out of detox, these mandatory group therapy sessions were my least favorite parts of the treatment. Not only did I have to suffer through the sob stories of my fellow tweakers, but I was expected to share in the process. Problem was, I had nothing to say. This wasn't some life-changing experience for me; it was punishment for a life squandered. I carried through the days with the jaded belief that I couldn't be cured, so all the pomp and circumstance was just make believe to me.

Determined to keep my issues to myself, I played along, focusing solely on the prize – going home. Pretending to be someone I wasn't became a little more difficult when a staff member let my last name slip, and suddenly I was beating the horny rehab girls off with towels. Oh, wouldn't that just be the icing on the cake if I came home with a druggie girlfriend? How proud would that make the parental units?

As those around me actively participated in the group setting, I jotted down my fake feelings. I was several days behind in my journal and I didn't want to get caught with empty pages, so I stole lines from Jake's songs and used kindergarten-sized letters to give the appearance of quantity.

"Keith, what about you?"

I jerked my head up and looked toward the source of the voice – the group leader. She was a young woman no older than myself, but the way she carried herself, with intellect and humility, told me age was where our similarities ended.

Clearing my voice, I asked, "Sorry. Could you repeat the question?"

"Sure. We were just discussing a defining moment in your life that triggered you to want to self medicate with drugs."

My fellow junkies eyed me hungrily, no doubt salivating at the chance to get the inside scoop on my notorious family. I struggled to mask my irritation. What did this woman want from me? I was showing up like a good boy and filling my notepad with someone else's feelings, but I'd be damned if I was going to air my dirty laundry in front of a bunch of strangers.

"I think we all know *his* defining moment," the guy to my left chimed in.

"Cory," Ms. Marshall corrected. "Remember the rules."

"What? It's not like it's a big secret what happened to his brother. That shit would mess anyone up."

Clenching my teeth, I bristled at the assumption that Jake's drama was responsible for my downfall. It wasn't. I'd seen the same reaction in my last outpatient rehabilitation therapy. I was basically forgiven for being a screw up because Jake's kidnapping had messed with my head. Why was it that siblings of kidnap victims got a bad rap? There was that pity thing involved, and people viewed us as a damaged lot by association alone. I'll admit, Jake's kidnapping did have a profound affect on my life, but that wasn't why I became a drug addict. I had no one to blame but myself, so why was I continually being forgiven?

Maybe… maybe if I faced the 'why' of my descent into drug abuse I could finally break the chains that bound me to this life. At the last rehab, when I was twenty-one, I'd sat back, half-listening, considering myself somehow above the other losers. I hadn't used the therapy as it was intended, and so I got nothing from it. I'd never taken the time to really evaluate myself and make the necessary changes. And look where it got me – right back where I started.

If I had any hope of turning this around, I had to face some hard truths… and they weren't about Jake and his trauma, they were about me and my low self-esteem. There was no smoking gun that made me who I was. There was no scandalous crime. It didn't always need to be some life-changing event that rewired one's brain. Sometimes it was simply small irritants that, left unchecked, grew into cancerous tumors. That's what had happened to me. I'd allowed life's little injustices to pull me down and make me feel less worthy.

The group leader warned the dude beside me before giving me an out. "I'm sorry for Cory's outburst, Keith. Of course, it's up to you what you decide to share with the group. Maybe next session. Eva, why don't you go next?"

"Actually…" I shut my notepad and glanced around the room. If they wanted a story out of me, I'd give them one, but it wouldn't be anything like they were expecting. "I want to share."

"Oh, that's excellent." She brightened, and I swear I saw everyone in the room sit up a little straighter. "Go on."

"Okay, so, I know what you're all thinking – that I'm here today because I couldn't cope with what happened to my family. And while it's true that event took my drug use to whole new levels, it's not the reason I started abusing them in the first place."

I could almost see Ms. Marshall taking mental notes.

"My defining moment goes all the way back to when I was five years old and playing in my first T-ball game. My half-brother Mitch, who was eight at the time, was playing on the adjacent field. I got up to bat, stood at that T, and whacked the shit out of that ball – hit it all the way to the outfield. It was the greatest triumph of my little life. As I was running the bases, I heard my father cheering from the sideline. Oh, man, you can't believe the pride I felt in that moment – my first time up to bat and I hit a goddamn homerun. I looked back to wave at my father with the biggest smile I think my face had ever produced. It was then that I saw his body was turned away facing the other field. He wasn't cheering for my homerun. He was cheering for Mitch."

CHAPTER TWENTY-FOUR

KEITH

Color-Coded

All I wanted to do the day I left rehab was go to some rundown motel and sleep. Lie low for a while. Being by myself while I readjusted to a new, clean way of living sounded pretty damn nice. But I knew what needed to be done, and putting it off would only delay the inevitable. So after getting picked up and driven home, I slipped out when my parental wardens weren't watching and began the trip to Arizona, where I was determined to right the biggest wrong of my life.

Driving through the night, I stopped only for gas and at a rest stop for a few of hours of sleep before continuing on my journey. It was 9:00 am when I pulled up to a townhouse on a tree-lined street. The anxious pounding in my chest kept me glued to my seat as I took in the place my brother called home. The bushes were trimmed to perfection, and colorful blooms were strategically placed in flowerbeds around the entryway to the front door. Everything was so orderly and fresh, like the man himself.

Those familiar pangs of jealously crept through me like a poisonous spider. But instead of gathering the eight-legged creature in a cup and taking it outside to live another day, I squashed the shit out of the black widow before it could strike me down first. There was no more room for negativity in my life. Today I would wipe the slate clean. It didn't matter if Mitch forgave me. All that mattered was that I finally manned up and apologized to my brother for the years of contempt I'd directed his way.

And that's why I continued knocking after the first round didn't produce any results. The fact that his truck was parked in the driveway inspired me to keep thumping my knuckles on his door. I was on round three of repetitive knocking when I finally heard movement on the other side, followed by what I was sure would be an eyeball peering at me through the peephole.

The door suddenly swung open and Mitch stood before me, bare-chested and barefoot in only a pair of sweats. It was clear by his sleepy eyes that he'd just stumbled out of bed. "Keith?"

"Hey, sorry," I replied, taking in his beefcake physique and smashing the imaginary spider threatening to crawl up my spine. "Did I wake you up?"

"I…" Mitch ran his fingers through his neatly trimmed brown hair, the look of surprise almost comical if it didn't reflect so poorly on me. "What are you doing here? I thought you were…"

"In rehab?" I finished his sentence before extending a full set of spirit fingers and exclaiming, "All done. Surprise."

Mitch's shocked expression didn't fade as he asked, "Is everything all right? Dad?"

I could see that his thought process was not on par with mine. For me to show up unannounced in his life, of course he'd be thinking the worst. "He's fine, Mitch. Everything's fine. I came to see you."

Because we weren't the type of brothers to show up unannounced at each other's doors, it took some time for Mitch to allow my words to sink in. I shifted back and forth while I waited. But once an uncomfortable amount of time had passed, I finally broke the silence. "Can I come in?"

"Oh, shit, yeah. I'm sorry." He stepped back, opening the door wider. "Come in."

Stepping over the threshold into his home, I allowed my eyes to wander. Everything was so neat and tidy, and he seemed to have a thing for organization. A long bookshelf was divided into cubbies, and three quarters of them held labeled storage and file boxes as well as color-coded pull out bins. And it was spotless. Not a thing out of place. Even the decorative pillows were all resting at 90-degree angles with the required 'V' smacked into the middle. Damn. This guy liked order in the house. Unlike me, he clearly didn't spend half the day searching for his keys.

Neither of us spoke past the customary greeting, and it was awkward enough that it began to feel a little like hugging a friend goodbye in a restaurant only to realize you are both going in the same direction.

"So, um… nice flowers outside," I said, scrapping my first idea of complimenting him on his organizational skills for fear he might want to share the details. "I didn't know you counted a green thumb among your many talents."

"I don't. My girlfriend does – she's the botanist."

"Really? Cool. Is that like a flower scientist?"

His eyes widened before he smiled. "I was…um… kidding. Kate's a business major, but she's the one with the green thumb, not me."

"Ah." I smiled back. "Sometimes you need to spell things out for me."

He nodded, amused. "I remember."

"Well, more power to her. I can't keep anything alive. Emma bought me a cactus once that only needed to be watered every three weeks. It was dead by week four. God help my future children."

"You and me both." Mitch laughed. "When I was a kid, I won a goldfish at a carnival and put it out on the back porch because I thought, you know, it might like to get some fresh air. Let's just say, the neighbor cat had a nice snack."

I chuckled, sliding down onto the sofa with the perfectly fluffed pillows.

He took a seat in the chair opposite me. "So do you want to tell me why you're here?"

Our eyes connected. "I think you know why."

"No, Keith. We haven't spoken in years, and then all of a sudden, you wake me from a dead sleep and want to talk about my girlfriend's flowers."

"The flowers were just a filler."

"Yeah, I got that." Mitch trapped me in his leading man stare. "Keith, straight up. What are you doing in my living room?"

"I'm here to apologize."

He just gaped at me. You would have thought I'd told him I didn't recycle my plastics. "Okay… for what?"

"For everything. Our whole lives. Every wrong I've ever done to you. I want you to know, Mitch, I'm so damn sorry. I really, truly am."

I stopped talking then, allowing him to chew over my words. And chew he did. I was pretty sure he was playing over every slight I'd ever perpetrated against him, big and small. It took my brother a surprisingly long time before he had a response for me.

"Even the time you dipped my carrot sticks in Orajel and caused my lips to go numb?" he asked, attempting to suppress a smile.

"Yes, even then." I laughed.

"Or the time you hardboiled all my eggs and put them back in the container?"

"Actually, I stand by that one. I ate deviled eggs for a week. They were delicious."

We laughed together, easing the tension between us.

"You were such a shithead."

"I know." I caught his eye. "But I think we both know the real reason I'm apologizing."

Mitch shifted in his chair and looked out the window. The pain on his face was clear to see. I'd hurt him more than maybe even I understood.

"That day at the hospital when I said you weren't Jake's real brother – that was such a shitty thing to say. It makes me sick that I was such a petty asshole."

"Yeah, you were," he said, leaning forward. "That stung like a bitch. Here's the thing, Keith: I've always felt like an imposter in your life. Do you have any idea what it was like for me to walk into your perfect little family and try to make myself relevant? And you – ah, shit, Keith, you were the best at twisting the knife in my chest."

"I know. I have no excuse. I was jealous, Mitch, pure and simple. You were perfect, and I was… not. I took out my insecurities on you. I can never take back all the horrible things I said, but I can try to make amends now. I'll do anything for you to forgive me… I mean, as long as it doesn't cost more than $84, because that's all I have left in my wallet."

His brow rose. "You're kidding, I hope."

I shook my head.

"What about in your savings account?"

"My what?" I flung my arms to the sides for affect.

"Credit cards?" He continued trying.

"Look at me, dude. Who's going to give me a line of credit?"

"Jesus, Keith. You need to stop living like a teenager."

"Don't I know? Number one on my 'to do' list is to 'Get Mitch to forgive me' and number two is 'Grow up.'"

"What's number three?"

I thought for a moment. Was Mitch trustworthy enough to reveal number three? By the earnest expression on his face, I decided he was.

"Number three. Find my own botanist."

A smile spread across his face. "Everyone needs a botanist."

"I already found her, dude. I just need to… find her again."

Rubbing the stubble on his chin, he met my eye. "Well, you can cross number one off your list. I forgive you."

"Just like that? You don't want me to grovel? Maybe… organize your pantry or wash your truck naked?"

"No. God, no. I don't want you touching anything in my house. You look like you have fleas. How long has it been since you showered?"

"Fuck you. I showered yesterday. I'm not dirty. I'm just going for the 'unkempt' vibe."

"Well, then, bravo, brother. You're killing it."

I shrugged. "Chicks dig the homeless look."

"No. No, they do not."

I smiled, buoyed by how easily he'd pardoned me yet also wise enough to know he might still be harboring some resentment.

"Why are you forgiving me so easily?" I asked.

His answer took time to formulate, but when it did, Mitch blew me away. "Because, if I'm being perfectly honest, it's not all your fault, Keith. I might have fanned the flames. See, every chance I got was spent trying to show you up. I made sure that everything you did, Dad could see me doing better. It's how I became a star athlete and an honors student. I pushed myself past every barrier, raising the bar each time, all to ensure that you, the kid who had everything, would never be better than me."

I leaned in, shocked by his admission. "You thought *I* had everything?"

"You did. Michelle has always adored you. I mean, I know she loves me in her own way, but I'm not hers. She was never vested in me like she was with her own kids. And you – you ran the pack. They all followed along like little ducklings. Jake especially. Even now, I don't think he likes me because he doesn't want to be unfaithful to you."

"Shit," I mumbled, realizing he spoke the truth. Their strained relationship had everything to do with me.

"Dad was the only one I could stand out for," Mitch continued. "So that's what I did. I stood out and made damn sure you were watching me do it. So, yeah, I twisted a few knives myself, but you just weren't bright enough to figure out what I was doing."

"Huh." I nodded, trying to process the information pinging through my brain. "Wait. Hold up… you were jealous? Of me?"

"Yes."

I let that awesome piece of reality soak in for a second before slapping his knee and laughing. "Well, fuck me! You petty little bitch!"

Mitch grinned, spreading his evil genius arms out to the sides.

"So then, are you saying you're not perfect after all?"

Puffing his chest out, Mitch smirked. "No. I'm perfect."

We laughed together, and an understanding passed between us. When it came right down to it, Mitch and I weren't all that different – except maybe for his chiseled good looks, bright future, and out-of-this-world organizational skills. But, you know, I could live with that. Because for the first time since we were kids, I had faith we could finally become friends.

"You wanna get some breakfast?" he asked.

"Depends. You wanna put on a shirt?"

Mitch chuckled as he stood up. "Depends. Are you buying?"

"Depends. Do you like McMuffins? 'Cuz that's all I can afford."

"I do."

"I figured you would – McMuffins are neatly stacked and organized."

"You're such a dick." He grinned and whacked me in the shoulder before heading off toward his room.

"Oh, and Mitch? I do have one more question."

He stopped, turning back and flashing me a quizzical expression.

"When there's discount day at The Container Store, do you turn that sales floor into your own personal sperm bank?"

Chapter Twenty-Five

Samantha

Unfinished Business

I jolted awake to the sounds of banging.

"Uugghh," I groaned, wrapping the pillow over my ears. Not again. With their headboard against my furthest wall, I'd thought I would be safe, but no. I just happened to be rooming with the horniest Harry Potter geeks this side of Hogwarts. Who knew the magically inclined were so prolific in the sack?

The only bright spot of being woken up on a weekend to thumping and pumping was that Stewart didn't have much staying power. Sometimes, as a way to pass the time, I even counted. Once he racked up a whole minute and thirty eight seconds. But more typically, by the time they got to the point where the headboard was bouncing against the wall, he didn't have much left in that skinny body of his.

Then came *the finish* – arguably the worst part of the uncomfortable eavesdropping forced upon me. Good god, they were like two snowy owls hooting. I half expected their Potter patronuses to shoot out of them and gallop around the house. Tightening my grip on the pillow, I cushioned my ears and hummed the theme song to *Friends*. It seemed appropriate under the circumstances. I mean, they were my friends... and roommates. But at nine o'clock on a Saturday morning, like clockwork, I hated their guts.

After I secured a job with an environmental survey firm, I took up Shannon and Stewart's offer to share a two-bedroom home only a few short miles from where I'd lived in high school. It hadn't been an easy decision, being so close to my mother again. She hadn't gone to prison, but she'd been required to undergo mandatory mental health treatment as part of her plea agreement. Auntie Kim had kept the specifics away from me, and I was glad for it. I had no desire to be part of my mother's life ever again, so what she was up to nowadays was not my concern. All I asked was not to accidentally run into her at the grocery store.

In the end, I took my friends up on the offer because it was the most fiscally responsible decision I could make. Once I saved up enough, I would find a place of my own and let the love birds fornicate in peace and harmony. And aside from their prolific love life, I really did enjoy their company. They included me in their life and never made me feel like a third wheel. If Shannon was cuddled up next to Stewart watching a movie, I was on the other side of him, resting my head on his shoulder as I shoveled popcorn into my mouth.

My besties were in love, and it was only a matter of time before Stewart got down on one knobby knee and proposed. They'd have some weird sci-fi wedding – no joke, they were already planning it – and there would be lots and lots of single tables for their scientist friends. A year or two later would come the little red-haired gingersnaps just as adorably precocious as their parents.

I was happy for Shannon. Truly, I was. But listening to her gush about her life and her future only reminded me of what I would never have. When you were born branded by Fate, there was no point in looking ahead. I'd chewed on Preston's cruel words for months, angry not only at him but at the world for strapping me to my mother's illness. But the more I thought about it, the more I realized that what Preston was saying was true. I couldn't risk passing on the disease to my own flesh and blood, much less forcing my special brand of crazy on an unsuspecting man.

Sometimes I wondered if I should've just taken Preston up on his offer. With him, I could have traveled the world, albeit in steerage when his parents were around, but at least

I would have had a good man by my side. Trouble was, I didn't love Preston anymore, and if I wanted to be totally honest with myself, I never had. Don't get me wrong, I tried – I really did – but Preston could never break into that place in my heart that was reserved for someone else.

After Shannon and Stewart's grand finale, I removed the pillow and stared at the ceiling, listening to the vibrations of my phone. Social media was blowing up, and for good reason. Today was the day we'd all been waiting for – the day the town's prodigal son returned for a benefit concert at the fairgrounds. And even though his name wasn't officially on the banner for the event, everyone knew who the surprise musician would be. Jake McKallister, the worst kept secret in the county.

Tickets were hard to come by, but luckily I had an ace in the hole by way of Shannon, one of Jake's unlikeliest of superfans. While many townsfolk followed his career, you'd have been hard-pressed to find one as committed as Shannon. She'd taken the extra creepy step of stalking him online and knowing where he was in the world at any given moment. So when the concert was announced with a mystery guest, and Shannon could pinpoint him back in town during that time, she was the first one online snapping up the tickets the minute they went on sale.

"Wake up. Wake up!" My McKallister-obsessed roommate burst through the door and into my room, instantly crawling over me like a six-foot spider.

"Go away." I shuddered. "You're covered in Stewart slime."

"Were you listening to us again?" she asked, fingers digging into my side.

"It's not listening if my ears just hear you."

"Oh, no. You were counting, weren't you?" She laughed. "How long did he last this time?"

"Forty-seven seconds."

"Huh." Shannon jutted out her bottom lip. "That long?"

We dissolved into a fit of giggles.

"I hate you both," Stewart said, apparently having been there the whole time to hear the unflattering attacks on his sexual prowess. "The thing is, Sam, you don't know what led up to those glorious forty-seven seconds. I have talents that you can't hear through the wall."

"No," Shannon replied, a mischievous smile stamped to her face. "I think Sam pretty much heard it all."

Suddenly Stewart was yanking Shannon off my bed by her legs. "Take it back."

On her way down, I grabbed my friend's arms and we played a game of tug of war with her lanky body, the three of us giggling like the dorks we were.

"Stew," I said. "I'm not sure if you're into polygamy, but once you marry Shannon, can I be like a sister-wife or something?"

Stewart slid a hand through his bowl cut, the corner of his lip hitched in a crooked grin. "I suppose I could spare forty-seven seconds for you once in a while."

"That's all I ask," I sighed, fanning myself for affect.

"Stop teasing my boyfriend." Shannon stretched her leg out and kicked me in the thigh. "You're going to give him a big head. I mean, look at her, Stew. Sam's way too hot for you."

"So are you," he replied. "But I reeled you in with my superpowers."

"Right, but we're heroes in the comic book world. Sam here, she's a real life one. Besides, she's beholden to only one man. And my bet is he'll be hanging around the stage today while his brother performs. If all goes as planned, my little sister-wife here will be getting some serious name-brand D tonight."

My eyes widened. Sure, I knew there was a good possibility Keith would be at the concert today, but it was the first time I realized Shannon was plotting something wicked. Per my request, she and I never talked about Keith. She'd brought him up plenty in the early days, but talking about him only made me sad, so I avoided the topic altogether until one day she stopped asking.

"You'd better not be thinking of doing something to get his attention."

"Me? No. That's your job."

"He probably doesn't even remember me."

Shannon rolled her eyes, knowing that statement to be as untrue as I did. No way had he forgotten me. We'd had something special – something I'd never managed to replicate with any other man I'd ever dated. So why was I fighting Shannon on this? If she had a way to get me close to my former flame, I should be jumping at the chance. But for some reason, Keith scared me now. The possibility of rejection hung heavy in the air, and after enduring Preston's proclamation, my trust in men had plummeted.

"Oh, please," Shannon scoffed. "You're a blast from the past. No way is he going to say 'no' to a visit from you."

"Unless he's married with children."

"Who gets married at twenty-four?"

"Lots of people, Shan. Not everyone has to wait on a *Star Wars* movie release schedule to get engaged and married."

"Yeah, well, if you ask me, he's too young, especially to have kids."

"Apparently you've never watched *Teen Mom*," I concluded.

"So, what's with this Keith guy, anyway? I mean aside from the fact he's the brother of Jake McKallister," Stewart asked. "I thought he was just some high school sweetheart."

"He was."

"Yes, but they never broke up," Shannon explained. "Neither of them ever got closure."

I swiveled my head in her direction, surprised by her take on things. After I'd moved away, Shannon had tried to give me updates on Jake and Keith, but I'd shut her down. In my mind, a clean break meant distancing myself from the McKallisters and the heartbreak of our sudden split. Not that that was so easy once Jake exploded onto the music scene. Suddenly Keith's surname was everywhere, making the memory of him hard to ignore. You couldn't turn the radio on without one of Jake's songs blasting from the speaker, nor could you go into a public place anywhere in the county without overhearing a discussion about the McKallister family. They were legendary in these parts, and ignoring their infamy was not an option.

Now I was wondering if forbidding all mention of him had been a mistake. Shannon was right. We'd never had closure. Could that be why I was having so much trouble committing myself to love? Maybe seeing Keith would be a good thing.

"What split you up then?" Stewart asked, swatting on the chains hanging down from my ceiling fan. His head barely cleared the rotating blades.

"A serial killer."

He stopped smacking the chains to address me directly. "So cliché, Sam. If I had a dollar for every time I've heard that excuse…"

"Oh, sorry." I laughed. "I didn't mean to bore you with my run-of-the-mill story of young love gone tragically awry."

He grinned, interested enough to press for more information. "After Jake disappeared, you never saw Keith again?"

"Only once, on the beach, the day before I left. It was awkward. Jake had escaped the week before, and Keith was struggling to keep everything together. We talked, but not in depth. I helped him gather items from the beach to share with Jake, and then we went our separate ways. I never saw him again."

"Like I said…" Shannon nodded. "Unfinished business."

"As in, *my* business, Shan, so no matchmaking and absolutely no dragging me backstage."

"Oh, please. Do I look like the kind of gal who gets summoned backstage? I'm a bleacher girl all the way. Now, listen up, Chicklet, my game plan is simple – we get you close enough to the action so you can at least get a look at the guy your seventeen-year-old mega-slut self shagged in the cab of his truck."

I gaped at her insult even as the two of us dissolved into giggles. I couldn't refute her claim. I had been a horny schoolgirl, that was for damn certain. Keith had revved my engines like no other, and to this day I still remembered every finger he'd strategically placed on my quivering body. There was no forty-seven-second sex in the Surfmobile, hell no.

"You had underage sex in his truck?" Stewart tsk tsk-ed. "And you give us crap about doing it missionary style in a comfortable queen-sized bed? Hypocrite."

Shannon smacked him. "We're lucky to be doing it at all. Sam here has options, and with any luck, she'll get to start using them tonight with the rock star's brother."

I'd be lying if I said I wasn't just a little curious about grown-up Keith. Certainly I wasn't expecting him to be an urban professional or anything, but I did hope he'd been able to pull himself together after the tragedy and make a decent life for himself. Over the years, I'd thought a lot about how he'd abandoned me and had come to the conclusion he hadn't done it to hurt me. No one knows how they'll react in a tragedy. Some seek out the comfort of a crowd, while others, like Keith – and like me – collapsed inward. I knew what it meant to implode. And I understood what it took to soar. My hope was that Keith had learned that difference too.

Maybe it was all the unanswered questions that kept him at the forefront of my mind. What if he was still a user, wandering homeless on the streets? What if he had it all together, complete with a beautiful woman by his side? What if – god, what if he were single?

"Fine, I'll play along," I huffed, pretending to be uncommitted to Shannon's plan when in reality, I was all for anything that got me a step closer to my lost love. The truth was I'd never gotten over him, nor had I been able to replicate the passion and excitement he'd brought to my life. "But don't embarrass me. No cowbells. Got it?"

"Relax. I already checked. They aren't allowed."

"Wait, why would you even think it would be a good thing to bring them to a concert?"

She shrugged. "I figured it would get his attention."

"Ah yes," Stewart smirked. "Cowbells are *moo*sic to everyone's ears."

"Oh, no." I waved my hand in his face. "You know the rules. No puns before noon."

"That's a real thing?" he asked. "I thought you were kidding."

"After the pun-streak the two of you had in our group text last month when Stew was on the airplane, yeah, I added it to the house rules. I'm not kidding. Check the chalkboard."

"You know what, Sam," he replied. "You have a lot of *baggage* to claim."

"Right?" Shannon jumped in. "She's so *Boeing*."

"I agree." He nodded. "Just *plane* exhausting!"

"Out!" I squealed, squishing the pillow back over my ears. There was only so much a girl could take.

Shannon's single-minded plan on getting us to the front of the stage had been an ambitious one. We'd made it within about fifty feet before the bodies formed a tight line of defense, blocking us from any further forward movement. With no other choice, we settled in where we stood.

"Sam?" Shannon grasped my shirt. "Look! Is that him?"

I didn't even bother to follow her finger this time as the same sentence had been repeated at least a dozen times now. Shannon had been scanning the crowds since the minute we'd arrived, convinced she'd find Keith in the crush of bodies, and even though I'd been hopeful before arriving at the fairgrounds, once I saw the crowds, I knew there was no way he and I would be reuniting.

"Over there, standing near the stage. I'm pretty sure that's him."

Her rising excitement drew my attention, and curiosity got the best of me. I glanced in the direction she was pointing. At first I didn't see what she was seeing, but then a brown-haired guy came into view, and even though I couldn't see him clearly, just like on the beach six years earlier, I knew it was him. The way his body moved with sinewy precision was the telltale sign I was looking at my former flame. I remembered the way he'd stirred in my embrace, the way my nails trailed up his back, and the way his lips pressed feather kisses into my skin. I'd known him intimately, and that wasn't something I could ever forget.

Swallowing hard, all I could do was nod in affirmation.

"Go to him," Shannon urged, pushing me forward.

Digging in, I held back shivers. "No, I can't."

"Sure you can."

This time I met her eyes and demanded her cooperation. This wasn't a game. Not to me. "No!"

"Fine." She sighed. "You leave me no choice. Stew? On your knees."

"Huh?" he replied in bewilderment but neither of us was paying him any mind.

"You wouldn't dare." I stared her down as I stepped between my best friend and her significant other.

"Watch me," she challenged, before addressing her man. "Stew!"

This time Stewart obediently dropped to his knees, allowing Shannon access to straddle his shoulders.

"What exactly are we doing here?" he asked.

"We're getting Samantha's shag buddy back."

CHAPTER TWENTY-SIX

KEITH

The Stilted Reunion

The sound of the roadie tumbling off the side of the stage drew our attention. Lassen and I were just making our way to the family area of the stadium when his body tumbled head over heels and landed in a clump by our feet.

"Dude!" I jumped to help, but he was on his feet in a flash.

"I'm okay. Happens all the time," he said, dusting himself off before hurrying away to rejoin his crew. An issue with the sound system had delayed the start of the benefit concert Jake was about to perform, and pandemonium among the crew had ensued. So frenzied was the atmosphere, Lassen had suggested an escape, and I'd taken him up on it. That stress was Kyle's problem now, although to be fair, I doubted my little brother did much more than follow Jake around like a puppy dog all day.

"Slinky is one of the new guys," Lassen announced gruffly. "I can't say exactly what he suffers from, but I'm sure it's hard to pronounce."

I let out an amused chuckle. That was Lassen – never a nice thing to say about anyone. If you had told me a year ago that I'd be palling around with the likes of this guy, I would have scoffed in your face; but times had changed, and ol' Grumpy Pants had unexpectedly become my friend. Jake had been right about Lassen. He was loyal to those he deemed worthy, and somehow, I'd made the cut.

"And yet, despite his obvious issues," I said, "the human Slinky is an improvement over me."

"How do you figure?"

"Well, he hasn't screwed himself out of a job yet."

Lassen grunted. "That's true, I suppose, but your contribution to the tour will live on forever."

"Oh, yeah? Tell me, what's my contribution again?"

"You introduced Jake to his Yogis."

I tossed my head back laughing. "Oh, shit. Yes, I did. Does he still have a steady stream of them coming and going?"

"It's stabilized. For a while there you could practically smell the syphilis."

His dry humor doubled me over. The mental image of poor Lassen banished to his camp chair outside the tour bus as Jake entertained a bevy of beautiful women was enough to keep me in stitches.

"If you tell your brother I said that…" He shook his bag of sunflower seeds. "I'll cut you off."

In my hands, I rattled an identical packet of seeds. It was like our ex-junky handshake. After I'd completed rehab nearly eight months ago, Lassen had stepped up for me in a big way, taking on the role as my AA mentor. Part of his duties, he'd claimed, was keeping me in a steady supply of sunflower seeds, his tried and true remedy for preventing a relapse. And although I'd never been a fan of the kernels myself, the dude had been sober for ten years, so who was I to question his methods? Soon I was carrying around my own emergency stash everywhere I went.

Not that I really needed it. After a rough decade of self-destruction, I'd finally made peace with the insecurities that had plagued me and was now ready for anything that came my way. It wasn't just post-rehab euphoria either. Drugs were my past, not my future. So convinced was I that not even the familiar smell of weed wafting through the stadium was enough to tempt my senses. I couldn't afford to waste any more brain cells on that stuff.

And with that in mind, I'd used the precious few I had left to earn a high school diploma. The milestone was huge for me, signaling the start of a new chapter in my life. More landmark moments followed – me enrolling in junior college. Me landing a job at a cellular store and quickly rising to the ranks of manager – not that it was much of a feat, considering the decision was between me and a greasy-haired guy with a really bad work place habit. I mean, just because your finger fits in your nose doesn't mean you should put it there.

Everything was in preparation for a future that was close enough for me to taste. If all went as planned, in a few months, Jake and I would be the proud owners of a surf and skate shop. Ever since we were kids, that had been our dream… well, that and Jake's little fantasy of becoming a rock star. And now that I was in a good place, taking business classes to supplement my education, and Jake had the overflowing capital to fund it, our vision was in reach. Finally, I was on my way to becoming someone I could be proud of.

"KEITH! KEITH MCKALLISTER!"

I spat the sunflower seeds out and looked around. All I could see were hordes of revelers packed inside the open-air stadium of the county fairgrounds. After Jake agreed to perform at the benefit concert, tickets to the event sold out within minutes, and the excitement around town was palatable. It was a chance to see their hometown boy perform, and since his fame had only intensified over the past year, this was a special happening in the community.

My name had turned into a chant.

"Who the hell is calling me?" I asked. "Literally everyone I know is backstage right now."

"Give yourself a little credit. I'm sure there's some baby mama out there you haven't accounted for."

"Says the guy with twelve kids from three women."

"Six kids."

"Interesting that you didn't correct me on the number of women. Honestly, Lassen, I don't know how you do it. I look at you and I think, 'Now that's an icky dude.'"

"Ha." As was customary, Lassen's enjoyment was abruptly cut off. Like those people who always sneezed three times, Lassen only laughed once. "Please, Keith, you're too kind."

"And I'm not even talking about your spare tires. You have a leaking problem. Like seriously, man, you need to get it checked. When you eat garlic, it oozes from your pores. I used to be able to smell you all the way back in my bunk. I swear you're the only thing standing between Jake and a pack of blood-sucking Yogi vampires. And, what's with the crumbs in your beard? Don't give me that bullshit about having something to eat if you get hungry, because I know you, Lassen, and you NEVER miss snack time."

He spit a mouthful of kernels to the ground, he tipped his upper lip the only indication he still found my judgment against him amusing, and as always, the mystery of his animal magnetism went unsolved.

My name continued to echo through the stands, and even though I assumed it to be a former fling I had no use for, curiosity got the best of me. I climbed up onto the second rung of fencing surrounding the stage and looked out over the sea of faces. The screaming grew louder and more intense as I shaded my eyes with my hand and followed the sound of my name. My eyes came to a complete stop on a woman standing heads above everyone else in the stadium. I'm not exaggerating here when I say she was a good ten feet tall.

"What the hell?" Was the woman on stilts? Did she not realize there was no more perfect way to get your ass kicked at a rock concert?

The wind picked up in that moment, and it was then I caught the bright red curls blowing in the breeze. That color. I'd only ever seen it on one other person.

My heart beat a little faster as I climbed to the third rung to get a better vantage point. I could now see the woman was not on stilts but on the shoulders of an equally tall man, and although her face was obscured by distance, I could see enough to know it was none other than…

"Shannon O'Malley?" I yelled, my voice easily soaring over the masses.

"Yes!" Her joyful screams filled the stadium as she waved. Shannon had an easy way about her that had always made me smile, and today was no exception. But she seemed in no mood for niceties, because the second she got my attention, she diverted it downward. I followed her overt gestures, but all I could see were the heads of thousands of people milling about.

And then a name floated through the fairground. "Samantha Anderson!"

It was almost as if the seas had parted and suddenly there she was, her face buried in her hands, as brown strands streaked with gold fanned out around her.

"Sam!" I screamed, not even trying to maintain a level of cool. It seemed only fitting that the only woman I'd ever loved – the one I'd been pining over for years – had come back only after I'd finally put my life back together. Sam was the prize – my chance to right the wrong and to close a wound I'd ripped open so long ago.

"SAM?" I hollered like a giddy little kid, and this time, she lifted her head. I couldn't see her eyes, but I knew she was staring back at me, and that was all the incentive I needed. I couldn't get to her fast enough.

"WAIT THERE! DON'T MOVE. I'M COMING TO YOU!"

And then I hastily scanned my surroundings. Lassen was standing there in surprise at my little chick-flick moment, a sunflower seed stuck to his drooping lip. Clearly, he was going to be of no help. My eyes continued the search. The only legitimate way out of this area was around the back and then out the left side of the stage. But that would take too long and get me even further away from her. Like Sam had taught me, the fastest way to get from point A to point B was a straight line, and I intended to honor that theory now.

Bounding off my perch, I shoved the bag of sunflower seeds into Lassen's hands and took off at a full sprint. Having worked on the tour, I knew leaping the barricade was a big no-no, and the security guards shot into action as I raced by. But I was too fast and too determined for them to stop. Profanities chased after me as I hurdled over the barrier and crash-landed into a pile of sweaty bodies. Instead of cradling my fall like what would have happened in that cheesy movie playing in my head, the extras – that is, the concertgoers – just let me drop to the ground in a heap of good intentions.

"Would it have killed you to catch me?" I complained to the crowds before leaping to my feet. Multiple bones in my body popped back into place. Yeah, that was going to smart in the morning.

An angry burly dude approached, ready and willing to ruin my romantic gesture, but if I'd learned one thing in life, it was to run the hell away from danger. And with that in mind, I darted past the strategically placed blocker and moved with purpose through the crowds. It wasn't until I was at ground level that I realized I was lost in a labyrinth of bodies and could no longer see the circus act that was Shannon and her human ladder.

"SAM!" I hollered.

And then, like honey to my ears, I heard her voice for the first time since that day on the beach when I'd walked out of her life.

"KEITH!"

With renewed vigor, I ducked, squeezed, and scurried my way through the milling factions toward the girl of my dreams. And I was getting closer until the screech of guitars put a stop to my forward motion. The first chords of Jake's song blasted through the speakers, effectively rendering me as helpless as a kid stuck in a maze.

"Sam!"

She couldn't hear me anymore. I knew that, but calling her name kept my eye on the trophy as I pushed through a crowd that had taken to jumping up and down to the beat. I wasn't sure which way I was going anymore, but I pressed on, determined. Somewhere in this mob was my future, and I would stop at nothing to get it started.

And then suddenly, behind a pack of college-aged revelers, there she was. I skidded to a halt, panting and hardly believing my eyes. Time stopped for the briefest of moments as I gaped at the woman before me. In my memory she was still a girl – young, vulnerable, and mine. I could still see Sam in there, but the years had changed her. Not only did her beauty stop me in my tracks, but the way she held herself with such poise and conviction told me all I needed to know. Unlike me, Sam hadn't wasted any time. The girl I'd left on the beach that day to fend for herself had moved forward with life, attacking it with the same commitment she'd invested in me all those years ago.

Would she be forgiving? Would she understand that my path to redemption had led me here? Or would she hold my past drug addiction against me? Sam had every reason to be angry with me. First I'd abandoned her, and then I'd never tried to find her. But if she knew the reason why, would she give me a second chance? I'd always intended to come for her, but I had to be a person she'd want back in her life. And now that I was, there was nothing to hold us back – as long as her heart had spent the years beating for me too.

Absorbing the gravity of our reunion, we were rendered speechless. The only sound penetrating our bubble was that of Shannon clapping her excitement. I would eventually acknowledge her, but right now I was a racehorse with blinders on and Sam was my finish line. I stepped forward, closing the gap between us. She swallowed hard, her lashes fluttering in that shy dance I remembered so well. And as she bit down on her lower lip, I was instantly reminded of that awkward girl from the library, the one I'd fallen hopelessly in love with. She might be an accomplished woman now, but my Sam – oh, yeah, she was still there.

"Look at you," I marveled, my greedy eyes trailing every inch of her. If Sam had a guy in her life, he would definitely not appreciate what I was thinking, but I didn't care. I wanted her, and I was done wasting time.

One more step was all it took to feel her warm breath on my skin. My fingers sank into her hair as I gripped the back of her neck and, so sure of our connection, pulled her into me. Lifting her gaze, she searched my eyes, and that's when I saw it. Against all odds and after all this time, there was still love in Sam's eyes. My lips parted. She shook. And I hovered, wanting the kiss but resisting only because once I took it, I could never have the second 'first kiss' with her ever again.

Surrounded by high-octane chaos, the world around us fell away as those precious seconds ticked by. Her trembling hands covered mine. There was no hesitation on her part. She didn't care about the meaning behind the moment. Sam was all quaking lust and dizzying passion, and I would do anything to see this desire every day for the rest of our lives. She brought my lips to hers, tenderly at first, but as if a jolt of electricity went crackling through me, I awoke. Gripping her tighter, my mouth braced against hers, moving harder, deeper, and with the urgency our years apart required. Her fingers tangled into my hair, trapping me against her hot tongue, and as it slid into my mouth, not even the mega-watt speakers could drown out the crazy loud beating of our reunited hearts.

CHAPTER TWENTY-SEVEN

SAMANTHA

Rediscovering Us

Everything fell away in that moment, as if time had sped in reverse and we were back in the Surfmobile, two kids – young, naïve, and in love – discovering each other for the first time. It felt so familiar and safe. Wild tremors surged through me, straight to the place between my legs that longed for his return. Oh, my god. How could I have forgotten what lust felt like? The yearning giddiness that swam around inside my belly like a ravenous vortex. All that time I'd wasted trying to convince myself that I felt something with other men, and I'd simply forgotten. It couldn't be forced; lust just was.

Suddenly everything made perfect sense. My mind had been made up long ago. The reason I hadn't bonded with other men wasn't because I was cold and heartless, as Preston had suggested, but because my heart had already pledged its allegiance to another. Due to circumstances beyond our control, Keith and I had been put on pause. Only now, six years later, were we finally in a place where we could push play on our relationship once more.

Hooking my arm around his neck, I gripped the back of his head and dragged him deeper into the kiss. Primal, instinctive, possessive, our tongues made a play for dominance. I moaned as his arm tightened around my back, pulling me flush against his heated body, and I knew I'd follow him anywhere he was willing to take me.

I was the one to finally break the kiss, not because I'd had my fill but because I needed to see him, touch him, experience him. Still clinging to his body, I leaned back to take him in – all of him. And what I saw sent the second wave of desire to skipping through me. Keith, bless him, he was still a looker. My eyes skimmed over that heartthrob face and I was reminded of why I'd so eagerly given myself over to him. Handsome in a bohemian sort of way, Keith wasn't classically gorgeous, like Preston, but he made up for it with a sexiness that reached up into another galaxy. I was squirming with desire for him. How stupid I'd been, thinking I could replicate him with other surfer dudes. It was like trying to pass margarine off as butter. A substitute could never measure up to the original – and Keith, with all his finger-licking goodness, was the real goddamn deal.

I allowed my fingers to wander over his tatted muscles that were showcased nicely in the form-fitting t-shirt that clung to him in all the right places. I felt like a kindergartener, finger painting on a living, breathing canvas. He was no longer the skinny guy I remembered. Adult Keith was taller and more strapping. The patches of haphazard scruff had been replaced with a closely trimmed stubble that looked downright sinful paired with the wavy hair tucked behind his ears. I noted its shorter length, hanging just past his jawline instead of all the way to his shoulders.

He was so familiar, yet at the same time, there was something different about him… something I couldn't quite put a finger on until he bowed down and dipped his head into my shoulder. Seaweed! Why didn't he smell like it? And for that matter, where were the telltale streaks of blond in his mane? There was no way to avoid the bleached hair that came with prolonged hours spent in the ocean. Could it be possible? Had the quintessential beach boy given up surfing?

Sensing the shift in my body language, Keith lifted his head and gave me a questioning look. I gently ran my hands through his hair, sad that whatever had happened in his life had taken him away from the one thing that made him feel alive. And as my fingers glided down his handsome face, they came to a stop at his collarbone where my agate necklace… was not hanging. Had he lost it? Or worse, had it meant so little to him that he'd thrown it in some drawer and forgotten about it? I had to swallow back the accusations threatening to put a damper on our reunion. Keith didn't owe me anything. The necklace had been a gift, and whether he wore it or not was his choice, not mine. Still, it felt strangely like a betrayal.

My eyes drifted back up, connecting with Keith's. He knew exactly what I was thinking, and his expression was nothing but apologetic. Whatever the reason for its absence, I felt certain Keith had been affected by the loss, and bringing it up would cast a somber cloud over this joyous moment.

"Sam, I…"

"Not now," I whispered.

Hooking my arms around his waist, I tucked into his snug embrace, enjoying the feel of his hair grazing over my neck.

Keith's low, contrite voice hummed for my ears only. "I promise it's not what you think."

"I don't care," I said, squeezing him tighter. And truly, I didn't. As long as he was happy, that was all that mattered.

"I missed you so much, babe," he whispered. "You have no idea."

With Keith, no games were required, and I felt free to tell it like it was. "I have some idea."

Tipping my chin up until we were staring into each other's eyes, he shot off a volley of questions. "Where have you been? *How* have you been? Are you happy?"

"I'm happy, but even happier now that I'm with you. And I moved back to town last year after earning a degree in marine biology."

Eyes widening, Keith took a step back. "You live *here?* In town?"

"I do."

"How… how haven't we reconnected?"

"I don't know, I surf at our spot all the time, but I've never seen you. I assumed you'd moved away."

There was no mistaking the wince that crept across his face. What was he not saying? "I'm proud of you, Sam. I knew you'd make something of yourself. You were always destined for greatness."

"Well, I wouldn't say it's greatness. I write environmental reports all day. And if you will recall, Keith, you were the one who showed me my strength. Without you – without the ocean – I never would have had the courage to pursue my dreams. You changed everything for me, and even if I uttered a thousand thank yous, it would never be enough to accurately convey my gratitude."

"It was all selfish angling, Sam. I just wanted to see you in a swimsuit."

"Oh, right, because I was such a catch back then."

"You were the most beautiful thing I'd ever seen. Still are."

A blush crept over my cheeks. "Thank you."

"No," he whispered in my ear. "Thank *you*."

"So what about you, Keith? What are you doing now? And, most importantly, why don't you smell like seaweed?"

Keith smiled, a hollow gesture. There was real pain behind the scenes, and I wanted to pull back the curtains and get immediate answers to his mystery, but I got the sense that beyond even the tragedy that had befallen his family, life had thrown some hard punches Keith's way.

"I have so much to tell you. But I can't do it here with the music and crowds. I promise you'll get your answers, though. Right now, I just want to look at you." His voice hummed a suggestive tune as he brushed his thumb over my cheek. "God, Sam, you're a knockout. How did I land a girl like you back in high school? It must have been all those prayers to the reefer gods."

"Yes." I laughed, feeling nothing but joy as my wandering hands continued to make up for lost time. "That must be it."

There was a cyclone stirring inside my gut. He was something I desperately wanted, and I wondered how long it would take us to get horizontal. My guess was before the clock struck midnight, and even that would be too long to satisfy the hunger surging just below the surface.

A high-pitched squeak caught our attention, and we both swiveled our heads in unison only to find Shannon hopping in place, a smile so wide it threatened to split her face in two. Damn, she was a good friend. In a world of cynicism and female jealousy, Shannon was celebrating my triumph right up alongside me. Sometimes I wondered if she was more than I deserved.

"Shannon!" Keith called out, opening his arm to her. "Get over here! Group hug."

As if she'd just been waiting for the invitation, Shannon squealed her way into our embrace with an enthusiasm typically reserved for the tiny organisms swimming under her microscope. Stewart stood off to the side, an awkward extra in our blockbuster movie.

"It's like high school all over again," Stewart quipped.

Keith glanced over at the lone giant waiting for an invite. "Dude, I have no idea who you are, but I'm feeling charitable, so if you need a hug, get on in here."

And then we were four. I got the distinct impression Keith instantly regretted it as Stewart, overexcited by inclusion, proved a needy addition to our circle of trust. Keith was forced to physically extract himself from Stew's loving embrace.

Once Keith had shaken himself loose, he extended a hand and properly introduced himself. "Hey, I'm Keith. Let me guess – you're Shannon's brother?"

Instead of politely correcting the mistake, Stewart snorted his amusement and went so far as to play along. "Yeah, okay, right. Yes, she's my *sister*."

Finger quotes completed the awkward exchange.

Shannon smacked him, rolling her eyes for our benefit.

"Or…uh… maybe not." Keith's brows drew together as he cast me a questioning glance. I grinned, shrugging.

"Keith," Shannon said. "This is my boyfriend, Stewart."

"Boyfriend?" Keith's eyes widened at the unbelievable news. "You're not related?"

"Nope," Stewart answered.

"Separated at birth?"

"No again."

"Distant cousins?"

"Nada."

Once Keith had run out of genetic pairings, he shrugged and gave up.

Stew, however, refused to let it go. "You're not the first person who has commented on our likeness. In fact, just last week, Shannon and I were confused for the Weasley siblings – which, by the way, is just beyond ridiculous given the fact that Shannon was clearly wearing a Hermione cloak."

It was evident by Keith's expression that he hadn't spent much time in the wizarding world. The clueless look on his face reminded me of the time I'd tried to explain to him that guerrilla warfare did not, in fact, mean that there'd been an uprising at the county zoo.

"All right, well… now that we got that out of the way…" Keith paused to raise his hand. "Who wants to go backstage?"

No more than ten minutes later, the four of us were watching the concert from the side of the stage. Keith made obtaining exclusive backstage access look easy. A few words here, a back slap there, and suddenly we were making our way past the scantily clad women crowded around the side entrance hoping for the coveted invitation that would bring them one step closer to their musical idol.

Snuggling into Keith's side, it felt like I'd never left it. "That was impressive back there. I thought scoring backstage passes was more challenging than that – like signing over your first born child or, at the very least, being on a list or something?"

"You don't need a list, Sammy, not when you've got me."

Keith spoke with the confidence of a man who was very familiar with the interworking of concert life. As if reading my mind, he nodded and confirmed what I'd been thinking.

"I worked for Jake for awhile."

Angling my head to get a better look at him, I asked, "But not anymore?"

"No." The slightest tense of his body belied his confidence. "I sort of wrote my own eviction notice."

"Uh-oh," I said, gripping his chin between my fingers and planting a smooth kiss upon his lips. "What did you do?"

Keith glanced over his shoulder surveying the area. "Let's go find someplace quiet to talk."

"At a rock concert?"

"Well, okay, quiet*er*." He ran his hand along my arm. "You think Stewart might stop hugging me long enough for us to slip away?"

Keith wasn't exaggerating. Stew really couldn't keep his hands to himself. It was like high school all over again – the geek trying to get the attention of the cool kid. Stewart took to nudging and patting and even made the misguided decision to massage Keith's shoulders.

"It's like no one ever taught him the maximum hug time rule. For guys, it's a strictly enforced three seconds. Anything over that is painfully awkward."

"He's just excited. I'm sure you're the coolest thing that's happened to him since he met Pikachu at last year's Comic Con."

Keith chuckled. "Well, then, we might want to keep him away from Jake. He's not big on the touchy-feely shit."

After letting Shannon know I'd find my own way home, I left hand in hand with Keith as he searched for that elusive quiet spot. I watched him intently, intrigued by the man he'd become. From just the snippets he'd provided, I knew he had a story to tell; how bad it would be was hard to tell. Although he certainly wasn't that goofy boy who'd condemned me for sprucing up his vocabulary all those years ago, he didn't appear to be overly damaged either.

"You up for a little hide and seek?" he asked, peeking his head around the corner before redirecting his attention to me.

Confused by the question, I stumbled on my words. "Um… I… I don't know. Is that something you like to play?"

He laughed. "I like to play it if I have Samantha Anderson with me and I need a quiet place to talk to her. So here's what's going to happen. I'm going to distract the guard, and you're going to slip into the first door on the right."

"What's the first door to the right?"

"Let's put it this way. If we let Stew inside, he'd be humping the furniture."

I gasped. "You'd better not be asking me to sneak into Jake's dressing room!"

"See, you're catching on to this game. Now, be ready. As soon as you hear the code word, bolt for the door."

"What? No," I whispered, panic beginning to rise. "What's the code word?"

With a grin, he replied, "You'll know when you hear it."

Before I could protest, Keith was gone, disappearing around the bend. With my ears peeled to the discussion he was having with the guard, I couldn't resist a peek – this was hide and seek, after all.

"So anyway," I heard Keith say. "Let me show you where I was thinking of getting a tattoo of a *platypus*."

The animal that haunted my dreams was practically hollered, leaving no doubt it was the elusive code word, and that set me in motion. I was slipping into the dressing room when I saw Keith flash his ass to the guard. "Right here on my left butt cheek."

A minute later he came strolling through the door with a satisfied smirk on his face.

"The guard wasn't the biggest fan of the idea."

"No," I laughed. "I can't imagine he would be. Come here."

Keith wasted no time. He practically swept me off my feet after bounding across the room. His enthusiasm was contagious, and the kiss that followed was just as wild. Unpredictability had always been his thing. Although while I applauded his spontaneity, sneaking into Jake McKallister's dressing room felt all kinds of risky.

"How will your brother feel about us being in here?"

"Um…you know," he replied, shrugging.

No, I didn't know, and now I had one foot pointed toward the door, ready to bolt at a moment's notice. "Well, that doesn't sound promising."

"Relax, Sam, we'll be out of here before he's done performing. Now do you want to hear my life story condensed into thirty minutes or not?"

I smiled, running my hand over his face. His humor and tell-it-like-it-is charm was what had hooked me in high school, and it was proving to be just as captivating to me as an adult.

Keith began his story the night ours had ended – the night Jake was abducted. He'd chosen to mask the pain instead of work through it with me by his side. He was remorseful. It was a decision that had changed both our lives, but had immeasurably shaped the last six years of his. And although he seemed hesitant to dive deep into a discussion about the hard years following Jake's return, he did speak freely of his descent into drugs, the withdrawals, the rehabs, and the relapses. I also got a sense of his rock bottom moment while on tour with his brother that led to him finally getting clean.

"I often wonder what my life would have been like if I'd made a different decision that night. Would I be further ahead or further behind? I think maybe I needed to go through all that to be where I am today. Even if nothing had happened to Jake and nothing had happened with your mom and we'd just gone about our lives as normal, I think I still would have found a way to screw us up somewhere else down the line. I mean, if you will recall, I was the king of bad decisions."

"Oh, yes, I recall."

The two of us smiled at the memory of his wayward self.

"I guess what I'm saying is it was only a matter of time before I did something stupid – something that would have ruined us to a point where there could be no reconciliation."

I wondered if maybe he wasn't giving himself enough credit. The boy I remembered had been committed to re-evaluating his life. But I understood his reasoning. We'd been so young back then. Even if he had chosen me the night Jake went missing, our chances of surviving the fall-out would have been slim.

"I know I don't have a lot to offer you yet, Sam, but I'm working on it. Being a drug dealer taught me I'm a good business man, so that's what I'm focusing on."

Only Keith could put a fun spin on a felony. "Maybe don't lead with that fun fact in job interviews," I teased.

He rubbed his stubble thoughtfully. "So, I should remove it from my resume? Is that what you're saying?"

"Yes," I laughed.

"Anyway, I just want you to know I don't plan to sell unlimited texting plans forever. Jake and I have a plan. As soon as I get some business classes out of the way, we're going to open that surf shop, Sam, just like I always said I would do."

It was indeed a dream he'd spoken of often. That he might realize it made my heart swell. "I'm so happy for you."

He grabbed my hands. "For us."

"Maybe we should get to know each other again before you start planning our future."

"I don't need more time to tell me what I already know." Keith gathered me in his arms, and my body melded to his.

"And just exactly what do you know, Keith McKallister?"

A sudden influx of voices outside of the dressing room drew our attention. Keith and I exchanged startled glances at the exact moment the door swung open, and Jake, drenched in an hour and twenty minutes' worth of sweat, stepped inside. We jumped to our feet and he halted in his tracks, all of us looking like we'd come upon a grizzly bear in the clearing.

Thirty minutes? Yeah, I don't think so. Why had I trusted Keith to accurately tell time when, back in high school, he'd struggled with the concept of counter clockwise? I slugged him in the arm.

"Ow." He rubbed the sore spot. "What're you hitting me for?"

I didn't answer because now I had the unenviable task of explaining myself to his rock star brother. "I can explain. It's all *his* fault." I poked Keith in the gut. "I told him no, but he wouldn't listen, and then, before I knew it, Keith was flashing his butt, and there was the platypus… it was all so disorienting."

Jake's look of bewilderment only made me talk faster, and when I was done with the apology, he raised a brow and replied, "Yeah, I can see where that might have gotten confusing."

Keith's amused chuckle was cut short by the daggers shooting from my eyes.

"What she means to say is that she's Samantha Anderson, my girlfriend from high school. You know, the one I told you about?"

Now Jake seemed more interested, less suspicious, and his gaze softened. "No shit?"

"We just found each other in the crowd. Dude, she practically fainted at my feet. It was a magical moment. She's so lucky."

Jake smiled, and for the first time, I was able to catch my breath.

"Huh." I grinned. "I remember it differently, but whatever."

"Don't worry," Jake answered. "I learned over the years to pass everything Keith says through a bullshit meter."

"Yes. I forgot those existed. Anyway, I'm happy to finally meet you, Jake."

"You too, Samantha."

"Actually, everyone just calls me Sam."

Keith swung his head around, gaping. "Since when?"

"Well." I paused. "Since you."

Ah, so smug Keith was, and that grin of his nearly irresistible. "See, Jake, this is how you make an impression on a girl."

"Yes Jake," I added helpfully. "Make sure you completely disregard her request to have her name pronounced properly so often that the girl finally just gives in."

Jake glanced between us. "Why do I feel like I'm no longer a part of this conversation?"

He was right. Our flirting had effectively forced him into the background.

"Anyway, you guys are free to... uh... to do whatever this is..." Jake made a wide sweeping gesture with his hand. "But I've got to sign autographs in twenty minutes, so I'm off to the shower. Nice meeting you, Sam."

And without waiting to make it to the bathroom, Jake pulled off his drenched shirt and tossed it to the floor. My eyes immediately zeroed in on his bare torso because there, hanging around his neck, was my grandfather's blue-laced stone.

CHAPTER TWENTY-EIGHT

KEITH

Enough

The second Jake pulled his shirt off I was in full defensive mode, waving my hand rapidly under my neck in a frantic aggressive cease-and-desist motion. Sam's eyes were as wide as bubbles, but she wisely kept her mouth from popping open until Jake had safely disappeared into the bathroom.

"Um… so… about that," I said, my finger over my lips as I kept my voice at a hush.

"Yes," she answered, trying but failing to keep a hushed tone as well. "About *that.* You think maybe you could have warned me first?"

"Jesus, Sam, where'd you learn to whisper – inside a helicopter?"

"Excuse me if I'm a little stunned to see my grandfather's stone around a rock star's neck."

"No. It's around my brother's neck."

That stopped Sam in her tracks, and I took the following seconds of blessed silence to explain myself. "I was going to tell you, but I only had thirty minutes."

"Try fifteen," she answered, her eyes going into the centrifugal stage of rolling. "I see your math reasoning skills haven't improved."

"Nor has your tact."

She met my eye and smiled. God, I'd almost forgotten how much I missed her. Sam never let me get away with anything, and it was her checks and balances that had kept me honest in high school – until I'd gone and ruined it all. But there was no reason to rehash the past, not when I had my future within arm's length. I closed the distance, grabbed her around the middle, and commenced laying waste to her long-untouched skin. She giggled as my fingers dug in. After a moment of reckless abandon, Sam knocked my hands away and arranged her shirt back into place.

"He's in the bathroom," she whispered, *finally*.

"Babe, if he couldn't hear you during the Apache helicopter phase of our conversation, I doubt he'll hear a little innocent tickling."

More eye rolls. I was already getting under her skin. "Can I just say thanks for making it weird between your brother and me? Jake probably hates me now."

"I wouldn't say hate." I grinned, now just trying to nettle her so I could continue seeing the irritated little crinkled of her nose. "He probably just mildly dislikes you."

"You think this is funny? We're trespassing. I can't afford to be arrested, Keith."

"I know. What would the dolphins think?"

A slow smile hitched one corner of her lips. "The dolphins work in another department."

"See? No harm, no foul. And trust me, Jake doesn't hate or even mildly dislike you."

"And you know this *how*?"

"It's a brother's bond, Sam. He wouldn't hate you because he knows how important you are to me. And stop worrying. That was Jake's 'like' face."

Sam wasn't convinced.

I reached for her hand. "Let's get out of here."

She didn't budge.

I eyeballed her. "Just take it, Sam. We both know you're coming with me."

"You're very confident for a guy I'm still considering kicking in the nuts."

Feisty Sam was my favorite kind. I thrust my hand out again and gave it an impatient wave. She sighed before grabbing it.

"Thank you." I smirked.

"You're welcome," she said, and then paused before adding, "… asshole."

We walked hand in hand as if it were the most natural thing in the world. The closeness was just there. Was it really possible to pick up where we left off? The way I was feeling now, I was pretty sure it was.

"Where are we going?" she asked, as we exited the backstage area.

"To your place."

"To *my* place? Why can't we go to your place?"

"Because my place comes with mandatory meal time, regular showers, and curfews – but I don't have to be home until 11:00 pm, so we're good."

Those eyes of hers were popping once more. "You still live with your parents?"

"Not still… I moved back in after rehab. And I was kidding about the curfew."

"I got that. What about meal time and showers?"

"No. My mom's militant about that shit."

Sam shook her head, fake cringing. "You know, Keith, on paper, you don't look like much of a catch."

I nodded, laughing. "I'm not much of a catch *off* paper either."

Conversation halted as we wove our way through the parking lot. I sensed a change in her demeanor, and as I glanced down at her, I noticed the tears glistening in her eyes. Now that we weren't volleying quips back and forth, Sam had the time to reflect on my betrayal. Dammit, an explanation about her necklace should have been the first thing out of my mouth. I knew she'd noticed it was missing out in the crowd when we first kissed, but I'd ambushed her with it when Jake unknowingly flashed her the evidence.

"You all right?" I asked, kissing the top of her head.

Sam's bottom lip quivered, and she put on a brave face to nod her reply.

I held open the car door for her but she didn't get in. My thumb swiped across the trail of tears on her cheek.

"Look, Sam, let me explain…"

"You gave my grandfather's stone to your brother?" she asked. Instead of being filled with anger, though, her voice was shaky and steeped in disbelief, as if the gravity of what I'd done was finally sinking in.

"I… it's complicated."

Sam laid her head against my chest and rewarded me with a warm, rich embrace. The sudden turn of events confused me, and I scrambled to catch up.

"You're not mad?"

"No. I'm crying because I'm touched. I'm happy. I'm… I don't know what I am. But I think what you did was a beautiful thing."

Relief swept through me. Years ago when I'd gifted it to Jake, I'd felt fairly certain she would approve, seeing that she'd done the same for her brother. But the necklace had been intended for me, so there'd always been that nagging doubt. My hands wrapped around her waist and I pulled her in tight. "As soon as I read your letter, I put the necklace on. I wore it proudly; I did. And strangely enough, I did feel its power. I credit it with helping me through withdrawal. There were times I didn't think I'd make it another second without a hit, but then I rubbed the stone like you used to do, and I swear it eased me through the rough patches. But…"

A sudden wave of emotion strangled my speech, just thinking about the time I'd found Jake in the closet with a baseball bat in hand, waiting for the ghost of his tormenter to come and finish him off. How could I not do everything in my power to help my little brother through? And so I gifted him the last thing I had left of my girl, telling him a pile of lies in an effort to make him believe the necklace had some special powers.

"But what?" she whispered, her grip on me tighter.

"But Jake needed it more than I did. It's not the stone itself that holds the power. It's the belief in it that does. You believed. I believed. I thought maybe Jake would too."

"Obviously he does if he still wears it."

"I think he does. We never talk about it. Here's the thing, Sam. He doesn't know it was yours. Jake never would have accepted it if he knew it was a gift you'd given me. That's why I silenced you back there."

"Where did you tell him it came from?"

"I told him a story about me being on the top of a cliff, flying high, inching closer to the edge. I said I was considering ending it all until I saw a flash of silver in the weeds. The sun was hitting it just right and it shone like a gift from the heavens. I told him the second I picked it up, I felt better; stronger. And once I put it on, I knew I was safe. You should have seen his eyes, Sam. He wanted to believe so bad. He needed some sort of hope to hold onto. So I took it off my neck and clasped it around his. He's worn it every day since."

She nodded, her hand grazing my skin. "Was it true?"

"Um… obviously not. You gave me the necklace."

"No, Keith, the story about you on the cliff edge."

My chest tightened as I looked away, not wanting to admit the truth. I still remembered her voice in my head, talking me off the ledge. She'd saved me that day, and no amount of physical evidence could convince me otherwise.

"Yes. That part was true."

The horror in her eyes was not lost on me. Sam knew all too well what happened to people teetering on the verge of no return. "And what made you walk away?"

I sought her out, my eyes connecting to hers in a way they'd never done with any woman before or after her. Time could not erase these feelings. I still loved her with all the intensity I'd had when I was still a screwed-up teen.

"You did, Sam."

She lay her head back against my chest, my arms wrapped around her like a shield in battle. The desire to protect her from life's tribulations was innate and stronger than any defensive weapon man could imagine. This woman had walked this world without my steely protection long enough, and now it was time for her to rest, knowing I had her back. And her front and every other part of her that required safeguarding.

The recognition that she was safe and loved was realized in every action she took while entrenched in my embrace – the kisses to my neck, the lazy trails she traced on my arms, the hum of her happiness encouraging my heart to skip a few beats. Sam angled her head, eyes half open as her sweet lips strained for mine. I dropped my head, my hair falling down between us. Sam swept it aside and pressed fluttery kisses along my jaw. I brushed a mellow kiss across her cheek.

It was as if the two of us were in slow motion, bathed in soft sepia tones. There was no need to rush. No need to prove ourselves. This was why I'd battled my way back from the brink… for her. For this. Sam had always made me better. If I didn't have a reason before to be the best version of myself, I sure as hell did now.

"Keith?" she whispered, and I could feel a shiver race through her body.

I drew her in, pressing my heated skin against hers to tame her trembling. "Yeah?"

"Let me be enough for you this time."

A lump instantly formed in my throat. I hated that she felt somehow responsible when our six-year absence was all on me. I was the one who'd chosen wrong time and time again. I was the one who'd put the distance between us – the one who hadn't fought to close the widening gap. The demons I'd wrestled were mine alone, cultivated over the years by an insecurity that had clung to me like a shy toddler. Sam had been the one shining light in a life filled with self-loathing. And I'd thrown that away.

"You were always enough, Sam."

"Then why did you leave me?"

"Because *I* wasn't enough."

CHAPTER TWENTY-NINE

SAMANTHA

At Long Last

"What are you thinking?" Keith asked, as his fingers tiptoed over my breasts. Moments earlier he'd amazed me with his one–handed bra extraction method, and now I was the beneficiary of his skills with miniaturized clasps.

I was in a state of quivers as I gazed into his handsome face. Oh, I doubted he really wanted to know what I was thinking. *I love you.* Those three words weren't typically what a guy wanted to hear right out of the gate. If the goal was to keep him in my life, hell, to keep him in the same state as me, then I needed to play this smart. Be cool. No declarations of love until I had him cornered and trapped like a lovesick animal. Only then would I pounce.

Affecting my sexiest smile, I pushed his face away playfully. If I couldn't confess my true feelings, I could at least work him up into a frenzy of lust. But Keith turned the tables on me, grabbing my dismissive hand and pinning it to the bed.

"Who do you think you are?" he asked, the hum of anticipation in his voice. He was being playful, but there was something more. Keith carried himself differently than I remembered. He was stronger and more powerful. Suddenly I wondered if it would be me quivering in a corner.

"I'm the woman who's going to take you over the edge." It was the right response, judging by the guttural sound from Keith's throat as he glided his tongue through the valley between my breasts. I gasped, tangling my fingers into his hair, not letting him up until that torturous tongue was giving me a proper lashing.

"What are you thinking?" he repeated.

"I was thinking…" I paused, moaning as my own hands found the playground that was his steely abdomen, littered with dips and swells. I shuddered at the thought of those muscles working in unison to transport me into rapturous bliss. "…that I like this new you."

He listed his head, a grin sweeping across his face. "Body or soul?"

"Less talk, bud. I just want your body."

He laughed, now leaning over me and tracing wet circles over my nipples. "I like shallow Samantha."

My breath hitched as I grabbed a wad of sheets in my fingers and heaved into his touch. "Yes," I panted. "Shallow."

Grabbing the hem of his t-shirt, I pulled it up and over his head, my tongue instantly on his bare skin and exploring what was at once familiar, but also unbelievably foreign to the touch. He'd left me a boy and come home a man.

I thrilled at the taste of him. His skin, though no longer dipped in the salty ocean, still had an earthy flavor. Mixed with the sex oozing from his pores and I was tipping into stalker territory. I raked my nails over his stomach, eager to mark him as my own.

While I was preoccupied by his Adonis-like torso, Keith had taken to kissing his way along my collarbone, the soft touch of his lips flittering across my skin as if he were painting on a canvas. Heat rose up through me, and I pulled him down on top of me with a force that surprised us both. Breathy with desire, I teased out each word. "I need you."

Keith panted into my neck as my body opened to him. I knew he'd feel good. I remembered the feeling of him deep inside, pushing me to my limits. That had always been Keith, my surfer boy taking me places I'd never gone before. He'd cracked me open, body and soul. Then, when I was lying vulnerable and for the taking, he'd put me back together, piece by agonizing piece, until I was stronger and braver than before. Everything I was today, the lengths I'd come, had his handprint all over it.

"God, Sam. I can't believe we're back," he said, puffing the words out with ecstasy accentuating his words. He wanted me as much as I wanted him. It was a powerful connection, one that had tethered us through the years. I couldn't imagine ever wanting another man the way I wanted Keith. It was beyond just the physical. We were bound by something stronger.

"I never left. It's always been you." I spoke softly into his ear as I draped my legs around his waist to let him know I was here, and eager. God, how I still craved him, every punishing inch.

The weight of his body pressed me flat to the mattress, and I could feel the power of him, sending a thrill of warmth and wetness pulsing through me. Gripping his back, I marveled at the changes his body had gone through since we'd last been intimate. Keith had not only grown broader through his back and shoulders but also taller. Where we'd once been near equals in length, he now surpassed me by several inches. And those wide shoulders tapered down into a lean waist. He was Keith, yes, but this was the upgraded model. I could only imagine how many women had lain beneath him as I did now. Had any of them meant something to him?

I gasped as he entered, the thrill of him rippling through my core and radiating out to my extremities as he filled me. Pulsing to his beat, I moved with him, the two of us in perfect harmony. He swelled inside and I screamed out, not concerned about the rapt audience I was certain was on the other side of the wall. I'd gone somewhere else in my mind, the place only Keith could take me, and I didn't care who knew. I just needed more of him.

Arching my back, I met his fury, both of us grunting and groaning as if we were rutting in the wilds. Pumping faster, he dug his fingers into my hips, the pain blending into pleasure with every punishing thrust. He was reaching places inside me that had long been neglected, and my spot pulsed as it neared release. My shaky breaths combined with his throaty grunts. We'd both crossed over into another realm where pleasure ruled.

"Oh, God," I moaned, surprising myself by the speed with which I was losing control. Keith released one hand from my hip and slid it down to the place where our bodies merged as one. My body constricted, pulsing in anticipation. Keith had already groomed me. I was ready for him to take me somewhere else. His touch was barely more than a whisper. No. I needed more. Curving into him, my body pleaded for more. His fingers were teasing me, not enough to set me off but enough to keep me on the edge of ecstasy. Keith grunted loud and wild, pulling out.

"Sam." His voice was hoarse yet frenzied in its need.

I grabbed his ass, imploring for him to come back to me – to finish me off. Every nerve in my body was on high alert, quivering with the promise of what was to come. He pushed back in, the entire length of him and, at the same instant his thumb pressed deeper into my center. I shuddered, my toes curling and my head lolling back and then, against the backdrop of his unrelenting drive, I exploded into waves of euphoria. Keith silenced my cries with his mouth and I probed him deep, still riding the rapturous surge. And then he paused, every muscle in his body constricting in the seconds before he shuddered and groaned. I wrapped my arms around him, thrilling in this moment with him. This was only the beginning. I could feel it. Keith and I were back.

CHAPTER THIRTY

KEITH

Skimming The Waves

The kiss started at my lips but quickly traveled the landscape of my face. A smile crossed my lips before I even opened my eyes to a whole new day – hell, a whole new life, if she'd have me. My lids blinked open only to find beauty and happiness staring down at me. My smile widened. She brought a harmony to me that I'd nearly forgotten existed. Tangling my hands into her hair, I dragged her mouth to mine, and as the kiss built in intensity, her body, soft and firm, sank into me.

So many sleepless nights and now finally I could rest easy once more. The what-ifs were gone. Sam hadn't moved on any more than I had. All that was left now was to build a life together with marriage, a house, a dog, and eventually kids. I wanted her in my arms, on my lips, till the end of days. And I saw no reason to wait.

Breaking the kiss, I groaned. "Do you know what you do to me?"

She nestled against me, nuzzling my neck. "I make you happy."

I thought about that a second, then tilted my head to kiss her forehead. "No, you make me cheer."

I'd have pumped my fists in the air if it wouldn't have made me look like a superficial frat boy. This feeling in my chest felt like a balloon that was about to burst. That build up and excitement – I never wanted the thrill to end. And it didn't have to. Now that we were back, there was no reason to ever be apart again.

"Sam?"

"Yeah?"

"Don't freak out when I say this, but… I'm in love with you."

Sam blinked me in with her pretty brown eyes, surprise evident in her reaction. I'd laid my heart on the line, only to hear static coming from the other end.

Suddenly I felt naked and vulnerable, and the words just fell from my mouth. "The truth is, Sam, I've never stopped loving you. I tried, but it just never worked. You were always on my mind, and any time I tried to get serious with a woman, I'd compare her to you, and... well, it was doomed to fail. You're like an infection that lives inside me, and no matter what medicine I take, I can't find a cure for you."

Her nose crinkled as she considered my declaration of love, but there was no disguising the pleased smile spreading from ear to ear. "You know, Keith, you're lucky I am a biologist. Not every girl would find it flattering to be compared to bacteria."

"But the good kind of bacteria, like what's in yogurt."

"Ah." She nodded. "That's yummy."

"I'm dying here, Sam. Say something."

"Don't die," she whispered, gripping my jaw in her hand and kissing me. "You know I love you, Keith. I always have."

I let out the breath I didn't know I'd been holding. "I'm not talking old friend kind of love. I'm talking the real deal shit."

"So am I," Sam replied, raising up to place a simple, sweet kiss to my lips. "Keith, I love you – with no pesky friendship attached."

I gripped my chest, exhaling heartily enough that wispy strands of her hair blew in my wind. "Way to give me a heart attack."

"Sorry," she laughed. "You just took me by surprise. I knew how I was feeling, but I didn't expect the same from you so soon."

I ran my thumb along her cheek. "I'm ready, babe."

"For what?"

"For everything. No more stupid shit. No more wavering. I'm all in with you."

"All in?" she asked, raising a brow.

I raised my own in question.

"Come to the beach with me." Sam glided her fingers along my stomach, effectively overriding all my free will. "I want to go surfing with you."

Surfing. It had been a very long time, and I wasn't entirely certain I knew how anymore. When I was a kid, I'd been oblivious to the dangers that lurked, but now, the dark vastness of the ocean freaked me out a bit.

Sam seemed to pick up on my hesitation. "I don't know why you stopped, but I want us to be together on the water like we used to be."

For reasons I didn't understand myself, the weight of the years slammed into me with a force I hadn't expected, and my eyes swelled.

"Keith." Sam jumped to her knees, gathering me in her arms. "What's wrong?"

"Nothing," I answered, wiping away the evidence. "I have no idea where that came from. Sorry."

"Don't be. Why does the beach make you sad? You used to love it."

"I'm not sure. I used to be so carefree. Nothing scared me."

"Except sinkholes."

"Yes, except those." I had to laugh. It was as if she'd hung on my every word when we were kids. "I never considered the dangers of anything I did back then, but once my world went to shit, suddenly everything was a potential death trap. The Keith Memorial Bench didn't seem all that cool anymore.

But, it went even deeper than that. Keeping myself away from the ocean became like a self-imposed punishment. Instead of flogging myself to a bloody pulp like normal crazies, I just deprive myself of the things I love, like you and surfing, and then I tell myself that once I'm worthy, I'll get them back. But the truth is, Sam, if you hadn't found me yesterday, I don't know if I ever would have felt good enough. I don't know why I've never been able to just be happy with who I am."

"I think everyone feels that way sometimes."

"You don't."

The turmoil that passed over her face gave me a glimpse into her own crippling insecurities. "Trust me, I do. I live in fear of becoming my mother, Keith. I feel like I'm tiptoeing my way through life, afraid of waking the demon. As long as it's hibernating, though, I'm safe."

"Jesus."

"Yep. So, don't think you're special by any means, you mutant freak."

The darkness faded, and we both laughed at our shared faults. Maybe that's why we'd worked all those years ago. We were a matching pair, like Shannon and Stewart – only without all the excessive hugging. Sam and I were more like gentle ocean waves, with the occasional tsunami tossed in to make things interesting.

"I deem you worthy, Keith McKallister." She stood up, offering her hand. "Now, come surfing with me."

I could not overstate the sensual, visceral power of the ocean. To use that force to ride a fast-moving wall of water was like nothing I'd ever known on dry land. The speed. The wind in my face. Skimming the waves was like connecting to some otherworldly energy through the surfboard. Like riding a bike, muscle memory kicked in, and it was as if I'd never spent a day away from the ocean. My legs remembered exactly how to absorb a drop and to generate the lightning speed required to harness the energy for a high-g bottom turn. It was sensory overload at its finest – the roar, the colors, the taste of salt, and Sam, the most beautiful girl I'd ever known. She was focused not only on her own ride but on making mine the best it could be. If

I hadn't loved her before today, this would have sealed the deal.

"You good?" she called out to me, water dripping off her eyelashes and sparkling in the early morning sun.

"Better than good," I replied, grabbing her board and drawing her to me so I could press a wet, salty kiss to her lips. The pieces of the puzzle were falling into place. I had my health. I had my family. I had my future all lined up. And now I had my Sam. There was nothing more I could want for. An idea sparked in my head, and once it had formed, there was no taming it. Snagging a long piece of seaweed floating near my board, I twisted and braided it until it resembled a crude ring.

I took her hand in mine, and without stopping for a single outside thought, I blurted out, "Will you marry me?"

She laughed, believing my gesture to be a joke. Of course she would. Who asked a girl to marry him less than twenty-four-hours after reconnecting? A mutant freak, that's who.

I slipped the seaweed ring onto her finger.

As my intentions slowly sank in, Sam ogled at me like one of those bottom dweller fish with gigantic nighttime eyeballs. "Wait – are you serious?"

"I know what I want, and it's always been you. Marry me, Sam?"

"I… I don't know what to say. I love you, Keith. I do, but…"

"But what?"

"But I need time. That doesn't mean I don't want to marry you, it just means… ask me again once we've been together for at least a day."

I got it. Maybe it was too sudden, too shocking. Plus the ring needed a serious upgrade. My grand gesture, along with the seaweed ring, sunk to the bottom of the ocean floor.

"Hey," she said, squeezing my hand. "I love the passion behind your delivery."

I nodded, grinning. "Thank you. And, just so you know, Samantha Anderson, that isn't my last proposal. You've been warned."

Five Years Later

CHAPTER THIRTY-ONE

SAMANTHA

The Writing on the Wall

I checked the phone for the twentieth time. Still nothing. I should have gone to her doctor's office. I could have hung out in the waiting room behind a potted plant. But this wasn't my experience to share. It was Shannon and Stewart's, and like it or not, the title of best friend didn't entitle me to share this moment with them.

Scooping Murphy off the floor, I flung the dog onto my shoulder. His breed, Wheaten terrier, was known for their sloth-like cuddling, and he didn't disappoint.

"Will you be my baby, Mur?"

He responded with a series of licks that had me forgetting about the phone call I was desperately awaiting. Typically, Murphy wouldn't be home with me on a Saturday as he had a permanent spot at Keith's side. An unofficial mascot, Murphy was a shop dog, going to work with Keith everyday. Fans even posted pics of him on social media.

Keith! Yes, he could help me pass the time. I rang him up.

"Hey, babe," he answered. "What's up?"

"Have you left for LA yet?"

A quick day trip Keith was making to Los Angeles to replenish supplies for his store was the reason for Murphy's banishment.

"Just did. I'm running late. A bus filled with tourists stopped by and gutted the place. Once they left, I had to wipe the bodily fluids off Jake's life-size cutout. It took a whole roll of toilet paper."

"Well, that's just..." I cringed. "Disturbing."

"You're telling me. I think I might need to laminate Jake."

"Or take him down. Even Cardboard Jake deserves his dignity."

Three years ago, Keith had realized his dream by opening Kali's Surf and Skate Shack. And that's where Cardboard Jake lived. Aided by the star power of its famous co-owner, Jake McKallister, Kali's grand opening was a Hollywood-worthy event. And it continued to draw crowds once word got out that it wasn't just a surf shop but also a museum of sorts, sporting a memorabilia wall with awards and old family photos of a young musical legend in the making.

"Have you heard from Shannon yet?"

"No, and I'm dying over here."

"I'm sure you'll be the first to know."

"No, I'm third in line. First her mom. Then his mom. *Then* me. It sucks."

Keith laughed. "God forbid you have to wait an extra hour."

My phone buzzed with an incoming call, and I screeched. "It's her. Bye! Call me on your way home. Squee."

I hung up on Keith, too excited to hear his reply, and before Shannon could say a word I blurted out, "Boy or girl?"

She laughed; such a beautiful sound. "Girl!"

I screamed, actually screamed, dancing around the room with Murphy. "Just what we wanted," I puffed. "Oh my god, Shannon, I'm so happy. The ultrasound was good? All her measurements are normal?"

"Uh, well, what is your definition of normal? She's perfect, but is already a giant. She's measuring way longer than normal babies her gestational age."

"Who wants a normal baby when we can have a super-sized one, right?"

I always spoke of this baby as *ours*, and it was, in a way. I loved her and her parents enough to officially refer to the collective whole as *us*, and certainly I wouldn't apologize for living vicariously through Shannon until I had one of those growing in my belly too.

We chattered on and on about all things baby until she shifted the conversation. "So, I'm assuming there was no marriage proposal last night? I didn't hear anything and didn't want to call and take you away from the tub of ice cream."

"So considerate of you. And no. No proposal."

"You should just ask him, Sam. Stewart and I had it all planned for months. There was no surprise, but it went down exactly as we wanted… except, you know, for your refusal to play along."

"Okay, look, we've been through this a thousand times. No way was I going to play the slave Princess Leia and be chained to Jabba the Hut all night. That would have set feminism back forty years!"

"So what happened last night?" Shannon pried. "You were convinced he was going to ask you."

"So after I got the dinner invitation, I left work early. Booked an appointment in a blowout bar and had my makeup done there too. Then I hurried home and changed into that dress I'd worn to the charity ball – remember the pink one that shimmers? Anyway, instead of telling me what restaurant we were going to, Keith said he'd ping me his location. I'm imagining some fairytale palace with snowflakes and twinkling lights."

"Snowflakes in Southern California?"

"It's my fantasy, so shut it!"

Only after we had a nice little chuckle did I jump into the nitty-gritty of my cautionary tale.

"I knew something was up the minute I pulled into the parking lot."

"Uh-oh." Shannon giggled. "Why?"

"Because it was Jorge's Mexican Restaurant. You know, the one with all the plastic owls?"

"Why would he propose to you at a hole in the wall like Jorge's?"

"Because, Shannon, he wasn't proposing. He was just *eating.*"

"So, you're saying he invited you to dinner – to *eat*? How dare he?"

"Exactly. And I walked into the owl nest looking like I was going to prom… yeah, it was embarrassing, to say the least."

"Did Keith notice? What did he say?"

"Obviously he noticed my glamour shots makeover, but he was so busy stuffing his face with nachos he couldn't really say much. Still, he was grinning at me all night like he was in on some secret I wasn't. I swear, Shannon, he's just playing with me. He knows I'm expecting it, so he's torturing me. And I only have myself to blame."

It was true. This was all my fault – and the biggest sore spot between us as a couple. The truth was he had proposed to me – twice. And I'd denied him – twice. But aside from Shannon, no one knew the truth. To the rest of the world, and by that I meant his family, Keith was viewed as the commitment-phobic chump who refused to settle down and I as the long-suffering girlfriend, longing for a marriage proposal that would never come.

I swear I tried to correct the assumption, not wanting Keith to take the blame for something I'd done, but he insisted he'd rather be seen as the bad guy than the poor sap that continually got shot down by the woman he loved. God, I was such a shithead.

The second proposal came nearly a year to the day after the seaweed proposal. Only this time, Keith proposed on dry land, down on one knee, and with a gleaming diamond ring ready and willing to be slipped onto my finger.

If the seaweed proposal was a victim of overeager spontaneity, the diamond ring proposal was the victim of poor timing. See, Keith had chosen to ask for my hand in marriage on the exact day I'd spotted my mother at the local mall, carrying on like a raving lunatic. She hadn't seen me, but I'd heard her. The entire mall had heard her. Her f-bomb-laden outburst was over tomatoes, and while she was still in the middle of aggressively chastising the food court worker for adding them to her burger, she'd been dragged from the area by mall cops as horrified mothers dove over their toddlers, shielding their innocent ears from harm.

Shaking from the encounter, I'd driven straight to the pier where I'd promised to meet Keith for an evening stroll. I hadn't had a chance to make sense of what I was feeling, or to tell him what had happened, before he was on the ground with my hand in his and a shiny diamond was being slipped onto my ring finger. I still cringed every time I thought back to that moment. Bursting into tears, I'd handed the ring back with some half-assed sob about him not wanting to marry me and then ran off into the night.

Yeah. Not my best moment.

That night, even after explaining to him why I'd freaked out, Keith was pissed and rightfully so. We didn't speak for a week, which was a little difficult seeing that we were living together by then. Eventually he got over it, and we went on with our lives. We only spoke about it one other time when he crushed my heart by asking if I'd ever marry him.

It was then that I made him a promise – and bought myself some much needed time. If, after five years together, I wasn't bat-shit crazy, he could propose to me again … and then, I'd say yes.

Well, that five-year mark came and went a week ago, and there was still no proposal. Keith didn't even act like he knew the significance of that date; or worse, that he'd remembered. And because of my past assholery, I couldn't say anything either. So Keith and I just existed in this weird expectant bubble, and last night… I couldn't shake the feeling he'd been messing with me.

After I hung up on Shannon, I flicked on the television to try to distract myself. Even though I expected a marriage proposal and would accept, it still scared the hell out of me. Each time I forgot my keys or became irrationally pissed about someone leaving their dog's shit pile on the walking path, I worried. Was I on my way to becoming my mother? Was it just a matter of time before I turned on Keith… on our eventual kids? But I also knew I couldn't postpone my future forever.

My phone rang again, but this time I didn't recognize the number. I sat up.

"Hello?"

"Is this Samantha Anderson?"

"Yes."

"I'm afraid I have some bad news."

I'd driven straight over to the hospital, and like the dutiful daughter they all thought me to be, I stood bravely as the sheet was pulled down to reveal my mother's body still cloaked in a hospital gown. I gasped. She was skeletal. My mother had been dwindling back when I was in high school, but now she was nothing more than skin and bones – dead skin and bones.

Aspiration pneumonia? What did that even mean? It had been fast, I'd been told. By the time she'd called the ambulance to take her to the hospital, she'd only had hours left. And since I was listed as her next of kin, it became my job to sort through the details of her life – and death.

As if identifying my dead mother's remains and dealing with her death weren't enough, the real kick in the gut came when her doctor pulled me aside to tell me the shocking truth. My mother's mental illness wasn't just some run-of-the-mill schizophrenia or manic-depressive disorder. Apparently, she'd been suffering from a progressive brain condition known as Huntington's disease.

I listened in horror as he described Huntington's as an inherited disorder that resulted in the death of brain cells. There was no cure. In its earliest stages, Huntington's disease manifested with jerky movements, a lack of coordination, and severe behavioral disorders. And, although symptoms of Huntington's disease most commonly became noticeable in one's thirties or forties, they could begin as young as infancy. Everything began falling into place. Sullivan's severe lack of coordination; his mood swings. Had he carried the gene? And what about my occasional clumsiness? Did I?

As I sat there and listened to the doctor explain the disease, I could feel the four walls closing in on me. It was a death sentence. *I* had a death sentence. At twenty-eight-years-old, I was fast approaching the age of no return. How had I not known such a horrible disease, one that slowly robbed the sufferer of his or her mind, was being passed down from generation to generation? Why had my relatives hidden this condition? Or had they even known?

In the midst of all the horrifying information settling in, my mind wandered back to Preston's mother. She really should demand her money back from the investigator she'd hired to gather dirt on me. He'd only provided her with half the truth. If only he'd dug a little deeper, Preston never would have asked me to be his barren plus one.

Armed with the devastating news, I gathered my mother's meager belongings and drove to the home I'd shared with her – the place once owned by my grandmother, who'd most likely passed away from the same degenerative disease that had cut a swath across my lineage. With the key I'd found in her bag, I opened the door and, by habit, peeked inside for the all clear.

The house remained largely the same, with one glaring exception – a heavy layering of dust. It was as if my normally perfection-oriented mother hadn't had the strength in her final days to tidy up, and from the look of her emaciated body, I could certainly see why.

Like a trespasser, I slowly made my way through her house. It wasn't that I was necessarily looking for something. Perhaps I just needed some sort of closure. But that was not what I found. While the rest of the house was tidy, her bedroom appeared to have been touched by a hurricane. Flashes of red caught my eye. All over the white walls were words, and phrases, and ominous warnings. *Die. Never grow old. Be Afraid. Death sentence.*

My hands shook as I read the inner ramblings of a diseased mind, and for the first time, I felt pity for the woman who'd birthed me. She hadn't been evil by choice. She hadn't asked for this disease. Maybe she would have been a lovely woman without it. Knowing that her cruelty couldn't have been helped brought me some measure of comfort… until I opened the bathroom door.

The writing was no longer on the wall. As I stared into the mirror, my reflection was covered in blood. Instead of using lipstick to communicate, my mother had chosen her own plasma. And the words she'd written weren't the cryptic ramblings of a crazy woman. No, this message was clear: my name written in blood.

Sam

And it was followed by two little words that put an end to the beautiful life I'd imagined with the man I loved.

You're next

Screaming, I sank to the floor.

Chapter Thirty-Two

Keith

No Easy Fix

The image of Sam all dressed for the Oscars last night made me laugh. She had obviously been expecting something, and it gave me the slightest bit of pleasure to make her squirm. After all, she hadn't made asking for her hand in marriage easy. It felt like I'd been jumping through hoops for five very long years. But no matter the restrictions she'd placed on us, I'd never been deterred either. It wasn't like I had much of a choice in the matter. I loved her. Only her. So, I was forced to wait out her ultimatum.

Now it was her turn to wait, if only because the ring I planned to propose with hadn't been ready until today. And now here it was gleaming under the lights. I picked it off the silver tray and inspected its brilliance from all angles. It was perfect – beyond perfect, actually. This ring was Sam.

The jeweler caught me salivating. "She must be one special woman."

"Oh, she is," I agreed, running my finger over the smooth stone. "I've proposed twice already."

He studied me more closely. "And you're finally buying her the ring?"

"No. The first time the ring was made of seaweed. The second time I was cock-blocked by her insane mother."

The slightest grin playing out over his face. "She said no twice?"

"She did indeed."

"You're a determined fella."

I shrugged. "You know what they say: the third time's the charm."

"Well, for your sake, I hope she says *yes*, because this ring is a special order and can't be returned."

"Way to have faith in me, dude," I replied, somewhat annoyed he'd brought the return policy into my otherwise landmark moment.

"Oh…" The man mumbled, realizing his mistake. "I didn't mean it that way."

"No worries," I said, too happy to be vindictive. I turned Sam's ring from side to side, examining its splendor. This was no ordinary diamond engagement ring I was buying for Sam. In the center lay a milky blue agate encircled by a bed of diamonds. It was beautiful and durable and delicate all at once – just like my girl. "Besides, this time, I'm not taking no for an answer."

"Good for you." Was that a hint of condescending asshole I heard in his tone? Why was I getting the distinct impression he wasn't liking my chances? Did he know something I didn't?

The jeweler placed my ring in a box and rang up the remainder of my purchase balance. As he was running my card, he glanced up at me several times.

"I thought you looked familiar. You're one of the McKallister boys, aren't you?"

Evidentially, I hadn't gone far enough out of my county to buy an engagement ring in peace. I wasn't even the famous one, and yet still I got recognized.

"Yep," I answered, hoping my curt reply would put an end to our chitchat.

"Well, I take it all back. Your lady will say yes, for sure. Who wouldn't want to marry a rock star's brother?"

Okay, now I was officially pissed. What a shithead. Did he really think Sam would only consider marrying me for my pedigree? If that had been the case we would have been betrothed long ago. My phone rang. Perfect timing.

Sam had effectively saved the opinionated jeweler from a tongue-lashing.

"Hey, babe," I answered, leaving the shop and heading for my car. "What's up?"

"Keith… help me."

By the time I got to Sam, I had to peel her off the bathroom floor. As far as I could tell, she'd been there for hours. The tile was slick with her tears as I scooped her into my arms and I carried her out of the house. Only after I'd clicked Sam into the passenger seat did she ask me to go back inside for her purse and the paperwork from the hospital. Leaving her alone was not an option, and I was about to tell her that when Shannon screeched to a halt in her Prius and bolted for my truck.

While the two were tucked into a tight embrace, I headed back to the house to fulfill Sam's request. It was only when I'd stepped inside a second time that I understood the full scope of what had happened. From her frantic sob-sodden phone call, I got that her mother had passed and that she'd gone to the house, but her incoherent comments made no sense until now.

My jaw twitched as I read the words Carol had left for her daughter. Scribbled on the wall were hateful words like *Abomination. Vengeance. Repulsive.* But the words Sam had repeated over and over to me were the ones written in blood.

The ones dripping down the mirror in an eerie warning. *You're next.*

I'd never wanted to hurt someone the way I wanted to hurt that woman. As if it weren't enough for Carol to wreak havoc in life, she'd found a way to reach her hand out of hell and wrap it around Sam's throat. How could it be that the kindest woman I'd ever known had been raised by the devil?

Sam took the week off work and spent most of it curled up under a blanket with Murphy by her side. She seemed inconsolable at times, and although I knew people handled grief differently, I wondered why she was mourning a woman who'd treated her so poorly. My hope had been that once the funeral was over, we could get back to our normal lives. I'd propose, and we'd spend our days planning for the wedding that had been such a long time coming. But Sam didn't get better. She cried a lot. Everyday. It had become noticeable enough at work that she was offered an extended leave.

But sitting home alone while I was at work was not helping her either, and slowly but inexorably, depression set in. Sam slept a lot and, when I attempted to comfort her, she always pushed me away. Even Murphy seemed at a loss to help her as no amount of face licks stopped the flow of tears.

So I was somewhat encouraged today when I arrived home from work to find her at the kitchen table, a pile of papers scattered about. She was freshly showered, an oddity as of late, and seemed more at peace than I'd seen her since her mother's death.

"Hey, hun," I said dropping my keys in the bowl and heading toward her for a kiss. She pulled back, and the thin line of her lips told me that perhaps she wasn't doing as well as I'd thought. Maybe I'd just arrived in the eye of her storm? Proceeding with caution, I asked, "Are you hungry? You want me to grill up some fish for dinner?"

Her eyes met mine. She was not all right. In fact, Sam was the opposite of all right. How could I have read her so wrong? Lifting her to her feet, I held her in a tight embrace. Sam was like a ragdoll, limp and heavy in my arms. My hand ran along her back, soothing her in the only way I knew how, while speaking softly in her ear. "Sam, talk to me. What's going on in your head?"

She pulled away and sank back into her chair. "I haven't been honest with you, Keith."

"Okay," I replied, already feeling the tension settle upon my shoulders. I took the seat opposite her as Murphy jumped onto my lap. It didn't matter what she'd done. I would forgive her, as I always did. There was nothing she could say that would push me away. "Whatever it is, we'll work it out."

"Not this."

The way she said it with such foreboding was my first indication that things would not be going my way. "What does that mean?"

"I found out in the hospital that my mother died from complications from Huntington's disease. I'd never even heard of it before. The doctor explained to me that the disease attacks the brain cells, causing mental illness and eventually death. There's no cure."

"Shit. And your mom had this?"

"Yes. The reason I've been so upset, Keith, is not because of my mother's death but because the disease is hereditary. It runs in families. And… and…"

Sam dissolved into tears. I let the dog down and dropped to my knees in front of her and lay my head on her stomach. "Just let me help you. We can figure this out. Everything will be all right."

"No!" She pushed me back, jumping from her seat. "I don't think you fully understand, Keith."

"No, Sam. I don't understand shit because you've been crying for a month straight. I'm trying to be supportive, but it's a little hard when every time I try to comfort you, I get brushed off."

"I have the disease!"

"You…" The left side of my face went numb. "Wait, how do you know?"

"The first signs are balance issues. Remember when I fell down those stairs last month?"

"So what? I regularly fall on my head. I ran into a wall yesterday. That doesn't make me sick, it just makes me stupid as fuck."

"I forget things."

"So do I. Remember when I biked to work the other day? Well, when I was getting ready to leave, I spent fifteen minutes searching for my car. I was on the phone with cops reporting it missing when it hit me that it hadn't been stolen – I was just a dumbass."

Sam sighed, long and heavy. "I understand you're trying to make me feel better, but nothing you say will change what's coming. Aside from me showing the early signs of the disease, the reason I know I have this is because pretty much everyone on my mom's side has died from it – including, I think, Sullivan. I've been combing through the family tree, and I'm telling you, Keith, my deranged ancestors are falling from the branches."

What was she saying? None of it made sense. Sam was the picture of health, or at least she had been until her mother passed. And now she was trying to tell me she was dying? No way would I accept that. "Okay, look, I'll talk to Jake and ask for a loan. We'll get you the finest doctors. If they're on the East Coast, we'll go there. If they're in Europe, we'll go there. Medical trials? Whatever it takes. Anything we have to do, Samantha, we'll fight this together."

Sam raised her head slowly and sluggishly. I noticed then, the light had faded from her eyes. Sam wasn't Sam anymore. I knew that look of defeat. I'd seen it in Jake's eyes after the kidnapping, and I'd seen it again in my own while in the midst of my drug issues. The hell if I'd let despair take my girl!

"There is no fighting this." Her voice matched the gloom in her eyes.

I swallowed the rising lump in my throat. This could not be happening.

Sam continued to rattle off words that laid siege to my ears. "Once the symptoms start, they get progressively worse. As my brain cells die off, mental illness will kick in, and I'll become just like her, spewing hate and vitriol to those I love. Most with Huntington's disease first start seeing symptoms in their early thirties, and then death comes 10 to 15 years later. I'm twenty-eight, Keith."

Sam paused as if waiting for my reply, but I was too stunned to formulate any coherent words. So she continued.

"By the end, I'll be completely gone, bed-ridden in a facility. My mother never got that far because the disease messed with her ability to swallow and she basically starved to death."

Tears welled in my eyes as I shook my head. No, way could I accept this. Not Sam. "No."

Now she was out of her chair, comforting me, her hand gliding through my hair. She held me tight as she repeated over and over, "I'm so sorry. I'm just so sorry."

"What about… what about all the things we want to do together?"

She shook her head, and the finality of it all ripped my heart in two.

"We can't. Not anymore." She spoke in hushed tones, all her strength depleted. "It's why I've been crying so much. I've been trying to come to terms with it. And today I finally accepted what I've known all along. This horrible disease is *my* future, but God help us, Keith, it won't be yours."

Chapter Thirty-Three

Samantha

Dead End

Cradling Murphy in my lap, I watched from the picture window in the living room as Keith packed up the last of his belongings. Getting him to this point had not been easy. Keith fought me all night and then into the next day, but I stayed strong and unwavering. After all, I had what he did not – the time to come to terms with my fate. If I gave Keith that same courtesy, I knew he'd find a way to talk me out of my decision. It wasn't that I didn't want him – I desperately did – but I refused to chain this loving man to my side when there was a full, rich life out there just waiting for him.

Yet Keith refused to accept the reality of our situation. Armed with his honorary medical degree off Wikipedia, he went back and forth from the computer to me, presenting the facts about the disease as if he somehow thought I hadn't already been beating myself over the head with them every single day for the past couple of weeks.

Huntington's was an open-ended disease, and one that didn't discriminate. Passed on from generation to generation, all who inherited it would eventually meet a horrible end. And even though the statistics were somewhat on my side – with a 50% chance of harboring the disease in my DNA, I didn't need genetic testing to tell me what I already knew – the monster lying dormant inside me all these years was lazily opening its evil eyes. I could tick off the symptoms as I experienced them. It was no longer a matter of *if*, but *when*.

Still, Keith clung to that 50% number like the glass half full kind of guy he was. I, on the other hand, had already anchored myself to despair. In my eyes, the glass wasn't just half empty – it was bone dry. No matter when I got the testing, I knew the outcome would be the same – I died at the end.

Despite it all, Keith was willing to stand by my side. It was noble and romantic in a 'doomed lover' sort of way, but it was also unrealistic. I, of all people, knew that getting to the curtain call would be the real battle. As my brain cells slowly withered away, Keith would take the brunt of the suffering, and slowly but surely, he would grow to resent me – just as I'd resented my mother and she'd resented hers.

There was no easy answer. Every path for us led to heartbreak. If we stayed together, we lost. If we split up, we lost. No matter what, our hearts would break, and we'd have to learn to live our lives apart. Sure, I could go through the effort and time and expense to get an official diagnosis, but that would only bring us closer together, winding him around my disease as if it coursed through his veins as well as my own. No, going our separate ways was the only answer to us each escaping with the least amount of suffering. Apart, we could still cling to our memories, and I comforted myself in knowing he would go on to love again. Keith had too much tenderness in his heart not to pass it on.

And me? Without having to worry about him, I could get back to work and make what I had left of my coherent life matter. With any luck, I could get to a place in my life where I wouldn't look back in sadness. Keith was my first love– my only love – my last love.

As he walked back into the house, Keith's shoulders were slumped and heavy. All that was left now was the fine print. I'd already worked out the bigger picture. My grandmother had left a sizable inheritance to my mother, which would soon be passed on to me. And once that money was in my account, I'd buy Keith out of the house we owned together. And Murphy... I hugged him tighter to me. I suppose I could have pushed for shared custody, but I couldn't bear the idea of Keith coming in and out of my life. It had to be a clean split for both our sakes. He got the dog.

"Are you all packed?" I asked, trying to sound unaffected in the face of such sorrow. I wanted desperately to postpone his departure, but why prolong the torture? I was a dead end, and the sooner he turned around, the better.

"Yeah." Keith's voice broke in the most grievous of ways. I resisted the urge to smother him in the love he deserved. No one had said this would be easy – but no one had said it would rip us to bloody shreds either.

I stood up, carried Murphy over, and transferred him to Keith's arms.

"Are you sure?" he asked, nothing but misery in his words.

I fought back the tears as I dipped my head into Murphy's soft fur and nuzzled him. Yes, I was sure. Even furry pups weren't safe from a deranged mind.

"I'm sure," I nodded, leaving a trail of tears in his unruly hair. "Mommy's going to miss you, baby."

"We'll come by and visit," Keith whispered, his hands sliding over my neck.

"No." I took a step back, away from Murphy. Away from Keith. Forever. "That'll just make it harder."

He shook his head. "You don't want this, Sam. I know you don't."

Of course I didn't… but I refused to feed Keith to the monster inside me. My bottom lip trembled as I swallowed back the sorrow and asked one last thing from the man I loved. "Please don't tell anyone why we split. If people find out, I might lose my job, and I want to hold onto that for as long as I can. I'll let people know when the time comes."

Keith stood there chewing over my words. "What do I tell my family?"

"Anything but the truth. Blame it on me, Keith. Tell them I cheated or that I broke it off. Just don't tell them about this. Please."

A storm passed over him. Anger. Despair. Hopelessness. He hated me. He loved me. I was destroying him – but only so he could live the life I could never give him.

"I would have stayed," he said.

"I know. And that's why you have to go. Someday, when you have a beautiful wife wrapped in your arms and a bunch of rowdy little kids crowding around, you'll think of this moment and you'll thank me."

Keith defiantly shook his head.

"No, Sam," he replied, carrying Murphy out the front door. "No, I won't."

Chapter Thirty-Four

Keith

Public Enemy #1

Like a refugee, I carried boxes of belongings into my parent's house – the only place I'd found that would allow dogs on such short notice– and unpacked my measly possessions with a sense of finality. This was not what I wanted. And it certainly wasn't what spoiled only-dog Murphy wanted. He now had to share attention with Mike, the golden retriever; Sally, the Shih Tzu mix; and Joshua, the tabby. And although Murphy didn't say as much, I knew he already missed his mom.

My parents' place might have been pet-friendly, but it came with judgmental disappointment. Sam had been a popular addition to the family, and because I wasn't able to disclose the real reason for our split, my family just assumed I was the dickhead who'd left her. And then if you paired my perceived heartless dumping with the recent death of her mother, I came out looking like a double dipping of dog shit.

A long, drawn-out sigh of discontentment from Murphy drew my attention.

"You and me both, Mur." I matched his canine melancholy with my own dismal sigh. "You and me both."

Mom came in sometime later to talk, and when I say talk, I mean she came in to torture me for information. Armed with the promise of my favorite meatball dinner, she pressed for details.

"I can go talk to her," she offered. "Maybe that will help."

"No, Mom, it would be the opposite of helping. She doesn't want to be part of my life anymore, and by default, that means you have to break up with her too."

I knew such a loss would haunt my mother. Over the past five years, she and Sam had grown as close as mother and daughter. It had been a slow growing relationship, with both women scarred by trust issues, but once they bonded over their shared interest – me – there was no stopping them.

Sam had been close to Quinn as well. The two had formed an attachment after she'd accidentally wandered into his room on her way to the bathroom in my parents' sprawling home. Although my mother had touted Quinn's musical abilities, Sam once claimed that she thought my mom might have actually been downplaying his talents.

Despite the fact that I hadn't cracked and disclosed to my mother why Sam and I broke up, dinner was still delivered to my room an hour later by none other than one very pissed off Quinn.

"What the hell did you do to her?" His words were steeped in accusation.

"It's none of your business," I fired back.

"You're an idiot, you know that? And don't think I'm going to stop seeing her just because you're a cataclysmic douchebag."

Tell me how you really feel, Quinn. I suppose I could have defended myself and blamed the breakup on Sam, as she'd requested, but despite the pain and anger I felt, I loved her too much to paint her as the villain. Plus, I was just too tired to fight. Today, I just wanted to lick my wounds. So I'd eat my meatball dinner in the sanctity of my own room, content playing the bad guy role if it let those around me stay hopelessly in love with Samantha Anderson.

Later, my dad popped his head in. "You wanna watch a movie?"

I eyed him suspiciously. A movie with my father was never just a movie. See, he liked historical dramas. Not, mind you, the cool kind like World War Two blood baths, oh no. Dad preferred those biopic snooze fests featuring historical figures that did nothing but talk for the first three hours before *finally* getting their heads blown off. "Depends. Which one are we talking?"

"You know…" He hesitated a second too long, giving himself away. "An action flick."

"Dad, I know you're lying. You get that twitch in your right eye. I can't believe you'd try to trick me into one of your shitty movies. You do realize this is the worst day of my life, right?"

"Oh," he said, his face contorting in fake concern. "I'm sorry about that, Mrs. Lincoln. Other than that, how was the play?"

So much for sympathy. I cast a pillow at his retreating form.

It wasn't until Grace came by that I got an offer I couldn't refuse.

Slipping into my room with her pedicure kit, she asked, "You want me to paint your toes?"

Well, damn. The fam was really pulling out all the stops tonight.

"Why the hell not?" I grumbled, extending my virgin digits.

And for the next half hour, she painstakingly painted my toes gray, the same color as my gloomy disposition. Then, with the steadiest hand I'd ever seen, the little artist in Grace delicately drew a colorful surfboard on each big toe. It was actually super cool and I felt a smidge of my spirit return.

Once she left, I crossed the room and rummaged through the bin until I found what I was looking for. Careful not to ruin my toenails, I sat on the bed and opened the box with the non-returnable engagement ring I was now never going to use. The smug face of the jeweler came to mind. He'd called this. Shaking my head, I threaded the ring through a leather band and triple-tied it for safety before slipping it over my neck and pressing my lips against the precious stone – effectively kissing my future goodbye.

I woke the next day to something slimy against my cheek. Without opening my eyes, I swatted Murphy away.

"Go away, Mur."

"Ruff!" My eyes shot open and I scrambled up. A pile of sunflower seeds slid from my soggy cheek and fell to a pile in my lap.

"What the fuck, dude?" I blasted Lassen as I fluffed the sheet, flinging discarded shells all over the place. "Were you spitting sunflower seeds on my cheek?"

"Maybe."

I narrowed in on my sleep time enemy. "You're disgusting, you know that? All of you. Always."

Lassen laughed – once – then stepped back and took a seat in the chair by the desk. "Aren't you a little ray of pitch black?"

"What are you doing here?"

"I'm your fairy godmother."

"No, you're the devil incarnate."

Another single-syllable laugh. "You say tomato, I say tomahto."

I was tired and cranky and in no mood for riddles. "What… do… you… want?"

"I brought you a box full of sunflower seeds."

I eyed him suspiciously. Since getting back together with Sam five years ago, I only partook in the seed addiction when she wasn't around since it made her gag. But Lassen's box of kernels had another meaning.

"You think I'm going to relapse?" I asked.

"You just lost your woman. I'm erring on the side of caution."

"Well, don't. I'm fine."

"At the moment, sure. But what happens weeks from now… months? You need to go back to AA meetings, Keith. Just to keep your mind strong. And lucky for us, since you slept until fucking four in the afternoon, there's actually one that starts in an hour. Get up. Let's go."

I last thing I wanted to do was spend what was left of the day with Lassen, but the man was strangely persistent, and I knew I wouldn't be getting rid of him anytime soon.

"Uuhhh." I flung the sheets off my body and headed for the shower.

Even though I hated to admit it, Lassen was right. I needed to get my head on straight. Even if my first thought wasn't drugs, it would be so easy to let myself go. I had to make sure that when the going got tough, I wouldn't reach for a bottle or a pill or a joint.

As the meeting was wrapping up, Lassen slapped my shoulder. "I gotta run."

"What's the hurry?" I replied.

"I have a date."

"With which wife?"

"None. I'm divorced."

"From which one?"

"All of them."

I scratched my head, confused. "So this is a new woman?"

"Yep."

Good god. How did he do it? "You're one of the Seven Wonders of the World."

One laugh. "Someday, maybe I'll share my secrets. But you're not ready to absorb my teachings just yet."

Lassen pushed his way down the row of AA members, knocking his ass into nearly every single face he passed. I couldn't help but laugh since I knew it wasn't an accident. He was such a jerk – and I loved the guy.

A minute later, the group leader called the meeting adjourned, and as I stood up to leave, I caught sight of a guy staring at me. Since I hadn't disclosed to this group who I was, I instantly found myself on edge and hastily searched for the nearest exit.

"Kali?"

That voice. I'd know it anywhere.

"Screensaver?" I couldn't believe my eyes. His hair was closely cropped and his body severely emaciated. Back in high school, Screensaver had been a shaggy-haired marshmallow, but now he looked more like a hollowed-out corpse.

"The name's James, asshole."

I laughed, giving my old friend a hug. "Damn, dude, long time no see. What have you been up to?"

He held his arms out to the side. No explanation was needed.

"Bad, huh?"

"The worst." James appeared so defeated.

I remembered that feeling well. "Sorry, man."

He shrugged. "Anyway, you look good, Kali. How you been?"

"Eh." I shrugged. "Broke up with my girl. Just making sure I don't relapse. Have you seen Valentine or Fire Crotch?"

"I haven't seen either one in years. Someone told me Fire Crotch got his act together after high school, but I have no idea where he is now. Last I heard, Valentine was in prison. He stabbed some guy a couple of years ago in a drug deal gone bad."

Valentine's fate wasn't necessarily a surprise, but it shocked me all the same. That could have been me had my father not stepped in and demanded change. It could have been me had Sam not taken me on and helped change my life.

I gripped James's shoulder. "I'd like to say you look good, but dude, I can tell you've had a rough go of it."

"Yeah. Real rough. I've been dealing with this shit since I smoked my first joint at twelve. Just finished my third rehab. It's a struggle. Can't hold down a job. Been living with my parents all these years. They finally had enough and tossed me out. I don't blame them. I was a mess. I really gotta get it together this time."

"You'll do it," I answered with all the encouragement I could muster. The truth of the matter was, Screensaver was fragile. One misstep and he'd be lost again.

"You're doing well, though," he said, seemingly eager to change the subject. "I heard you opened a surf shop. Good for you, man."

"Well, you know, I had a little help from my rich and famous brother."

He smiled without an ounce of jealously. James had always been a nice kid, if more than a little dopey. "Congrats on Jake's success too. You must be so proud of him."

"I am. Thanks. How come you never came to the shop to say hi?"

He shifted from heel to heel, his head hanging low. "I've been on the outs for a while. Homeless. Last thing I wanted was for people I knew to see me that way."

I nodded, understanding his predicament perfectly. "But you're clean now."

He lip edged up as he bowed his head. "I am, but you know how it is. I've got to fight to keep it…"

I stopped him. "Do you want it?"

"Want what? To be clean?"

"Yeah. Do you want it?"

"I do, Kali." His eyes filled with tears. "I want it so bad. I'm just… I'm so damn tired."

I thought back to Lassen and how much he'd helped me when I was hopeless like James. I'd reeked of a man in need of help and compassion. That same smell was now drifting off James. Building my old friend back up would take a considerable amount of time. Luckily for him, my schedule had recently been cleared.

"You got a mentor?" I asked.

He shook his head. "Nah."

I laid my arm over his shoulder and walked him toward the door. "How do you feel about sunflower seeds?"

Chapter Thirty-Five

Keith

Lunch Intervention

"I like raisins too."

Oh, god. James was speaking again. When would he learn? I looked up from the safety of the merchandise boxes only to find him making a play for Taylor again. I glanced over at my manager, Nick, who was already silently chuckling; and that, of course, made me stifle a laugh.

Since the day James had started working for me at Kali's, he'd formed a massive, unrequited crush on Taylor, the hottest surfer chick this side of the equator. None of us had the heart to tell him his chances with her were about as good as him getting out of a revolving door in one pass, but still he insisted.

James was nothing if not persistent. He was pursuing Taylor with the same determination he'd employed in tackling his addiction. That day I took him home like a stray dog in need of a bath, I hadn't had the highest hopes for him. Yes, I was determined to do what I could, but I wasn't sure he had the strength of mind to overcome his cravings. But what I also hadn't banked on was my parents welcoming scruffy James in like one of their own and nurturing him back to health.

Soon my old friend was his goofy self, just without the puff of smoke that used to settle over him like stinky smog. Together we moved into a condo on the beach and became Murphy's platonic co-parents. And now, nearly a year clean, James was in a good place and ready for love. Unfortunately his heart had imprinted on Taylor, the sea goddess he had absolutely no business making a play for.

"These are blueberries, James."

I could almost hear her eyes roll. Taylor's patience was wearing thin. This was, after all, a multiple-times-a-day occurrence.

"Oh. I like blueberries too."

"That's nice."

I cringed. Those two words were some of the worst a guy would hear from the love of his life. James was going down.

"Actually," he hesitated. "I lied. I don't really like blueberries because they turn my teeth blue."

Taylor's eyes widened, perhaps realizing for the first time that she too might suffer such a fruit-related malady. I could see her vain attempt at cleansing her pearly whites with her tongue.

James saw it too and jumped at the chance to correct his mistake. "But you look good with blue teeth."

Oh, well, shit. His plane just hit the ground, exploding. So painful. I turned away, my cheeks burning hot for him. I needed to take James to a library or a Starbucks, somewhere he could meet a girl who might appreciate his unique ramblings. Yet I knew my friend. He'd be back at it tomorrow, trying desperately to get the girl to notice him. I had to hand it to him – even with his awkward attempts at bonding, James was further than I was with women. At least he was trying, which was more than I could claim.

The door chimed as a tall brunette walked in, and I had to do a double take. Emma? I was still getting used to the drastic change in her. Not only was her hair not bleach blonde, but her belly was swollen and her smile was ear to ear. Who was this woman and what had she done with my cranky sister?

Heading straight for her, I wrapped her in a hug. "What are you doing here?"

"Taking you to lunch."

We hadn't done our biweekly lunch dates since she'd met and fallen in love with Finn. I'd only initiated them years back when she needed the company, but now that she was a happy and fulfilled woman, she didn't need her big brother anymore.

"Well, hot damn. Are you paying?"

She glanced around the busy shop. "I should think you could afford it."

She was right, I could. "Nick, take over. James, leave Taylor alone and watch Murphy for me."

Settled into a booth at a restaurant down the street, Emma talked about all the new and exciting happenings in her life – Finn and the baby who was only a few more weeks away. I'd never thought I'd see the day when Emma let her guard down and opened herself up to love. I was so proud of her.

"So, tell me what's happening with you. I see you still have your stray."

"Murphy?" I asked.

"No, James."

I laughed, taking a gulp of my soda before she covered my hand with hers. "How are you doing, really?"

"I'm okay."

"Are you? Because I get the distinct impression you're still stuck on Sam. Have you seen her?"

"No. Sam and I are not getting back together, if that's what you're thinking."

"But Keith, if you're not moving on, maybe you should turn around and go back. Beg for her forgiveness."

"Why does everyone just naturally assume I'm to blame? Has it ever occurred to you, or to anyone in this family, that she broke it off with me for her own reasons, and she doesn't want me back?"

Emma's lips parted and her eyes widened. "Is that what happened? You didn't cheat on her?"

"No, I didn't cheat on her. Jesus, what kind of person do you think I am? Does everyone think I cheated?"

"Not everyone," Emma answered in halted speech. "Just me and Mom. And Dad and Quinn and Jake. And the dry cleaning lady down the street."

"No, not Nancy too." I laughed despite myself. "Look, if you must know, Sam is going through some big things, and she didn't want to..."

"To what?"

"Drag me along with her. She shut me out of her life, Em. I can't go back even if I wanted to. Do you understand now?"

Rocking back in her seat, Emma focused on the tabletop, running her fingers along the wood before finally glancing up at me. "I didn't know. I'm so sorry, Keith. Why didn't you say something?"

"It's complicated."

"But you still love her?"

"Yes."

She sighed, focusing on the grooves, and without looking up, she said, "Sometimes love sucks, doesn't it? It's designed to hurt you. The more you love, the worse the pain of losing is. I tried to hold it off, hardened my heart to it, but what I learned was that not having love is worse than losing it in the end."

"I don't know about that. Right about now I wish I'd never loved her."

"Do you?"

Folding my arms on the table, I dropped my head into them. "I don't know. I hate this. The whole thing – it feels unfinished. It's been this way since we were teenagers. There's so much history between us, but things beyond our control always get in the way. You want to know the worst part of our breakup, Em? Sam broke up with me not because she hates me but because she loves me. She wanted me to have everything she couldn't give me. I think that's why I can't move on. We never fell out of love. It's the story of our lives."

"I did the same thing to Finn, but then I saw the error of my ways, and I begged his forgiveness. She might see it too and come back to you, Keith."

I shook my head, feeling the heaviness. "She can't."

"Why?"

"Because, this isn't about hang-ups, Emma, it's about life and death and she's… she's dying."

For a second there I thought I might need to check my sister for a pulse. Maybe it hadn't been the best idea to shock her this way when she was eight months pregnant.

"You can't tell anyone I told you. Not even the dry cleaning lady. Do you understand?"

Her mouth had yet to close. "How?"

"Sam has Huntington's disease. It attacks the brain cells…"

Her face faded to ashen white. "I know what Huntington's is."

"And so you know what's going to happen to her?"

Emma was stone-still for a moment before she reluctantly nodded her head.

"She's trying to spare me, Em, to give me a chance at a life with a wife and kids I can grow old with. But the problem is, I don't want to grow old with anyone but her. And that's why I'm stuck spinning in circles until the bitter end."

"I don't even know what to say."

"Don't say anything. No one can know. I promised Sam, and I plan to honor that one promise for her, do you understand?"

"I do." She reached across the table and tangled her fingers in my hair. "I'm so sorry."

"Who died?" A familiar voice broke into our deep discussion.

I jerked my head up just as Kyle slid into the booth next to me, and Jake beside Emma.

"What the hell?" I laughed, the dark cloud dissipating. "Is that you guys under all that hair?"

The two acknowledged their identities, hidden behind bushy beards and long straggly tresses.

"I get why Jake's in disguise," Emma said. "But don't you think it's a bit overkill for you, Kyle? I mean, last I checked, you were still a C-list celebrity."

"For your information, Emma, people recognize me all the time, and if someone in here is a fan, it wouldn't be too hard to figure out who Sasquatch here is. So let's try not to be a bitch, shall we?"

"Okay, fine, all I was implying was that you were giving yourself a lot of credit."

"Oh, I know what you were implying. And speaking of your unplanned pregnancy, did you and Finn use a Ziploc sandwich baggie as protection?"

"Haha. Good one. Is there a reason your armpits smell like horse slobber?"

"Oh god," Jake whined, dropping his head to the table. "Somebody please shut them up."

"As the oldest," I interceded. "I'm calling a truce. You two hug and make up, or get off my planet."

Kyle stood and leaned over the table, giving Emma a hug. "You look beautiful, sis."

"And you smell wonderful."

Kyle beamed, plopping back down into his seat. "Thank you.

"So, why are you all here?" I asked. "Is this an intervention?"

"Why does it have to be an intervention for us to hang out together?" Jake asked.

"Because we never hang out together unless Mom guilts us into it."

"Is there a particular reason why we need an intervention, Keith?" Emma asked.

I thought about it and realized that, no, there actually wasn't. "Oh, yeah. You're right. Old habits die hard."

"Although…" Jake said, hesitating just enough that I knew whatever he was about to say wouldn't please me. "I did want to get your take on something. Casey would like to invite Sam to our wedding. It's just in the planning stages, so if you're against it, I'll put up a fight."

Kyle coughed out a laugh.

"You have something to say?"

"Um…actually, yes, I do, Jake. Did you give up your balls right away, or did she give you a grieving period?"

"Like you can talk."

"Dude, I'm not trying to deny it. Kenzie is my queen. I've accepted that. But you… you still seem to think you've got some sort of power. Face it. Casey is your Commander in Chief. If she's decided Sam is coming, there is nothing short of an executive order that will stop her, so stop pretending like you have any say in the wedding planning."

Jake was silent for an extended period of time before raising his hand. "I vote that Kyle not be invited to any further intervention lunches."

"I second that," Emma laughed.

"Hey," Kyle scoffed. "I thought we kissed and made up."

"We only hugged, so I still don't like you."

Kyle tossed his head back, laughing, and the rest of us joined in. Luckily our younger brother was one of those guys who was *very* hard to offend.

"So what's your decision, Keith?" Jake asked. "Yes or no? Do you want Sam to be cut from the guest list or not?"

I thought about it a moment, knowing Sam would probably say no anyway, and shrugged. "Go ahead. Invite her."

"Oh, thank god," Kyle blurted out. "Jake gets to live another day."

The two tussled from across the table, Kyle grabbing ahold of Jake's shirt and pulling down on the collar. Something caught my eye. Or actually, something *didn't* catch my eye. I reached over and yanked on the collar myself. The agate necklace. It was gone.

"What the hell?" Jake asked, knocking my hand away.

"The necklace you always wore – where is it?"

Emma and Kyle glanced between us, as confused by the encounter as Jake.

"I took it off. Jesus." Jake rearranged his shirt. "What's your problem? I didn't realize I needed to clear my jewelry selection with you."

"You never take it off."

"Well, I did. What's wrong with you?" Jake stared at me curiously. "Are you mad?"

I realized I was probably sounding like a lunatic, so I took a deep breath and calmed myself down. "Look, I'm sorry. I'm just surprised. Can I ask why you took it off?"

"I don't know. After you gave me that whole line of bull-shit that the stone had healing powers, I guess I thought of it like my safety net for a while. But once I met Casey, I realized I didn't need it anymore. So I took it off. It's in my safe. It's nothing against you or the gift you gave me. I mean, I honestly didn't think you'd care. And I definitely didn't think you'd accost me over it."

"I'm sorry. That was totally uncalled for," I said, fidget-ing long enough that everyone at the table was eyeing me with interest. "Okay, fine. I wasn't totally honest with you about that necklace. I didn't find it in the weeds on a cliff. Sam gave it to me. It was her grandfather's. She believed it protected her, and before she moved away, she gave it to me because she knew I was in a bad place."

Jake's eyes narrowed in on me. "Why didn't you tell me that?"

"Because you wouldn't have taken it."

"Obviously I wouldn't have taken it."

"But it helped you."

"But it wasn't mine. Did Sam even know you gave it to me?"

"Not until that day in your dressing room. She saw it around your neck."

"Oh, my god, Keith. You put me in such a bad position."

"No, she was happy you had it. I'm not kidding. The necklace had always brought her comfort, and she was proud to have you wearing it. The thing is, Sam's going through some pretty heavy stuff, and it might help her to..."

"I'll get it back to you tomorrow."

"Are you sure? You don't have to if you don't want. It was a gift."

"I'm sure." No longer pissed at me, Jake relaxed and sat back in his seat. "I don't need it anymore. Casey's my agate."

CHAPTER THIRTY-SIX

SAMANTHA

On the Winning Side

Weeks passed, then months, and each day got a little easier. The loneliness was something I would have to battle the rest of my life, and the sooner I came to terms with it, the better. I went back to working full time, taking the long way around to avoid Kali's Surf Shack. As long as I didn't think too much about what was missing, the pain was bearable. But some nights, alone in my bed, I still wept.

The last thing I had to tackle was my mother's house, which had sat untouched for nearly a year. I'd tried several times to walk through those front doors, but for whatever reason, I couldn't. Although, leaving it to decay wasn't an option either and it made poor fiscal sense to continue to pour money into a place I never planned to live in again.

Weeks before I gathered the courage to return, Stewart had gone in and painted over the nasty messages Mom had left for me on the walls. He'd also sold off the antiques and given the rest of the furniture away. Now all that was left for me to do was to box and bag up whatever was left. I doubted I'd find anything I wanted to keep, but the need to uncover more of my past made me take the sorting process seriously.

"Suck it up, chicky."

I dutifully held my breath as Shannon gripped the fastener to the form-fitting gold dress and yanked. The wind sucked out of me, I expelled a very loud swear word.

"Shhh," she warned, placing a finger over her lips and gesturing with her eyes to the little bundle of cuteness sleeping in the car seat. "If Audrey wakes up, feeding time's on you."

"Well, then, it won't take long because the only thing these nipples are secreting is dust."

"Speaking of dust," Shannon said, waving her hand around. "We need to finish up this *Pretty Woman* makeover montage before I have an asthma attack."

Our quest for hidden treasures had led us here, into my mother's closet and her vast collection of evening gowns.

In her early days, Mom had been something of a starlet. Her dream of becoming a movie star was never realized, but she had for a time lived amongst the Hollywood elite. I tried to imagine what she would have been like back when she was my age and still filled with such promise and aspirations. She'd been beautiful and joyful once; the pictures proved it. But that was before disease struck her down like a bolt of lightning and before she'd morphed into the fiend I knew her to be.

Earlier in the day, on my knees in her closet sifting through what remained of her life, I finally made my peace. The hate I'd been holding onto for so long fell away once I could admit that she too had been a victim of circumstances. I had no choice but to forgive her sins because someday, they would be my own. Shannon had given me ample time to grieve, but once there was a break in the waterworks, she'd offered me a Kleenex with one hand, and held up a gold dress in the other.

"Oomph," I groaned, as my organs rearranged just enough for Shannon to get the zipper past the small of my back. This was no small undertaking. Shannon was attempting to squeeze my sporty, size six body into a model-worthy size zero gown.

"I knew my mom was thin, but I thought she'd just gotten smaller because of the disease. Now I know she was always tiny. I swear, that woman didn't eat when she was my age."

"Um… yeah, I already figured that out." Shannon stepped out from behind me in her own Hollywood gown – only hers looked like it had been made for a doll. Not only did her forearms stick out several inches from the sleeve, but the floor length number she'd chosen to model fell only to her calf.

And just like that, my bestie had come through for me again. Our hushed laughter chased away the negative energy. I would get through this somehow.

"Shannon?"

Her eyes rolling in their socket, she answered, "Yes, my pretty?"

"I can't breathe. My toes are going numb."

"This brings up an interesting question," Shannon said, taking her damn time unzipping me. "If you had to choose between eating tacos every day or being super skinny for the rest of your life, what would you choose – hard or soft tacos?"

Laughing only obstructed my airflow further. "They're tacos, who cares?"

"Exactly!" she exclaimed, finally pushing past the resistance and setting me free. "You'd be surprised how many people get that question wrong."

"Well, you know, that's why we're friends."

"Yes, it is." And while we were still looking into the mirror, Shannon stroked my hair and said, "You know you have to get the genetic testing done, right?"

"We've been through this a hundred times. There's no point. I already know the answer."

"No, you don't, Samantha. 50% means just that. It's the flip of a coin; the difference between having a boy or a girl."

I sighed. "I have symptoms, Shan."

"Here's the thing about symptoms. Our minds can trick us into believing something is true when it's not. How many times have you felt nauseous when someone else has the stomach flu?"

"I know, it's just… I'm scared. Right now, I still have hope. If the results come back and I'm on the wrong side of the percentage, then it's all over for me."

"But what if it's on the right side?"

"But what if it's on the wrong?"

We stood there quietly for a moment, reflecting, before Shannon repeated her earlier line.

"But what if it's on the right?"

With the exception of some of my mother's dresses and jewelry and boxes of paperwork I'd sort through later, I gave Stewart the green light to donate the rest of her things to charity, hoping something good could come of her difficult life. When I arrived home later that day, exhausted from both the mental and physical toll it had taken on me, I noticed a manila envelope propped against my door. There was no postage. No writing.

A shiver ran through me. I don't know how I knew, I just did. It was from Keith. Picking it up with shaky hands, I carried it in as if it were a newborn baby. But once I had it safely on my kitchen table, I couldn't get myself to open it. Why I wasn't sure, but I flitted around the house, completing chores, until finally I could avoid it no longer. Pouring myself a glass of wine, I sat down on the chair and carefully separated the sticky paper flap. I pulled out a framed photo and immediately brought it to my chest to give it a hug. Murphy. My baby. I missed him so much, and here he was now, that toothy grin of his brightening my day.

My smile reached wide as I gave a silent thank you to Keith. Even from afar, he was still looking out for me in his own way. I'd heard a rumor that he was dating again, and although I stayed away from the details, I was comforted by knowing he was doing okay – even if the nagging jealousy ate me up inside on occasion.

As I laid the envelope down, I noticed a swell at the bottom of the packaging, and when I reached my hand inside and pulled out a small item covered in tissue paper, I knew exactly what it was. With shaking fingers, I tore through the wrapping, squealing when the prize was revealed with a little note that read, "I thought you might need this."

Elated, I raised my grandfather's lucky stone to my lips and whispered, "Yes, I do."

Chapter Thirty-Seven

Samantha

The Imposter

I could have waited to be escorted to my seat but, since two thirds of the ushers at Jake and Casey's wedding had McKallister DNA coursing through their veins, the odds were low I'd make it to a pew without some awkward encounter. Best-case scenario I got a Caldwell brother. Worst case? I got my ex, the man whose heart I'd shoved into a trash compactor and selected 'power pack' just to be sure it was sufficiently crushed. No, it was best to find my own seat as far away from the action as possible.

At the ready, I stood just outside the door to the church, waiting for the coast to clear so I could make my 3-inch-heeled run for it. And I was about to make my move when Keith's laugh traveled outside, wafting into my ears like a beautiful melody. A hopeful smile crossed my lips. Maybe I hadn't totally squashed him. Or, more likely, another woman had brought that joy back into his life. I could almost feel the color draining from my face at just the thought of Keith in a happily ever after with a woman who was not me, and I had to actively remind my possessive mind that this was what I had wanted – what I'd asked him to do.

Someday you'll think of this moment and thank me.

No, Sam. No, I won't.

I shook off the memory, refocusing on the here and now. Keith's voice drifted further away as he escorted another lucky lady down the aisle. I pictured him mesmerizing her with his witty charm and unparalleled good looks while she tittered all the way to her seat. He had a way with the ladies, all right. I mean he'd effectively turned me into a pile of goo for the rest of my life. And I bet he was as handsome as ever, too. Of course he would be. A person couldn't just cease being attractive. He'd captivated me as a seventeen-year-old girl, and I was still hopelessly stuck on him all these years later. I wondered if I'd ever fully recover from Keith McKallister or if he would be like one of those chronic inflammations that flared up from time to time.

Maybe I shouldn't have come. After the wedding invitation arrived by personal courier, I'd wavered back and forth for days. Don't get me wrong, it was an honor to have been invited, and I wanted nothing more than to celebrate with Jake and Casey, but I couldn't help but feel like an imposter; or worse, the ghost of girlfriends past.

Yes, I'd remained friendly with Casey in the aftermath of the breakup, but the rest of the McKallisters, with one exception, had rallied around their own as if the years I'd spent with them had been erased from their memory. I understood. They were family, albeit one I'd once considered myself a part of. But even though I was the cause of all the strife, I'd be lying if I said being blocked from their huddle hadn't hurt. But then, what did I expect? They weren't my family anymore, and the sooner I accepted it, the easier it would be.

With Keith a safe distance, I darted through the foyer and into the church before ducking behind the first bench and sliding into the second-to-last pew. The mother and daughter duo beside me wearing colorful hats seemed distracting enough that no one would bother looking past the peacock feathers to notice a callous heart-stomper like myself.

I was wrong.

I hadn't even had time to wipe the sweat from my brow before Keith strolled down the aisle. It wasn't my first experience with him in a tuxedo, but I can tell you, it was always a show-stopping experience. The measly collection of tissues I'd brought wouldn't be enough to collect the drool pooling in the corners of my mouth. Unable to rip my eyes away, I peeked up at him from behind the feathery glamour lashes I'd applied earlier in the day, not at all expecting anything in return. But as if by some invisible force, Keith turned in my direction, and his eyes zeroed in on me. He seemed surprised at first. Then hurt. Then angry. And finally, his features softened, and I saw what I'd desperately been searching for – love.

My own emotions were on full display, the moment so raw and real that it felt as if my heart was skipping way too many beats. His face an open book of feels, Keith faltered in his stride. He seemed uncertain; conflicted. I had the feeling he wanted to come to me, but the voice in his head was telling him not to. The rational part of his brain won out, and Keith continued down the aisle, never to glance my way again.

As the ceremony got underway, it became immediately apparent that the Kleenex I'd shoved in my clutch wasn't even going to be enough to cover the walk down the aisle, much less the heartfelt vows. Still, it had been worth the sacrifice of my soggy tissues. There was nothing more beautiful to witness than the union of two people meant to be.

Keith and I – we were meant to be.

Yeah, shut up there, Sam. You suck!

The reception was spent deflecting the attention of a man at the singles table. He was handsome and accomplished. Ask me how I knew this? Well, I'll tell you. Because he felt the need to continually remind me how handsome and accomplished he was. He also spent the down time rattling off a list of his high-powered friends. As if I cared about superficial crap like prestige and titles. It only took one brain-zapping disease to set your priorities straight… or… well… at least to prioritize what was real and what was bullshit. Keith. The McKallisters. The Caldwells. Real. Flawed. Beautiful. Men with high-powered jobs and impressive friends, step aside.

I liked pirates who frosted cupcakes and surfer boys who made engagement rings out of seaweed. I suppose I was just simple like that.

"Sam?"

My head turned to the sound, knowing who I'd find before ever laying eyes on him. Quinn – Keith's kid brother and my unofficial musical crush. I flung my arms around him and we hugged for the longest time. The first Christmas I'd spent with the McKallisters, I'd wandered into the wrong room and heard a then-twelve-year-old kid singing his heart out. From that point on I was hooked. I suppose maybe my devotion went further back than that - all the way back to the disheveled little boy on the porch –

the one struggling to understand the world that was crumbling down around him. Yes, I'd loved him since then.

"Quinn, I missed you so much," I said peppering his cheeks with kisses. "My favorite singer ever."

He grinned. "You've always been biased."

"I just know what my ears like to hear."

Quinn humbly accepted my compliments before anxious energy got the best of him and he shifted nervously in place. "I'm sorry I haven't kept in touch. I wanted to but you know, the bro code and all."

"Of course." I smiled. "I understand."

And I did. I wouldn't have wanted my problems to cause issues with Keith and his family and the fact that Quinn stuck with his brothers despite our tight bond said something about his commitment to family – of which I was no longer a part of.

"But believe me, I was so pissed at Keith. I wanted to smack him upside the head for hurting you."

My smile wilted. Keith hadn't told him. He'd taken the blame for our breakup. That wasn't what I'd wanted at all. Did I tell Quinn? Did I not? In the end, I let the decision be Keith's.

"That song, Quinn, it was beautiful. You should have seen Jake's face. He was so impressed."

There was an instant dampening of his mood. "I doubt that. We had it out last night."

"Uh-oh. What happened?"

"I asked him to help me with my songs, and he basically told me I was looking for handouts. He doesn't care about my career, Sam. He never will."

"Then you carve your own path. If Jake can't see your talent, that's his loss, but don't let his indifference deter you. You're just too talented to walk away."

Quinn stared off in the distance, then shrugged. "It's whatever."

"No, it's 'you will show them all.'"

He lifted his eyes. "Sure, Sam. Whatever you say."

"That's better. And remember, I get a front row seat to your first show."

Finally a grin swept over his face. "If I'm doing it right, there won't be any front row seating."

Quinn wasn't the only McKallister to come calling. Michelle sidled up, her arms wrapping around me in the maternal hug I'd been craving since I'd broken her son's heart over a year ago. Then it was Scott and Emma and Kyle and Kenzie. And, just like that, I felt welcome and no longer wanting to make the quick exit I'd planned upon entering the reception.

Glancing in Keith's direction, my heart kept telling me to go to him, but my brain continually talked me out of it. Just because his family seemed okay with me being there didn't mean Keith would. He didn't need me popping back into his life and stirring up memories better left buried. He'd moved on, and I'd… um… sort of moved on. I needed to give the poor guy a break. *Over is over, Sam.* And Keith and I – we were over.

Maybe it was time to leave. There was nothing I could do here that I couldn't do at home with a good bottle of wine. I'd find Jake and Casey, congratulate them, and be on my way to a nice drunken night of self-loathing. *Sounds like a solid plan.*

And as fate would have it, Jake nearly stumbled right into me. Obviously the universe wanted me gone too.

"Congratulations," I said, grabbing his arm to keep him from tumbling on by.

"Sam," he said, hugging me. Like his family before him, Jake was warm and welcoming. I wanted to hold him a little tighter and soak in his acceptance. Why it meant so much to me I couldn't say, but it did.

As he pulled back, I caught him staring at my necklace. He looked up, our eyes met, and he smiled. Jake knew. Keith must have told him of its origin, and he'd chosen to give it up – for me. The power of my stone had worked on him. Jake knew that tiny slivers of his strength had come from all those who'd worn it before him: me, Keith, my grandfather, and yes, even Sullivan, who'd held on as long as he could.

"Thank you," he mouthed.

Sentiment stopped the flow of words I wanted to speak to him, so I simply smiled in reply.

"Samantha Anderson!" Casey squealed, her energy instantly erasing the emotional exchange. Jake stepped back, happily allowing his wife to take the lead. Casey and I hugged it out. "You came, girl."

"Of course. Like I'd miss this for the world. Jake, you should have seen your face when Casey punked you in the church."

As the three of us laughed, I'd lost track of Keith in the crowd until he suddenly appeared by Jake's side, hanging an arm over his brother's shoulder. "What did I miss?"

"Nothing. We were just making fun of Jake," Casey said. "Like always."

Keith nodded before shifting his gaze toward mine.

"Sam," he said, tipping his head in greeting.

"Keith," I replied, mimicking his exact acknowledgement.

"You look good."

"So do you."

Then silence. The four of us stood there awkwardly until Casey filled in the gaps with a well-placed poop joke, instantly lightening the mood. Keith's face relaxed as he and Jake dropped into a conversation about a woman in a wedding dress flashing them some serious nipple. Such things didn't happen in the real world, but it did in theirs. Over-the-top unpredictability was part of the McKallister charm.

"Only in this family," I said, giggling along with their story. "See, this is what I miss about not hanging out with you guys."

"Breasts?" Keith asked, feigning ignorance.

Remembering everything I loved about this big, crazy family, I gave into the moment and laughed with abandon. Without thinking, I reached out and spontaneously touched Keith's arm. Shocked by the unplanned moment of contact, I immediately pulled away, but not before locking eyes with him. The world around me swam out of focus, and I was only partially aware of the bride and groom slipping away. All I could see was the man before me, and instead of the anger and indifference I'd expected from him, I got love and understanding.

"I gotta tell ya, Sam. I nearly passed out when I saw you in the church."

"I didn't want it to be awkward, so I was trying to hide."

"I know you were," he said, his hand gliding along my back as if no time had passed. "But you should know by now that we always find each other. It's just what we do."

His words hit me hard, forcing me to swallow down the lump that instantly formed in my throat. "Yes, it is what we do, isn't it?"

We stood staring at one another. There were so many things I needed to tell him – huge, important things – but was it right to upend his life all over again?

"I'm sorry you had to lie to your family for me. They blamed you for the breakup. Keith, that wasn't what I wanted."

"*That's* what you're worried about?" Keith asked. "Trust me, I didn't do it for you. I prefer scorn over sympathy any day."

"Regardless. I'm sorry."

Keith bent down and whispered in my ear. "I missed you."

The moment was so intimate – so sweet – that every truth I'd held so tightly slipped out. "I missed you too. And I miss Murphy and your family and our life together. I miss it all so much. I think… I'm just not meant to live without you."

As if unable to keep his hands off me, his fingers traveled over my skin. "No, you're not. Good or bad, Sam, I would have stayed by your side. You made that choice to go it alone, not me."

"I know. And, I promise you, every single day after you left I wanted to run to you, but… I was like a wave that was never going to make it to shore. At some point, you had to get off of it for your own good."

"But who are you to tell me what I need? Maybe I wanted to ride your wave to the end. Have you ever thought of that?"

There was nothing I could say to defend myself. I'd chosen my fate, but I hadn't allowed him to do the same.

Somehow I'd fooled myself into thinking I was doing what was best for him when, in reality, I was only feeding my own ravenous self-pity. Oh god. I'd done this. I'd made us two halves of a whole.

Keith tipped my chin, studying me. "You look beautiful, Sammy. Healthy. Have you experienced any symptoms? Have you been to the doctor? I've researched a lot about Huntington's and, I know you're still on the young side of a diagnosis, but why torture yourself? Find out for sure if you carry the gene. At the very least you'll have your answer."

My bottom lip quivered as I fought the tears, but it was no use, there was no stopping the flow. "I did the genetic testing, Keith."

Interpreting the results by way of my emotional reaction, the color drained from his face. "Oh."

Sliding my fingers into his hair, I drew his head closer and whispered the words in his ear. "I'm not my mother."

Keith jerked his head back and the words fell from his lips, almost hesitant.

"What does that mean?"

I stared at him, willing him not to make me say it.

He repeated the question.

"It means I don't carry the gene. I can't get the disease, and I can't pass it on."

A draft of air flowed between us as Keith stood up straighter. His mouth hung open, and I couldn't tell if he was more pissed or stunned. Anger won out and he pushed me away. "When? When did you find this out?"

"I got the results a couple of weeks ago."

"And you're just telling me this now?"

"I was trying to figure out how to tell you… or even *if* I should tell you."

"*If*?" He demanded.

"It goes back to the wave, Keith. You finally got off it. I heard you were dating. I didn't want to uproot your life again."

"What is it with you, deciding what you think is best for me?" His voice rose above acceptable levels and, although I deserved the scorn, I still pulled him out into the hallway for a proper tongue-lashing.

"So, let me get this straight, Samantha. Are you saying you don't have Huntington's disease, and you will never get it?"

Unable to meet his eye, I nodded to an unforgiving floor.

Keith stood motionless for a moment before dropping into a crouched position and covering his mouth with his open palm. I could see him trying desperately to process the information. Once he'd had ample time, I reached out to touch him. Keith flinched like I was setting him on fire. Jumping to his feet, he stomped down the hallway, gripping his hair in his hands as a low growl bubbled from his gut.

"Keith…"

"No. Don't talk to me. Don't even look at me! You... you should've taken the test before breaking it off. We lost over a year. A year, Sam! Dammit."

"I know. I was so sure. I thought... I thought I had it. No, I was convinced I had Huntington's. Nothing anyone could say would change my mind. It wasn't until you sent me back the necklace that I finally had the courage to face the truth. I'm so sorry for all the pain I've caused you. I truly am."

"Stop saying that! I'm so... I'm going to..."

More angry marches up and down the corridor kept me rooted in place.

"Uuhhh. I don't know if I should be pissed or jump for fucking joy."

In a voice barely above a whisper, I replied, "I vote for fucking joy."

Keith stopped, glaring at me. "Oh, I'm sure you do."

I swear I heard the tiniest bit of amusement in his words, and I offered him up my own itty-bitty grin. I didn't deserve his forgiveness but I'd accept if it were offered. Keith continued to stare – no, gawk – and then, unbelievably, the anger in his eyes began to fade, replaced not quite with 'fucking joy' but something damn near close to it.

Keith shook his head before grabbing my hand and leading me outside. I followed without protest. He was in charge now, and whatever he decided, I'd abide by. We stopped in the middle of a rose garden bursting with fragrance and color.

"You understand that I'm mad as hell, right?"

"Yes."

"And you know you should have told me the second you found out, correct?"

"Yes."

"And you understand that I'm not going to forgive you for a very long time, got it?

"Yes."

Keith sighed long and hard before reaching up around the back of his neck and untying a leather band. Pulling the necklace out from under the collar of his tuxedo shirt, his large hands shielded it from view.

When he finally looked back up, tears had flooded his eyes. "I never got off the wave, Sam. You of all people should know that."

I could barely hear him over the wild beating of my heart. "What are you saying?"

"I'm saying you're the only one for me. And even though I sort of hate you right now, I love you more."

Without breaking eye contact, Keith lowered himself to one knee, drawing a gasp from my lips. He gently placed his palm against my stomach, staring up at me with the look I knew so well. Time had not dimmed his love. And why would it? Keith had always believed. It was me who'd lagged behind.

"I asked you once with a seaweed ring. I asked you twice with a diamond. And now, Samantha Anderson, I ask you to marry me one last time with the ring that belongs only to you."

He opened his hand to reveal the stunning surprise. A ring of diamonds sparkled like twinkling lights, but it was the stone that sat in the middle of them all that caught my eye – the ocean captured in an agate.

This time, there were no unanswered questions.

This time, our future wasn't in jeopardy.

This time, I said yes.

CHAPTER THIRTY-EIGHT

KEITH

Long Time Coming

"Are you sure you don't want to wear the bowtie?" my father asked, holding the unraveled cloth in his hands. "Just asking for a friend."

"No, and you don't, either. This is a beach wedding, Dad. Informal is the name of the game. Come here."

"Why?" He stepped forward.

"So I can loosen a few of these buttons. You look like a priest."

And as we stood facing one another I purposely avoided his gaze. He'd been trying to corner me all day, and now that we were alone, I could feel the energy pulsing off him.

He grabbed my hand. "Keith, I need to tell you something."

"Dad, I swear if you tell me the honeybee story, you're out of the wedding party."

"I hate that you boys talk amongst yourselves. Jake ruined a perfectly good bachelor party story. I hope he's happy because now everyone loses. Anyway, no, I want you to know how unbelievably proud I am of you."

"Thank you."

"And I think maybe I need to apologize."

"Dad, you, of all people, have no reason to apologize. I'm only standing here today because of you."

"Oh, but I do. You were right. I did favor Mitch. I see that now, but it was only because I felt guilty for not having him in my life as much as I should have. So when he was home, I overcompensated, putting him on a pedestal without really noticing it."

I put my hand up. "Let me stop you right there. I am not that insecure kid anymore, and I don't hold you responsible for anything. Hell, without you, I'd probably be a prison bitch."

"Oh, yes, there's no doubt."

We laughed, a sense of humor being one of the most important things I'd inherited from him.

"And I'm glad you gave Mitch the attention he deserved. We had you all the time. He needed you. And he's like the perfect human, so you did a good job."

"You're perfect too."

We both saw the humor in that at the same time and laughed accordingly.

"Or… like perfect in a recycled furniture kind of way."

"I'll take it. And someday when I'm a father, I want to be just like you… only handsomer and thinner and with more hair. And without all the uncontrollable gas."

"You're such a jerk," he said, grinning. "You and your siblings are ingrates. All of you."

"We are what you made us."

"Then I'll die a happy man. I couldn't be prouder of my kids – of you. You're the exact man I always knew you could be, and I just couldn't love you more."

We hugged it out, only breaking apart when the motorhome we were using as a dressing room began to shake. Mitch opened the door, halting when he understood he'd just interrupted something.

"You want me to come back?" he asked, already turning to leave.

"Hey." I opened my arm and motioned him in. "Get over here."

Mitch strode over and wrapped his arms around the both of us.

"So, I don't mean to rush you, but your bride is ready. And, oh, James is trying to ride one of the tortoises."

"I'm ready," I said, patting his shoulder. "I was just waiting on my best man to arrive."

Mitch's smile couldn't get any wider or more blinding. "I'm here, little brother. Let me lead the way."

My bare feet burrowed into the sand as I watched Sam pace toward me holding a small bouquet of flowers in one hand and her arm hooked though my father's on the other. Her white dress flowed out around her in gentle waves. She resembled a water fairy with flowers braided into her hair. I blinked away the tears as she made her way toward me, the picture of beauty and health.

I scanned the small gathering of people – everyone we loved. There were no sides separating the bride and groom's family, just an intimate blending of the two. A small, laid-back wedding was all we required, and what better place to celebrate our union than on our beach where it all started?

My father stopped, lifted Sam's hand, and kissed it before turning her over to me. Maybe I expected her to be a swirl of emotion, but there were no tears in her eyes. No fear. Sam knew exactly what she wanted: me, every day for the rest of her life.

"Look," I said, pointing to the area behind the altar. There, in roughly the same spot in the sand I'd once asked her to by my girlfriend, was a heart with the words, *Will you be my wife?*

She placed her hand on my chest. Only the slight tremble of her bottom lip spoke to her sentiment. "Thank you for never giving up on us, Keith."

I leaned in, brushing a kiss upon her sun-lit cheek.

"It's just what we do."

EPILOGUE

"Scoot all the way down, Bud." I bumped Wyatt along with my ass to make way for his mother and little brother.

"I don't want to sit too close to the edge," Wyatt said, his innocent eyes peering up at me. "What if a pirate gets me?"

"Impossible, bud. And you know why? Professional courtesy."

"He's four, Keith." Sam elbowed me, casting me a sly smile as she adjusted our baby on her other hip in order to comfort her oldest son. "What Daddy means to say is they are toys, and toys are fun – nothing to fear."

"Actually, that's not at all what *Daddy* meant to say, but thank you for putting words in my mouth, *Mommy*."

Finn leaned in from behind. "At least you can get a word in edgewise. That was a luxury I lost after daughter number three exited the birth canal."

"And whose fault is that, Finn?" I asked, glancing back at his all-female crew. With her curly brown hair and agreeable personality, Indiana was a copy of her father, while identical twins Kimi and Paige were blonde and straight-laced like their mother. "You're physically incapable of producing a male heir."

"If your sister would have given me one more shot, I'm confident I would have proven all you dickhead haters wrong. But nooo. I have one little mishap with a condom… no offense, honey." He squeezed Indiana to him. "And then a few years after that, I make the grave error of forgetting to mention the prevalence of twins in my family. Suddenly, I'm the one with the vasectomy? How's that fair?"

Offering no sympathy, Emma countered his complaint. "Look, if I could trust your sperm, there'd be no need for such drastic measures. But you Perrys insist on populating the world one broken condom at a time."

The adult talk going straight over his head, Wyatt pulled on my sleeve, eager for my undivided attention, and I gave it to him, no questions asked. My little sandy-haired, bronzed-skin cutie was already a beach bum, spending hours playing in the sand and dipping his toes in the Pacific. On the adorable scale from one to ten, I could objectively report that he scored a twenty.

His little brother Thomas enjoyed the same high ranking, even though he wasn't nearly as interactive as his brother. At thirteen months old, Tommy was a one-syllable kind of guy, who babbled his way through any conversation. He was also a competitive eater and would shove into his mouth whatever was handy: dog toys, onions, sand. Nothing was safe. In one glaring lapse of supervision, I even discovered our little food connoisseur chowing down on a paperback book. By the time I figured out what he was doing, Thomas was a third of the way through the novel. Let's just say the story didn't read as well coming out the back end.

Just thinking about my little family caused bursts of happiness to pop through my chest. It seemed I had a limitless capacity to love. Who knew? I'd thought marrying Sam on the beach that day was the pinnacle of all things awesome, but I found that with each addition to our tribe, my heart expanded a little wider. And it gave me a new appreciation for my own parents, who'd raised us all into adulthood with a focus on family, a sense of right and wrong, and clear hearts primed for love.

I picked up Wyatt and wrapped him in my arms protectively. "Don't worry, kiddo. I got you."

Grasping my face in his little hands, he tipped my head to the side and whispered into my ear. "I'm still scared of the pirates."

Obviously his mother's fairytale explanation hadn't been enough to ease his concerns, so it was time to explain professional courtesy to my preschooler in a way he could understand. "Listen up. The pirates won't bother us because they like me." I dropped my voice and looked around for spies. "I haven't told you this before, Wyatt, but before I met your mommy, I was a pirate myself."

"Really?" My boy stared up at me with eyes so wide and trusting I wanted to live in his magical world forever. Sure, it wasn't the full truth, the whole truth, and nothing but the truth. But like my own dad had before me, I'd learned that I could feed little Wyatt a big boy plate of yummy old white lies and he'd eat up every last bite.

"Yep, I had the long hair, stinky clothes, dopey smile; the works."

Kyle tipped his head back from the bench directly in front of us. "Back when your dad and I were kids, Wyatt, pirates were also known as stoners."

Sam smacked him. "Do not bring that word into my son's vocabulary. Don't you have your own kids to parent?"

Smugly, Kyle hooked his arms behind his head. "I don't have to. He parents me."

And, sadly, he wasn't kidding. I glanced over at Kyle and Kenzie's firstborn son, who'd inexplicably been born a genius. Talk about a miracle of science. Little Arlo was already at a junior high school reading level, and he was only six. There was talk amongst the family that maybe the kid had somehow been switched at birth, but his resemblance to Kyle was too strong to make a legal case against the hospital. Somehow my younger brother and his Bigfoot-loving wife had sired a child with a Nobel Prize-level IQ.

I glanced over at Arlo, who'd been looking up at the vast darkness of the artificial dome ceiling that created the fantasy that was the Pirates of the Caribbean ride.

"Dad," Arlo finally spoke. I listened in, always enjoying the profound words that carefully exited his mouth. "How many years are there in a millennium?"

"Is this one of those questions you already know the answer to but you ask it just to make me look bad?"

He shrugged his little shoulders.

"Um, okay well." Kyle scratched his head searching for an answer – always searching. "Like ten, maybe."

"No," he sighed. "That's a decade."

"Oh…huh. Really?"

"Yes. The correct answer is one thousand."

Kyle tipped his head back again. "See what I'm saying? No need to parent."

I reached up and manually turned my little brother's head to something that did require his attention. "I was actually talking about that one."

Our eyes both diverted to Kenzie trying desperately to pry their unruly three-year-old off a wheelchair he'd commandeered on his way into the boat.

"That's not a ride, Axel," Kenzie said, yanking on his little body while blowing the hair out of her exasperated eyes.

At least there was some justice in the world – a balancing act of sorts. It seemed all the dominant genes had been depleted making Arlo, leaving poor Axel with little more than the ability to wander around with a bucket on his head, ramming himself into walls.

"You gonna help with that?" I asked him, flicking my head in Kenzie's direction.

"Nah, she's got it."

"Kyle!" Kenzie snapped, and he jumped to attention like he'd been pierced with a pirate's sword. He was out of the boat before the exclamation point attached itself to the end of his name.

Yep, my siblings and I were learning that there were no Fast Passes in parenting.

There were, however, VIP tours for the rich and famous, and that's where we were now, celebrating one of Dad's birthday week days in the happiest place on Earth. Having the benefit of a celebrity in our ranks, we enjoyed certain privileges that most did not. Case in point: the temporary shut down of the pirate ride so our swelling group of twenty-six – twelve of which were children – could get into the waiting boats without sinking the wooden pier.

Mitch, sandwiched into the first bench between his wife, Kate, and their two kids, had to raise his arms to disengage from the crush of his family. His son Max insisted on sitting in the front row, which he called the splash zone, and because he was the oldest of the grandkids, all his worshipping cousins fell in line. Along with his sister, Madison, they were the stars of the show anytime they arrived for a family function. It was like Mitch déjà vu all over again… but now I embraced it. As I saw it, the more family I could surround myself with, the happier my life would be in the long run. So I embraced crazy situations like this, bobbing in a pirate boat while thousands of inconvenienced park-goers eagerly awaited my famous brother to make his move.

"Where are the others?" Mitch asked, glancing over in the direction we'd come from moments before getting on the ride. "I thought they were right behind us."

"They were having some security issues, I think," Finn said. "It's not so easy for him to get through the crowds these days."

Kyle rocked the boat as he stepped back in, dangling his rowdy son over his shoulder. "I've never seen it this bad, and I'm used to screaming fans."

Right on cue, a group of female admirers called out, but it was Finn they'd set their sights on. He waved back amicably.

"Hey," Mitch called to him. "Shouldn't you be in the second wave – where the important people are?"

"Are you kidding? I'm but a speck in the ocean of the tsunami that's about to slam into the pirate cove."

On a hit television show, Finn was a celebrity in his own right, but given the high-caliber company he kept, he wasn't wrong about his self-assessed level of fame. His place was rightfully here with the rest of us nobodies.

A scream went up, echoing through the cavernous room.

"Speaking of the tsunami..." Sam said, covering her hands over Tommy's sensitive ears. "Here he comes."

The main attractions came into view as they made their way onto the loading dock. Fans standing in the lines cheered wildly as Jake climbed into the boat with his sons Miles and Slater before turning to help Casey, who was cradling baby Lily in her arms. Mom, Dad, and Grace took their seats just behind.

Then a strange hush filled the dusky cavern as security guards flanked the last member of our twenty-six-person party, steering him towards the others.

Kyle turned toward me, shaking his head. "Here we go again."

A frenzy of screams erupted as our brother emerged from the protective barrier and stepped into the boat, a chant echoing throughout the vaulted chamber.

"Quinn."

"Quinn."

"Quinn!"

The End

Made in the USA
Coppell, TX
31 October 2020

40519877R10281